AWAY
TO ME

PATRICIA McCONNELL

KENSINGTON PUBLISHING CORP.
kensingtonbooks.com

This book is a work of fiction. Names, characters, businesses, organizations, places, events, and incidents either are the product of the author's imagination or are used fictitiously. Any resemblance to actual persons, living or dead, events, or locales is entirely coincidental.

To the extent that the image or images on the cover of this book depict a person or persons, such person or persons are merely models, and are not intended to portray any character or characters featured in the book.

KENSINGTON BOOKS are published by

Kensington Publishing Corp.
900 Third Avenue
New York, NY 10022

Copyright © 2025 by Patricia McConnell

All rights reserved. No part of this book may be reproduced in any form or by any means without the prior written consent of the Publisher, excepting brief quotes used in reviews.

Without limiting the author's and publisher's exclusive rights, any unauthorized use of this publication to train generative artificial intelligence (AI) technologies is expressly prohibited.

All Kensington titles, imprints and distributed lines are available at special quantity discounts for bulk purchases for sales promotion, premiums, fund-raising, educational or institutional use. Special book excerpts or customized printings can also be created to fit specific needs. For details, write or phone the office of the Kensington Special Sales Manager: Kensington Publishing Corp., 900 Third Avenue, New York, NY, 10022. Attn. Special Sales Department. Phone: 1-800-221-2647.

KENSINGTON and the K with book logo Reg. U.S. Pat. & TM Off.

Library of Congress Control Number: TK

ISBN: 978-1-4967-5711-1

First Kensington Hardcover Edition: March 2026

ISBN: 978-1-4967-5713-5 (e-book)

10 9 8 7 6 5 4 3 2 1

Printed in the United States of America

The authorized representative in the EU for product safety and compliance
is eucomply OU, Parnu mnt 139b-14, Apt 123
Tallinn, Berlin 11317, hello@eucompliancepartner.com

To Cat Warren

Writing Coach, Cheerleader, Friend

"Away to Me" is a cue used by sheepdog handlers to ask their dog to run counterclockwise around the sheep.

CHAPTER 1

On that day, burned into my brain like a cattle brand, the woods stood dark and silent, an audience to the fog rising in an amphitheater of spring-green grass. The air was fuzzy with moisture, so the Twin Oaks Championship Sheepdog Trial outside Portage, Wisconsin, had been delayed until one could see the sheep, four hundred yards away. A barred owl called in the distance. *Who cooks for you? Who cooks for you?* Finally, the fog began to lift and the forest hummed with songbirds, so the first team walked up to the post.

George and Jess had drawn the first run of the day. George, all six foot four of him, was a top hand at trialing, and most of the other handlers had gathered to watch his run. He had a lot of wins under his belt, but his little bitch, Jess, was young and inexperienced. Her sire had won the Nationals, so there was a lot of interest in her performance. Few were more interested than I. Not only was George my friend and mentor, my own dog was Jess's brother, a young male Border collie who infatuated and infuriated me with equal intensity. His name was Jack, aka Mr. Wonderful. Or, on a bad day, something else I'd rather not say.

George and I had talked earlier that morning, when he gave me some last-minute advice about running Jack on this particular course. George wasn't just a great dog trainer; he could read sheep as if he'd been one in a former life. "Watch the pull to the exhaust pen, Maddie. The sheep are gonna charge down the field to your left and you'll need Jack to cover them sooner than you think unless you want a wreck." As usual, he was generous with his support. "Go get 'em," he said, with a gentle squeeze around my shoulders.

"Good luck yourself," I laughed. "Heaven knows you'll need it, Georgie."

Calling a man "Georgie" who looked like he walked out of a 1950s TV Western—his body lanky, his face chiseled—was patently ridiculous. Which is why it was so much fun. I'll never know why George adopted me as if I was his long-lost daughter, letting me tease him relentlessly and giving me free advice and lessons, no matter how much I protested. We spent countless sun-speckled afternoons on his porch nursing a beer while we shot the shit after we worked dogs. He had become, over the three years since I'd bought Jack from him, one of my best friends. I'd add in cheerleader, if cheerleaders expressed their enthusiasm with a raspy whisper of "Good enough," and a barely perceptible dip of the head.

His face looked drawn that morning—I wondered if it was the high expectations everyone had for his run with Jess. He smiled his cowboy grin when I wished him luck, and said he'd need it. I turned to go, not wanting to interfere with him getting ready to run, but he grabbed my hand, pulled me back, and looked straight into my eyes.

"You take care of yourself now, girl." He was the only man who could call me, a forty-two-year-old woman, "girl," and not piss me off. I had enough trouble being taken seriously, being only five foot two and, as my aunt used to say, "a little hefty," with vaguely red hair that I battled into submission every day. George walked away, Jess trotting beside him, looking up at his face with a gaze of adoration. A man for all species. Something in me wanted to run after him and give him a hug.

As George walked away, Jack was standing transfixed by my side, watching a group of four sheep, a faraway blur of cottony white, that was being carefully moved into position by another handler and her dog. The *caw caw caw* of a crow rolled through the valley as wisps of mist swirled above the grass.

Jess, a small Border collie with a foxy feminine face and a curly ruff, stood beside George looking for the sheep, her pointed ears toggling left and right. Her jaw chattered from excitement. I could barely hear George whisper "away to me," the signal for Jess to run counterclockwise around to the back of the flock. Jess bolted forward, a black and white bullet, hitting full speed in three strides and beginning her run around to the back of the sheep.

What is more beautiful than watching a dog, all muscle and mind and heart, run free across a field of green to gather a flock of sheep? My heart swells up every time I see it. Every time. And I see it a lot. Being an applied animal behaviorist is my career, but working sheepdogs is my passion. It's an addictive sport—imagine playing chess with all the pieces alive and full of their own opinions, moving at twenty miles an hour. It's like *Through the Looking Glass*, except for real.

Jess turned in behind the sheep at exactly the right point, her body low to the ground. She crept toward the sheep like a lion on the hunt, easing the sheep forward with controlled determination. She moved the sheep quietly but with authority toward George, pushing them forward as if she'd put them into a shopping cart. But then, the lead ewe turned and put her hoof down. Literally. A big wooly thing with black legs and a speckled face, she turned to face Jess, stomping her hoof and ducking her head, presenting an anvil-like forehead that threatened to send Jess flying. She stomped again. Jess didn't flinch.

We spectators took a collective breath, riveted by the standoff between a thirty-five pound dog and a hundred-and-thirty-pound ewe. Many a dog, especially a young one, would give in to the pressure by backing away, or by panicking and biting, an automatic disqualification. What happened next would make or break the run and let us know if Jess had the chops to be a top competitor.

It was silent, every spectator caught up in the drama. Jess leaned forward, just an inch. The ewe bent her head down farther and made a mock charge. Jess crept forward another inch, looking directly into the ewe's eyes. Finally, the sheep lifted her chin and turned her head. She began trotting away, Jess behind her, leading her flock in the right direction.

I exhaled, not realizing until then I had been holding my breath. I looked down at Jack.

"See that? That's how you do it, bud."

As I did, an audible crack split the air, so loud I felt it in my chest. I startled, not expecting anyone to be hunting this time of year. Gunshots are common in the country, but we rarely hear them in spring. They're usually the boom of shotguns, not the air-splitting sound of a rifle.

I started to shake it off, but suddenly heard Stephanie, a fierce competitor in her own right, yell, "Oh God. George!"

I looked up to see George sprawled on the grass where he had stood moments ago, a pool of blood expanding in the grass beneath him. He lay on his back, his blue eyes wide open, as if surprised. His left leg was bent at an unnatural angle underneath him. For a moment we were all frozen in place. Even the birds went still.

I started to run to George, but someone behind me yelled "Get down!" grabbed my arm, and pulled me back behind a Ford F-150 with chrome wheels and a teardrop trailer. I can see the image of its silver hubcaps to this day, but I cannot for the life of me remember who pulled me away from George. Trauma does weird stuff to your brain.

No new shot rang out. A lone robin began to sing, two dogs began howling behind us.

"What the hell?" said someone behind me, and stood up

slowly. Suddenly there was action everywhere; two handlers ran to their trucks and started loading their rifles and pointing to the woods, looking for the dumb-ass hunter who must have shot George. Others pulled out their phones and called 911, while running over to George. I ran after them, desperate to help him, save him.

I took his face in my hands while the pool of blood underneath him grew. Another handler joined me and put her fingers on his neck. "Oh no. Oh no," she said so quietly I could barely hear her. "He's dead."

I started to crumble and then someone wrapped their arms around me. It was Dorothy, a top-level handler and my best friend. Except for George, she was the only other person I would call a good friend, at least the human kind. She wrapped me in her arms and tried to pull me away. I fought to stay with George—I couldn't bear to leave him, alone in the wet grass. But as I struggled, I realized that I had left Jack by the truck, abandoning him when I ran to George.

"Jack? Oh my God, where's Jack?" I looked around in desperation.

Jack was standing by the truck I'd hidden behind, trembling. He could've run away in a panic, and then there would have been two tragedies. Border collies are known for their sensitivity to loud noises; he could have been running away in fear, a mile away by now. But there he was, his eyes huge, his mouth closed tight, and if I didn't do something soon, he could forever be fearful of loud noises. Or sheepdog trials.

I ran to him, crooning "Good boy, stay there, good boy," and slumped down to the ground beside him. I wanted to go back to George, but couldn't bear to leave Jack. Dorothy leaned down beside me and gave me an awkward hug.

"Take Jack back to the truck, Maddie, there's nothing you can do here. I'll call Tom."

Tom was George's business partner and co-owner of the

H & H Working Dog Center, a dog-training facility where George had worked with stock dogs, and Tom raised and trained K9s for the police.

I took some deep breaths to try to stop my own hands from shaking. "Wanna go for a ride?" I said to Jack, as I picked up his leash and walked him back to the truck, parked a hundred yards behind the trial field. Jack looked calmer, but his eyes were still huge and dilated. "Take a bow, bud." I'd learned years ago that asking a dog to do a play bow helps them relax. Jack knew the trick well and complied instantly.

"Good boy." I took a few deep breaths as I fished into my pocket for dried liver treats.

Jack slurped them up. Good. At least he wasn't too frightened to eat. I asked him for a few more play bows, and after that some high fives. Jack's eyes returned to normal. To my relief, his mouth relaxed, so I popped him into his crate and walked back to the cluster of handlers on the field.

George had been shot in the chest. Someone had covered his body with a purple blanket. And yet . . . George couldn't be dead. It had only been ten minutes since we talked. This could not have happened: "shooters" don't happen at sheepdog trials, and although hunting accidents happen too often in the country, who could mistake a man standing alone in a field for a deer? One of George's friends had collected Jess, who pathetically had brought the sheep to George's body. She seemed a bit disoriented but had willingly responded. The rest of us stood in stunned disbelief, needing to talk, not knowing what to say.

I walked over to sit beside his body, just to be there, with him, one last time. The birds were singing their cheerful spring songs full volume. It sounded wrong, like heavy metal music at a funeral. I pulled George's hand out from under the blanket and held it. For the first time in my life, I understood that it can actually feel, physically, like your heart is breaking.

A sheriff's car pulled me out of my reverie, speeding down the dirt road leading to the parking area, the Dodge Charger's front end flapping up and down over the bumpy grass. Within minutes there was an EMT vehicle and several other law enforcement cars, lights flashing. We didn't need a medical examiner to confirm what we already knew. It wasn't George anymore; it was his body.

The site began to swarm with people in uniforms. Two officers surrounded the body with a tent, with bright yellow crime-scene tape around it. One squad car backed up and flew down the side road toward the area we thought the shots came from. Three officers, two male, one female, herded us away from the body and asked us to stay put until they could talk to us. Another siren, the loudest of all, announced the arrival of an ambulance, and behind it a car with what looked like a forensic team.

It was chaos. And noisy. Jesus, it was noisy. Between the sirens, the car engines, and the dogs barking, I began shaking again. I ran toward the truck—surely, I should check on Jack again—when a cop yelled "Hey! Stay with the group."

"My dog. I've got to check on my dog. He's just right over there, please, in the Toyota

Tacoma, right there." He stood silent for a moment, and then said, "Okay, but come right back."

"Hey, bud," I said, opening the door leading to Jack's crate. His pupils were huge. I took some breaths before I let him out and, glancing over my shoulder at the nearest cop, took him for a short walk toward the woods and away from the noise. He squatted beside an old buckthorn stump and deposited a puddle of diarrhea. After a bit more walking and a few tricks, there was nothing for me to do but put him back in his crate and return to the other handlers. They were standing in clumps, phones in their hands, trying to make the unreal feel real by telling the world what happened.

We all agreed that the shot had come from the woods northwest of the field. From who? During the fall hunting season the woods are full of out-of-towners who do stupid, and sometimes fatal, things. In spring you might hear a local going after squirrels, but not with a high-powered rifle. Besides, it was hard to imagine anyone confusing the figure of a man, standing in the open, for a squirrel or a deer. But then, plenty of cows have been shot at or killed over the years by trigger-happy people, so who knows. The only thing we knew for sure was that George was dead.

I spotted Dorothy over by her truck, sitting on the ground, petting Jess. We exchanged looks of disbelief and hugged when she stood up. As always, tall, slender Dorothy looked like she'd just left a photo shoot for an outdoor clothing line. No matter the weather, her hair looked gorgeous and her mascara never ran. Runny mascara wasn't a problem for me. I hadn't worn makeup in decades, not since my husband insisted I wear it all the time. I could be mucking out a horse stall and he'd tell me to go inside and "fix yourself up."

But Dorothy looked like she was born with the makeup of a cover model. Dorothy was a wildlife rehabilitator; once I had found her with a cadre of volunteers trying to treat an injured otter. Everyone but Dorothy had been covered in shit and fur and mud. She looked ready to go on a dinner date.

"Holy fuck," said Dorothy, "Is this really happening?" The face of an actress, the mouth of a sailor. I shook my head from side to side and wrapped my arms around her.

I lifted my head up as two members of the Jefferson County Sheriff's Office walked toward us. They had gold stars, actual gold stars as if in a TV western, pinned onto the left side of their dark brown shirts. The embroidered patches sown onto their shirts below their shoulders said "Sheriff" or "Deputy Sheriff, County of Jefferson." They reminded me of Girl Scout badges. They began interviewing us one at a time, while others drove back to the road to investigate the area where we thought the shot had originated. I had little to say: "No, I don't know if people usually hunt around here off season, I don't live around here. No, I couldn't imagine why anyone would want to kill George, that was impossible. No, he seemed no different than usual earlier this morning."

After getting all my contact information, the deputy snapped his notebook shut, left me a card, and turned toward another handler. I went back to the truck, let Jack out, and sat down beside him, wondering. Had George been really "no different than usual" this morning? That's what I'd said, but as I thought about it, why the drawn face, and why did he pull me back to tell me to "take care of myself"?

After endless hours, we were released by the sheriff. I didn't want to go home. Dorothy came back over and said, "Want me to come home with you?" She turned me to face her and looked into my eyes when she said it. This was a generous offer. Dorothy and I live a good three hours apart, and she had three dogs and a litter of puppies to take care of, not to mention her own farm and full-time job as a wildlife rehabber.

Our jobs had gotten us together—she'd heard about my work with dangerous dogs, and called to see if I could help her manage an injured bobcat. She couldn't get near the thing to treat its mangled paw. Eager for the challenge, I drove up curious, having waived my usual fees. I drove home having made a best friend, as if I'd known Dorothy all my life. No one could lighten me up like Dorothy, and few people could put up with her flat-out honesty and, uh, colorful speech.

"No, I'll be fine," I said to Dorothy. "What about you, you okay? Maybe let's talk on the phone later today?"

"Yeah. Good, okay." Dorothy gave me another hug and walked back to her Chevy Silverado. I stood beside my truck, knowing there was nothing to do but to leave.

I couldn't bear to go home. I asked one of the deputies if I could stay if I didn't interfere. He looked at me intently, made a valiant effort to suppress an eye roll, and said, "Suit yourself, just stay over there out of our way." I sat beside the truck, almost immobile, while tides of grief ebbed and flowed. I stroked Jack's head robotically until he went to sleep. A pair of sandhill cranes landed in the field behind me, where previously there had been rows of cars and trucks, all full of Border collies waiting for their chance.

The activity calmed down as the sun rose higher in the sky. Some of the uniformed people walked to their cars, drove away. Nothing seemed to be happening. I walked over to the tent, expecting at any moment to be confronted. No one noticed me, except some sparrows who flushed out of the grass as I crept forward. I stood on the outside and peeked in as one EMT, a young woman with electric blue hair and bright white gloves, supported George's head as he was put into a body bag. I was reminded of carrying my first Border collie to the grave I'd dug for him. I still remember how his head lolled over my arm and how important it felt for it not to do so. I couldn't comprehend then, and still can't now, how someone who means the world to you can, in an instant, turn into nothing more than a floppy sack of skin and bones.

I stood watching his body being loaded into the funeral home's van. Then I turned, loaded up Jack, and drove away.

Chapter 2

It was a two-hour drive from the trial field to my farm outside Clear Creek, give or take the time dawdling behind the springtime farm implements that migrate on the roads like massive metal reptiles. I usually don't mind being stuck behind them; driving in May here is like flowing through a calendar cover, the trees with leaves so soft you want to pet them. The forest is sprinkled with milky-white trillium, the pastures have turned Irish green, and the air bubbles with oriole song. But today all I wanted was to get home. I swerved to pass an interminably slow tractor pulling a bright green plow. I barely got back into my lane, tires squealing, before I would have slammed headfirst into a milk truck. I pulled over, took some breaths, and said, "I'm sorry Jack, I'm so sorry!" The poor dog must have been thrown against his crate. I turned back to check on him and he grinned and wagged his tail at me as if nothing had happened. I sat deep breathing in the cab, as I had learned to do so many years ago, after New Mexico. Inhale, 1-2-3-4. Hold, 1-2-3-4. Exhale, 1-2-3-4. Hold, 1-2-3-4.

Soon I began the gradual ascent up to my little farm. Lonely Owl Farm is forty acres of heaven and hell on a bluff overlooking the south branch of Clear Creek. It's the view that sold me on the place, that caused me to beg and borrow every dollar I could manage for a down payment eight years ago when I stumbled upon it, bumping my way down a dirt road, following a faded FOR SALE sign by the side of a county highway.

I had imagined accomplishing a long list of renovations when I signed the papers, after convincing the local bank to loan me more than they should have. I didn't care that the old farmhouse was in such disrepair that you couldn't lock the doors, or the barn was on the verge of collapse, or the gate to the yard around the house almost impossible to open. Barns can be salvaged, doors can be repaired and locks added, gates mended. All I cared about was the land and the view. It wasn't my smartest financial decision; I didn't have much money to fix things up. But I needed it, knowing that the land and the view and the birds would be better than therapy or drugs to make me whole again after running away from the nightmare that was my marriage. Best decision I ever made.

I let Jack out of his crate after parking the truck. Unlike his sister Jess, Jack is a big Border collie, forty-seven pounds of muscle and sinew. He has a lustrous collar of white fur, like the ruffle around the necks of seventeenth-century royalty. He is also full of himself. He strides toward unfamiliar females like John Travolta in Saturday Night Fever; you can practically hear "Staying Alive" in the background. He also sneaks under the fence to work the sheep on his own and wakes me up at four in the morning for his breakfast. And, I adore him, and I think he adores me, and at night when he lies beside me on the couch and lays his silky head on my lap, we forgive each other everything.

That afternoon it was all I could do to unpack the truck. I carried armfuls of dog supplies, jackets and boots out of the truck, and threw them down in the mudroom. I let Jack outside where he marked his territory while I let Clementine, a fifteen-year-old, ginger-colored terrier mix, out to potty. Adopted from a client who couldn't take care of her anymore, Clementine suffers from heart disease and a tendency toward intestinal upset. She sleeps twenty-three hours a day and is occasionally mistaken for a stuffed animal.

Clementine and Jack are joined by forty Katahdin ewes with lambs, a flock of obnoxious Muscovy ducks that I consider butchering every day, and a thirty-year-old pinto mare that I rescued from an auction and creatively call Old Horse. We are all managed by the farm bosses: two calico cats named Thelma and Louise.

I called Jack and hiked down into the pasture to check on Bo Peep, a Great Pyrenees livestock-guarding dog who lives with the sheep. I was glad to find her in her usual spot that time of day, zoned out in the shade of an old hay wagon. Sheep guarding dogs sleep during the day because coyotes usually do their hunting between dusk and dawn. Bo Peep woke up as we approached, thumped her tail, and slowly rose to her feet. She traded butt sniffs with Jack, and I bent down to rub her neck.

She licked my face, and I gazed up the hill to see that the flock was resting comfortably under a stand of oaks, peaceful as a Victorian painting. The ewes lay with floppy ears and folded legs, mouths moving rhythmically, the lambs cuddled up beside them. A bucolic scene, spoiled by the image of George's bloody body, as if it was a filter that had been superimposed onto my eyes. I bent over and put my hands on my knees. Old Horse lumbered over and rested her forehead against me. I stroked her cheeks and rested my head on hers. Finally, I collected myself and went back to the house.

My first job was to let Vince, a retired dairy farmer who lived down the road and did the farm chores when I was gone, know that I was home early. I was glad I got his answering machine; I didn't want to talk to anyone. I checked my phone messages, including the ones that came in on my business line.

Luckily there were just a few, with none of the crisis calls I had learned to expect on a weekly basis, begging me to see them TODAY because their dog was scheduled to be euthanized TOMORROW because of a bite. "You're Champ's last chance. Please, please can you fit us in tomorrow morning?"

I unpacked slowly, hanging the jackets more carefully than usual. I folded my T-shirts and socks, placing them in the drawers in order of color, instead of the usual kaleidoscope of chaos. I went to the kitchen and scrubbed the sink. I shook out the blankets in the dog beds and swept the floors. I turned on the TV, then turned it off.

I sat down on the couch and stared at the only photograph on the living room wall that had people in it—all the rest were of dogs, horses, and sheep. George and I were crouched beside Jack, maybe nine, ten months old then, with gangly legs and a goofy face full of innocent expectations. I looked over the moon with excitement. George looked serious, although one corner of his mouth was turned up; you had to look hard to see it.

Vince, my neighbor with the voice of a gravel road and the heart of a dove, called while I sat staring at the photo. He was a friend, in the way that good neighbors are. I couldn't count the number of times he bailed me out—from pulling my skid steer out of the ditch, to minding the farm when I left for sheepdog trials. I helped him care for his aging German shepherd before she died, and took him rotisserie chicken when he mangled his hand in a friend's manure spreader. We knew each other's land, animals, and the state of our farm equipment, but, like many country neighbors, not much of each other's back stories. I knew his wife had died, and that he had a son somewhere in Kansas. I'd heard from another neighbor that it broke his heart to sell his cows the month before I moved in—yet another casualty of the dairy industry. He'd never said a word to me about it.

Shocked by my news about George, he asked if I wanted him to come over. I said thanks, no, and settled with Jack and Clementine on the porch to watch the sunset over the creek.

I didn't sleep much that night. I kept seeing George's face, those kind eyes, that subtle

grin. I first saw them when I went to meet Jack, a mewling ten-week-old puppy out of George's top bitch and an imported sire from Scotland. George had been working a young dog when I arrived, and called her off when he heard my truck drive up. I twirled my hair as he approached.

I was about to meet a litter from two nationally known parents. I felt like an imposter hoping to get one.

George was famous. He'd won the Nationals five times, sold trained dogs for five figures, and gave clinics all over North America. I was a nobody, certainly not in the sheepdog world. I may have had a devoted clientele and a number of veterinary clinics who referred to me for my work with family dogs, but I kept my head down, even in my own field, stayed in my lane. No weekend seminars on canine aggression for me, like some of my colleagues; no television appearances in spite of local reporters begging for a story to fill their morning shows. I was surprised George had even considered selling me a pup from such a well-bred litter; usually such a breeding would be reserved for other top handlers.

The dog he had been working, a lanky adolescent, ran over and leapt up to greet me. George started to call her off, but I love a dog who wants to say hello with enthusiasm, rather than stand stiffly, contemplating how best to sink their teeth into my thigh.

"She's lovely!" I said, and extended my hand to George while I stroked her soft face with the other. "Glad to meet you. Thanks for letting me come look at the litter."

"Shouldn't let her do that, I suppose," he said, assuming

like many that I thought well-behaved dogs always kept four paws on the floor. I shrugged my shoulders. "I don't care, we're on a farm, right? I'm always happy to see a friendly dog."

"So . . ." George picked his cap up and smoothed his hair, settled it back down. "You work with pet dogs, is that right? But want to get into working dogs?"

I hate the word "pet." It started as a term for domestic animals, but morphed into something meaning spoiled and indulged, like "teacher's pet." "Family dogs" is what we call them in the behavior business, or "companion animals." Something about the word "pet" feels like it diminishes them and what we do. I swallowed.

"Mostly I see clients for aggression problems, but also for problems based on fear, like thunder phobia, separation anxiety. Things like that." I squared my shoulders, forced my hand to stop twirling my hair. My hair was getting tangled.

"But, I've worked with a lot of Border collies, and now I've caught the sheepdog bug."

"Well, I'll bet you do interesting work, then. I've got a new dog who is terrified of strangers. Got her from Wales. Maybe you could help me with her sometime?" George turned and began walking toward the barn, nodding at me to follow. "But first, let's go meet the litter."

The puppies were sound asleep in a pile of adorableness, nestled on clean straw in an old horse stall. They woke when George opened the stall door, scrambling over each other to greet us. George and I sat down and were instantly covered in five fuzz balls, with velvety round bellies and hot little tongues. George picked up a female with beautiful markings. She had a wide, white stripe down her face, one all-white leg, and a big white collar.

George said, "I think this might be a good pup for you. She's not too bold, but not too soft. Seems pretty mellow and easy to be with. I call her Jess. Listens well for her age too." He plopped her in my lap. There is a level of cuteness that defies description; all I can say is that, while I held this little packet of life against my chest, I felt soft and warm and like life would always be good.

I spent some time with her and did a few standard puppy evaluation tests. I liked her responses, and was about to say "I'll take her" when a bigger, darker puppy weaseled his way into my lap. He pushed Jess aside, crawled up my chest, and started licking my face as if it was covered with chicken fat. I picked him up, laughing, and held him in front of me while he squirmed in protest. He had a squiggly, off-center, white line down his face, a big white collar, and a fluffy collie coat. He was going to be a big boy.

"So, who is this handsome stranger?" I asked George.

"Uh, well, that's Jack. He's sort of the opposite of Jess. Super bold, always the first to try new things out. Pretty sure of himself, and busy. Busy, busy, busy. First to get up and last to go to sleep. I like his attitude though. I've had my eye on him either to keep myself or give to Simon"—who I knew was the other top handler/trainer in the country. "I'm not sure he's the best pick for a novice handler. He's going to have his own opinions about how to work sheep."

I put him down, knowing well the importance of personality matches between dog and owner. Who was I to not take George's advice? I retrieved Jess and pulled her back to my chest. Jack leapt, LEAPT, like a pouncing cat, back into my lap. Before I could stop him he was back up in my face. I gently pushed him away, stood up with Jess in my arms, and got ready to settle the business part of the arrangement with George. George put Jack back in the stall and shut the door. We walked out, Jess's heart thrumming against my own. We hadn't gone ten yards when I almost tripped on a black and white bullet who had thrown itself in front of my feet. Jack.

"How the hell did he get out?" said George. Shaking his head, he picked up the pup and tucked him into his arm to take him back. Jack squiggled and whined, thrashing like an out-of-control three-year-old child. Without thinking, I traded puppies. I pulled Jack, flailing and complaining, against my chest, and said, quietly, "Hey, bud. It's okay. Settle down." He instantly relaxed, and pushed his head farther into me, making whimpers of contentment. In less than a second, I wanted him as much as I'd ever wanted anything in my entire life. I looked up at George and shrugged.

George laughed, to my relief, and said, "Well, if he wants you that bad, I guess maybe he knows something we don't. He's a lot of dog, Maddie. I'm still not sure he's the best dog for a novice handler like you. But you're a professional dog trainer, so that has to count for something. I'll tell you what, you can have Jack, IF you promise to let me work with you on his training. Working a sheepdog is all about trust—he has to trust you as much as you trust him, and you're gonna make mistakes starting out, it's impossible not to. Maybe I could help you avoid most of them."

That was the beginning of a friendship with a man who became, besides Dorothy, the most important person in my life. He had thrown me a lifeline of respect and treated me like an equal within minutes of our meeting. I learned through the years that he was like that around everyone—respectful, curious, generous, never defensive or competitive. George was that rare individual—I've known horses and dogs like this too—who was so comfortable in their own skin that everyone wanted to stand next to them, bathing in the halo of their quiet confidence. You could trust him. To say what he thought, to be kind, and to be there when you needed him.

And now he was gone.

That night, I couldn't get the image of George's body out of my mind. How one moment he was brimming with life, and the next moment, an empty shell. Life can be extinguished in less than a second, no matter how elaborate and miraculous its creation. This information is important to know, and essential to ignore most of the time, because otherwise, we'd go mad.

CHAPTER 3

The weekend went by in a haze. I spent a lot of time in the office, doing paperwork, scrubbing the bathroom sink. Dorothy and I talked on Sunday. I gave her some advice about handling a frightened fawn. She teased me about the crappy coffee I drink. We heard on the news that the police were investigating George's death, but there were no suspects. Anyone with any knowledge of someone hunting in the area was asked to come forward.

Years ago, one of the bank's tellers had been shot during hunting season by a trigger-happy FIB (Wisconsin speak for "Fucking Illinois Bastard") who ran as soon as he realized what had happened. The cops found him within a day. Hard to hide in the country, where we all tend to know our neighbors' business, in spite of the distance between houses.

Dorothy and I ended on a happier note, chatting about her new litter and the weirdly sweet, skunky scent of puppy bellies. I complained about my hair, frizzy in the moist spring air and almost impossible to domesticate under a cap. She said, "Oh shut up. I'd kill for your hair. You look like a fairy goddess. Even your freckles are cute."

"Exactly," I said. I hate cute.

I did the chores, ate canned beans and burritos, locked up

the house, and spent the evening curled up with Jack and Clementine, watching bad television until the late night informercials came on, hawking new ways to lose weight and use vegetable choppers. No vegetable has been harmed in the making of my dinner since I moved to Wisconsin, and having a little bit of heft never hurts when you have to flip a ewe onto her back to treat an injury, so I turned off the television and dragged myself up the stairs.

I drove into my office Monday morning, smack in the middle of Clear Creek. It's a small town, one of those "don't blink or you'll miss it" kind of places. The main street is five blocks long, with architecture that can't seem to settle into a particular time or style. Some buildings are old, built in the bulky, sandstone blocks of midwestern tradition, but they alternate with squat, flat-roofed structures from the sixties. A timeless gas station/convenience store anchors the end of town, where you can still buy the daily paper and grouse about the weather to Pat or Kristi behind the counter. The Dodd County Community Bank stands square in the middle of town, a drive-up window at the back attesting to its efforts to keep up with the times.

The Feed Bucket Café is across the street from my office. It opens at five in the morning, feeding hungry farmers done with the early milking, and droopy-eyed county workers waking up over bottomless cups of coffee. Both the township and the café are shared by fourth-generation farmers whose great-grandparents had come from the old country, and by newbies like me, people born in cities or suburbs and drawn to the scenery. You could find us there together on Sunday mornings, the dairy farmers commiserating over a new low in milk prices, the newly landed arguing over an op-ed in the *New York Times* or the *Wall Street Journal*. We talk together about a late snow or a dry summer, bound together by the weather that humbles us, and the land that holds us like a cupped set of hands.

The café is great, but Clear Creek was not the ideal place to open an animal behaviorist's office. It's a small town, primarily rural, and a good thirty minutes from a town of any size. But it's ten minutes from the farm, and the rent is cheap, so I thought I'd give it a go when I opened up my office seven years ago.

I work with animals with serious behavioral problems, which mostly translates into dogs who bite. Or try to. I love these dogs, no matter what their reasons for threatening aggression. Most of them are frightened and don't know any other way to protect themselves. They need someone to stand up for them.

Many of these dogs are dangerous, but that's okay. I have my share of fears—don't even talk to me about caves or elevators, much less ask me to go into one—but I've never been afraid of dogs, even big ones with jaws strong enough to bend steel. But they don't frighten me; they *interest* me. I want to get into their heads. What are they thinking, what are they feeling? What can their postures, their eyebrows, their tails tell me about what they are about to do?

It's not just dogs. There's just nothing about an animal that has ever scared me. I had a pet tarantula when I was a little girl, Lady Schick. I did some of my research in graduate school on wasps, getting stung multiple times in search of more data. I worked at a stable in my teens; my favorite horse, Buzzword, was a bite specialist. He liked to pin his ears back and corner you in his stall, snaking his head forward to sink his yellow teeth into your shoulder. He became my special project when I was fourteen. I loved trying to figure him out. What was it that set him off?

What was he getting out of threatening people? He was a puzzle, a living, breathing Rubik's Cube, and I loved trying to solve it. I did too. In six weeks, anyone could walk into his stall, and he'd lower his head for a head rub.

I love horses; they are intuitive and super social, and incomprehensibly, are often as noble as they look. But dogs, oh God . . . dogs. I adore them, cherish them, need them, live and breathe them. I've never been afraid of them. When they threaten me—eyes blazing and teeth flashing, or worse, their body going stiff and silent—I thank them for the information they are providing me. I don't need time to know how to respond. I just do. I don't have a lot of social skills outside my office—I'm worthless at a cocktail party—but I can talk dog all day long. I have another advantage: my height, or lack of it. Being short doesn't give you any gravitas with people, but it's an advantage around dogs who are frightened of tall people looming over them. I do have to tame my feral hair—to a dog, a mass of big hair looks like someone with their hackles up—so I pull my hair back in a tight bun, but loosen my face and body to help them relax.

I discovered the profession before I left New Mexico, my bank account full of money from my divorce settlement. Listening to the radio one morning a few months later, I heard a behaviorist talk about applied animal behavior, using what science has discovered about why animals do what they do, and how to use that to work with problem dogs. I had loved my science classes, a passion long forgotten after I'd married and became a housewife. Inspired, I loaded my sweet mare Neriffa, the only good thing that had come from my marriage to Tyler, in an old horse trailer hitched to the truck and began driving east. I'd managed to get myself into the animal behavior program at the University of Minnesota, after learning that one could study behavior like veterinarians study medicine. I found an old farmhouse to rent for cheap, where I could keep Neriffa, not too far from town. Making a living working with animals hadn't been in my game plan when I was younger; marrying someone who had horses, like Tyler, seemed much more realistic.

I spent years studying the basis of behavior, from genetics to in-utero development to neurophysiology. I learned all about learning—how to use positive reinforcement to teach a new behavior and change a problematic one, why to avoid punishment if at all possible. I went to classes with the dogs of friends to learn the art and sport of dog training, I read volumes on evaluating and treating behavioral problems in dogs and cats; I attended conferences and watched videos. I sat in on cases with a mentor, and got certified as an applied animal behaviorist by the Animal Behavior Society. I created a brochure, visited vet clinics to drum up referrals, and waited for business.

I'd thought I was ready to start working on serious behavior problems. Turns out I wasn't as ready as I thought I was. Neither was Clear Creek. Several people poked their heads in the door and asked if they could bring their dogs in for grooming on the day I opened. I put on my glasses, used only in an attempt to create gravitas in a short woman with too much hair, and patiently explained that I was an applied animal behaviorist who treated serious behavioral problems in pet dogs and cats. Not to mention that I couldn't groom a poodle to save my life.

One neighbor, the owner of Heavenly Styles Hair Salon apologized for her mistake.

"Oh honey, I'm sorry. I thought you were a groomer. Town sure does need one. What is it you said you did?"

"I help people when their cats or dogs get into trouble, like if your dog bit the neighbor or panics when it thunders. I studied behavior in school just like veterinarians study medicine. So many dogs are euthanized or given away because of behavior problems, and my job is to help the family treat the problems so that both the dog and the family are safe and happy.

"Oh," she said, looking away from me, toward the street. "We had a dog who bit someone once. Had to shoot him."

But people did come in for appointments, at first mostly referred by their vets. It was a trickle during the first months, but a steady stream by the time I'd been in business for six months. I saw a cocker spaniel who bit the mailman and a golden retriever who bit the neighbor's dog. I met a pony-sized Great Dane who killed a Yorkie and a German shepherd who growled at garbage cans. Mostly, I saw dogs who growled or bit because they were frightened, many of them having been neglected or traumatized at some point in their life. Their fear was palpable, at least to me. It didn't take long for them to realize that, finally, someone understood them, and was on their side. I adored them all.

On that first workday morning after George died, my first clients came in promptly at nine o'clock. I knew little about them except that Animal Control had asked me to see them over a dog-dog aggression issue. Three men strolled into the front office and introduced themselves as Joe, Clyde, and Marvin. After a brief hello, we moved to the inner office and they set themselves down on the chairs across from my desk. Their one-hundred-pound sorta-maybe Labrador settled at their feet.

They wore rumpled jackets straight out of army surplus, jeans distressed by work rather than design, and boots with leather so cracked I could see a suggestion of socks through the slits. These were not socks you wanted to think much about. The guys sat across from me sporting a collection of headwear, including a denim newsboy's cap on one and a backward facing Milwaukee Bucks cap on the other. I immediately thought of them as "the boys," although their gray hair suggested that they were well acquainted with their sixties.

They were not the kind of pet owners I usually saw. Although none of my clients had been rich, old ladies with diamond-collared dogs (as was often assumed), I didn't see a lot of people who looked like they lived under a bridge. The people who came to see me were pretty much straight out of middle America—they taught school, or fought fires, or wrote grant proposals to fund research at the university. They could be twenty or eighty years old, single or married, gay or straight, but they all shared two things: they loved their dog, and they could afford—sometimes easily, sometimes not—to pay an animal behaviorist eighty-five dollars an hour for help solving a serious behavioral problem. Actually, they shared something else. They usually came dressed in clean clothes and had combed their hair.

"So . . ." I began, squelching the urge to call them Larry, Darryl, and my other brother Darryl, like the "Anything for a Buck" handymen on the *Bob Newhart Show*.

"So, how can I help?"

Joe, the only one clean shaven, but with feral eyebrows that threatened to take over his face, was the apparent spokesman. He answered the question while the massive dog snored, his plump torso rising and falling.

"We're only here because Animal Control made us. Gave us a goddamn 'dangerous dog' ticket. Two hundred and twenty dollars, and for what? Just because Harpo here was protecting us? Isn't that what dogs are supposed to do? And now we have to pay you another goddamn bunch of money, just to keep them from taking Harpo away." Clyde and Marvin said nothing but shook their heads in mutual disgust.

There are times when a PhD is useful. My graduate work in animal behavior made veterinarians more likely to refer their clients to me. But an advanced degree wasn't going to score points with these boys. They didn't want to be there, and they didn't want my advice. The only way to their hearts was through Harpo, who lay snoring on the rug, his yellow-brown flews bubbling up saliva with each breath.

"He's a good dog, Harpo, a damn good dog." This was from Clyde, who leaned over arthritically to stroke Harpo's flanks.

I looked carefully at Harpo, who radiated good health. His tawny coat glistened. He was at a perfect weight. His nails were trimmed. He had on a clean, new collar and a set of dog tags with a heart-shaped identification disc. In contrast to his owners, Harpo could have come off the pages of a canine *Gentlemen's Quarterly*.

The only problem was that Harpo's well-maintained teeth had sunk themselves into the neck of someone's shih tzu, almost killing her. It hadn't been the first time he'd attacked another dog. A colleague at Animal Control had told me that the residents of the neighborhood lived in fear of Harpo, who often jumped over the yard's sagging chicken wire fence, terrorizing anyone walking their dog. This was the first serious attack, but there had been at least six incidents in the past two years.

Joe and friends sat back, arms crossed, with pursed lips and glaring, narrowed eyes. I left the shelter of my ship-sized mahogany desk and walked toward Harpo.

"Hey, handsome," I said.

Harpo's head rose up a few inches, and his tail began to thump. I clapped my hands softly to encourage him to come up and say hello. His body arose initially one section at a time—first one front leg, then the second, then followed by a lurch as he rose lopsidedly to his feet and shook his entire body as if he'd just taken a bath. Then he stood still, looked at me, and grinned. I grinned back.

I turned to the side as he ambled toward me, always careful to avoid a face-to-face greeting with a dog I'd never met. Any other approach in our own species is creepy—ever met someone who wouldn't look you in the eye? But it's rude in the society of dogs. Polite dogs greet from the side, with bodies bending in semicircles. There's the sniffing of each other's butts too, but I tend to skip that part.

I was looking for a sign that Harpo would stiffen his body, a good predictor of a dog who was uncomfortable with strangers. But Harpo's torso was loose and loopy and his mouth was open and relaxed. Aggression to people, at least on neutral territory, didn't seem to be a problem.

Within a few seconds I was sitting happily on the floor, face covered in slobber, hands deep into Harpo's fur.

Harpo wagged from the shoulders back and licked my face while I cooed about what a good dog he was. And he clearly was, at least with people. There's almost no such thing as an "aggressive dog" who attacks everything in sight. Like most of my client's dogs, Harpo was dangerous in one context, but a sweetheart in others.

I could see out of the corner of my eye that Joe had uncrossed his arms as Harpo and I had a love fest. Clyde moved forward so that he could pet one end of Harpo while I was petting the other. Marvin stayed sitting back in his chair, eyes narrowed under the bill of his cap, watching me intently.

I stroked Harpo's belly as I explained how "good" dogs can get into a lot of trouble. I asked how they'd feel if a three-hundred-pound animal leapt over their fence and attacked Harpo, almost killing him while they attempted to rescue him.

Silence. Joe and Clyde looked at the floor. Marvin looked out the window. Finally, Joe said, "Yeah. Okay." Pause. "So now what?"

We talked some more, and I got more details about the previous incidents. I explained that management was going to be as important as training, but I didn't know enough about their yard and fencing. Could I come out and do a house call?

Joe looked at Clyde, who looked at Marvin. All three looked at Harpo, who was now half asleep at my feet. I broke the silence by yet again ignoring the advice of a business consultant who begged me to stop giving away my time and knowledge. I told them I'd waive my house call fee and go to their home to create a treatment plan, knowing that just talking in the office wouldn't be enough. Business be damned; who else was going to help Harpo and the boys? Harpo was a good dog in so many ways, and they clearly adored him. I didn't see how I could ignore them.

After we set a date for a house call, I sat back and took a breath as they paraded out of my office. And realized that, for the first time since Friday, I hadn't thought about George's death for over an hour. Dogs, my best friends, yet again.

CHAPTER 4

A week passed, the image of George's bloody body on repeat, over and over and over again. At night I'd lie on the couch and look at the photograph on the wall of me, George, and Jack, thinking about the day he'd called me a few months after I brought Jack home, and asked how he was doing. I'd spluttered for a moment, surprised he'd called, but recovered to say that Jack was growing so fast I could barely recognize him every morning. He acted like every visitor was a Christmas present, and was learning so fast I could barely keep up with him. He also drove me crazy, chasing the ducks and throwing toys in my face at four in the morning. Standard stuff for an adolescent. I told George that, in spite of it all, I adored him, trying not to gush, failing miserably.

"Well, glad you like him. He sounds a lot like his momma, one of my favorites of all time. I kept his sister, Jess, and she's coming along nicely." He paused; I looked down at Jack, chewing on a stuffed Kong toy, and smiled. "Say," George said, "could I ask you about that dog I told you about? The one from Wales who is bad with strangers? She damn near bit someone yesterday, and if I can't get her turned around, I'm going to have to put her down or find a safe place to send her. I've tried correcting her, but she's just getting worse. I have people here for lessons all the time, and can't afford to have a dangerous dog around. But I paid a fortune for her, and she's sweet with me, so . . ." He trailed off.

I went there the next weekend, happy to soak up George's wisdom about stock dogs, curious about this little, imported female, name of Gael. She was a tiny thing, with a busy nose, pointy ears, and a body radiating terror when she saw me. For a microsecond, her eyes softened; I turned my head away to look unthreatening, sank down to the ground well away from her, and tossed chicken in her direction. In twenty minutes she was licking my face.

"Well, I'll be damned," he said. I got in a chance for a second session when his next client appeared for a lesson; Gael got more chicken as they approached and then let me take her back to her kennel before the stranger got too close and set her back.

"Just go slow, George, one person at a time. Always quit when you're ahead. You don't want to rush this kind of counterconditioning. Call me anytime if you have any questions. I'm guessing she's going to be fine if you don't go too far too fast."

Thus began a friendship between us that I counted on every day. He asked me about family dog training, I picked his brain about stock dog training—how "giving dogs the sheep" is all the reinforcement a Border collie needs, how to read the sheep better, how to help my dog rather than setting him up to fail. We talked trial strategies, and crazy, funny things people did, and most of all, dogs, the center of our lives.

My farm and animals were my only solace after his death. I sat on the porch for hours with Jack and Bo Peep at my side, staring across the valley to the soft purple hills rising in the south, the verdant fields in the foreground. When I first saw Lonely Owl Farm, I actually twirled around with my arms raised, like a fuzzy-haired Julie Andrews, circling in unbridled joy at the view. As a wren burbled its liquid song in a downed oak tree, I decided then and there that I just had to make it my home.

I've never regretted it. Except maybe when hordes of disoriented mice were forced to find new housing. Or, the year of the ice storm when all the pipes froze in the barn and I had to slide down the hill on my butt to water the sheep, hauling buckets on a sled that I pulled behind me. I fixed it up as best I could. I can now walk in through the front door without danger of falling through the porch. The makeshift root cellar that's dug under the house has yet to collapse the foundation, as the home inspector warned. Water runs reliably through the pipes, unless it gets under twenty-five degrees below zero, but even then, a few minutes with a hair dryer under the kitchen sink and I'm good to go. I never fixed the sticky gate that leads into the fenced yard around the house; that way people I don't know have to mess with it before getting to the door. Gives me time to check them out.

The morning of George's funeral dawned sweet and clear, an introduction to those rare spring days that reward us northern gamblers who live through the dark days of winter, counting on a jackpot of Kodacolor skies and cotton ball clouds in spring. As I pulled away, the wild geraniums in the ditch waved in the breeze beside the driveway, as pale pink as a newborn rabbit. I drove by them numbly. As always, I ignored the piles of farm debris I'd promised to dispose of after I moved in. Time flies.

It was about an hour to the funeral, held in the outskirts of town. I blasted 106.1 on the radio—country music's elemental stories of love and loss keeping me company. I pulled off the highway into the parking lot and wedged my truck between a faded '88 Chevy pickup and a smoke-colored Lincoln Town Car. George's friends were nothing if not eclectic. The dress code inside the dimly lit funeral home continued to reflect

George's mix of friends, from clean jeans to suits and ties, and lots of men in dark blue jackets that looked rarely worn. We were all a bit spiffed up, so much so that I barely recognized some of George's friends from the sheepdog world. Turns out I wasn't the only one.

"Maddie? Is that you?" Jeremy, one of the handlers at the trial who had gone in search of the hunter who shot George, stood in front of me as if planted there like a tree. "You look great!" he said, and then added abashedly, "It's such a shame about George." He had me trapped against a door; it being easier to corner me in a funeral home than in the expanses of a sheepdog trial. Did he know he was staring at my chest? I struggled to come up with some snappy remark, but was rescued by a familiar voice, saying "Hey, girlfriend, hi, Jeremy."

I turned to see Dorothy standing behind me, her dark green pants and fitted vest fading into the dim light of the room. She moved between me and Jeremy like a dog splitting up a group of sheep, turned her head, and said, "Excuse, Jeremy, but I need to talk to my girlfriend a minute." He smiled ruefully and walked away.

"Jesus, that guy never gives up," I said.

"Yeah, well, he's single and you are too, and you are not weird or crazy and you are NOT HEFTY like your stupid-ass aunt said—when are you EVER going to get over that? You are curvy and you have no fucking idea how many men ask me if you are available."

"Sure I do. Jeremy and who else? Who else is single in our sheepdog community?"

"Who said anything about single?"

We were saved by Mary, another handler, who came up and gave us both hugs. "George. Poor George. What the hell?" That was the unspoken question that lay over the room like ground fog. Who had shot George, and why? It seemed improbable that some idiot hunter had aimed for a deer with no idea that his shot could carry five hundred yards across an open field. But it seemed even more impossible that someone would want to kill George. Murders happen on TV, not at sheepdog trials in Wisconsin.

Dorothy and I moved with the crowd toward Tom, George's best friend and business partner. Tom was greeting guests along with his wife, Joan, George's brother, and nephew. George's wife had died years ago; he used to tell me how much he missed her when we sat on his porch, our dogs cooling off after training, their tongues long and velvet pink. He said once, after a few more beers than usual, that his business partner Tom and I were his "only family, now." His brother lived in California; George rarely spoke of him.

Tom stood stiffly, as if his body would collapse if he didn't consciously hold it together, his eyes sorrowful. Tom didn't work with sheepdogs like George, but he often came to trials as a getaway from his own work with sniffer dogs. While George had been a man of few words, Tom was the life of the party. Tom was the extrovert who always had a hug for you when your dog's run went badly, who never forgot that you had relatives in wherever, and who could be counted on to haul out glasses, ice, and drinks for everyone after the competition was over. Tom was the yang to George's yin. George was tall and spare with a quiet, benevolent strength. Tom couldn't be over five foot seven, with the wiry build of a soccer player. He radiated energy as if he carried around his own internal sun.

"Oh God, Tom," I said. "I'm so sorry."

"I know, Maddie. Thank you so much for coming." He held on to my hand but looked down at the floor for a moment. "I just can't imagine life without him, you know?" I squeezed his hand and tried not to dissolve when I leaned forward to hug him. I took a breath, drew back, and looked one more time into his haunted eyes. We nodded, a tiny head bob in solidarity, and I moved a half step over to be in front of Tom's wife, Joan.

I didn't quite know what to say to her. I didn't know her all that well, and I was surprised when Tom married her two years ago. It seemed like he hadn't known her long before the wedding—she was a police dispatcher in Milwaukee—but Tom was clearly gobsmacked in love with her. She was gorgeous in a city kind of way, with straight blond hair that angled shorter toward the back of her head, razor-edged cheekbones, and the slender build of someone who hadn't seen a potato chip in years. She didn't seem to love dogs all that much, but she seemed intelligent and cheerful, and Tom adored her, so we were all happy for him.

I shook her hand, her fingers cool and thin. She said, "Maddie, I am so sorry. George was so fond you, he used to talk about you a lot." My eyes got all gooey, and I told her how glad I was that she'd be there for Tom; he'd need a lot of support after losing both a good friend and a business partner. I moved down the short line, expressing my sympathies to George's brother and nephew. Dorothy and I took our seats and chatted quietly for a few minutes. Soon the reception line cleared and everyone took their seats.

As they did, the double set of doors behind us squeaked open and two men entered the room, backlit by the lights in the lobby. They were dressed in identical suits, with white shirts, dark blue ties, and unnaturally shiny shoes. They might as well have had the word "COPS" emblazoned on their jackets. There was nothing remarkable about their entrance besides their late appearance; there were a lot of people from law enforcement in attendance. Tom sold working dogs to police departments all over the country, and it was no surprise that some would come out to support him. All eyes had shifted toward the noisy door, but once the men were seated at the back, everyone turned their heads toward the front of the room.

Except me. I couldn't take my eyes off one of them. Something in his face drew me in. I stared for so long that he turned his face and looked directly at me. As he did, I felt a familiar tightening in my gut.

His eyes were flint. "Hard eye" is what we call it in the dog world, when a dog's eyes go still and flat, right before they try to bite you. I was warned about this before I started seeing cases, but I could never get anyone to describe exactly what I was supposed to be looking for. Then one day a visiting dog grabbed a barn swallow that had fluttered to the ground. I reached toward him to rescue the bird, but before my brain had sorted out what I was seeing—that the dog's body had gone stiff and his eyes flat—my internal alert system flashed. We all have one, a primitive part of our brains that screams DIVE DIVE like a siren in a submarine when it senses danger. As I pulled my hand away, I saw that his eyes, normally soft and friendly, looked cold and hard. The temperature inside my body plummeted.

It turns out that the phrase "my blood ran cold" is actually literal. Oh, I thought. Now I get it. That's what "hard eye" looks like. And there it was, on the face of the tall guy, the one with stringy black hair, and a big nose. I turned my head back to the front and fiddled with the program.

I looked at Dorothy, tilted my head and crunched my eyebrows in a "Who are they?" expression. Sometimes Tom's friends and colleagues from law enforcement came to sheepdog trials; I thought she might have met them. She shook her head. We turned our heads when "Amazing Grace" began to play, and I reached for the tissue in my pocket.

After the service we were invited to an adjacent room where folding tables groaned under the weight of food brought by friends. The array included everything from cheese balls to the green bean casseroles that define the Midwest as much as the map. I think I ate most of a cheese plate by myself; people who can't eat when they are stressed are aliens to me. My body screams for fat and sugar, no doubt why my contribution was a plastic plate of cookies from Costco. I passed on the beer, which was going faster than the cheese dip. The food and the friendship, and, clearly, in some cases, the booze, lightened our hearts. And loosened our mouths. Dorothy and I told stories to George's brother about how many times he had helped us on the trial field. Everyone laughed about the time George took me to the shooting range that Tom used to condition his police dogs to gunshots. I ended up on the ground, not understanding that when George said, "Be ready for the kick," he meant an invisible mule would smash a hoof into my shoulder.

But who shot George crept into the conversation, speculations arising that it made no sense that it had been an accident. Hunters mistake people or livestock for deer in dense woods, not an open field. One handler started bad-mouthing one of George's top competitors, as if she had something to do with it. A group over in the corner kept turning to look at me while chatting with their heads down. They might as well have screamed WE'RE TALKING ABOUT YOU. I knew there was gossip about me and George, that we were more than friends; no surprise it continued. Did they think I had something to do with it? Dorothy and I began giggling about their ridiculous attempts to be discreet. We quieted when Jeremy came over, his eyes laser focused. Time to go.

Once home, I changed into a pair of old jeans, pulling them out of a sloppy pile of pants too stained or worn out to wear anywhere else. An infinite trial learner when it comes to clothes, I'm always thinking "It'll be okay just this one time," and wear my new pair of jeans/shoes/jackets into the barn, "just this once." And end up ruining them with detergent-proof manure.

I put on my books, called Jack, and headed out to the pasture. Working a dog on sheep is a kind of meditation unto itself. You have to focus on the sheep and little else, because their behavior tells you if your dog is working correctly and what you need to do next. "Next" can happen in a split second, so you'd better be ready.

Things didn't go well. I tried to work on driving the sheep in a straight line, but they zigzagged all over the place. Twice they bolted back to their buddies in the barn and Jack had to peel them off the fence and bring them back to me. I finally called Jack off. He was happy to quit; dogs know when things aren't going well. I sat down on the grass knowing it was me that was the problem, not Jack. He lay down beside me, his tongue long, his sides heaving.

Chickadees sang in the trees down by the creek. *Whoo-hee,* they repeated, their high, musical voices interspersed with the nasal *yank yank* of the nuthatches. We sat in the field for the longest time, the five sheep noisily ripping up grass not far away.

I hate it when things don't go well. Herding is a team sport, and you can let down your dog just like you can let down your teammates in other sports. If a good dog learns not to trust you, they'll either take over completely or never learn to trust themselves. Mistakes are inevitable, but you can't apologize to your dog over a beer, so you are left sick to your stomach that you've failed to help your dog. You can't even say you're sorry. I knew the problem was mine—Jack is too talented a dog not to be able to do the exercise. But what was I doing wrong?

A few days ago I would've called George and asked him.

Okay, I said to myself, *what would George say if he was here?* I closed my eyes, conjuring up his weathered face with a hint of a smile on it. The birds by the river sang, the sheep noisily tore up grass, Jack panted. And then I remembered George, his voice quiet and low, saying, "Too much, too late, girl, too much, too late," in recent lessons. I'd been late with my signals, and kept overcompensating by giving Jack too many verbal and whistle signals.

My feeling of relief about what to work on was countered by the tension on George's face on the day he was killed. *Was* there something wrong, something bothering him? I knew it wasn't the trial; he was far too experienced for that, but he looked different, worried in a way I hadn't seen before. I felt confident I was reading him right; making snap judgments about the faces of aggressive dogs to keep from being bitten can teach you a lot about human facial expressions. But it's one thing to know the emotion behind an expression, it's another thing to know what caused it.

And then I remembered the last time we had sat on his porch and talked, when he turned to me and said, his voice low and quiet, that he had something personal he wanted to talk to me about. I looked up from watching a finch foraging in the dirt to see that his face was pale.

Surprised, I lay my hand on his forearm and said, "Of course. What is it?"

"Yo, mateys!" Tom had appeared around the corner of the house, his face lit up like a Christmas tree. "Who wants another beer?" George and I exchanged a quick glance; he shrugged his shoulders so subtly I doubt that most people would have noticed. I rose up as Tom settled into a chair beside us, saying I needed to get home. "Give me a call anytime, George. See you guys later," I said as I walked to the truck.

As I drove home, I reflected on how George and I had always kept our talks focused on dogs. Or sheep and sheepdog trials. Plenty to talk and laugh about, no need to get into personal stuff. What had changed? I resolved to give him a call sometime soon. . . .

The light had faded, and the birds began to roost, so Jack and I walked back to the house together. Thelma and Louise met me on the porch, bunting the back of my legs, reminding me that it was dinnertime. I fed them and Clementine, then went back out to grain the lambs, feed the ducks, and give Old Horse her geriatric supplements. By then Jack had cooled off enough to eat, so I fed him too. Chores done, I cracked open a Spotted Cow and went out onto the porch. I sipped my beer and let my heart ache for failing George when he needed me. The sun sank behind the trees along the creek while I rubbed Jack's belly, the light glowing like coals before fading into nothing.

CHAPTER 5

On Sunday I spent the day cleaning out the barn with the ancient skid steer I'd bought for two thousand bucks, the price an indication of how little optimism the former owner had for its longevity. My neighbor Vince is a brilliant mechanic, as all dairy farmers have to be, and he brought it back to life for me in mysterious ways that I imagined involved incantations over lizards in soup. Cleaning out the barn took the better part of the day; by the time I was done it was all I could do to feed the animals and walk Jack.

Old Horse and the flock were grazing together in the west field, their bodies backlit by the sun behind the willows lining the creek banks. Bo Peep had woken up from her afternoon nap, and was silently patrolling the perimeter of the field, stopping every fifty yards to squat and pee. The message to the coyotes was clear: "Don't even think about it."

I lost my first guard dog to cancer a few years ago, an Anatolian shepherd named Karli, and within a few weeks of her death the coyotes began circling the field at night, yip-yowling by the creek, their eyes blazing blue-white in the shine of my spotlight.

A few weeks later I drove to a farm up north and brought back a Great Pyrenees, a one-year-old, hundred-pound, cream-colored fluff-ball, bred to be a working guard dog who was raised with sheep as litter mates. Within a few days my own sheep accepted her as part of the flock, and although my neighbors struggle with coyote predation on their livestock, I haven't had a problem since she arrived.

After Bo Peep finished her evening patrol, she ambled over to me and put her big, square head on my thigh. I stroked that magical, silky area that all dogs have under their ear flaps. Together, we watched the sun float down behind the trees like a hot air balloon, round and full and weightless.

Monday morning came all too soon, but I had an atypical case on the docket and I drove to the office feeling curious. Ranger was a working K9, coming in from Milwaukee on his handler's day off. A detection dog trained to sniff out drugs like heroin and cocaine, Ranger was apparently brilliant at his job. He had helped the police solve several drug-related cases and was so friendly that the department used him in demonstrations for the public. Only one problem:

Ranger was terrified of thunder.

Thunder phobia is an issue for a lot of dogs here in the Midwest, aka Thunder Alley, where every summer we get storms loud enough to shake your house. Dogs of every description become fearful, and for good reason. Thunder is basically one loud, all-encompassing growl, as if the entire sky is about to attack. No wonder so many dogs are afraid of it.

Officer Ryan Conners was coming in to see me because last week Ranger had leapt through a second-story window during a particularly violent storm. Ryan wasn't just worried about Ranger's safety; his supervisor had given him an ultimatum: get it fixed soon or he's off the force. Dogs who are thunder phobic often become afraid of any loud sound—like a gunshot.

Not the dog you need by your side if you're a cop in a crisis. It seemed like an interesting case.

Officer Conners and Ranger entered my office together as I ended a phone call with another client. I put on my glasses, anything to counter the "cute little girl" look that I was cursed with. I looked up and couldn't take my eyes off Ranger, who had enough presence to stop the talk at a cocktail party. A seventy-five-pound Belgian Malinois with the body of an athlete and the eyes of a scholar, Ranger strolled into the office, turned his head, and looked deep into my eyes. I loved him in an instant.

Officer Conners, on the other hand, would barely look me in the eye, and looked nothing like I expected. I've had a lot of contact with cops—my ex-husband took care of that. Most of the ones I dealt with out west were burly dudes with buzzed haircuts and big jaws. But this guy was all slim and slender, with a narrow face, gray eyes, and John Lennon glasses. He looked like a physics professor. He introduced himself quietly, shook my hand with an earnest face, and sat down with Ranger beside him. I noticed some lacerations on the dog's front legs. Poor guy.

"Lie down and stay," he said quietly to the dog. Ranger did, without the slightest hesitation. Good boy.

"What do you want to know, Dr. McGowan?" he said to me as he fiddled with the leash, briefly looking me in the eye again before looking down toward Ranger. His desire to pet his dog was palpable.

"Please call me Maddie, Officer Conners. May I call you Ryan in return? I see us as equal members of Ranger's team, doing everything we can to help him, so if it's okay with you, we can just be Ryan, Ranger, and Maddie. That okay?"

Good grief. I sounded like a telemarketer reading a script.

Ryan gave me small smile and a nod in response. Ranger lay quietly, looking directly at me, eyes soft, mouth open and relaxed, body sleek and chiseled.

"Why don't you start by telling me what happened last week, and then we can go back in time and get more information."

Ryan nodded, and gave in to the luxury of stroking Ranger's head.

"It was during that storm we had last week. There were tornado warnings, so even though I was off duty we were all on call. The thunder got louder and louder, and Ranger started pacing and panting. I went into my den to check in with the department when there was a thunderclap so loud that the windows rattled, and I heard the sound of breaking glass. I ran into the bedroom and saw that Ranger had gone through the window.

"I couldn't believe he'd do that." Ryan shook his head while he looked down at Ranger.

He spoke so softly I barely heard him.

"I looked out and saw Ranger sprawled on the sidewalk. I tore down the stairs and by the time I got to him he had stood up and was staggering in a circle. He had minor cuts on his face and some worse ones on his legs, so I ran him to the emergency clinic. They didn't find any broken bones, but kept him overnight for observation; they said he might have a concussion. In the morning he seemed fine except for a few lacerations from the glass. He seems like himself now, but he's off the force if I can't get this fixed. And he's—Ryan's voice caught; he turned his head to look out the window—"my partner," he finished. I sat quietly, waiting for Ryan to collect himself.

After a long pause, Ryan turned back to tell me that Ranger, a six-year-old veteran on the force, had always been fearless until recently. An early spring storm had sailed in, a maelstrom of rain and hail and snow and thunder. ("Thunder snow." It's a thing.) Ranger had run to Ryan and tried to crawl up his body, as if he wanted to hide inside his mouth.

Poor Ranger. Thunder phobia can be a nightmare for any dog. Ranger isn't the first dog I'd seen who had gone through a window, and I knew he wouldn't be the last. Thunder phobia is usually treatable, but the scientific term for the process is "pain in the ass." It can take a massive amount of time and energy to turn around. I'm never sure an owner is up to it.

After I got more background information, we spent a long time talking about a treatment plan for Ranger. I explained how to use classical conditioning to change Ranger's emotional response to loud noises, how to build a safe house for Ranger to go into if he felt scared, and other options like body wraps and the value of talking to his vet about possible medications. I told Ryan to tell his vet to call me if he'd like, and to call me himself if he had questions.

As he stood up to go and approached the door, Ryan turned back to me and said, "You never tried to pet Ranger. Everyone always does." He cocked his head, his question unspoken but clear enough.

"I have a working dog too," I said. "A sheepdog, and at big trials spectators always come over and try to pet him while he's in work mode. He tolerates it because he's a polite dog, but it's just an annoyance to him. Ranger is in work mode here too; I figured he'd appreciate the space."

Ryan's eyes softened, and for the first time his body relaxed, as if he himself had been in "work mode" during our appointment. "Sheepdogs, really? I've seen them work on TV, but never in person. I've always wanted to watch them do their thing. My friend Kevin has a K9 he got from a guy whose partner trains sheepdogs. He was at his funeral just a few days ago, as a matter of fact. Maybe you knew him?"

"Uh, yeah, I did. I knew him well," I said after I took a breath and found my voice. "He was my mentor, as a matter of fact." My throat started closing up, but I was damned if I was going to start crying in front of a cop. I took a deep breath, let it out. I stood up, hoping Ryan would get the hint and leave. Ranger stood up too, looking at me with huge, liquid eyes. What a beautiful dog. "Yeah, maybe you saw my friend? Kevin is a tall guy with a big nose, sort of hard to miss. We all tease him about it."

Oh, I saw Kevin, all right. The guy with the pit viper eyes. Great.

"Sorry, Ryan, but I have to go. I have another client coming soon." I wanted to add "because the dog hates cops," just to get him out of there as soon as I could, but I managed to restrain myself and tell Ryan to call if anything came up. I watched them walk down the hall to the outside door, Ranger in a perfect heel. He turned his head and looked back at me with those soft brown eyes as Ryan paused to open the door. "Good luck, bud," I whispered. Ranger blinked and trotted outside beside Ryan, where they disappeared into the parking lot.

I went into the tiny restroom, with its stained sink and crumbling linoleum, and stared into the mirror. So much for my work with dogs being an escape from the pain of George's death.

I splashed water on my face and went back into my office. I had another client coming, a basset hound who had bitten a delivery man, and I needed to get it together. Good thing too, because Harvey, the basset, was early. I welcomed him into my office and managed to get lost yet again in trying to help a creature who couldn't use words to tell me what was wrong.

Chapter 6

The next few days were full of clients and farm chores. One morning Dorothy sent me videos of her litter to cheer me up. I showed them to Jack and asked if he'd like a little sister. He licked the screen of my phone, farted, and started his favorite solo game—dropping a stuffed bunny down the stairs, so that he could run down and fetch it back up. While he did, I lay in bed in a cozy fog, and then felt my heart break when I remembered that George was dead.

On Wednesday afternoon I got a call from Catherine, the director of the Southeast Wisconsin Humane Society. They'd picked up a half-dead German shepherd beside the highway, and no one could get near him after he got out of intensive care. I'd done volunteer work for the shelter before, impressed with their skill at working with dogs with behavior problems. If their highly trained employees were having trouble with the dog, I knew the issue was serious.

"We should probably put him down, Maddie. He's barely alive, he won't eat or drink, and yet he's still dangerous. We just can't figure out how to get through to him. He alternates between being shut down to looking ready to kill anyone who makes eye contact. My staff is overwhelmed with all the dogs that just came in from a hoarding case, and I can't put my volunteers at risk. Is there any way you could come out and volunteer a little more of your time?

Your skills with traumatized dogs would be a life saver here."

I didn't want to go. It had been a hard enough week already. I wasn't sleeping well and spent too long staring at the photograph of me and George and Jack. Every night I'd tell George I was sorry I had driven away before he said what he wanted to tell me. Every night I'd wonder what it was he wanted to say. Maybe it was nothing. Maybe it was the answer to why he looked anxious the day he was shot.

My clients had been tricky too. On Tuesday I'd seen a heartbroken couple with a miniature poodle who put a three-inch gash in their five-year-old son's face, a Weimaraner with separation anxiety who destroyed an eight-thousand-dollar couch, and a Border collie with eyes as crazy as Jack Nicholson in *The Shining*.

This is not how most people envision the life of an applied animal behaviorist. "Oh, I wish I had your job!" they say, when I explain what I do for a living. They seem to imagine me running through fields of daisies with golden retriever puppies. More often it is sitting in a small room with heartsick clients who love their dog but may not be able to provide the best home for him. Or just as often, with dogs whose owners smile obliviously while their dog stares at me, stiff as a statue, like a farm cat watches a mouse. But Catherine and the Humane Society were doing great work, often with too few resources, and needed help. I'd kept my life simple to be able to help dogs in crisis—no dating, no travel, no interviews. Just the farm, clients, and dogs. I couldn't bring myself to say no.

I drove out the next day, on an afternoon I'd reserved for catching up on paperwork, arriving forty-five minutes later at the shelter, a series of sprawling flat-roofed buildings, surrounded by muddy fields dotted with spikes of corn seedlings. Volunteers were walking dogs in an adjacent field, and a few puppies played in a small grassy area fenced off from the parking lot.

The dog I came to see was being held in quarantine, well away from the public areas where potential adopters chose between the dogs with pleading eyes, desperate to belong to someone, anyone. The shepherd was in an attached building, curled up in the far corner of a kennel, his head on his back legs. His black eyes were open but flat. The skin on his face was hollowed out, as if someone had inserted a straw between his skin and skull and sucked out everything in between. His ears, the semaphore flags of a healthy shepherd, flopped to the side, like soggy, black tissues. A sign on his kennel door said CISCO. DO NOT ENTER.

The dog growled, a soft smudge of a noise, when I said "Hey, bud." Catherine filled me in as we stood looking into his kennel. "We have no idea about an owner, no tag, no microchip. Once we'd revived him with an IV of fluids, no one has been able to get near him, not with chicken or toys. We can't get him to eat or drink. We are all afraid he is just going to waste away."

Poor guy.

"Okay," I said. "How about I just hang out with him for a while? I've cleared the afternoon, and we can't force anything here."

"You're a life saver, Maddie, thanks so much." Catherine turned to go back to her office, and said over her shoulder, "Just let me know if you need anything."

I sat down in front of Cisco's kennel and got out a book that had sat on my nightstand for months. Forcing anything with Cisco would just cause harm, and by sitting quietly beside his kennel I hoped that he would at least habituate to my presence.

* * *

A few hours later my butt was sore from sitting on the concrete floor, my eyes were tired from reading in bad light, and my ears were exhausted from the buzz of a fluorescent light about to die. Cisco was sound asleep, at least relaxed enough to shut his eyes. Could I count that as a victory? It had been quiet, since this area was reserved for convalescing animals, but suddenly the door down the hall opened and Chris, a volunteer I'd worked with before, entered and said, "Hey, Dr. McGowan! Good to see you!" Chris was six foot two, with tattoos of dogs and cats on his arms. He wasn't rom-com handsome, but he had tousled, flaxen hair, and a quiet kindness to him that relaxed even the shyest of dogs.

Out of the corner of my eye I saw Cisco's head rise a few inches and his ears twitch as Chris spoke. I motioned for Chris to stop, moving my hand in such a way that Cisco couldn't see it. I didn't want anything to set him off, but wanted to see how he would react to someone standing further away. Chris stood still in the dimly lit hallway, the building's exhaust fans whirring quietly above us.

Cisco stood up slowly, rising without moving his head or his feet, as if his torso had been lifted up by a puppeteer's strings. He stared at Chris for several seconds, his hindquarters wobbling, while he attempted to stay standing. His head turned so slowly toward me it was riveting. This time his eyes had a spark of light in them. And then, again ever so slowly, he sank his hindquarters into a sit while turning his head back toward Chris. Still sitting, still in slow motion, he turned his head back toward me and looked straight into my eyes.

I knew, I just knew, that he was trying to tell me something.

Chris began to walk forward a few steps before I could stop him, and said, "Wow! That's the first normal reaction we've ever seen from him." At that, Cisco leapt up and tried to charge the kennel gate, but fell down in a heap. Even lying down his ruff was up, his ears were on full forward alert, and his black lips retracted, emphasizing the size of his shiny white teeth. Chris backed up a few paces, but Cisco continued to growl. Now I had a chance to look at his face more clearly. It radiated pure, unadulterated fear.

Dogs who are on offense push the corners of their mouth forward. But dogs who are scared, like Cisco, pull the corners of their mouths back toward their ears, just like we do when we are frightened. Cisco stayed still, eighty pounds of living weaponry, his face spilling the secret of his fears. All standard behavior for a frightened dog. I motioned to Chris to back up to the door, telling him we'd talk later. Cisco retreated to his corner. I sat motionless on the hard floor trying to figure out what had just happened. Why did Cisco sit down and then look at me so pointedly?

I left Cisco's kennel and walked over to talk to Chris. It turns out that it had been Chris himself who found Cisco while driving by, lying like a rag between two warehouses beside the tracks off National Avenue in Milwaukee.

"Yeah, I didn't think it was a dog at first; I thought it was maybe an old coat or something someone had tossed out of a truck. But then I saw his ears flick at some flies, so I pulled off the highway and walked over to him. He was so weak at that point he barely responded when I picked him up and brought him to the shelter. Poor guy, looks like he might have been a nice dog once."

Chris gave him a quick glance before turning away and saying, "I gotta go exercise some dogs, but good luck with him. I sure hope you can save him."

After another fifteen minutes, Cisco fell asleep again, so I got up, legs stiff, neck aching, and went to Catherine's office to tell her I had to get home. I'd give her a call about Cisco tomorrow. She'd left for the day, but I sent her a voice mail message about when I might be able to come back, and to ask if a female volunteer could sit by his kennel and offer him chicken-flavored water after a few hours. Like a lot of fearful dogs, it could have been that men bothered him more than women.

It took forever to get home, rush hour traffic adding thirty minutes to my drive, but finally I pulled off the county highway onto the farm's gravel road, the truck bouncing over the ruts I'd planned to smooth out months ago. Bo Peep's woofs boomed from the south pasture as I drove in. Jack and Clementine barked at the window as I got out of the truck and danced the universal canine happy dance when I entered the house. After the expected chest rubs and ear scratches, I called Dorothy to tell her about Cisco.

"Oh lordy, girlfriend, now what?" Dorothy was used to my obsession with difficult cases. "Don't you have enough going on now? I know you, you're going to move heaven and earth for this dog and never give up until the bitter end. You know you are one stubborn bitch? Seriously, Maddie, don't get more involved unless it is going to help you get over George, okay?"

"Okay. Promise." I hung up, grabbed a pair of boots from the pile of muddy footwear by the screen door, and went out to do the chores.

Bo Peep was waiting on me when Jack and I went out to bring in the sheep, trotting over to get her special dose of loving. The flock was up and grazing, ripping grass with sharp, inward tugs, swallowing fast and storing the food for later, when they could lie in the evening light and chew their cud. Jack and I needed to gather the sheep into the barn, where we could sort out the lambs and give them some grain, their mothers bawling objections behind the fence. Jack knew the drill, and kept running forward and back, eyes glowing, waiting for a cue to gather them together and bring them to the sorting chute by the barn.

"Away!" I said, sending Jack to our right. He ran off, his black and white body stretched out like a ribbon as he ran through the grass toward the oaks by the creek. "Lie down!" I called, when Jack got to the back of them, working on keeping my voice low and confident.

Good boy, he did indeed, and brought them politely toward the sorting chute. If only he'd be so good at a trial, where he tends to blast in like a shotgun. In no time at all we had the lambs eating their evening meal, their flexible lips nibbling kernels of corn and oats out of the long, black feeder pans. After they were done, I let the ewes come in to clean up the crumbs, and Jack and I went on to other chores.

As always, Jack and I took a long walk after everyone had cleaned their plates, his tail swishing in that circle dogs can make with their tails that says *I AM SO HAPPY!* We walked for almost an hour, Jack snuffling down rabbit trails, dashing back to me to check in, lifting his leg every hundred yards or so to mark territory.

It couldn't have been sweeter that evening, the sky fading into pale pink, the robin's flutelike song backed by the tympani of red-winged blackbirds calling in the marsh across the creek. I try to be like Jack on these walks, staying in the present as I learned in meditation class. *Feel the breeze. Focus on the birdsong. Notice the feel of the earth beneath my feet.* But my brain couldn't stop going back to Cisco and his behavior that afternoon. Why did he sit down when Chris got closer to his kennel? Or were his hindquarters just collapsing? Why did he look at me as if trying to tell me something? Or was I just seeing something that wasn't there?

There were no answers to be had on this walk, and eventually my thoughts shifted to how I could help Catherine and the trainers at the shelter. How much time, really, could I spend doing pro bono work on this one dog? I decided that I could spend at least tomorrow with Cisco. I had only one client and I knew they'd be okay with a reschedule for such a good cause. I'd call Catherine first thing in the morning and tell her I'd come over again as soon as I could get there, hoping by then that he had eaten something since I'd left.

A ground fog crept in and it was twilight now, that magical in-between time when everything shifts, ever so slightly, and it feels like anything could happen. Jack and I were beside the creek when a great horned owl called behind us, *Who Who Whooooo, Whoo Whoo?* A rabbit froze in the dim light, twenty yards ahead. Jack was oblivious, his head down, following a track unseen and unscented by me. The air was heavy, full of moisture and the scent of newly plowed earth.

Vince must have done some work in his north field, the one on the other side of the creek.

The rabbit lost its nerve as we got closer and bolted before we walked on top of it. The movement caught Jack's eye; he perked his ears up and stared at the hole in space where it had been.

I could feel him turn his head to the right at same time that I did. A tall shadow across the creek, moving toward us. I couldn't see much, just a dark shape, moving forward steadily, the figure of a man. Vince? He didn't take a lot of walks around his farm like Jack and I did, but it was his land and I knew he was trying to get more exercise ever since he had to sell off his cows.

"Vince?" I called.

The figure stopped, but no response. "Hey, Vince!" I said it louder this time. Silence. Jack and I stood motionless, staring. Once, years ago, I had called out to a hunter in a deer stand while looking in the woods for a friend's dog. The hunter, unmistakable in bright orange, was close enough for me to see his beard, his tight grip on the rifle. He didn't move, didn't turn his head, didn't answer. It was a warm day, and yet I was instantly chilled to the bone. I backed away like a single ewe being worked by a Border collie, afraid to turn my back on what I knew could kill me.

I felt the same chill that evening, that same sense of dread. Until the shadow turned sideways and began to bolt away, and Jack leapt forward to chase it. A young buck. I laughed and clapped for Jack to come back, and he did and I collapsed on the wet grass and ran my hands all over him and he rolled over and waved his paws in the air and looked like he was laughing back at me. We ran together back to the house, away from the fog, the mystery of Cisco and George's death, me flapping my arms in my cartoonish running style, Jack's long, luxurious tail streaming behind him.

I ate my usual dinner of refried beans (canned) and tortillas (frozen), smothered with bargain-rate salsa. Putting Cisco and George out of my mind as best I could, I settled in on the couch with a beer and a bag of sweet potato chips. Sweet potatoes—good for you, right? On my right, Clementine snored like a three-hundred-pound drunk at a bar. Jack rolled onto his back so that I could rub his belly while I binge-watched *House* on the tiny TV in the corner of the living room. Around eleven, I took both the dogs out for one last pee and climbed the creaky, wooden stairs up to bed.

A party. Wild laughter, sloshing drinks, Reba blasting on the radio. No one I knew, no one I didn't. Some guy—sort of my ex, sort of not—grabbed my ass, and I elbowed him in the chest and ran toward a closed door. It opened into the entrance of a black cavern. I ran into it, pursued by some man-as-monster, running deeper and deeper into a lightless, shrinking tunnel, so small I had to bend down to move forward. Until I couldn't go any farther. I tried to back up, but now I couldn't move either way. It was getting hard to breathe.

Someone started screaming. I didn't know it was me until Jack woke me up by pawing at my face and whining. I threw my arms around him, hugging him in the way that I know most dogs hate. But he pressed his body against me and licked my face until my breathing slowed. He finally went to sleep beside me, but I lay in bed for hours, practicing my breathing, trying to meditate. I drifted back to sleep.

CHAPTER 7

I woke up around four, instantly, as if snatched out of a hypnotized daze by a finger snap. One moment I was sound asleep, then I was awake. Wide awake, because I knew why Cisco had tried to sit when Chris approached his kennel. At least I thought I did. What if Cisco was a scent-detection dog, trained to sit when he detected drugs, or bombs, or the body of a lost hiker? Sitting down is the "alert," the signal that sniffer dogs use to communicate that they have found the oxycodone, or the C-5 explosive, or the dead body. Dogs used to be trained with a more "active alert," pawing at the area with the target substance. Pawing at a bomb or a corpse isn't a particularly good idea, so the protocol for almost all detection dogs now is to sit when they find something.

Maybe that's what Cisco was trying to tell me. *I found it! It's here.* Could Chris have had something in his pockets? Or just smoked some dope? Either way, I was sure, as sure as I have been about anything, that the look in Cisco's eyes wasn't just *I've detected something,* it was: *Please, please, do you understand what I am trying to tell you?*

I leapt out of bed, practically knocking Clementine off, startling Jack, who had been quietly snoring at my feet. "That's it, that's it," I repeated nonsensically as I threw on clothes and ran down to my computer. This was just a guess, possibly a wild one at that, but it felt right in my gut, and long ago I'd learned the cost of ignoring what my body was trying to tell me.

How do I confirm this? *What* do I know? *Who* do I know? Scent detection dogs weren't in my wheelhouse. I turned on my laptop and found some sites about training scent detection dogs, but I needed more information than I could get on the Internet. Luckily, I knew just where to get it. Tom, George's partner at the H & H Working Dog Center, worked with narcotic detection dogs, so I sent him a text asking if we could talk as soon as possible. I needed to learn a lot more about how handlers communicate to their dogs. If Cisco was trying to "talk" to me with his body, I needed to be able to talk back.

By six a.m. I'd heard back from Tom. He was about to go out to the kennels to begin the morning round of chores, but he said he'd be happy to talk briefly before he left the house. I called him right away and explained my hypothesis.

"Am I crazy?"

"Well, probably."

My heart fell. I had expected to be congratulated for my brilliant deduction, and I yearned to solve the mystery of Cisco. The image of his shell-shocked face was breaking my heart. I began twisting a lock of hair around my finger.

"Sorry, Maddie, it just doesn't make any sense. First of all, what would a highly trained drug dog be doing half dead by the side of highway? Detection dogs are expensive; mine go for twenty-five thousand dollars. Who the hell would dump one by the side of the road? And I'm pretty sure that the guy didn't have explosives in his pocket; none of it makes any sense."

"Okay." I paused. "But what about drugs?" The hair twirled around my fingers started to knot up.

"Possible. But I want to warn you: detection dogs aren't machines. They make mistakes, especially in the early phases of training. And if this dog was barely alive and as stressed as you describe, I wouldn't put much of anything into what he did or didn't do. One question for you though: does the dog have a tattoo in his ear? That's how military K9s are identified; the tattoos are big, hard to miss."

"No, no tattoo. I'm sure I would've noticed it."

Damn. I'd been so excited about my theory. But in the time-honored tendency of people to not let facts interfere with their beliefs, I said, "But if there weren't any drugs, why did the dog alert and then look at me with such intensity?"

Tom said, "Hell if I know. You're the animal behaviorist."

I was about to hang up, deflated, but blurted out, "Wait! Could you at least tell me some of the cues that are commonly used with police dogs? Just humor me, Tom. I know it doesn't make any sense."

"That's tricky, 'cause K9s are trained with different languages—German, Dutch, Czech. German is probably the most common, that's what I use. You can find all the commands online, including visual ones that are universally used."

"Okay, thanks. But one more thing. I know you think it's foolish, but I still have to try this out for myself. I need some drugs. Could I borrow some samples from you that you use for training?"

"Are you fucking out of your mind? Seriously, Maddie, I go through more hoops than you can imagine to get drugs for training. If I got caught giving them to you I'd be screwed. You were a good friend to George, but good God, girl. And what about you? Want to drive around with illegal drugs in your pocket? I told you that your theory doesn't make sense. Give up on it and use your own skills to help the dog."

Pause. "Jesus, Maddie," he said, and hung up.

Okay. Tom was right. That was a stupid ask. I needed to calm down, put on my animal behaviorist's hat, and find another way to get through to Cisco. I sat down and started writing out a treatment plan. Written out plans are great: They get you focused; they give you clarity. They give you an excuse to doodle in the corner of the paper, as I began doing that morning, because I couldn't give up on the idea that Cisco had been alerting me to something, something he'd been trained to find, and was asking if I was listening.

I pushed the paper away and threw down my Graphgear 1000 pencil, the one I can't think without. I knew I was being stubborn, not a new thing for me. My ex-husband, Tyler, would be happy to send you examples of what a stubborn bitch I can be. But stubborn isn't always bad and my gut kept telling me that something about my theory was right.

I sketched out a treatment plan, took Clementine out to pee again, and made coffee in the ancient Corningware percolator I'd found at Goodwill. Cup in hand, I went back online to find information about the standard commands given to working police dogs. I knew that most of the dogs working in the states are raised in Europe; Tom's midwestern kennel was an exception. If he used German commands to his dogs because they were so common, no reason not to learn a few.

After another cup of coffee and a quick run-through of the morning's chores, I gave the shelter a call as soon as they opened and asked how Cisco was doing. "Not well," the volunteer answered. "It doesn't look like he drank any water and he won't touch any food we've left for him. We're bringing the veterinarian in to see if he needs to be put back on an IV for hydration, but we have to sedate him to do so and the only way to do that is with a dart gun. It's beyond me how this dog who is barely alive gets the energy to go after anyone who comes near him, but he does. Right now, they're wondering if they should just put him down and relieve him of his misery. He doesn't want anyone in with him in his kennel, he doesn't respond to other dogs, and the whole place is running out of ideas of how to help him. Honestly, it's just heartbreaking."

"Don't let anyone put him down, please, not yet. Tell everyone that I have an idea; just give me a few more hours and I'll be over there."

Easy for me to say, but now what? Somehow someone had to get through to this dog, and I thought he just had to be a trained detection dog, in spite of what Tom said. Ideally, I'd get some drugs to test my theory, but I'd given up pot many years ago and been too chicken to mess around with anything else.

But wait. Vince! God bless him, Vince, my sixty-nine-year-old, ham-handed, farmer friend who loved his weed, illegal as it was in Wisconsin. I never knew where he got it, but he seemed to have a never-ending supply. He'd stopped offering it to me after I'd turned him down a gazillion times. I have no objection to anyone using it, but it slows my reaction time, even a day later. Not a good thing if you spend your time with dogs who can put you in the hospital if you make a split-second mistake.

"Vince. You up?"

"I am now." His voice was a little raspier than usual. I figured it might have been a late night with his girlfriend, Ms. Merlot.

"I need to borrow some pot."

Pause. There'd been a lot of pauses lately during my phone conversations.

"What? Did I hear you right? And did you say borrow? It's pretty hard to bring it back once you've smoked it."

I explained the situation, told him my theory was crazy but that I still just couldn't quite give it up. He chortled, coughed, and said, "Holy moly, woman, what have you gotten yourself into this time?" It was my turn to answer with silence.

Finally, he said, "Okay, Maddie, just don't get yourself caught. That'd be ironic."

It took way too long to get to the shelter after picking up the small, ziplock bag full of cannabis from Vince. I stuffed it into the glove compartment and then worried for the entire drive thinking that'd be the first place someone would look if I got pulled over. But it felt like Cisco's time was running out, so I kept driving, faster than I should have, slower than I wanted to. I considered ramming into the manure spreader that blocked my progress soon after leaving the farm, but took a breath and watched the fields alongside the highway being planted with corn. I sped around a van going too slowly on the interstate and honked at a car that sat too long after a traffic light turned green. It wasn't the smartest way to drive with illegal drugs in the truck, but I'd pretty much thrown rationality out the window when I refused to accept what Tom told me. I finally pulled up to the shelter around nine, just as Catherine's car drove in beside mine in the almost empty parking lot.

"Maddie! Here already?"

"I have an idea, Catherine, and I need to test it out ASAP. It's crazy, but it sounds like Cisco isn't doing well, and I don't think we have a lot of time left." My words came out in a continuous stream. *IhaveanideaCatherineandIneedtotestitout.* . . . I didn't know why it felt so important. I didn't know why my heart was racing. I'd learned years before that I couldn't save all the dogs who desperately needed help. I love what I do, and I want to do it for decades to come. If I made desperate attempts to save every dog in trouble, I'd have been burned out years ago.

But Cisco was different. Maybe I could save him, since I couldn't save George. Like someone had saved me once.

I explained my theory to Catherine, leaving out the name of the volunteer who had entered the kennel, but explaining that Cisco's response, given his condition, might have been a mistake. She smiled ruefully at this part, and wisely said, "We can talk about that later." She frowned when I told her what I had in my truck. "Good grief, Maddie, I can't let you bring that stuff into the shelter. If word got out we could be closed down.

I could be fired." I was about to push back, but stopped and took a breath. I've gotten in enough trouble in my life by being impulsive. Stubborn is one thing. Stubborn and impulsive is another.

"You're right. I'm sorry, bad idea. I won't bring anything into the shelter. I'll start by seeing what I can do with some signals that I learned online this morning."

Vickie, a young pink-haired volunteer with three nose rings, escorted me to Cisco's kennel. He looked worse, a sack of bones lying like a crumpled, black garbage bag in the back corner of the kennel. His eyes, when he finally opened them, were black holes of misery. He didn't raise his head as I approached the door and looked into his kennel.

I took a breath. *"Zooch!"* I said, the sound of the German command for *Seek!* Cisco's head whipped toward me so fast that I barely saw it move. One moment his head was lying limp on his paws, the next he was looking directly at me. His eyes burned into mine, the flame so intense that I stopped breathing. *"Sitzen,"* I asked after a moment, while raising my forearm up toward my shoulder, a common visual signal for *Sit*. Cisco struggled to get his body into a proper sit, still looking at my face. He couldn't quite manage it, but I whispered, "Good boy!" to reward the effort. I clapped my hands quietly and said, "Good boy!" again.

Cisco melted and sagged back to the floor. His eyes softened and his tail began to thump, ever so slightly. "Good boy," I said again, quietly, as I opened the kennel door and walked in.

Vickie's quiet gasp of alarm could barely be heard over the sound of the metal latch closing behind me.

The risk was obvious. Once inside both Cisco and I would be trapped, making him more likely to be defensively aggressive and me more likely to be injured. A bite from a dog his size could put me out of business for months, if not cause permanent injury. One of my colleagues had been attacked by a ninety-pound dog who lunged at his face, her massive jaws engulfing his face like a snake on a mouse. Her teeth sunk in above his eyes and below his chin. He's designing websites now.

I also knew it was now or never, and if I was going to convince Cisco that I was his friend and handler, I had to come in with calm and benevolent confidence. I crooned "Good boy" again, my voice low and steady, as I stepped past the door into the wire enclosure.

Cisco welcomed me into his kennel like a rescued kidnapping victim. Weak as he was, his tail wagged hard enough to move his hindquarters. He began making short, high-pitched squeaks, looking up at my face. I sank down and he began licking my face, his tongue thick and dry and raspy.

"Vickie, quick, go get some water, he's so dehydrated. And could you mix a tiny bit of canned dog food in?" Vickie stood immobile, her eyes focused on Cisco.

"Vickie? Go!" I said, trying to keep my voice quiet and calm. She nodded and raced out of the building, only to return with a bowl of water, colored light brown from the food mixed into it. Cisco drank and drank and drank until I finally stopped him, worried he'd make himself sick.

Vickie stood outside the kennel watching Cisco drink and then turned to go tell Catherine what had happened. Cisco lay with his head on my thigh while I stroked the side of his head. At one moment I thought he was growling at me, but then realized he was moaning.

"Hey, bud, you are going to be okay," I said quietly, my eyes getting moist. His tail thumped again, but froze when Catherine, Vickie, and Chris approached the kennel. Cisco's tail stopped and he closed his mouth, his body going stiff again.

"Whoa," I said to Catherine, who was standing in the front of the others. "Let's not push things too far. Maybe not so many people right now? Catherine, would you stay where you are, so we can talk?"

"Of course. Okay, everyone, let's give Cisco some space. I'll fill you in soon." Chris and Vickie practically ran into the door on the way out because they couldn't take their eyes off me and Cisco.

"I want to take him home." The words came out of my mouth before I knew what I was saying. "He's a trained K9, Catherine, he must be. How the hell he ended up half dead beside a busy highway is beyond me. I know he looks like hell right now, but the light in his eyes just turned on and I swear there must be a way to get through to him. Can I take him back to my farm and foster him?"

"Oh my God, Maddie! I would saint you if I could. I'll bring in the paperwork for you to sign and you can take him home right away. We can skip the usual neutering requirement until he is healthy enough for a surgery." She disappeared out the door, leaving me and Cisco sitting alone in the building.

It was quiet. I could hear the lights buzzing and a fan running with a low frequency *burrrr-rrrrr-rrrrr,* counterpoint to Cisco's quiet panting. I turned and looked toward him, my hand resting on the ruff above his make-shift collar. He licked my face and lay his head down on my lap.

What the hell had I just done? What happened to my policy of not letting client dogs interfere with my own life? Saving Cisco was not going to save George—it was just going to make my life more difficult.

Cisco drank more water and ate a few bites of canned food off the palm of my hand.

After a half hour it was time to get him up and out.

"Okay, bud, time to go." I stood up and said, *"Heeee-a,"* remembering that is the pronunciation for *Hier,* the German word for come. Cisco slowly got himself to his feet but was still wobbly. I slung my sweatshirt—an ugly-ass pink one with a snowy owl image on the front that I'd gotten from a bargain bin—under his hindquarters to stabilize him.

I was halfway to the truck when I remembered what I'd stashed in the glove compartment. I couldn't resist seeing if it had any effect. I smooched to get his full attention, and then said, *"Zooch!"* Cisco, still propped up by my sweatshirt, pushed his head forward and put his nose down. I helped him walk around to the passenger side of the truck and waited for him to alert. Nothing. Cisco kept sniffing the ground around the truck, sniffing, sniffing, and sniffing, and looked at me as if defeated. I opened the door of the cab, got out the bag and tossed it on the ground in front of Cisco. He sniffed it indifferently, then wobbled away to sniff a more interesting piece of gravel.

Great. There went that theory. Disappointed, I picked up the bag of weed and hefted Cisco into Jack's crate in the back of the cab. It was a tight fit, but I didn't have a lot of choices.

My mind buzzed all the way home. If Cisco wasn't a drug dog, why did he respond to the signals that handlers use? Maybe he was a bomb dog, but why then would he alert when Chris walked in? It seemed beyond credibility that this dedicated volunteer, who I'd worked with for a couple of years and seemed like a sweet guy, would be carrying around explosives. Best guess was that Cisco had been trained by a private group for home protection, and in his semiconscious state, saw Chris as a threat. I kept rolling it over and over in my mind as I drove home, my brain so busy that I almost missed the turnoff to home.

CHAPTER 8

Home, however, was where Jack, an intact male (like most working trial dogs), had no idea that I was bringing home a testosterone-fueled dog twice his size. Home, where Bo Peep, the dog who viewed Cisco look-alikes as mortal enemies, was dedicated to protecting her flock. Clementine would be fine, but things with the boy dogs or Bo Peep could go bad fast; I spent much of the drive home strategizing how to handle the introductions.

I knew what to do in general; literally hundreds of my cases involved helping dogs become friends instead of enemies. But *exactly* how to do it always takes some thought. This wasn't the only issue: Cisco had been aggressive to people at the shelter, and I had no idea how he'd behave once he healed up.

One thing at a time; at least I could see if I could get him and Jack settled. Having two male dogs in the house who don't get along isn't much fun. The standard routine for first introductions has dogs meeting off territory, in a large, open area, both on leash and allowed to sniff each other's urine marks but not each other. Simple enough, but it requires two people.

I knew who to call. Vince was close by, and had a large, fenced area where the dogs wouldn't feel any pressure. Even better, he'd helped me out on a few cases, especially with dogs who were afraid of men. Vince was one of the few men who actually did what I asked when working with a fearful dog. He's worked with cattle all his life, animals who can kill you when they're frightened, simply because of their size. A panicked cow can move like a gymnast and crush you like a bug against a fence. Aware of the importance of "reading" an animal, Vince respected my knowledge about dog behavior and followed my suggestions to the letter. Too bad the man wasn't younger. Not that I wanted a man in my life.

"Vince? You home?" I said into my cell phone after dialing his number and getting his voice mail. "Pick up if you are! I need to talk to you."

"Hey, I'm here. I was just getting ready to do some planting. What's up?"

I told him about Cisco, that he was maybe a drug dog but maybe not, and that I need his help to introduce him to Jack. There was a pause that went on so long that I wasn't sure he'd actually heard me, until he said, "What are you getting into this time?"

"Fair question, but right now I could really use some help."

"Uh . . . okay."

It did not sound okay. Which wasn't like Vince; usually he was all-in for whatever adventure I concocted.

"Vince?"

"Uh, how close does a drug dog have to get before they can smell pot?"

I covered my mouth just in time to turn my burst of laughter into a kind of snorty sound that I hoped was impossible to classify.

"You're good, Vince. The dog paid no attention to your bag of weed. If you could come over in a few minutes, that'd be great. I'll call you soon as I get home. Once I do, you could come over, put Jack in your truck, and take him to the field behind your back shed. But don't try to greet Cisco—that's his name now—he's fearful of strangers and I don't trust him around you." I went on to explain I'd like to walk the dogs with a good distance between them to see how they responded to each other. Vince said—I could just see him rolling his eyes as he spoke—that he thought I was crazy, but he'd help.

Cisco had been silent for the entire drive and stayed quiet when Jack and Clementine began barking as we approached the house. I left Cisco in the truck, let the other dogs out to potty, and then gave Vince a call.

"Okay, Vince, I'm here. I'll keep Cisco in my truck while you load Jack into yours. Go back to your place, put Jack on leash, and start walking him in the middle of the field."

Five minutes later Vince pulled up, made a fuss over Jack and Clementine, then asked Jack to hop into his truck. Jack stood still and looked at me, his eyebrows going a little squinty.

"It's okay, bud, I'll be right there." Jack gave me one more look of concern—*You know this isn't our truck, right?*—and then leapt into it as if gravity was taking a rest. Soon our two vehicles caravanned down the hill to Vince's place.

As planned, Vince and Jack got out first and disappeared behind a weathered shed, complete with enough rusty farm equipment to inspire a "found art" opening at a modern art museum. Cisco and I followed, although slowly because of Cisco's condition. I had thought about waiting to make the introduction when Cisco was healthier, but they were going to have to live in the same house, even if separated by gates and crates, and it would be so much better if I could get things started right off on the right paw. It was worth a try.

I caught a break. Water and a little food had energized Cisco enough to walk slowly—very slowly, with the help of a sling under his belly and lots of breaks for resting. Vince and I walked the dogs in parallel for a few minutes, going east to west, with a good thirty feet between them. Cisco looked askance at Vince a few times, so I warned him to stay well away. Jack and Cisco, however, looked at each other off and on, without any sign of tension.

I was just about to call it quits; Cisco was clearly tiring and it had been a good start. That's when Jack bowed in one glorious slow-motion swoop, his mouth open, his eyes gleaming, his butt high in the air. A play bow, the universal canine invitation to play. Cisco stared, and then, glory hallelujah, attempted to bow back. He couldn't manage it, and almost fell over, but the signal was clear enough to Jack, who starting wagging his tail from the shoulders back.

"Okay, Vince, stay where you are but let Jack off the leash."

Jack trotted over and sniffed Cisco's butt. Cisco reciprocated. Both dogs looked relaxed and eager to play. Jack even play bowed again, and Cisco tried to respond, but collapsed on the ground with a grin on his face. Smiling, melting with relief, I said, "Let's go!" and walked the dogs back to the truck. I hefted Cisco into Jack's crate and crammed poor Jack in a smaller one I had in the back of the truck.

"Sorry, bud, it's only five minutes."

I remembered the package in my glove compartment as I started to drive away. "Vince! Wait! I don't need this anymore." He reached through the window, took the bag, and shook his head as I drove away.

I settled Cisco in the mudroom in my largest crate, gave him a small amount of food and water, and told him to be a good boy. I let Jack in next; aware that dogs might be friendly when outside but not necessarily in the house. Jack sniffed the door to Cisco's room, but returned quickly to the kitchen to hang out while I grabbed some lunch, sitting alongside Clementine on the couch, who treated all visiting dogs like mobile furniture.

I did my work as best I could for the next few days, but all I really wanted to do was work with Cisco. He had gained strength every day, and within just a few days was able to go on short walks with no assistance. Bo Peep, safely on the other side of a fence, had barked nonstop for two days whenever Cisco was outside, the air filled to bursting with her outrage. But, thankfully, my ears got a rest by the beginning of the third day. Bo Peep began to bark less, and by the next morning she curtsied up to the fence and ducked her head in greeting. Jack and Cisco began to play in the house, and before I knew it they had a full-blown bromance going on, play fighting on the threadbare oriental rug, licking each other's ears, and sleeping side by side. I asked them at one point if they needed a room.

I was busy with clients that week, including a Siamese cat who attacked the resident King Charles Cavalier, a Pomeranian afraid to leave the house, and a bull terrier who couldn't stop chasing his own tail. Between working with clients, doing farm chores, and nursing Cisco back to health, there wasn't much time to do anything else. But Saturday finally brought a break, and after a long morning cuddle with Jack, Clementine, and the cats on the bed, I took Cisco and Jack on a walk. Cisco was still a bit weak, but healthy enough to beat me in a foot race, so I kept him on a long line. No point in tempting him in a countryside full of animals with *CHASE ME* written on their butts.

Whoo hee. Whoo hee. The high, thin notes of the chickadees played counterpoint to the nasal *yank yank yank* of the nuthatches as we walked beside the creek. I began wondering again where Cisco came from and how he ended up abandoned on the side of a road. I was sure he'd been trained as a police or military dog. But for what? As a protection dog? Competitor in ring sports? Bomb dog? None of that would explain why he'd alerted when he saw Chris, but he clearly had some kind of similar training based on his response to me. But where did he come from?

After we returned from the walk and I put Cisco in his crate, I left a message for Tom and began sorting through the laundry pile of underwear and T-shirts, dirty dog towels, and washable cat cozies. The largest pile contained pants caked with mud and manure. Tom called back between the underwear and dirty jeans.

"Hey, Maddie, good to hear from you. How are you doing? I've been thinking about you." "And me you," I said. We talked for a bit about how much we missed George, whether either of us had heard anything. (Nope) I wondered if I should ask him what might have been bothering George, and decided against it. I told Tom what had happened at the shelter.

"He's clearly not a narcotics dog, because he ignored a bag of pot right at his feet."

"Whoa, let me stop you right there," Tom said. "Most dogs aren't trained on cannabis. It's too confusing. Legal here, illegal there, CBD oil legal here, sort of there. Hardly anybody trains drug dogs on pot anymore. It's confusing enough, between coke and heroin and meth and all their variations, so only older dogs trained a long time ago would alert to pot."

"Well, that explains a lot. So, he *could* be a drug dog, or bomb dog, or a protection dog of some kind. He's got to have that kind of background, because as soon as I said 'Zooch' he perked up and responded. He knows the language, Tom, he had to learn it somewhere. So how do I go about trying to figure out where he came from?"

I waited for a response, figuring Tom was thinking of people for me to call.

"Sorry, Maddie, but I haven't heard a word about a missing K9. I'm about to leave town now, doing a seminar outside LA and delivering a dog for explosives detection. How about I ask around after I get back?"

"Okay, have a good trip. Talk to you when you get home."

I hung up, but stood standing, the phone still in my hand, staring at the photo of me, Jack, and George. I realized I hadn't thought about George's horrific death all day. *Thank you, Cisco*, I thought, until Jack bumped his nose into the back of my leg. It was one of his endearing habits, until it wasn't. *Come on! Let's go!* Jack bumped me again and then turned his head toward the sheep in the field, backlit by the morning sun and visible through the window. He looked back at me, then back at the sheep.

"Okay, bud. Let's go."

I left Cisco in his crate and Clementine snoring in the sun, grabbed my brass whistle from the nail by the door, and went out into the early summer sun with Jack. We split out five sheep, a good-size group for competition practice, and set to work on driving the sheep in a straight line between cones I'd set out. This time we made some progress before it was time to give the sheep a rest, and we walked back to the house together, Jack's tongue lolling, my mind going over what had gone well, what I needed to work on next time. I heard the phone ring as we entered the house.

"Maddie, it's Catherine. We found the collar that was on Cisco when he was brought in.

Want me to keep it in case it might give you a clue where he came from?"

"I would! Could you put it in the mail for me?" It probably wouldn't come to anything, but I was grasping at straws at this point.

Catherine said it would be sent out on Monday or Tuesday, asked how Cisco was doing, and thanked me again for fostering him.

I said good-bye and turned to see Cisco watching me. "Hey, dude. Where the hell did you come from anyway?" Cisco's tail wagged in a slow figure eight as his eyes looked into mine.

"Wait!" I said out loud, so abruptly that Jack's head snapped toward me. What was I thinking? I could ask Officer Conners, the cop with thunder-phobic Ranger, how a trained K9 could have ended up half dead on the street. Like the sport of sheepdog trialing, working K9s live in a small world, in which a tight community of trainers and handlers stay in touch over a wide area. Someone, somewhere, had to know where Cisco came from.

CHAPTER 9

I got a hold of Ryan Conners the next morning. He sounded hesitant, but his voice held something underneath it. Intrigue? After talking about how busy he was, he finally said that he was off duty on the upcoming Saturday. He offered to come out to meet Cisco if he could update me on Ranger's progress and get some more ideas without a fee. A win/win. Perfect.

Saturday morning dawned warm and sunny. I did the usual chores, and then took the dogs on a walk, Cisco still on a long line. Overall, he was doing well, although I'd been careful to feed him light dinners because his digestive system was struggling. That's another way of saying I cleaned up a lot of stinky shit. But he was gaining strength and energy, his ears twitching back and forth to follow the symphony of birdsong, squirrels chattering, and a chain saw throbbing in the distance. I'd been doing some training, and he was an eager student. Job one, besides house training, was to teach him to respond to "Cisco."

Dogs' names are actually just like ours—if someone says your name it means they want your attention, and that's what I wanted "Cisco" to mean to him. That morning I gave him a tiny piece of chicken when he turned his head back to me at the sound of his name. I'm pretty sure he thought this was the easiest work he'd ever done. I interspersed the chicken with a few short chase games—shepherds were bred to move and they love doing it—but not enough to tire him out. Cisco lapped up some water after our walk, before I hefted him up in the truck to go meet Ryan at my office.

Ryan was there when I arrived. You couldn't call him demonstrative when I got out of the truck to say hello, but his lips moved up a bit at the corners into an almost-smile, and his eyes seemed warmer than before. I dug my glasses out of my purse, put them on, and left Cisco in the truck so that Ryan and I could talk about how Ranger was doing.

So far, so good. Ryan had gotten a barometer, turned his closet into a safe house, and started giving Ranger treats for settling down inside it. He'd yet to install a speaker system that played barely perceptive thunder from the ceiling, but he was working on it. I had to give the guy credit. Anyone who crawls into a closet in the middle of the night to sit beside his dog couldn't be all bad.

After we talked, we went outside to let Ranger relieve himself before going back into the cruiser. As the dog sniffed around, I got up my courage and asked Ryan if he'd heard anything about George's death, and if there was any evidence of some idiot hunting in the area.

"Uh, I can't say much, but every gun death is treated like a homicide until proven otherwise. And the logistics are pretty clear—a clean shot from a high-powered rifle toward a man standing in an open field, surrounded by spectators behind him?"

Homicide. Someone had intentionally killed George. We had all sensed that this had to be the case, but I had nevertheless worked hard to imagine it being an accident. I put my hand onto the truck to steady myself.

Ryan started to move toward me, stopped, and asked, "Are you okay?" I nodded numbly, and turned to look at Ranger, who was lifting his leg on the scrubby cypress by the back door that Jack pees on all the time. Ranger seemed to be staring at me too, his leg jacked up as if on a string.

"Okay, yeah, sure, I'm fine. Just surprised," I said, forcing myself to take a breath. I considered asking for more details, managing to squelch my curiosity and drop it.

"Can we talk about this dog I found?"

Ryan said sure and put Ranger in this cruiser. I asked him to stand well away from my truck, explaining that Cisco had been afraid of everyone at the shelter and I didn't want him to be forced onto defense. Right now, I wanted to focus on just one thing: eliminating the possibility that Cisco was a drug dog.

I put one forearm under his belly and the other under his chest, and set him down gently on the pavement, cursing my ridiculously small frame. I may be strong for my size, and he may have been mostly bones, but he was still almost half my weight.

"Okay," I said, turning toward Ryan, who was about twenty feet away, "go ahead and say something to him. Let's see how he responds." I expected Ryan to start with a command, but he stood quietly, slightly sideways from Cisco to avoid looking threatening, and clicked his tongue.

As Cisco's head turned toward him, his body stiffened and his mouth closed. Okay, clear enough. Cisco was nervous.

"Hey, son," Ryan said, his voice like velvet. Cisco stood immobile, but his eyes softened and his head cocked almost imperceptibly. His tail began the slow swish of a dog who wants to be happy, but isn't sure it's safe to relax into it. I knew the feeling.

Ryan repeated, "Hey, son," and then raised his forearm and said, *"Sitzen."* Cisco's head cocked sideways another half inch, and his hindquarters sunk into a squatty sit. His mouth was still closed, and his ears were back, so I told Ryan to stay where he was. It was too soon to push Cisco into an interaction he wasn't ready for.

"Good boy!" said Ryan, in a quiet voice far lower than I would have expected from his thin frame.

"Platz," he said. Cisco lay down, slowly and cautiously, his eyes never leaving Ryan as if it was dangerous to lose track of him.

"Okay," I said to Cisco in a bright voice, wanting him to be released from lying down in a strange place while feeling nervous. Cisco stood up and shook off a cloak of tension. "So, what'd ya think? Doesn't Cisco act as if he's been trained in some kind of police or protection dog training?"

"He does, but I'd guess he's been trained by some private sporting club, or maybe a private company that sells protection dogs to the public. I can't believe he's been trained for law enforcement; no police department is going to lose track of a dog this expensive. You know what they cost, right?"

I nodded. $20,000 to $25,000 just for the initial training, and most departments have to fund the dogs through donations, not through their regular budget. "Didn't you say something about thinking he might have been trained as a drug dog?"

Uh. Now what? Do I tell him about how Cisco alerted when Chris walked into the building? I didn't want to get Chris in trouble. Ryan seemed nice but, still, he was a cop.

"It was just a guess, cuz, uh, he did a clear alert on something—that's what started this whole story. I can't say *where* that happened, but *what* happened only makes sense if he was a detection dog or if he was so addled with exhausted and starvation that he made a mistake. But he was trained as a working K9, that's for sure, and you are the only person who could help me sort all this out." I looked toward Ranger in the squad car. "I'll give you free consults forever if you'll help me."

It occurred to me that I just tried to bribe a policeman.

"Look. I don't want to put you in a difficult position. And I'll admit that I'm a bit obsessive with this dog, I just . . ." I didn't know what else to say. I sat down, defeated, beside Cisco in the gravel and stroked his chest. I was spent. Too little sleep, too much worry.

Ryan didn't answer for the longest time, looking down toward the cracked asphalt.

After an eternity, while Cisco sat silent and I memorized the pattern of brown and black on the back of his ears, Ryan said, "Just a minute." He opened the back door to his patrol car, rummaged around, opened a metal box, and pulled out a small piece of what looked like PVC pipe with lids screwed on either end.

"I am NOT doing this, got it?"

I nodded, almost too surprised to stand up. Ryan placed the pipe, which I figured held some kind of heavy-duty illegal drug or explosive, behind the front tire of my truck. I started to move Cisco toward the truck, but Ryan held out his hand to stop me.

"We have to let it "cook" for a few minutes, let the scent disperse."

After what seemed like way too long, he turned toward Cisco, and said, *"Zooch!"*

"Now walk him around the truck, starting on the other side, and we'll see what happens."

I hadn't needed to do anything to get Cisco up. His ears pricked forward as soon as he heard the word from Ryan, and he pulled me toward the truck. He began sniffing on the driver's side, his nostrils flaring in and out, taking fast, shallow breaths as he examined the edges of the door. I walked him around to the other side of the truck, close to the tire with the mysterious white cylinder. Cisco sat. Then he turned and looked me in the eye, exactly as he had when Chris entered the kennel building. His message couldn't have been clearer if he'd held up a sign that said, "I found stuff. I am looking right at it. Copy that?"

Ryan said, "I'll be damned," as he threw a Kong toy he'd been hiding in his pocket to Cisco, who pounced on it like a cat on a mouse.

"Where did this dog come from, anyway? Where did they find him?"

I told him what I had learned from Chris and the shelter. Ryan shook his head. "That's weird. Never heard anything like that."

"Would you ask around? See if any departments have lost a dog? Any reports of a dog stolen from a training facility?" He said he would, put the cylinder back in the cruiser, and opened the door to his cruiser.

He settled into the driver's seat and said: "Hey, I have one more quick question about Ranger." I keep my face neutral, but if I had ten dollars for every time a client said "just one more question" on his way out the door, I would be at a beachside bar in Hawaii. But he'd just done me a huge favor, so I said, "Sure, what's up?"

"Ranger did something he's never done before. We had gotten a tip about a huge delivery of cocaine that was going to be held in a warehouse for a couple of days. It should have been good information—from a reliable source and all that. But here's what was weird: after Ranger had been inside the warehouse for just a few minutes, he gave us a positive ID, but then negated it by standing up right away. He'd slammed his butt on the ground as if he'd found the mother lode, but then, completely out of character, he stood up and looked left and right. I swear he looked confused. When I told him to search again, he sniffed in another area, and sat down again. But, just like before, he stood up right away. Honest to God he looked at me as if he was apologizing. And then, get this, he lifted his leg and peed right where he stood while staring at me. I was so shocked at first that I didn't know what to say. All our dogs are trained to pee before they enter a building, and Ranger has never lifted his leg inside, anywhere. Ever.

"Not anywhere," Ryan repeated, his voice louder and emphatic. "Finally, I yelled 'No!' and then called him to me. My partner said I should have given him a heavy correction, but honestly, by the time I had my head together it was too late and what would I have corrected him for anyway? I had no idea why or what he was doing."

Points for Officer Ryan. Good boy.

"We searched the area for another hour after that, with three different dogs, but couldn't find the slightest sign of drugs, not even an aspirin." Another long pause. "What was that about?" Good question. I didn't have a clue, but it seemed clear yet again that a dog was trying to tell his human something. We just couldn't imagine what it was. We both wondered if there had been drugs there before, which might explain Ranger's ambiguous alert. We all know about "residual smells," scents that remain in a room after what caused them were gone, like the smell of cooked liver or fresh bread long after it is consumed. But why did Ranger lift his leg? While looking directly at Ryan?

I told Ryan I'd think about it, and to let me know if any other mysteries came up. He agreed to ask around if anyone knew of a missing police dog.

As he started to roll up his window and back out, I couldn't resist asking: "What was in the cylinder, can you tell me?"

"Heroin," he said. "Some of my buddies and I are getting together today to do some training." Cisco and I stood staring at the cruiser as he drove away.

Heroin? Was that what Cisco alerted to in the shelter? Did Chris, the dog lover and volunteer extraordinaire, have heroin in his pocket? That seemed hard to believe, given what a hardworking and dedicated volunteer he'd been. But I knew that life is complicated, and that everyone has their secrets. And too, I remembered Tom's words that detection dogs make mistakes, which seemed especially likely if a dog is semiconscious and barely alive. All I knew for sure was that Cisco was trained by someone as a working K9, but I still had no idea where he might have come from and why he was found by the side of the road. More confused than ever, I drove back to the farm with my head spinning.

I was so distracted that it was getting dark by the time I finally took Jack on our usual long walk at the end of the day. Bo Peep came along for the ride, but Cisco seemed tired, so I left him in the house. We startled some sparrows roosting in the brush as we approached the edge of the creek, black shadows fluttering in front of our faces, so close their wings fanned my face. The moon, just a narrow sliver of light, was rising behind me as I cursed not bringing my flashlight. It was getting dark enough that I needed to get away from the brush and back onto the grazed pasture lest I ended up blundering into something by mistake.

As I turned toward the house, a good four hundred hundred yards away, I thought I heard something move, just on the other edge of the creek. I looked back to see the dim shape of a man, barely perceptible, standing at the creek's edge. Everything went still when I startled. Then I laughed. Ha! Deer again. Not going to be fooled this time. I looked down to see Jack's reaction, ready to call him back to prevent a chase. He was staring, his eyes fixed, on the immobile shape. Something about Jack's expression made me stop breathing and look back up. As I did, I heard a growl behind me. Bo Peep was frozen, her ears up and her body leaning forward, staring across the creek. Jack looked at me and then back toward the . . . the what? A deer again? But Bo Peep wouldn't growl at a deer. A black bear? One of the rare ones who wandered down from the north woods? A man? That's what it looked like.

"Vince? Is that you?" It was all I could do to get the words out. The shadow didn't move, didn't turn away like a wild animal would. "Vince?"

I stood in the dark in a heavy silence, not a sound except the quiet burble of the creek. It became hard to breathe. Whatever it was moved, maybe just a step, the crunch of dead leaves from last winter giving it away.

I caved. I started running, only turning back to look to see if the dogs were coming with me. Jack was about to overtake me, but I couldn't see Bo Peep at first.

"Bo Bo! Bo Bo!" A fuzz of white appeared behind me, loping easily to keep up. She slowed when we approached the flock, their eyes lit up by the barn light. Jack and I left her with the sheep and ran into the house.

After locking the doors and latching the windows, I got out a beer and sat on the couch stroking Jack and Cisco both. "Holy shit, guys. What was that?" Or was it anything? Was I just losing it? Was I seeing things, tired and wired by everything that had happened? I'd been doing so well since I'd left New Mexico, but I had to admit that George's death, no, his murder, was bringing things back. My chest was getting tight again, like it used to.

"It's okay," I said to myself. I knew what to do. Breathe, one, two, three, four. Hold, one, two, three, four. Exhale, one, two, three, four. Hold, one, two, three, four. Repeat.

I hadn't known I'd fallen asleep until the dream woke me up. Trapped in a closet this time, where disembodied hands had reached out to grab me and pull me in. I struggled off the couch, stiff and foggy headed, to see Jack and Cisco staring at me, their eyebrows pinched, their faces worried.

"It's okay, guys. Really. I'm okay. Want some breakfast?"

Chapter 10

The next week went by slowly. Too many riddles to solve. I fought to keep my concentration on a poodle puppy who bit his owner, hard, when he went to trim his nails, and the Border collie/Aussie mix who couldn't tolerate an unfamiliar dog anywhere near him. Bless them for helping me get through the days. The early evenings were the best part of the day, when I walked Jack and Cisco and the wood thrush sang while the light softened and the boys played chase games, eyes sparkling, tongues lolling. I avoided the creek.

The nights were the worst—when I lay on the couch and wanted to call George, when I couldn't sleep and stared for hours at the TV screen, barely tracking what I saw.

On Friday afternoon my client called and canceled, so I got home in time to get in a bit of work with Jack. A trial was coming up soon, and we had a lot of work to do. So many things to work on, including the first part of our run. Jack had a nice, natural outrun like his sister Jess, but too often he'd blow the "lift," when the dog gets the sheep moving. The lift can make or break your run—boisterous dogs scare them and set up a fight or a panicked escape, while an overly cautious dog is instantly known by the sheep as someone they can bully. Everyone wants a Goldilocks dog, a dog who is just right—not too soft, not too pushy.

Jack is not that dog. Jack may understand sheep as well as any dog George has worked with, but he has the impulse control of a teenage boy when his parents leave for the weekend. He likes to come in hard and fast on the sheep, scaring them and setting up trouble for the rest of the course. George thought there was fear hiding underneath Jack's cowboy persona. His busting in at trials was some combination of "Oh No!" and "Eee Ha!" I had to find a fine line between shoring up his sense of security, and preventing him from releasing tension by charging forward.

George suggested that the tension on a trial course brought out his anxiety, and counseled me to focus less on practicing driving, and more on doing practical chores with sheep, especially in close quarters, off the farm. I could do it a home too, just get him comfortable being in a small pen with sheep, with no expectations. "Don't ask him to do anything, just hang out together, you, Jack, and the sheep. Put a leash on him in case he starts to lunge, but the idea is to make being close to the sheep no big deal."

Before I knew it, the first day of the trial arrived. Dorothy and I had talked about whether we wanted to go, given what happened at the last one. I wanted to skip it. I told Dorothy I had enough going on, what with Cisco, clients, and the young lambs on the farm. I didn't mention that I had barely slept for weeks.

She knew the other reason that I'd left unspoken. "There's always going to be a 'first trial after George died,' Maddie, so we might as well get it over with."

She was right, so at dark-thirty on Friday morning I lugged jackets, water jugs, and rain gear into the truck. I brought Cisco with me because I wasn't sure yet that he'd be okay with Vince. Jack leapt and pranced, experienced enough to know we were off to a trial; Cisco didn't get the excitement, but was strong enough now to leap into the truck himself. I knew I'd have to be careful with him around strangers, but trial people understand better than the general public about dogs who need space, so I thought it'd be a good opportunity to help him meet people who wouldn't overwhelm him.

It was only a couple of hours to the Big River Stock Dog Classic, with a smallish, fenced field bound on one side by houses that couldn't decide if they were suburban or rural, and two county roads that defined the east and south sides. The challenge for the competitors was not the size of the field, or the noise of the traffic. It was the sheep. The sheep in this trial were famous for beating the dogs at their own game. They were experienced professionals, having been shipped around the Midwest every trial season, and could read a dog's commitment and experience in an instant. Sheep may not be Mensa candidates, but they are smart at what they need to be smart about, and I'd seen this group make good dogs look bad over and over again. Jack's lack of experience at this level of competition meant we'd have to bring our A game in order to manage them. We had worked hard the last few weeks, especially on lift, but if he didn't stay calm on these sheep, they'd have him for lunch.

I thought about how best to handle all this while I parked the truck in the little shade that was available. As I got out, I looked around for George's truck to see if he had any last-minute advice for me.

Reality hit hard. I stood still beside the truck, the door to the cab still open, concentrating on my breathing. In and out. In and out.

Dorothy pulled up beside me while I was still standing by the truck. I took one last deep breath and let Jack out to stretch his legs. He hit the ground looking for sheep; I had to smooch to him to get his attention back onto me. Dorothy got out her two trial dogs and we walked our dogs together, off leash, the usual practice of sheepdog handlers who have dogs easily trained to stop or lie down when asked. Jack flirted with Dorothy's younger bitch, his ears erect in that silly sideways posture adopted by lusty male dogs. We laughed when she began flirting back. I called Mr. Wonderful back in case things between the two got out of hand. A robin began to sing, and a light breeze ruffled the leaves on the scrubby buckthorn trees outlining the field.

"How're you doing?" Dorothy asked, looking, as usual, camera-ready in a rust-colored L.L. Bean jacket that matched her jaunty hat. I adjusted my bedraggled Packers cap and thought about how to answer. Depressed? Grieving? Obsessed with Cisco? Exhausted? All of the above?

She turned to stop me from walking forward, put her hands on my shoulders, and looked straight into my eyes. "No, really, Maddie, how are you doing?" It came out like five sentences.

No, really, Maddie. How. Are. You. Doing?

"I don't know," I finally answered, stopping to pause while Jack squatted to poop. We both watched him intently.

"How are *you*?" I finally said. I paused to pick up Jack's poop, still steaming, in a plastic bag. I tied the ends together, focusing hard on getting the ends tucked in just so, then letting the bag swing from my left hand as we continued walking.

"I don't know either," she answered. "It's all just so otherworldly. But mostly I keep asking myself 'why.' Why the hell did someone kill George? Or were they trying to kill George at all? And I worry about you. Are you sleeping?"

"Jack! That'll do," I called. Maybe what he was sniffing wasn't safe. Dorothy took one more look at me and called her dog Kip back to her. She knew me well enough to not push it. We continued walking, our dogs trotting from scent to scent, warming up their legs and emptying their bladders, while my stomach knotted up and my throat tightened. Just the usual nerves before a trial, I told myself. Nothing to see here.

We walked toward a cluster of handlers, grouped together

in anticipation of the "handler's meeting," when the judge and course director explains the course and the time limit. "Maddie," said Peter, a handler who had also worked with George as his coach, "have you heard anything about the shooting?" The chatter around us went silent, and I saw several handlers move forward, the better to hear my answer.

"Not a thing, sorry." It was the last thing I wanted to talk about. The course director saved me by clapping his hands and saying, "Handler's meeting!" I swallowed, tried to focus on Jack instead of the image of George lying dead on the grass, as the judge, a tall, plain-spoken woman from Virginia, explained the details of the course: "Ten minutes, left-hand drive, pen before the shed, take two off the back. Any abuse of the sheep and I'll call your dog off. Good luck." That's shorthand for: You get ten minutes to complete the course; start the drive by moving your sheep to the gate panels on the left of the field; after the drive portion put the sheep into a free-standing pen before attempting to split two off from the other two. Abuse equals biting, unless the dog has to defend itself, or chasing the sheep rather than herding them.

The first dog was off by 7:15 a.m., and as predicted, the sheep were doing better than the dogs. Almost half the runs ended with the sheep running pell-mell back to where they came from, the dogs unable to control them.

"Heaven help us," I said to Dorothy as our turns drew closer and we watched a dog being run over by a freight train of four sheep who had spent the night strategizing in their pen. She laughed and told me about all the times she'd failed on a trial course. "Don't worry, whatever happens to you and Jack has happened to all of us at one point or another."

Still, I began checking the running order repeatedly and stressing about whether I should take Jack out to warm him up three runs before ours, or four. I visited the porta potty twice in ten minutes. Standard procedure before a run.

Finally, it was my turn. Dorothy and a few others called "Good luck!" as Jack and I walked onto the field, my chest tight and my mouth dry. Everyone told me I'd get over my nerves once I had more experience, but I wasn't there yet. Not in this class, where the sheep were so far away your dog was a tiny black dot when he picked them up. I took a deep breath, smiled to Jack, and said, "We got this, bud!" as we walked out to the post.

We waited there, Jack's body tense and his mouth closed tight, for the sheep to appear three hundred yards away. Finally, they settled in position, their white bodies highlighted by the sun. It was time to send Jack. I opened my mouth to say *Come bye*, but as I did, someone wrapped a steel band around my chest. My throat began to close up, and it became hard to breathe. It all happened in less than a second, but I knew, just knew, that I was going to die. Just like George did, standing at the post. Where I also stood, with a "Shoot Me" sign on my chest.

My eyes were open but everything started going dim. I grabbed onto the post to stay upright. Jack looked up at me, sensing something was wrong, but then turned back to keep his eyes on the sheep. I held on to the post and forced myself to remember what I'd learned when the panic attacks began years ago. Slow, deep breaths. Feel your feet on the ground. Focus on something far away. Remind yourself over and over that you are not dying, that this is temporary.

"Right Here, Right Now," I chanted under my breath, trying to stay in the present and avoid getting lost in the terror that is an anxiety attack. I heard the traffic hum. A light breeze made music through the trees lining the course.

I also heard that the usual chatter of the handlers behind me had stopped. You can't stand forever at the post when it's your turn. After a minute or two, the sheep are too hard for the spotter to contain, your own dog begins to stiffen up, and you're taking up valuable time when there is barely enough daylight to get in all the runs.

Get it together, Maddie, I silently said to myself. I considered giving up and going back to my truck, saying I felt sick. But there was Jack beside me, counting on me, tensed with excitement, ready to spring forward and be all that he could be. I didn't want to confuse him. I didn't want to turn and face the other handlers either, so finally, after an eternity, I was able to croak out a feeble "Come bye" to Jack. He leaned forward as if to run, then paused to look at me again, confused. I managed a second signal with a bit more conviction, and he took off slowly, looking back at me once more, then gaining speed and confidence, running his beautiful, black and white body in a sweeping circle around to the back of the sheep. As he did, my throat loosened up a little, and my legs gained some strength.

Jack's run could have been worse. He did a lovely outrun and praise be, started to pause at the top when I asked him to lie down. But then he leapt forward and bolted toward the sheep, scattering them like balls on a pool table. So much for all the work we'd been doing. He gathered them back together and got them down the field to me, albeit way too fast and in a wavy line that lost us points. We managed to start them around the drive part of the course, but after I whistled and called "LIE DOWN!" a few times to no avail, I got Jack back and walked off the field, taking my option to "retire" before things went from bad to worse. No point in letting him learn bad habits. We joined the long list of handlers who got no points, earning either a RT for "retired," or a DQ for "disqualified."

We walked off the field, Jack's tongue long and fuchsia pink, my heart still racing and legs weak. Jack plopped into the water tank set out to help dogs cool off, panting in water up to his shoulders. I stood to the side, breathing deeply, in and out, in and out. I was grateful for the time alone, having to stay by the water tank to gather the sheep after the next team's run before leaving the field. Dorothy walked over, smiled ruefully, and gave me a one-armed hug. The three of us watched the next run in silence while the sparrows discussed their plans for the day and the breeze chattered to the trees.

The next run was over quickly, the sheep having outsmarted the dog and run to the rest area to join their friends. I opened the gate for them and walked off the field with Jack, through the line of chairs that handlers had set up to watch the runs. Several friends called out encouragement as we walked past them toward my truck. "Well, that happened!" said Tony, grinning his bashful grin. "Good for you for retiring. Good choice!" Violet said, always ready to praise something good about your run. I nodded and smiled. "Gotta go walk Jack to cool him down," I said as I waved acknowledgment, looking toward the back of the parking area where you could walk dogs.

Dorothy had to get her own dog ready to run, so Jack and I walked alone beside a fence in the shade of the scruffy box elders. I threw up behind some bushes. Jack looked ready to clean it up for me, so I called him away and we walked some more, until his breathing had slowed and his tongue had shrunk back into his mouth. I gave him some more water, popped him into his crate, and let Cisco out to stretch his legs.

As I did, a police car turned off the road and parked behind a row of trucks and campers. I kept moving toward a quiet area where I could keep Cisco out of trouble while he sniffed around. I heard a door slam and turned to see two people get out of the cruiser, one male, one female, both with sunglasses. The guy was tall and tricked out in full cop gear, complete with a Glock, collapsible baton, and cell phone carriers. The woman had on civilian clothes, with a navy suit jacket and matching pants. Detective? I'd never met a female cop in New Mexico, much less a detective, but that was then, and this was now. It didn't matter. Either way, I didn't want to talk to them.

But they walked straight toward me, so I turned and faced them as they approached.

"Hello," I said as they got closer. "This dog is a rescue from the local shelter, and he's frightened of strangers. Could I put him back in the truck before we talk?"

"We'll just be a minute," the woman said. "Just a few questions." I inhaled and straightened my back. "Okay, but please don't come any closer, I don't want him set off."

They exchanged glances. The cop was at least six foot two, dark haired, bulked up like a weight lifter. He looked a little familiar, probably because he looked like the offensive lineman of every college football team in the Midwest. The woman, with badly cut bangs and at least six inches on my paltry five feet two inches, managed to look equally imposing, as sculptured as an Olympic athlete. I disliked her immediately.

After introducing herself as Detective McCraig and her partner as Officer Thompson, she said they had a few questions to ask about George and the morning he died.

"Sure," I said, fiddling with the brass whistle hanging around my neck on a red, fabric lanyard. I dropped it when I realized my hands were shaking. Officer Thompson looked at my hands, then up to my face, his eyes flat. I swore I'd seen him before.

After a pause, he checked off a list of questions. "Did you see anything out of the ordinary on the morning George was shot?" I thought of George's face before he was shot. Why was he so tense before his run? Did it have something to do with what he had wanted to talk about? I felt sick to my stomach that I hadn't called him back to find out what it was, and longed for another chance. That I'd never get.

I didn't answer, just stared at him.

He continued: "Were there any people there who didn't belong? How well did you know George? What do you know about his business partner, Tom?" He had a voice like polished steel.

I took a breath, told them that nothing seemed unusual that

morning, that George was divorced, had a brother who lived in California, and was like an uncle to me. He lived in a farm/kennel facility with his friend and business partner, Tom, who raised and trained scent detection dogs. Maybe they knew him? No, Tom was not there when George died.

"Do you know how he reacted to George's death?"

Good grief. I thought of his stunned face at the funeral. "He looked devastated."

Finally, out of questions, McCraig reached her hand out with a business card and told me to call if I thought of anything. I stretched forward to take it while keeping Cisco behind me, while she looked me in the eyes, her own a cold blue that made me feel guilty just for standing there.

As we had talked, Cisco had been quiet. I thought I had stayed far enough away to avoid any defensive aggression, but lost focus on him once I started talking to the cops. As I turned my head to put the card in my pocket, I saw him staring, fixated on Officer Thompson. That's when I heard a growl, so quiet it was barely perceptible. Shoot, I wasn't doing my job, keeping Cisco far enough away from strangers to keep him comfortable. I clicked my tongue to get Cisco's attention, backed up a few steps, and gave him some liver treats as he relaxed. I turned to walk to the truck, but Cisco turned his head back and took one more look at Officer Thompson. I wasn't surprised that he focused on the guy; shy dogs are almost always more worried about men than women. Men move more assertively, have lower voices, and bigger jaws, the better to bite you with. I've always wondered too if dogs can pick up on the scent of testosterone, a dangerous drug if there ever was one. As I clicked my tongue to get Cisco focused back on me, Thompson turned his own head and took one more look at me as he walked away.

Oh. It was him, that guy, the guy at the funeral with the dark hair, flat eyes, big nose. Ryan's friend. My throat began to close.

Right here, right now, I repeated as we walked to the truck.

I decided to go home. I loaded up Cisco into the truck and told Dorothy I was leaving.

"You sure?" she said. "Maybe it'd be good to . . ." I cut her off. "Sorry, Dorothy, I just have to go. Sorry I'll miss your run. Good luck!"

"Call me," she said. "Promise?"

I promised.

I left Vince a message I'd be home early, and drove home numb, blasting Madonna the rest of the way. A male bluebird flew across the driveway as I pulled into the farm, luminous blue against pea-green leaves. I got the dogs out, and left everything else in the truck. I let Clementine out to potty, said hi to Bo Peep, and went to bed.

It was dark when I woke up, after eight o'clock. Holy shit, I hadn't fed anyone. I fed the house dogs, put a bowl down for Thelma and Louise, and gave Bo Peep her dinner along with an apology. Old Horse nickered a complaint, but soon had her velvet nose tucked into his grain. The sheep were far out in the field. I could see their eyes shining when I scanned my torch light across the pasture. The lambs had missed their evening grain, but they'd live through it. I went back to bed, and dreamt of bad things.

Chapter 11

Cisco kept me distracted through the rest of the weekend. His ribs, though still wash boards, were softened by a thin layer of fat under his fur. I started working on his recall, clapping and calling while I ran away from him to get him into chase mode. Everyone had a good time except my own short, stumpy legs, which are designed to stride up Scottish hills at a determined walk. Running is not in their repertoire, as they never fail to remind me.

After training I'd sit down and rub that baby soft place behind his ears. He'd close his eyes and make little groany noises. My mind buzzed. *What happened that you ended up by the side of the highway half dead? Why are Jack and I falling in love with you? And, mostly, what am I going to do with you?*

What *was* I going to do with him? I didn't want or need another dog right now, and if I got one, it would be a working Border collie. Besides, surely Cisco should have a chance to use his skills and training to do his own kind of work. Dogs like Cisco are bred to be detectives, their noses finding clues that we humans never could.

As I lay there, I realized I hadn't talked again to Tom, my best option to figure out where Cisco came from. I called him, a little surprised I hadn't heard back from him. Surely, he was home from his trip? I got his voice mail, so I left a message. "Hey, Tom, Maddie here. I'm still trying to figure out where this shepherd I've got came from. Have you had a chance to ask around yet? Give me call, thanks."

I waited awhile for him to call back, finally settling in on the couch with Jack and Cisco, who were determined to share it with me and Clementine. It was a tight fit, made tighter by the dogs hovering over me while I ate a plate of refried beans. I ate, they drooled, and we all finally slumped into some semblance of comfort and snored our way through multiple episodes of *House*.

Monday arrived cool and crisp, one of those rare spring days with bluebird skies and cotton clouds that keep me living here, in spite of hot summers and iceberg winters. The day's schedule included the house call I'd agree to do for Harpo, that big lug of a dog whose disheveled owners were going to lose him without my help. Shadows dappled the road as I drove away from the farm, the maple leaves still Irish green and fat with promise. As I got closer to town, the rural landscape shifted inevitably to a smattering of gas stations, hardware stores, and fast-food joints.

By the time I pulled up in front of Harpo's house, a good hour from the farm and on the other side of town, the scenery had flipped from scenic rural to blighted urban. I drove past sad, old houses in a neighborhood where no one called the authorities if a front yard looked like a dump site. Most of the houses, classic wood-framed midwestern cottages, sat close to the road, but the boys' salmon-colored house was a good hundred feet back. The front yard was surrounded by a chicken wire fence that wouldn't keep chickens inside unless they were agoraphobic.

After I parked on pitted asphalt, I sat in the truck wondering what I had gotten myself into. Being a behaviorist meant taking on someone's burdens, and it can sit heavily on your shoulders. In spite of my optimism at the end of our first appointment, I knew that training dogs is easy compared to changing the habits of humans. Without my clients' total commitment to changing Harpo's behavior, he was going to terrorize another dog, and the boys were going to lose him.

I looked in the mirror to ensure I was presentable. Before I got out, I called Dorothy and left a message with the address and time of my house call. I said if I didn't call her in two hours to send a Saint Bernard. I had started that years ago, when a simple "nuisance barking" house call turned into something else altogether. The dog was a retriever mix, the kind that fills the cages of every animal shelter within five hundred miles. The owner was a single guy, IT consultant he told me, with lips as thin as his belly was full.

It was his eyes that saved me, the eyes of a dog before it attacks, when I suggested we go into the backyard to work on his dog's barking.

"No, I'd rather work in the house," he said, moving between me and the back door. I had been looking at his dog when he spoke, but when I looked up he was looking straight at me, his back against the door, his eyes flat, locked onto mine.

There it was, that internal chill, that gut wrench, that I had experienced long ago when a pointer's eyes had become reptilian when I reached toward his toy. I learned after that to read the same look in the eyes of people. I saw it when a client bragged that her dog would kill me if she let him. And, years after the fact, I realized that's why my heart froze when my ex came looking for me after a night in the bars.

That is why I knew what to do in that client's house. Timing is everything in dog training, especially if a dog is about to bite you. Without hesitation, I had turned and fast walked out the front door, striding purposefully to my truck, locking the door, and turning the key.

"Hey! Hey!" he yelled after me. "Where are you going?" I shifted into gear and drove away.

Harpo interrupted my reverie. He came barreling out of the house, a hundred pounds of glorious, uncontrolled momentum, and smashed into the flimsy fence. I leapt out before he trashed it completely and ended up in the road.

"Hey, gorgeous! How's my guy?"

After Harpo behaved as if I was the love of his life, and I apologized for abandoning him, we again declared our eternal commitment and walked into the house together.

Joe opened the door and said, "Uh, sorry. We keep meaning to fix that back door so he can't get out, but . . . ." His voice trailed off as if the reasons not to repair the door were too complex to explain. He motioned me over to a couch so low that getting out was going to be gymnastic.

The living room was tiny and dark, made smaller by the five of us clustered within it. Marvin sat in a chair so weathered and unique it deserved its own name. Clyde settled into a creaky rocking chair in a dark corner while Joe leaned against the door to the kitchen. Harpo lay his head on my lap and licked my hands.

I asked Joe if he could open the curtains—an improbable set of yellow calico ruffles—so that I could see to take notes. After he did, I listened for a good ten minutes while they complained again how unfairly they had been treated, and how Harpo was a wonderful dog and would never hurt anybody. After they'd had their say, I explained again that this was all about protecting Harpo. If he hurt another dog, very bad things would happen. They might never see him again.

It got very quiet. Joe looked out the window toward a mourning dove cooing on a phone wire. Marvin chewed on his thumbnail. Clyde rubbed the stubble on his face with his huge, pawlike hands and said, "Okay, what do we do?"

It was the first time that Clyde had done much more than grunt at me, and I considered his question a victory.

"Okay, boys, here's what we need to do." I'd never addressed my clients this way before—"boys?"—but something about the cozy living room and the rapt attention of three grizzled men who worshipped their dog got to me. Maybe it was the calico curtains.

"First, we need to manage the situation. No matter how hard you work on changing Harpo's behavior toward dogs from aggressive to friendly, stuff happens. We need to make management our first priority and make it impossible for Harpo to get over the fence. Once that's done, we can talk about teaching him to respond to other dogs in a different and less dangerous way. Make sense?"

We went first to the back door and discussed what it needed to stay shut once closed. Then we trooped out to the front yard, Harpo on leash this time, and inspected the tangle of wires that was a fence in name only. I nixed their suggestion of a new three-foot fence; Harpo could practically walk over it. Four feet? Not good enough. Five was safer. Six even better.

Things got tense again when we began talking about materials. The fence had to be sturdy, which would involve wood, and that meant money, probably more than they had to spare. Joe and Clyde began to argue. Marvin walked back into the house. Harpo stood between the house and the three of us in the front yard, looking back and forth at his disputing pack members, his tongue flicking in and out anxiously.

Somewhere around the fourth "Damn it" from Joe, I glanced in Harpo's direction. His head had turned, ears up, mouth snapped shut. I followed his glance to the left, where a young woman walked down the sidewalk with a pumpkin-shaped pug by her side. I tightened my grip on Harpo's leash and reached for his collar at the same moment that he lunged upward, like a charging bear.

Harpo had the muscles of a sumo wrestler, but I'm strong for my size, and I knew more about physics than he did. Although we ended up sprawled in the mud together, I successfully redirected his lunge and stopped him from scaling the fence. Out of the corner of my eye I could see that the dog walker had wisely decided to turn around.

"Oh damn, are you okay?" said Joe, bending down to haul me up. I ignored him because Clyde began yelling at Harpo, and I turned my attention to calm him. At the moment Harpo wasn't doing anything but standing in the yard looking confused, and yelling at him now wouldn't do anything good.

"I'm fine," I said, as if my arm didn't feel as if it had been pulled out of my shoulder socket.

"But look, first we have to keep Harpo out of the front yard until you can create a safe barrier. (When had it become "we"?) For now, let him potty only on leash in the backyard and fix the back door. It won't cost much of anything but a few new screws. And about the fence: I know you want Harpo to be able spend time out here in the yard, but you just have to build a better fence. I have tons of old wooden posts piled up in my barn. You're welcome to them. Why don't you come out and pick out what you want? I could bring it out in my truck if you don't have another way of transporting it."

We settled on a time for them to come out to the farm and gather wood and materials for the fence. Harpo licked my face when I said good-bye and did a little dance at the door that made him look like a WWE wrestler trying to tap dance. As I left, I didn't say anything about a house call fee, or payment for another consultation. That's me, Dr. Maddie McGowan, a paragon of business acumen. I drove home wondering what the hell was wrong with me that I kept getting myself involved in other people's problems, when I was supposed to be making a living at it.

Damn dogs.

CHAPTER 12

Something was wrong when I arrived home. But what? The sheep were grazing quietly in the small field behind the house, grabbing mouthfuls of grass with little jerking motions, tearing off the nutritious tips. The door to the house was closed, the front porch still had its elliptical sag in the middle. The barn swallows were swooping in and out of the shed, feeding their second clutch of babies with insects snatched on the wing.

But something wasn't right. I could feel it, like stray voltage in the air. I parked the truck, turned the key to off, and suddenly realized what was wrong. It was quiet. Too quiet. Yes, the barn swallows chittered, a catbird repeated *meowee* from the bushes by the barn, and I could hear the breeze through the aspens along the driveway. But Bo Peep wasn't barking, and her silence was tangible. She always barked when I drove up, the notes rapid and high-pitched. It's her excitement bark, easily distinguished from the noise she makes when we patrol the fields each evening, barking "I'm on guard now" in a low, mildly threatening tone to no one and everyone, like an actress belting out her lines to an audience she can't see.

I sat stiffly in the truck, unable to do anything but try to sort out what was going on. Suddenly Jack, who had been safely inside the house when I left, came running to me from behind the barn. I opened the truck's door and he leapt inside, pupils dilated into black pools, the skin over his skull stretched tight. He ran smack into me, head and ears down, and began thrashing against me, smashing me into the seat. He whined high, keening notes I'd never heard from him before.

What the hell? I felt sick to my stomach. Something had happened, something bad. How did Jack get outside? Where was Bo Peep? What about Clementine? Cisco? I stroked Jack's head for a moment, spoke low and slow to him, and then leapt out of the truck and ran inside. Clementine was sound asleep on the couch. Thank God. She blinked blearily at me as I turned and ran into the back room where Cisco slept in his huge crate when I was away.

His crate was empty. I stared at it in disbelief, my brain not processing what I was seeing. Finally, I whirled around and called his name, my voice high and screechy. I dashed through the house, barely breathing, my heart slamming against my chest. "CISCO? CISCO?" I kept yelling as I ran up the stairs, and down into the cellar. Jack followed me, eyes huge and round.

"Oh Jesus, Jack, where is Cisco? Where is Bo Peep?"

I searched for Cisco in empty room after empty room. I ran outside and called for Cisco and Bo Peep repeatedly, running into the barn, the shed, dashing through the high weeds around buildings, into the fields, where the sheep raised their heads and stood in mild alarm as I ran and ran and called and called until I was covered in sweat and burrs and my voice gave out.

Panting, heartsick with fear, I found Bo Peep, or Jack did, as we trotted back to the house. She was lying in some high grass under the scrubby buckthorn trees I'd meant to remove earlier in the summer. I would have missed her if Jack hadn't run over to sniff her limp body. Not knowing what he'd found, I called him to come, wanting him close to me. He turned toward me when I called, but held his body still, as if posing for a photograph. I was about to call him again when I saw a smudge of white in the brush beside him. It was Bo Peep, lying on her side, unconscious. Her lips were pale and flecked with blood. Jack nudged her muzzle. No response. She was alive, but barely.

"Oh my God, oh my God," I chanted, as I tried to pick her up and get her into the truck. It wasn't easy. I'm strong, really strong, but Bo Peep weighed close to ninety pounds. I ran back to the house and got a blanket, rolled her onto it so I could drag her to the truck. I finally got her lifted into the truck. It wasn't elegant. But I knew she needed emergency medical care, and I couldn't wait to find someone to help me. I ran back into the house to get my wallet, told Jack to jump into his crate in the backseat of the cab, and drove like a maniac to the closest vet, the dust swirling behind the truck as I roared out the driveway.

The clinic staff met me in the parking lot with a gurney; I had called to alert them that I was coming.

They took Bo Peep into the back room for diagnosis, her white body sprawled over the edges of the shiny aluminum surface. Her eyes looked vacant. Her tongue hung out of her mouth, saliva pooled onto the surface of the gurney.

Jack and I stood in the lobby of the clinic—I couldn't bear to let him out of my sight, even in a locked truck. I sat down on the tile floor, stunned, motionless, my mind swirling. Bo Peep was dying and might be dead already. Cisco was gone. Jack had been loose outside. What the hell could have happened? Did I leave a door open? Did Cisco get out of his crate somehow? Had Bo Peep gotten into poison? But what could have poisoned her? I scrupulously kept dangerous chemicals off the farm, or with rare exceptions, carefully locked up.

Before I could even sit down, Dr. Reynolds threw open a door and ran into the lobby, looking as wild-eyed as Jack had.

"What?" I said.

"She's crashing, Maddie, we have to work fast. Her breathing is abnormal, extremely slow, and even with support it's not stabilizing. If anything, it's becoming slower and shallower. She's at risk of brain damage due to lack of oxygen at this point; that's why we have her on oxygen. I have to be honest, though, and tell you that already might have happened."

"But what's wrong? Why is she crashing like this?"

"I don't know, but if I didn't know better, I'd think she overdosed on fentanyl. Do you have any fentanyl on the farm? It's a painkiller—has your doctor prescribed it?"

Fentanyl? That superstrong pain medicine that's fifty times stronger than other opioids and is killing people all over the country when it's mixed with cocaine or heroin? We've all heard about it on the news.

I stood stunned, staring at her face. She said my name again, louder.

"Maddie! Do you have any fentanyl in the house?"

"No! No, I don't."

She motioned for me to follow her into the treatment area as she continued talking.

"All I can do at this point is give her naloxone; it's an opioid antagonist and can reverse the effects of fentanyl if that's what it is. Do I have your permission to use it? She's slipping, Maddie, we're going to lose her soon. I've already had the staff get the naloxone out; we keep it because we use fentanyl sometimes as a painkiller after surgery."

"Yes! Yes, of course." I asked the receptionist to hold Jack for a moment while I went to see my big, white, fluff puddle of a dog. Maybe for the last time. Bo Peep's body was half hidden by medical paraphernalia. She had a mask over her muzzle and a tangle of rubber tubes draped over her. I reached out and stroked her ears, her silky, cream-colored ears. I told her I loved her, while tears streamed down my face. Dr. Reynolds took a white vial from the vet tech and sprayed it into Bo

Peep's nostrils. Within seconds, her chest rose and fell, and she coughed into the mask. She began to stir while the mask was taken off her face.

"Good grief. It *was* fentanyl, look at what's happening," the doctor said. Already, Bo Peep's lips and mouth were gaining color.

"There are some possible side effects—vomiting, weakness—so we'll need to keep her here at least overnight. I have to warn you, she may have brain damage. That was a long time for her to get so little oxygen into her brain. It's too soon to say how she'll be once she's fully awake."

I started crying for real, gasping with snotty sobs that took me over as if I'd been drugged myself. I sank down against a wall, head tucked into my legs, when I felt a warm tongue lick my face. The vet tech had brought Jack in. Oh Jack. Jack, Jack. What the hell? First George, now this.

Eventually I got it together and drove home with Jack, begging the universe to send a healthy Bo Peep back to us tomorrow. I couldn't imagine life without her. I had thought she might be a bust when I first got her, a shaggy twelve-month-old, who was too playful and silly to be trusted with the sheep, seemingly too sweet to stand up to a pack of coyotes. And then one day, a few months later, I was attacked by Beavis, my 250-pound, anvil-headed ram. I knew never to turn my back on a mature ram, but Beavis had surprised me, charging out of the flock like a bull and smashing me into the ground. As I struggled to get my breath back, I saw him backing up for another go.

Bo Peep, still a gangly adolescent, dashed in so fast to protect me that I didn't realize what had happened until it was over. I heard a visceral growl-bark, loud and low, accompanied by a flash of white between me and the ram. Bo Peep had dashed between us and gone straight for his nose. She bit him hard enough to draw blood, and then backed up and looked straight into his eyes. Beavis decided discretion was the better part of valor and trotted away. Bo Peep came over to me, sprawled in a pile of sheep shit, and licked my face. Bo Peep grew up that day; she stopped playing with the sheep and settled into life as the farm cop, always on duty. I trusted her completely to keep the sheep safe. But what about her? How could I keep her safe now when I didn't even know what had happened?

And Cisco? Where was Cisco? I began calling my neighbors as soon as I got home, asking if anyone had seen him. No one had, but they said they'd keep an eye out. Vince, bless him, asked if there was anything he could do. I asked if he'd search the surrounding woods. I made flyers to post over the southern part of the state, found phone numbers for the sheriff, and wrote down the phone numbers of nearby shelters to call in the morning. But here's the thing. Cisco had been in his crate. Someone had to come inside the house and open it. They wouldn't do that and then just let him run into the woods. Would they?

My mind looping between panic and fury, I fed Jack, heartsick at having no bowls to fill for Bo Peep or Cisco. I did the rest of the chores, ate a bag of chips, drank too much beer, and drifted to sleep.

The nightmares came back, this time with Tyler in them.

I had met him when I was eighteen, drooling over the muscled-up quarter horses running the barrels at the New Mexico State Fair Rodeo. I had dreamed about a horse like that, with huge eyes and a warm neck to throw my arms around; to be one of those girls, hair flying behind my cowboy hat, astride a powerful horse wrapping itself around a barrel, turning so fast that his body was almost parallel to the ground.

My girlfriend and I had left the stands to get some lunch and a cold drink. We stood in line in our new western shirts—the kind with frills down the front—and talked about the palomino we both wanted the moment he entered the ring.

And then there was Tyler Jones, the famous bull rider, standing in front of me, ordering a hot dog with chili. Successful bull riders, the highlight of every rodeo, make millions now every year. Back then, making a couple hundred grand was big news, and Tyler was on track to earn it and be the bull rider of the year. If rodeo had a celebrity, he was it.

He got his lunch and bumped into me when he turned to leave the food stand.

"Sorry, ma'am." He had electric blue eyes, a dirty white hat, and a movie-star grin. He started to turn away again, but then turned back and looked me up and down.

"Why don't you let me buy you lunch to apologize?" I was too stunned to answer. Tyler was a star. Girls followed him everywhere for his autograph. I nodded my head. Yes.

The tiniest of movements. Which almost got me killed.

CHAPTER 13

First thing in the morning I called the vet clinic and was told that Bo Peep was stable and resting comfortably. We wouldn't really know much about brain damage until I got her home and put her in her usual environment. But at least she seemed okay in the clinic. I sighed in relief, and said I'd be there as soon as I could.

I called Dorothy and told her the story, trying to keep it together enough to be coherent.

"What the fuck?" she said.

"I know, I know. First George, now this?"

"I'm coming out," Dorothy said. She hung up before I could answer.

While I waited for Dorothy to arrive, I called the vet clinic to say I'd pick Bo Peep up in the early afternoon, afraid to leave the farm until Dorothy arrived. I called Vince but had to leave a message, figuring he was out in the woods searching for Cisco. I wanted to join him, but first called the sheriff's office and explained as best I could what had happened, repeating myself so often that I was ready to scream.

"Yes, she was poisoned with fentanyl. The vet will confirm that. Yes, fentanyl, the drug. But another dog has been kidnapped." The dispatcher said she'd talk to a deputy, reminding me that missing dogs don't usually result in visits from a busy county sheriff. I reminded her, again, about the fentanyl. And that my house had been burglarized. She said she'd see what she could do.

I began printing the flyers with Cisco's photo, grateful that I had a few good ones on my phone. I offered a hefty reward for information. A Dodd County sheriff's car drove up as I was printing out the last of them. Sheriff Wallenberg lumbered out of his car, his belly and cop paraphernalia preceding the rest of him. I always wondered if they actually chase suspects anymore, covered as they are with massive leather belts holding guns and tasers and batons and who knows what else hidden away in multiple black leather pockets. It looked like his gear added twenty pounds to Wallenberg's own heft. He weighed at least 230 and had white-blond hair that fit with the name Wallenberg, a good Swedish name if there ever was one. I put on my glasses, scrunched my hair under a cap, and went out to let him in through the sticky gate.

"What's this about a drugged dog?" he said, after introducing himself and glaring at Jack, as

if Jack had been dealing smack at the local bar. Jack treats strangers like long-lost lovers, but I wasn't sure I trusted Wallenberg around him, so I thanked the sheriff for coming and popped Jack into his crate in the mudroom.

"Well, that's part of the mystery," I said in answer to his question. "The important part now is that a valuable dog has disappeared, and he must have been stolen. One of your own, Officer Ryan Conners from the Milwaukee K9 Unit, said he thought he had been trained as a drug detection dog, and we know how valuable they can be. I've been fostering him since he was found half dead and taken to the shelter. It looks as though he'd been trained as a K9. But someone broke into my house and stole him, and I have to find him. I just have to."

I shouldn't have added that last sentence. I was using all of my energy to speak in a measured, low voice, rather than the panicked woman that I was. I knew full well how little respect is given to "emotional" women by law enforcement, not to mention short, "cute" ones. I wanted to scream, because every single second that Cisco was gone was a second too long. I'd had Cisco for just a month, but he had a hold of my heart the moment he looked into my eyes at the shelter. I took some breaths, noting that Wallenberg's expression was skeptical, if not amused.

"What kind of guard dog was it that was supposedly drugged?" Supposedly? More deep breaths.

"Was she a shepherd or a Malinois, maybe?" Wallenberg added, filling the silence.

"No, she was, I mean is, a livestock guarding dog, a Great Pyrenees, about ninety pounds of a living, breathing, anti-coyote security system. She is at the vet clinic now. The dog who was stolen was, I mean is, a shepherd; he looks like half the police dogs in the state."

"So, you think someone came in here, drugged your 'guard' dog (he actually made finger quotes) and stole this other dog you say was a K9?" Three breaths.

"All I can say is that when I arrived home, my livestock guardian dog didn't bark as usual and I found her barely breathing in the bushes. The vet diagnosed it as a probable fentanyl overdose, and administered naloxone, which brought her back almost instantly and confirmed the diagnosis. My Border collie, Jack, who is always in the house, was loose in the yard when I drove up, and the German shepherd that Officer Ryan thinks was trained as a drug detection dog wasn't in the crate in the house where I left him."

"Okay," he said, snapping shut his unused notebook. "Let's look around."

He looked for tire tracks that wouldn't fit with my vehicle. The driveway is mostly dirt and gravel, but he thought he might have found something in some soft ground by the side of where

I usually park. He called me over and asked if I ever parked exactly in that spot. I don't, and told him so. He took a cell phone out of one of his many leather belt pockets and took a few photos.

I followed him toward the house where he looked carefully at the bronze doorknob that I'd carefully locked before leaving for the house call. He found no sign of disturbance, but surprised me by opening the door, turning the knob on the inside, locking the door, and then shutting it. He got out a thin metal wire, and proceeded to try to pick the lock. He got it open in about six seconds. Oh.

"You live alone out here?" I nodded. "Ever thought about getting some kind of security camera and better locks? You're pretty vulnerable, so isolated and all."

I had thought my locks were fine. My house is tucked safely far off the road in rural Wisconsin. I had learned self-defense years ago.

But reality hit hard. I can protect myself, Bo Peep can protect the sheep, but who protects my dogs when I'm gone? Why did I think living tucked away in the hills meant my dogs were safe when I was gone?

He looked at me, waiting for me to say something. All I could do was nod, and then I had to look away, my eyes starting to burn. I took some deep breaths.

"Okay Miz McGowan, I'll file a burglary report and put out an alert about the dog. I can talk to some of the guys in narcotics to see what they think about all this. Have any photos of the dog?"

Grateful for the distraction, I gave him several of the flyers I'd just created.

"I'm going to set up some drive-bys so that we can keep an eye on you and your place." His face softened and suddenly he looked more like a kindly uncle than a character from a TV show.

I sort of wanted to hug him.

"Do you have friends who can stay with you for a while?" he asked.

I turned my face away, my throat tight, as I said, "I'm good, I have a friend coming, thanks so much for your help."

Dorothy arrived midday. She walked in carting a massive silver thing, which turned out to be

an expresso coffeemaker, a De'Longhi Magnifica. "I will do just about anything for you, girlfriend, but I will not drink your god-awful coffee one more time." Apparently, my ancient Mr. Coffee machine wasn't good enough for her. She also brought her litter of puppies as therapy, along with a bag of takeout Mexican food. Enchiladas with mole sauce, corn chips made that morning, guacamole, and salty red beans sprinkled with cheese. I ate ravenously, having forgotten about food for almost twenty-four hours. After lunch we took Jack and the puppies for a long walk toward the creek, the puppies scrambling, shiny-eyed and determined, over the agility course of high grass and bushes provided free of charge by nature. Jack had given them each a quick sniff and a lick, and then ran forward to look for rabbits.

"Okay, what's the plan?" Dorothy asked, always practical and on point.

"First things first: I have to beef up my security. Would you stay here while I go to the hardware store and then the vet's to pick up Bo Peep?"

"Of course. If I'm lucky the bad guys will come so I can slaughter them like rats. Remind me where your shotgun is. And . . . oh yeah, I brought my Glock."

I stopped walking and looked at her. She knows how I feel about handguns.

"I know, I know, but good grief, Maddie, George got murdered and now someone has almost killed your dog. And got into your house. I know you know how to use a handgun. Just keep it hidden, empty, so you can't even see it. It'll be okay."

I said, "Okay," but so quietly I'm not sure she heard me. I

plumped down on a relatively dry rise in the field, and smooched to attract the puppies. A little bitch with three tiny white paws squiggled into my lap and began licking my face.

Puppy breath, the best smell in the world—milky, and sweetly skunky. I breathed it in like life-saving oxygen.

"Okay," I said again, louder this time. "Here's the list: After I get Bo Peep, I get new locks, secure the windows, and get a home security system. At the same time, we look for Cisco. We search the woods, several times a day. We can alternate putting up flyers so someone is always home, call shelters, and alert the neighbors. We go on social media and ask neighbors to look out for her. I'll call Southeast Humane and ask for their help spreading the word. Maybe I can talk to Chris and learn more about where he found him. Maybe the people who had him lost him, found out where he was, and wanted him back?"

"What about that cop you saw as a client?" Dorothy added. "The one with the thunder-phobic dog? Maybe he could help."

"Good idea." I kissed the pup on her sweet little face, put her down, and stood up. "Okay, let's get started."

Dorothy stayed at the house while I drove to the local hardware store, not wanting to leave Bo Peep unguarded in the truck after I picked her up. The saleswoman, Martha, who'd been at the store since time began, greeted me and listened to my story in horror.

"Okay," she said, "follow me." We walked through aisles full of plastic packets of tiny things whose purpose mortals like me can't imagine, and finally got to the locks. The selections were endless, but I finally picked out keyless entry locks with deadbolts and codes that prevented them from being picked. I bought two packages of those indoor security guards that motels have with swing bars that keep the doors from opening. Those only help when you're inside, but it was beginning to occur to me that feeling secure at night was going to be more important than ever. We talked about my old, warped windows, and ended up agreeing that the best defense was a home security system with a built-in burglar alarm.

Be Peep greeted me in the lobby of the vet clinic as if she'd been to the spa. Bathed into bright white glory, brushed out and full of herself, she talked to me as soon as I entered.

"Wurrr, wurr, wurr," she trilled, her nose pointed to the ceiling while she strained against the leash. I ran to her and collapsed on the floor, burying my face in her thick ruff. Tears were shed. Again.

Dr. Reynolds came out and said, "We are so lucky, Maddie. I can't believe she is doing so well. We came so close to losing her, and I was worried she'd have brain damage. But she looks great. Thank heavens you brought her in when you did."

I nodded, my throat too tight to answer. I stood up, waving my hand aside my face in the universal sign of "Can't talk, crying," and hugged Dr. Reynolds.

"I'll call you later to settle up the bill, okay?"

"Of course, Maddie, take care of yourself."

A vet tech helped me heft Bo Peep in the truck. After making sure she was settled in, I drove the few miles to the Clear Creek bank, where I put up a flyer on their window. Then I sat in the truck and called the shelter and asked for Catherine.

"Catherine, you're never going to believe what happened." I still didn't believe it either. Maybe talking about it would make it seem more real.

"Cisco's kidnapped. I got home to find Jack loose outside, my Great Pyr almost dead from fentanyl poisoning, and Cisco's crate was wide open and empty."

"What? What? What did you say?"

"I know, it's insane, but Bo Peep came through thanks to the vet, and now I have to find Cisco. I know I've only had him for a few weeks, but I adore him. He's doing so much better, Catherine, you should see him. Can you help? I'll email you some flyers to put up, but could you put me in contact with Chris too? I'd like to learn more about where Cisco came from. Someone must want him back, but who? And why? Maybe Chris can tell me more about where he found him and that'll be a starting place."

"He's not here today, but I'll contact him and have him get a hold of you as soon as he can."

I sat in the truck, the phone sitting in my lap, set on speaker. I had nothing else to say, but disconnecting meant driving home, to the vireo singing counterpoint to the breeze through the trees, the sheep snoozing in the high grass, the lilac-hued hills to the south, hazy in the distance.

The place I'd established years ago as my safe house. Which was no longer safe.

Chapter 14

Once home, I hefted Bo Peep out of the truck and brought her into the house for the night—I wanted her in my sight at every moment. She'd never been inside and leaned back in horror at the door, having lived outside as a livestock guardian dog her entire life. It took a lot of patience and a lot of dried liver to lure her inside, but she finally lifted one paw, and then the other, and made her way into the living room.

I saw Vince and Dorothy through an arched doorway, seated around the kitchen table, drinking coffee. Vince got up to give me an awkward hug, our first. He smelled like grass—the kind you mow and the kind you smoke. He told me he'd scoured the woods for hours, but hadn't found anything but a deer skeleton. Dorothy had written out a to-do list, with checks beside most of the items. Very Dorothy. Very helpful.

She had already called the shelters within two hundred miles. Check. I'd put up flyers every possible place I could imagine and had contacted my neighbors. Check. I'd gone to the hardware store and bought better locks. Check. Home security cameras and alarms had been ordered. Check. I should hear soon from Chris. Check. A police report was filed. Check.

We couldn't think of anything else to do except install the new locks. Vince worked on the front door while Dorothy and

I worked on the back. It didn't go smoothly. Carpentry never does in an old farmhouse. Some of the wood on the back door was so rotted that we couldn't secure the new locks, so Vince drove into town and bought me a new back door. Installing all of that took a couple of hours, and by then it was time to do chores and settle the farm in for the night. I told Vince to go home and take care of his own place; he had a couple of horses, an ancient Guernsey, and an itinerant dairy goat (Motto: *Fences are for Losers)* who needed feeding. Dorothy and the puppies were staying overnight; she'd already called and asked a neighbor to farm sit.

Vince left reluctantly, turning back twice, saying, "Are you sure you'll be all right?" Dorothy looked straight into his eyes and patted her hip like a gunslinger in a fifties Western. "Yup. Now get out of here." Dorothy shooed him away as if she was shaking out a rug.

She turned toward me. "Okay, let's get the chores done. And you need a long walk."

Eventually, with the animals fed and exercised, and the light fading, there was nothing to do but get out the leftovers from lunch. I wasn't hungry, but managed a few bites of an enchilada, and then topped that off with a bottle of beer. I turned on the TV, then four of us—me, Dorothy, Jack, and Clementine—scrunched up together on the made-for-one-couch. Bo Peep snored on the braided rug below us. Somehow, I must have made it upstairs, because I woke up around two a.m., in my own bed, needing to pee, with Jack, warm as a water bottle, snuggled against me. He blinked as I got up, then yawned and rolled over, belly up, legs sprawled. I padded downstairs to find Dorothy asleep on the couch, Bo Peep whuffling in harmony on the rug beside her. I crept back up, not wanting to wake either of them.

Sleep was hard to come by after that. I lay quietly beside

Jack, stroking his silky head, listening to a barred owl calling, *Who cooks for you? Who cooks for you?*

"Where is Cisco? Where is Cisco?" the owl might as well have been saying. It felt unbearable to know he might be somewhere, suffering, in danger. Nothing I could do at two a.m. I tried my breathing exercises, meditation, and my own version of prayer. Nothing worked. Finally, the sky relieved me by lightening, the house wren woke up and called for the sun, so I got up, made coffee, and let the dogs out.

Dorothy was starting to stir when I took Bo Peep outside. Never house trained, it was a miracle she hadn't peed in the house. She rewarded me by squatting and peeing a racehorse quantity of urine two steps from the front porch. She began straining on the leash, barking her announcement bark, ready to go back on duty. I let her go into the small fenced area around the house, promising I'd check on her often and run outside if I heard a car come down the driveway.

After we fed everyone else, Dorothy and I ate some peanut butter toast while we talked about the red-tailed hawk she was rehabbing. It had been hit by a car and had a broken wing. She wasn't having a lot of luck getting it to eat, even though she had years of experience with avian patients. I suggested she try my favorite trick for getting dogs to eat—offer them the food and then snatch it away. Repeat three times and on the fourth try just about every dog in the world can't resist grabbing it before you pull it away.

She said she'd try it, then stood up. Time to walk the dogs. The dewy grass turned the puppies into soggy bundles of enthusiasm, so we toweled them off when we got back before putting them back into the X-pen we'd set up inside the house.

We poured out more coffee and checked our texts and emails. There it was, a text from Chris late last night that said to call him today. I punched in the numbers immediately.

"Yeah?" A groggy voice greeted me. "Who is this?"

"Is this Chris?" It didn't sound like him. At the shelter, he had a kind, quiet voice that mesmerized fearful dogs and cats. The guy on the phone had a gravelly voice that sounded sort of pissy. I flashed back to Cisco growling at him in the shelter and almost hung up. Who is this guy, anyway?

"Uh, Chris? This is Maddie McGowan. I'm afraid I have bad news: Cisco was kidnapped and I'm desperate to find him. Whoever did it drugged my guard dog and almost killed her."

"What?" I could see him jerking up into a sit, starting to wake up. I waited, not sure what else to say.

"Uh, wait, what? Dr. McGowan? I'm sorry, I was asleep. Kidnapped? What do you mean? What happened?" I told him the whole story.

"Jeez, I'm sorry, that's horrible," he said, sounding fully awake now.

"I'm desperate to find him, Chris. He's a wonderful dog, honest, he was just so stressed and sick when you found him. Why would anyone steal him? Unless it was the people who had him before, and why would they want him back? Would you take me to where you found him to see if we can get any ideas about where he came from?"

"Uh, gee. Today?" Long pause. "I've got class this morning and there's an exam tomorrow." I knew Chris was in community college, studying computer coding. But it felt like every minute Cisco was gone was another minute I had less chance to find him.

I poured another cup of coffee, the phone scrunched to my ear by my shoulder.

"Can you get the notes? Catch up online? I'm so sorry, Chris, I know this is a big ask." I could hear my voice thicken as my throat started to swell. I took some deep breaths and pulled my finger out of my hair.

I waited, drank a few sips of the coffee. It was cold and acidic.

"Okay, I guess. I'm not sure that I remember exactly where it was, but I can try. Give me an hour and come pick me up?"

I wrote down his address and looked it up, figuring out how to get there and how long it would take. Dorothy said she'd be fine staying the day, but she'd have to leave before nightfall. I checked my messages and emails, answered a few that couldn't be put off, and put a message on my phone and email that I was out of the office. I called the clients I had scheduled and explained that I had an emergency and had to rebook.

Soon I was in the truck, turning on GPS and following its directions to Chris's place. He lived in an apartment complex that was somewhere between a little scruffy and downright shabby. I parked in the lot, the asphalt pocked with holes, with little ponds of greasy water. Chris's apartment was up a metal flight of stairs, paint peeling, rust blooming on the edges of the steps. My feet made a clanging sound at each step, as if the stairs objected to being disturbed.

There was no doorbell, so I knocked. Chris opened the door right away. He looked older, more serious than at the shelter. He had a day's worth of a blond stubble on his face, his usual rumpled hair, and a navy blue backpack slung over his shoulder. I had to bend my neck to look up to his face.

"Take your car, that okay?" he said.

"Sure, of course," I answered. We fast-walked down the stairs and got to my truck. Why had I not thought to clear off the front passenger seat? It was covered in papers and jackets and some catsup-covered McDonald's wrappers.

"Oh lordy, I'm sorry." I used my forearms like a backhoe and scooped everything into the backseat, thankful I'd sprung for a club cab with a seating area in the back.

"Okay, where to?"

Chris directed me toward an industrial area in West Allis, just outside Milwaukee proper.

We drove in an awkward silence, my mind full of George's death and Cisco's disappearance, while Chris checked his phone. I knew he was shy and didn't want to push him, so I let the silence sit with us, like another passenger. Chris had never asked a question at some of the workshops I'd done at the shelter until everyone else had left. He'd hang around pretending to mess with his backpack or a book, slide out of his seat, and walk over looking anywhere but at me. And then he'd ask the most insightful question of the day, and I'd say I wished he'd asked that earlier so everyone could hear, and the corners of his mouth would raise microscopically, the gestation of a smile.

After a while, I turned on the radio and let the talk show chatter propel us onto a street of warehouses and flat-roofed buildings surrounded by dumpsters and old trucks. The roadside was a mix of weeds and trash—wild mustard, blooming dandelions, an empty can of beer here, a crushed bag of chips there.

"I think we're getting close," Chris said. He peered out the window toward a set of warehouses with faded blue siding. "Slow down."

I had traffic behind me, so I pulled over to the shoulder and stopped to let it pass. "Go up a ways, maybe a hundred yards." I eased the truck forward until Chris said to stop. He got out of the truck without saying another word, so I switched off the ignition and followed him.

It was surprisingly quiet at midmorning on a weekday. The only noise was the squabble of English sparrows on the lines above us, and a few cars going by on the street. The building on our right looked unused, if not totally abandoned.

We kept walking, one hundred, maybe two hundred yards. Chris stopped a few times and looked around, then continued onward.

Finally, he said, "Here. I recognize that garbage bin, the one with the gang tags on it. He was lying beside it in a heap."

We walked over to the green metal bin, its ridged, plastic cover bent awkwardly to the side.

Chris pointed to a patch of weedy gravel. "He was lying right here. I'm sure." We stared together at the spot, indistinguishable from the scrubby soil around it. It had nothing to tell me.

I felt like an idiot. What was I expecting? A note from Cisco's former owner with his name and address on it? Most likely he'd been dumped here, as people do, discarding unwanted dogs and cats like broken appliances by the roadside. But we'd come all this way; I wasn't going to give up now.

I looked around, trying to find a place Cisco might have wandered away from. I took out my phone and took photos 360 degrees around the spot.

"Let's go knock on some doors," I said to Chris. "Maybe we can find out if he wandered away from someone or something here."

Chris looked around at the neighborhood. "Uh, I'm not sure that's such a good idea. It's not exactly a place for a casual walk, Doc."

"It's Maddie, Chris, and look, it's the middle of the day, there are two of us. We'll be fine." I figured it didn't hurt that Chris was six foot two and built like a muscled-up steer. I strode toward the closest building, a car parked on the side by a metal door, the scratches in its paint like abstract cave paintings. Chris followed behind me, looking right and left for traffic.

I knocked, hard, three times, the door responding with a deep, hollow boom. Nothing. I knocked again, waited. Silence. I turned to walk up the steps of the building's loading dock and knocked on the large doors. Something skittered on the other side, a mouse or a rat? Maybe a feral cat? We waited. Still nothing.

I walked over to the two cars, parked on the other side of the lot, a gun-metal gray Honda Civic and an old Chevy station wagon with wood paneling on the sides. The Civic had a flat tire, the Chevy was full of trash, but neither gave me any clues about who might own them and where they were.

"Okay, let's check out a few more of the buildings before we go back," I said. I turned to see Chris halfway back to the truck.

"Hey, sorry," he said, his body walking away, but his head turned toward me. "I need to go back to check my phone, I left it in the truck. I'll keep an eye on you though. Be careful."

"I will." I knocked on the door of the other warehouse; no one home there either. I walked across the street to a flat, light green building that had a half dozen cars parked in front of it. I knocked on a door under a sign that said WESTERN AUTOMOTIVE and opened the door.

Mateo, his name emblazoned on his orange shirt over a company logo, looked up from behind a counter covered in wrinkled papers.

"Good morning," I said.

"Buenos días," he responded, looking equally confused and amused by my presence.

"A few weeks ago, a German shepherd dog was found across the street. Had you seen him around the area before that?"

He stared. *"Perro?"*

"Si, perro. Mucho grande y mucho . . ." I didn't know the word for sick in Spanish.

"Almost *muerto?*"

"Muerto?" His eyes rounded and he began speaking a stream of rapid-fire Spanish. I cursed not knowing the language better.

Just then the door behind me opened and Chris appeared.

"Any luck?" he said.

"I'm trying to ask if he'd ever seen Cisco around the area before you found him, but my Spanish sucks."

Chris turned to Mateo and spoke in Spanish so fast I couldn't begin to sort out individual words beyond *"Mateo,"* and *"perro,"* and *"por favor."*

Mateo shrugged and said, *"No, lo siento, no perro."* Chris spoke again. Mateo turned and went through a door behind the counter. Chris explained he'd asked him to talk to the others in the back.

Mateo returned, shaking his head. *"Lo siento,"* he repeated.

"Gracias," Chris and I said simultaneously, and walked out.

"Your Spanish is good! I didn't know you were fluent," I said.

"Yeah, my stepmom was from Guadalajara, and I have some Latino friends now who speak it much of the time, so I've picked a lot of it up." Clearly, I had a lot to learn about Chris.

I wanted to look around more, but Chris said he had to get back. I'd already taken up most of his morning, so of course I said yes, but I asked him for a few more minutes while I took photos of all the buildings in the area, just in case. In case of what I couldn't say, but I'd come all this way and felt like I had to do more. We walked back to the truck while I looked around for some miraculous sign—a billboard that said "Cisco Was Here," any kind of clue that might help me find him.

I got the truck started and pulled forward. Chris's head was down as he answered texts on his phone. I have no idea how thumbs that large managed to hit the right keys so fast.

I drove on past the dumpster where Chris had found Cisco and turned in the parking lot to reverse direction. As I pulled onto the interstate something nagged at me; like a jacket caught on a barbed-wire fence. To distract myself I asked Chris more about his knowledge of Spanish, and if he knew any other languages well.

"No, not really, just a little French from high school." He

bent his head back to his phone. I concentrated on finding my way back to the interstate.

After another fifteen minutes, the silence felt too heavy to carry, so I asked him what he was studying. He sounded as excited about learning computer coding as I would be. Not. He sighed and said he'd had a variety of jobs, none that paid well and nothing seemed to stick. At least there should be jobs in this field, and he didn't find it difficult, just a little boring.

"I wanted to be a vet, but there's no way I could afford to go to vet school. Or get in; I wasn't exactly a great student. And I can't imagine going to graduate school like you did."

"What about working as staff in shelters or rescues? Or dog training?" I asked. "There are so many careers you could have with animals that don't need degrees. What about being a professional dog trainer? You'd be great. You can study, work with the pros, and eventually get certified. Why not?"

He started to answer, then paused. I made myself shut up, squashing the urge to keep at it. I thought it was a great idea. Dogs adored Chris, and he seemed eager to learn. The challenge for him wouldn't be the dogs, it'd be the owners. Dogs are easy, people are harder. I can always tell when I'm tired in a consult because I start working the dog instead of training the people. But Chris, although seeming a bit shy, surely could do well enough to make it his profession? Lots of people make a living at it, although it's hardly a way to make big bucks. But then, neither is what I do, and I get by.

I turned to look at him to say something else, the need to encourage him winning out, and was stunned by the look on his face. Defenseless.

"Chris?"

He turned his head away, looking out his window. I had the sense to shut up for a while, and turned on the radio.

We drove along the interstate through fields of corn and soybeans, their green shoots thriving in the sun. Navy blue silos rose above the crops every mile or so, some on farms with clean white houses and carefully tended yards, others abandoned, scattered beside sheds losing the fight with gravity, the roofs too much for their tired walls.

"I'm just not great with people," he said, his voice surprising me over the wail of a country singer's broken heart. "You're so good with people; I could never be like that." He looked away again, out his window. "I guess I have some kind of anxiety disorder, 'social anxiety' they called it at school. That's why I'm studying coding—I don't have to meet a lot of new people. I'd love to be a professional dog trainer, but I'd never be able to do it. It's challenging enough to get myself to the shelter."

I clenched my jaw to keep from jumping in to fix Chris's problem. I fix things for a living, which makes it hard to stay out of it when someone we know has a behavioral problem.

Our minds start writing treatment plans as soon as we hear about it.

Desensitizing. Counterconditioning. Working with a therapist. Herbs, acupuncture, carefully considered medication . . . The list went on, but I managed to restrain myself. "That sounds hard. Let me know if there's anything I could do to help."

It occurred to me that it must have been hard for Chris to come this morning, given our close quarters. I almost asked him if there'd been an exam at all that he needed to go to class for, but managed to leave it at, "Thanks then, for coming this morning. It was good of you." He nodded and said he was glad he had.

When we pulled up to his apartment complex I sat in the cab, engine running, and thanked him again as he bent his head to get out of the truck. Before he left he leaned into the cab, looking straight into my eyes, his own soft and surprisingly green, and said, "I'm so sorry, Maddie, about Cisco. I really am. Let me know if there's anything else I can do to help." I drove away unsettled, discouraged, blasting Madonna's "Ray of Light" on the radio.

It wasn't until I was almost home that I realized what else

had been bothering me. Chris said he'd seen Cisco lying in a heap beside the dumpster when he was driving by. But when I drove by to leave, I saw that you couldn't see that spot from the road. The road curved and Cisco would have been behind the dumpster, out of sight, to anyone in a car. Yet, Chris had seemed so sure. Did he just remember it wrong?

Now what?

Chapter 15

After dropping off Chris, I made it back to the house feeling physically sick. How could I ever find Cisco? If he was even alive. Dorothy gave me a hug when she heard that the trip with Chris was a bust, then she popped the puppies into a crate in her truck. As she climbed into the truck to leave, she said, "I've left the Glock in the bedroom dresser beside your bed. It has a trigger spring so you have to mean it when you pull the trigger, but it has an extended slide release so it's easier to reload. The ammunition is in another drawer. Underneath."

Dorothy knew I'd taken gun safety classes after New Mexico, and that I knew how to use a Glock. She also knew I hated handguns, but she drove away before I had a chance to answer. Standing on the porch, I exhaled so hard that Jack turned to look at my face.

"Holy shit, Jack," I said, "what am I getting myself into?" Good thing dogs can't talk.

I went upstairs to check on the gun. It was, no surprise, unloaded, easily accessible in the top drawer of my bedside dresser. It lay there, in all its blunt, black power, pointing toward the bed. Glocks look nothing like you'd think. The smaller ones are light, comfy to hold, and almost cute, which is all the more reason to find them terrifying. Illogically, I turned it around so that it faced away from the bed and covered it up with a Premier sheep supply catalogue. Good reading when you can't go to sleep.

I checked the answering machine when I went back downstairs. Three messages, one from a woman whose shelter dog had bitten her last night over a steak bone, the second from a widower whose dachshund had stopped eating after his wife died. The third was from Ryan, about Ranger. I called him back.

There'd been a thunderstorm in Milwaukee, and Ranger had a setback. He had been fine at the beginning of the storm, but refused toys and treats once thunder began to shake the house. He went into the safe house with Ryan, but then clung to him as if to a lifeboat in a tempest.

The storm had started around three a.m.—when midwestern storms seem to most often occur, the better to ruin our sleep. Ryan stayed up with him the rest of the night but was worried that he wasn't doing the treatment protocol correctly. I assured him that he'd done nothing wrong, it was fine to comfort Ranger when he was panicked, and to keep up with the plan. I had talked to his vet a few days ago, who recommended an anti-anxiety medication when logistically possible, but Ryan hadn't had a chance to pick up the prescription yet.

Ryan didn't seem to want to get off the phone. He wasn't convinced he was doing the counterconditioning right and he wasn't sure that the safe house was designed correctly. Could I come out to check on things myself?

I told Ryan that I had clients for the next few days, but could come out on Saturday. I had planned to go to Dorothy's to practice for the next trial, but Ranger was such a good dog, and Ryan such a good owner. Besides, we were moving into the height of thunder season and we needed to do all we could for Ranger as soon as possible. (I made a mental note: stop saying "we.")

Ryan lived a good hour and a half away, and I explained I'd have to charge him for the driving time as well as the consult. "Could your department pay for it? It is for a working dog, after all."

"I wish," he said. "I'm on shaky ground here. My boss is ready to cut Ranger from the force altogether. I don't want word spreading that things aren't going well. But it's okay. I'll find the money somehow."

Ouch. Should I donate my fee? I struggle with this on a regular basis. My heart says "of course," and my financial dude—that term is appropriate, given his sartorial choice of Hawaiian shirts and sandals even in winter—says no.

"We'll figure it out," I said. Pause. "Ryan, do you have a minute for me to ask about that dog you met, Cisco?"

"Sure," he answered. "How's he doing?"

"He's gone. He was kidnapped out of my house. My house was broken into, Cisco was taken, and my guard dog was poisoned with fentanyl and almost died. She's okay, but I'm desperately trying to find Cisco. The sheriff came out and said he'd try to help, but I'm looking for any help I can get in the world of K9s. I don't know what you can do, but . . ."

I gave up talking. My throat was all messed up again—me, the one who almost never cried, even the time I slashed my forehead on a table's edge, blood pouring down my face like a tiny, red river.

"Where are you now?" Ryan said, his voice lowering from dog lover to cop-on-duty. "Are you alone? Don't you live in the country? Are you married, is someone else there?"

I was too surprised to answer at first. Was this really another guy in law enforcement who actually cared? News at eleven.

"I'm okay, really." That's what I said, because that's what you say. What I wanted to say was, "No. I'm not close to okay."

But, of course, what I did was tell him all the safety precautions I'd taken, and that I was sure I'd be fine. "But what the hell is going on?" I said. "First my friend George is killed, and then this. I'm heartsick about this dog, Ryan. He was half starved when they found him, so surely the old owner wouldn't want him back. And how would they know where he was anyway?"

I paused to take a breath. Jack came over and pressed his head against my thigh. I leaned down to inhale the scent of his fur, deep and rich and earthy. I stroked his silky head and listened to a cardinal singing outside the window.

"It doesn't make any sense to me either," Ryan said. "I did ask around about Cisco, but no one had heard about a missing dog. All the dogs in our unit are healthy and accounted for. But I'll tell you what. I'll ask Kevin again. He hadn't heard anything, but he's more plugged into the K9 training world than I am."

Kevin? Great. Mr. Snake Eyes.

"Thanks," I said, exhaling hard for the second time that day. "We can talk more when I come out Saturday. But if you hear anything before that, you'll call me, okay?" He promised.

After I hung up, I called the potential clients back, and left messages for both about days and times I could see them. I checked in with a few other clients, aware I'd been paying too little attention to my work. After an hour on the phone, I finally called Tom to see if he'd heard anything.

Tom didn't answer, but I wasn't surprised. He was often back in the kennels or working outside with the dogs. I tried a text message, and got a text back immediately.

Trg, ttyl? Tom was not one to waste characters on a text.
You around Saturday about 10? I'm driving by.
K.

I worked hard the next few days. I had six clients to see, past clients to check up on, notes to update, and new appointments to schedule. The lambs needed worming, I needed to pick up more grain, and, of course, Jack needed to work every day to keep him fit. I continued calling shelters and neighbors about Cisco whenever I got a break, but no one had seen or heard anything. Cisco had disappeared into thin air.

I managed to keep busy enough during the day to keep my stomach from turning over, but the nights were something else again. I tossed and turned the next three nights, listening to the barred owls calling. *Who cooks for you, who cooks for you?* I startled on Friday night when a tree branch brushed the bedroom window in the wind. I pulled open the drawer with the Glock in a panic before my brain engaged. Jack's head flew up when I leapt out of bed, but then he blinked, yawned, and went back to sleep.

By the time Saturday morning dawned I was bleary from too little sleep. As tired as I was, I had to do the chores before driving out to Tom's on the way to Ryan's. I made myself do the feedings, moved the sheep to a new pasture, and confirmed that Vince could come out to mind the farm for the day. I passed on breakfast, my stomach not pleased with its last occupants, but put the rest of the coffee in a mug as Vince drove up.

"Vince, you are a lifesaver. I don't know how I am ever going to repay you."

"I do," he said. "You're going to keep yourself safe whether you find that dog or not. That's thanks enough."

He patted my head as if I was an obedient Labrador, and pulled away, clearing his throat. "You go on, now. Don't be late."

I couldn't stop thinking about Cisco while I drove to Tom's, so much so that I was surprised by the lump in my throat when I pulled into the training center's driveway. How many times had I met George in the barn, he with some long-legged, adolescent Border collie at his side, looking up at him in adoration? How many times had we sat on the porch and talked the sun down? And, what was it he had wanted to talk to me about the last time we were here together? I could see his face the morning he died as plain as day. Taut. Pinched.

I took a minute to sit in the car, the air busy around me with barking. I could hear deep-throated barks from shepherds and Malinois on my right, and higher-pitched ones from the Border collies on the left who had not yet been sent to new homes. A sandy-colored Yorkie leapt at my truck's door, barking so hard she ejected herself backward, a pocket rocket propelled by outrage.

"Tillie!" I gushed, as I bent down to pet her. Tillie had been George's lapdog, a little one he could spoil all he wanted and never worry about mud or sheep shit in his sheets. I stood by the truck, cupping a hand over Tillie's tiny head after I picked her up. She lapped her sweet, tiny tongue over my cheeks, quick little darts, tickling my face.

A wave of guilt joined the tide of grief I was feeling. I'd been so involved in my own problems I hadn't done much to help find good homes for George's dogs. I had heard that several top handlers had taken some of his best dogs, and his nephew took one sweet old bitch home as a house dog. But what of Tillie? Did Tom's new wife want to keep her? I'd heard Joan wasn't a big dog lover, which had seemed crazy to me when she married him. If she didn't love dogs, you'd think Tom would've been pretty low on a list of guys to go out with. But he's fun, and friendly, and not all that hard to look at it. I figured she deserved a pass, given how few guys are available in their forties and fifties. Not that I'd care myself.

What if Joan didn't want Tillie? George would never have let her run loose outside—tiny dogs are hard to see when you're driving up in pickup trucks. Maybe I should take her home, given all that was going on? She was pretty old and probably would need a lot of care in the near future. But what would Clementine say?

I was saved from my ruminations by Joan opening the door and yelling, "Tillie! Get in here!" and then, "Oh Maddie! I didn't realize that was you." Her face broke into a smile as she walked up and took Tillie out of my hands.

"I just worry when she runs outside, you know. She's so tiny, she could get squished like a bug out here." She kissed Tillie on the top of her head and said that she hoped I was doing okay. "Just let me know if there's anything Tom or I could do—I know you must miss George an awful lot."

I started to say something about Cisco, but we were interrupted by Tom coming out of the kennels with a black shepherd on a leash beside him. Joan nodded to me and said, "I'll just run Tillie back inside while you talk to Tom."

The shepherd sat quietly as the two of them stopped in front of me, turning his head toward Tom as if awaiting the next instruction.

"Hey, Maddie. Good to see you."

"Hey, Tom, good to see you too," I answered. I would've given him a hug, but felt it would interfere with his work with the shepherd. "Poor Tillie. How is she doing?"

"Okay, although she wasn't for a couple of days. My aunt is going to take her in a few days when she gets back into town. She'll be a great home for Tillie, so that's a relief."

Whew.

"Uh, hey, Tom, I know you're busy, but I'm desperate to find this shepherd I told you about. I was hoping you'd have some ideas about where to look next."

"Makes no sense, Maddie. The word would have gone out in a minute if a working K9 was lost, and I'd have heard about it the same day. You said you found him by the road outside Milwaukee?"

"Not me, but a shelter volunteer. I took him out of the shelter to foster him, and that's when he was stolen."

"Jesus. Someone sure wants that dog back." Tom raised and lowered his yellow and black Brewers' cap, snugging it over his hair. "Sure you want to get involved?"

"I am involved. My house was broken into and Bo Peep was

poisoned, for God's sake." I could hear my voice rising. I took a breath. "I'm going to find that dog, Tom. I'm not giving up." I stood silent for a moment, looking into Tom's face; his eyes shaded from the sun by his cap. "Please, Tom, any ideas? What would you do if you were me?"

He turned his head, scratched his chin. "I don't know, but I think I'd stay out of it if I were you. It doesn't sound safe. And I don't want to worry about losing you too. But, okay, I'll put the word out to other trainers. I'll reach out to some guys I know. You might want to talk to someone at one of the national organizations, like NAPWDA." I cocked my head.

"The North American Police Work Dog Association. They do a lot of seminars that are open to anyone interested in this kind of work, so that would be a good place to start. Go online too and contact some of the other private trainers around the area. I wouldn't mention my name; some of these guys are a little, uh, competitive." He listed some names.

"Okay, thanks. I will." Before I got into the truck, I asked Tom who the handsome stranger was sitting beside him.

"Oh, this is Sergeant. I've been working with him awhile, got him as an adolescent from a friend. I think he's gonna work out well, seems smart and motivated. Hey, boy?" Tom said.

Sergeant's tail wagged slowly, and his jaw relaxed. His black coat was lustrous, the muscles in his hind legs visible beneath his fur. I was happy to see that instead of the choke or prong collars that are often used on K9s, Sergeant had on a wide, leather collar, with a large, brass nameplate riveted on to it. I have a similar plate on Jack's collar; they don't come off as easily as regular dog tags and can't catch on anything besides.

"Maddie, we're having a memorial party here for George next week. Joan will send out the details soon. It's a potluck. We hope you can come."

"Yes, yes, absolutely, that's a great idea. Thanks for doing it." I mentally listed the food I could bring without feeling completely humiliated. Cookies from the bakery one town over, maybe a salad from the deli section of the supermarket?

"I'll be here, Tom. See you next week then." I turned to Sergeant, still sitting patiently, looking straight at me, eyes soft. "Good luck with Sergeant, and thanks again."

"Good luck to you too, Maddie," Tom said, as he turned and started back to the kennels. Sergeant turned with him, as if physically attached to his leg. I watched the two of them walk toward the kennels, the dog's long tail swooping down like a swan's neck.

CHAPTER 16

It was another forty-five minutes to Ryan's place, a green and brown ranch in New Berlin on the west side of Milwaukee. There was a muddy, black Ford F-150 and a dark green SUV in the driveway, parked end to end between rows of boxwood hedges. I could hear barking as I grabbed my bag, put on my glasses, and got out of the truck.

Two dogs appeared in the window beside the front door, both barking hard. I could see spittle flying out of the mouth of a German shepherd. Ranger stood shoulder to shoulder with him, barking fast and high, and occasionally turning his head to check in with the other dog. Ryan's second dog? He didn't mention that he had another one.

Ryan opened the door, turning his head to his right, and saying, "Hey! Guys, settle down." Ranger closed his mouth and sat down. The shepherd, with classic black and tan markings, kept barking until a deep voice from the back of the house yelled, "Cut it out, Cujo!"

"Cujo? Seriously?" I blurted.

Ryan laughed. "I know," he said. "It's just a nickname. Sort of Kevin's joke. His real name is Coop. He's harmless, don't worry about him."

I never take anyone else's word for a dog's behavior, even

someone trained to work with a K9. If I had ten dollars for every time an owner said "Oh, he's fine!" when the dog was ready to bite, I'd buy an RV with two bathrooms and a TV screen the size of my truck.

Coop was looking at me, still barking, but with less arousal. His tail was wagging, but a wagging tail doesn't mean a dog is friendly. Coop's body was still statue stiff. Best to leave him alone for a while.

Ranger, on the other hand, was doing his best impression of a golden retriever in a Disney cartoon, not having read the chapter that describes a Malinois as "reserved and sometimes aggressive with strangers." I gave him a scratch behind his ear, and then said, "Hey, bud," to Coop, keeping my face turned sideways while I extended my hand just a few inches from my body. If a dog wants to come up to sniff it, fine. If not, he's basically told me to keep my hands to myself.

Ranger pushed in and sniffed my hand, and then began an in-depth appraisal of my pants. Coop couldn't let his friend have all the fun, so soon two seventy-five-pound dogs put their noses to work and examined every inch of my clothing they could manage while keeping all four paws on the ground.

"Maddie, this is my friend Kevin. You probably figured he's on the force too. It's okay," he said, in answer to my tilted head and barely raised eyebrow, "he knows about Ranger." I stood stock still for a moment, staring at Kevin's face.

Kevin said, "Hey, glad to meet you."

"Oh hi," I finally forced myself to say. I did not say: "So, you're the guy who came to Tom's funeral, interviewed me at the trial, and always looks like a hawk about to eat a mouse?"

I turned to the dogs, and said, "Hey, Ranger, how's my guy doing?" He began wagging his tail again so hard his entire body followed his tail as it shifted left and right, a silly grin on his face. Relieved to have a distraction, I sunk down to Ranger's level and massaged his neck. He was kissing my face as Ryan invited us to his living room to talk.

"Get you anything?"

"No, I'm good," I said. "Let's talk about how things are going for a minute and then check out the 'safe house.'" I settled on a burgundy leather couch, while Ryan sat down in a La-Z-Boy carefully positioned in front of a massive big-screen TV. It was a nice room, comfortable, with floor to ceiling bookcases on the far wall. No photographs anywhere. I got the feeling that Ryan lived alone.

Kevin leaned against the door to the kitchen, Coop sitting beside him. I could see both of them looking at me out of the corner of my eye. Ranger came over to sit beside me, ruffling the magazines on the coffee table with his tail before he sat down.

One was *The Atlantic*. *"The Atlantic?"* I thought to myself. "A cop?" Embarrassed by my own prejudice, I focused on my job, asking Ryan how things were going and how I could help, while I stroked Ranger's head.

It sounded like things were going well. Ryan played tug with Ranger when the barometer went down, tossed beef and chicken pieces when the wind came up or there was barely perceptible thunder. As long as the thunder wasn't too loud, Ranger happily played along. Ryan, Ranger, and I checked out the "safe house," which Ryan had constructed in his bedroom's walk-in closet, out of a folding table draped with blankets. As instructed, he'd put the entrance to the side, so that any lightning strikes couldn't be visible once inside. Good thing Ryan wasn't a big man, maybe five foot eight, because crawling in with Ranger was no easy task.

He'd also picked up the prescription for an anti-anxiety medication that he could use when he knew a big storm was coming, and was starting to teach Ranger to go into the safe house by himself to chew on a bully stick. Our goal was for

Ranger to go into the safe house by himself if he felt frightened. Ryan wasn't sure if the body wraps he'd purchased had helped at all, but he'd keep giving them a try since Ranger didn't object to them. Most importantly, I told Ryan not to lose heart if the intensity of the storm overwhelmed everything else. "If Ranger gets frightened, it's fine to comfort him all you want," I said.

Kevin stood in the bedroom behind us as we faced the closet, Coop at his feet. I heard him snort. "So you're going to give him cookies for being a wuss?" He managed to suppress an eye roll, but I couldn't miss the impulse.

"Good question," I answered, in my most neutral, professional voice. "You can't actually 'train' an emotion. Think of it this way: if you had a three-year-old child who was frightened of a storm, would you think comforting him would make him worse?"

"My dad would," Kevin said, "But, okay, I see your point."

I told Ryan he was doing a great job, and we walked back into the living room. Without an invitation, I sat myself back down on the couch. I wanted to be sure to get Ryan's full attention when I asked about Cisco.

"Are we okay to talk about Cisco now?" I asked.

"Sure," he said, as he turned toward Kevin. "That's that dog I was telling you about."

I leaned forward toward Kevin, hoping, in spite of my feelings toward him, I could enroll him in helping. "Here's all we really know: We know he was abandoned on the outskirts of Milwaukee in an industrial district, starved and half dead. We know he was trained in narcotics. We know he doesn't have any identification, like an ear tattoo or a microchip. We know he was stolen from my house, by someone with access to fentanyl. That's it. It's not much, I know. But I'm gonna find this dog. . . ."

I sat back, realizing I was leaning forward so far that I was at risk of falling off the couch. *Take a breath, Maddie.*

"I went out with the shelter volunteer who found him beside a warehouse outside Milwaukee." Kevin's eyes narrowed. Maybe he really was serious about trying to help?

"Where was that?"

I told him the street, said it was across from a Western Automotive shop.

Kevin said, "Well, that's probably irrelevant. Someone probably drove him there on purpose to dump him, specifically because there'd be no one around at night to see anything." He turned and looked at Coop, who was now sound asleep on a dog bed in the corner. "People dump dogs all the time. I'll keep asking around, but it's hard to imagine how you're going to find this dog again. And if you're messing with someone willing and able to drug your Great Pyr, you might be dealing with people in the drug trade. Better off dropping it. I wouldn't mess with them if I were you."

"Kevin is right." Ryan sat on the edge of his La-Z-Boy, his fingers running over a stain in the leather. "Most people don't know how active drug cartels are in this area. They don't play nice."

I sat staring. No one had yet used the term "drug cartel" before, and you might as well have hit me in the stomach with a bat. I sat still, holding my breath, remembering the horrific stories I'd heard about what drug cartels do to people they don't like. Feed them to alligators. Or worse. This was not the world I wanted to even think about. So not.

"Shit." Not something I usually say in the presence of a client. I was twirling my hair. I put my hand down.

"I just can't give up looking for this dog. I just can't." I straightened my spine, in danger of starting to cry.

Kevin's face softened. "I get it. Coop is my best friend, besides Ryan. Well, maybe more than Ryan—he never talks back."

He turned toward Coop, who seemed attached to his left leg, and I swear his eyes got soft. He cleared his throat and turned to look at me.

"Do not mess with this, Maddie. You need to leave this to law enforcement."

"What do you mean leave it to law enforcement? Who is looking for Cisco besides me?" I could hear my voice rise in pitch. Ranger came over and put his head on my thigh.

"Kevin is right," Ryan said in a quiet, measured voice. "You need to be careful here. I'm glad you have a neighbor looking after you, but the more you pursue this, the more danger you're going to be in. I'll give your sheriff a call and see if he's gotten any leads. You should check in with him too and see if anything has come up. Those county guys can get pretty busy. Or, sometimes, pretty lazy." A little grin. "Don't quote me on that."

"Okay, thanks. I'll check in with the sheriff." I blew out a breath. I looked at Ryan, then Kevin, who was typing something on his cell phone.

"I stopped off at Tom Hutch's on the way here. Kevin, you must know him, given his work training detection dogs? He said he'd help too, so there's that."

"Yeah, Tom? I know him pretty well; he trained Coop. Tom does a good job," he said, as Coop looked up at him with adoration.

I stood up, inhaled. "Well, I'm just glad you all are in my corner. And I don't think anyone is going to kill me over a damn dog, so I'm not stopping. I'm going to find Cisco if it's the last thing I do."

"Let's hope it's not," Kevin said. I had looked up at his face to say thanks, but his words closed my throat. Just for a millisecond, I thought his eyes went hard again. Maybe not.

I drove away thinking about their warning to drop it. Forget about Cisco? Cisco of the huge, intelligent eyes that talked to me as if speaking English? Who seemed as smart and sentient as most of the people I know? Who Jack already adored? I'd been helpless about George's death, and I hadn't been there for him when he needed me, but that wasn't going to happen again. If there was anything I could do to save Cisco, I was going to do it.

CHAPTER 17

The days went by with consults, emails, phone calls, and farm chores. The lambs were growing like weeds, so large now that their mother's back legs rose off the ground as they pushed for milk. They needed more grain and more management, so Jack was in heaven.

I got a text from Chris, who said he'd be in my area next week and would drop off Cisco's collar. I called the boys to check up on Harpo. Good news: they'd repaired the back door and seemingly were doing a good job keeping Harpo away from the front fence. We confirmed the date for them to come out to the farm to scavenge wood. Nights I settled in front of the TV after eating ramen or boxed mac and cheese. It all tasted like cardboard.

In late evening I lay on the couch, my heart aching for George, my mind full of Cisco's absence. It felt crazy-making that George was the one, besides Dorothy, who I would have called after the break-in. He was the one who would have sat with me on his porch, a bottle of Spotted Cow in hand, and listened to how worried I was about Cisco. He would've told me to be careful, but he wouldn't have tried to stop me from finding him. He would've told me to forgive myself when I went home abruptly that day, instead of letting him tell me what was bothering him.

Finally, I'd doze off in front of the TV, eventually hike up the stairs and fall into bed, sometimes dreaming in a panic about darkness so black nothing could penetrate it. Sometimes lying still until the sky turned silver and the house wren's melodious chatter bounced through the window.

I kept doing what I could about Cisco. I called the local shelters every day. I stopped in at each of them every few days, knowing that busy shelters can have trouble keeping their "found dog" notices updated. I contacted some folks in the NAPWDA and told them about Cisco, asking them to let me know if they heard anything.

After playing phone tag a few times with Catherine at the shelter, we finally connected. She said she'd asked Chris to send the collar he must have forgotten. I sent him a text asking if he'd mail it. He answered right away, said maybe he could drop it off at the farm; he was going to check on a dog close to where he thought I lived. We agreed on a date, I texted the address, and thought little more about it. I called Sheriff Wallenberg and left a message asking if he'd turned up anything. I called Vince, who'd been babysitting the farm every day for a week and a half every time I left.

"I think you can stop now, Vince. Nothing has happened, and why would it? Whoever came in got what they wanted—Cisco. Why would they come back? And thanks for installing the security camera. You rock." I didn't mention that I was feeling like he'd done too much already, and I had no idea how to repay him. Being a good neighbor is one thing, but he'd taken my problems on as if I were family.

Vince tried halfheartedly to talk me out of him dropping the security detail when I was gone, but I knew he wanted his life back, and my logic was pretty compelling. He said he'd drive by often, told me to be sure to keep my phone on in case the security camera sent me an alert, and to call him the second it did.

Eventually the day of the memorial party came. I wanted to go to the party, and I didn't. I knew it would be good for me to be around other friends of George, but I was exhausted from worry and grief. Driving back to the training center earlier had been yet another way to throw it all in my face. But the only thing worse than going was not going, so I pulled myself together on a hot Saturday morning and drove over to H & H.

The place was packed. There must have been sixty cars and trucks in the driveway, and maybe one hundred people, all milling in the yard beside the house, red plastic cups in hand, while the kennel dogs barked like a discordant band hired to provide entertainment. Most of the crowd was made up of handlers, all people who had worked with George, or, at least, admired him, over the years. A small group of Tom's friends, some with "COPS" written in invisible ink on their face, grouped together beside the food tables.

I put my grocery store cookies, carefully overlapped in a circle and covered with foil, onto a table sagging with the weight of cheese plates and snap pea salads and bumbleberry pies with crusts so flaky that even I would moan when I ate them. I pulled a Coke out of the big blue ice chest under one of the tables and went over to thank Tom for hosting the memorial. He nodded and said, "Of course," his eyes moist and his voice scratchy.

I hated to do it, but didn't know when I'd get another chance to talk to him. "I hate to ask now, Tom, but I'm still looking for that shepherd I was fostering. Have you had a chance to ask around?"

"Not yet, but I will, promise, Maddie." He looked carefully at my face, his eyes soft and kind, and said, "You doing okay?"

I tried to answer, but couldn't seem to get any words to come out of my mouth. I shrugged and asked how he was doing. "I won't lie, this sucks. Miss him every day." He patted my shoulder, excused himself, and turned to greet another guest.

I found Dorothy over by the rosebushes, talking to Violet, our mutual friend from the sheepdog world. Violet never says a bad word about anyone and has a childlike optimism that surrounds her like a magic cloak.

"Hi, Maddie!" Violet said, quieter than usual. "How are you holding up?" Violet knew that George was a friend as much as a coach to me. Dorothy answered Violet's question. "She'd be better if this dog she was fostering hadn't been kidnapped from her house. And her guard dog poisoned."

Violet looked at me with her eyes round, her raised eyebrows wrinkling her forehead. "Holy moly, Maddie," she said. "That's awful." It was, but I didn't want to talk about it right then. Facing George's death was enough to deal with at the moment, so I thanked Violet for her concern and walked away, shifting my eyes sideways to encourage Dorothy to come with me.

After we'd walked away a few feet, Dorothy looked at me and wordlessly asked how I was doing. Amazing how little one actually needs language sometimes. I shrugged my shoulders upwards a quarter of an inch, moved my head left and right even less, looking down at the grass. When I looked back up into Dorothy's eyes, perfectly emphasized with mascara and eye liner, I could feel my eyes going soft. I knew moisture was coming soon, and I didn't want to start crying in the middle of the yard, holding a sweaty plastic cup of lukewarm soda. I blew out a breath.

"Let's go tell funny stories about George," I said, putting my arm around Dorothy's shoulder, careful not to knock off her perfect hat. "That's why we're here, right?"

We walked over to a cluster of handlers standing under a maple tree, talking in raspy whispers—the kind easier to hear than regular speech—about who killed George. The group went silent as I approached, until Jeremy spoke up.

"Heard anything about who killed George, Maddie?" Faces

turned toward me expectantly. I explained I hadn't, and kept my mouth shut while speculations ranged from a drunken hunter to a jealous competitor. A few names were named as possible killers, superficially in jest, but with a palpable undertow of accusation.

I changed the subject by talking about the time that George went to the post with Tillie the Yorkshire terrier, a tease to a well-known judge who didn't always pay attention to the first seconds of a dog's run.

That got more stories about George flowing, in between catching up on whose bitch had a litter, how the young dogs' training was going, and the best ways to heal up a dog after she tears a cruciate ligament. After forty-five minutes of chatting and munching on salad and cookies, Tom clapped to get our attention. "Thank you for coming and honoring George! I just wish he could be here to see all of you all cleaned up. Not sure he'd recognize you!" The crowd laughed politely.

"A few of you have asked if anything has come out of the investigation, but I don't have much news. Several deputies have been out to interview me and Joan, and I know they've scoured the woods at the trial site for any evidence of a shooter. I guess they found a site in the woods where they think the shooter set up—it was a good five to six hundred yards away, so it wasn't some asshole deer hunter who shot George, unless they were also a trained sharpshooter who hunted with some kind of kick-ass high-powered setup and was too drunk to see straight. But it's being treated like a murder investigation, I can tell you that."

The crowd had been shifting around, some still chatting when Tom began speaking, but his news acted like the pause button on a video. Everyone went still, shocked by the news, even though none of us could imagine how it could have been a hunting accident. It got so quiet that Dorothy's "fucking-A," meant just for me, was clearly audible to everyone. Someone tittered in response. The guy next to me, nursing a glass of bourbon I could smell without trying, said, "Jesus."

At least half the faces in the crowd turned toward me. As if I had known. As if, somehow, because of our relationship, I had something to do with it. I glanced at Dorothy and started to walk to my truck. Dorothy put her hand on my arm and gently pulled me back.

"Don't. Don't let them get to you. George wouldn't want you to." I stopped and took a breath. Tom continued talking.

"What we do know is that George would want you all to keep on keepin' on, and to remember that your job is to be a good shepherd to the sheep, and that's always how you should train your dog."

Tom turned to his side as his wife, Joan, tapped him on the arm. "Just a minute," Tom said, leaning over to hear what she was whispering in his ear. "Oh, okay. Joan would like to say a few words."

This was a bit of a surprise, since Joan never came to trials, and none of us knew her very well. But then, she'd been sharing a house with George ever since she married Tom, so she must have known George pretty well. I realized the card I sent was addressed to Tom only, and felt bad about it.

"Thank you again for coming," Joan said, her hair ruffling in a light breeze. I tried to focus on what she had to say, instead of her tall, slender frame. I always felt extra short and dumpy around her model-thin build. As she spoke, I realized that she looked thinner than ever, even a little gaunt.

"Most of you have known George longer than I have, but I'd grown to love him like a brother. I loved his sense of humor, his talent, and his commitment to dogs. But most of all, that man could make lasagna!" We all laughed, the handlers remembering how Tom would bring George's lasagna to trials sometimes, and dish it out on Saturday nights at the handlers' dinner. George, with his craggy face straight out of a television Western, just didn't seem like the type to make lasagna. Cowboy beans maybe, but not lasagna. But he did, and it was great. He'd give me a piece some evenings when our training had run late. We'd sit at an old wooden table on the porch, stuff ourselves with carbohydrates, chased down with a beer.

"Tom and I wanted you to know that although we've lost both a friend and a partner, we'll be keeping H & H going. We're looking for another top sheepdog trainer to come in; we've got some leads out already. We'll let you know soon as we have some news. Stay safe, and again,

I'm sorry that we have all lost such a great trainer, competitor, and friend."

We clapped politely in unison, still stunned by the reality of George's death. An old-time trainer raised his glass and said, "To George!" "To George!" we all called out, raising our plastic glasses to the sky. But no amount of clapping could drown out the question that was stuck like a burr in everyone's mind. If it wasn't a deer hunter, who was it who killed George? Was it someone upset with him in the world of sheepdogs? Someone we knew? Granted, there was another famous trainer who never missed a chance to throw shade on George's dogs, but that's a far cry from murder. Of all the trainers I knew, he was the most universally loved. If it was someone related to sheepdogs, then was it someone here at the party?

Dorothy broke the ice. "Okay, now let's go honor George and do some work!" This from Dorothy. I had almost forgotten that several of us had decided we could help out by checking on the sheep and putting our dogs to good use. It was a relief to get Jack out of the truck. I had started walking toward the barn when Joan called out my name.

"Maddie!" she said, pushing her huge sunglasses on top of her head, pulling her hair back away from her forehead. I could feel my hair get frizzy. I definitely gained five pounds.

"Maddie, Tom told me about this dog of yours that was stolen. I'm so sorry! That must be awful."

"It is . . . Thanks, Joan, I'm still working hard trying to find him. I sort of fell in love with him. If you or Tom hear anything, please, please let me know. I'm not going to give up." I could feel my jaw setting into stone. "I'm not," I repeated. George always said he could tell when I was getting stubborn just by looking at my chin.

"Of course," Joan assured me. "We'll help however we can. Have you gotten any leads at all?" It was a relief having someone take me seriously and not tell me to give up. Most of the world seemed to think I was an idiot to keep looking for this dog.

"Not a damn thing really. But if you hear anything in the K9 world, please give me a call."

I paused, not sure if it was appropriate to ask about Tom. Impulse overrode discretion, and I asked, "How's Tom doing?" Joan had started to move toward the house, but turned back quickly.

"Oh, the poor man, he's gutted. I'm just so glad I can be here for him. I think it's good for him to visit with George's friends. Come by any time. You're always welcome." She walked toward the house, and I continued walking to the barn.

Jack had long left my side, and was staring, motionless, at the flock of Cheviots enclosed inside a pen. Their classy white faces were surrounded by a ruff of wool, their three-month-old lambs sprawled beside them, dozing in the sun. People often think that Border collies "transfix" the sheep with their laser-focused stare, but really, it's the other way around. Dogs with a "strong eye" can get stuck, unable to move, as if hypnotized themselves by the sheep. Lucky for me, that was not one of Jack's problems, and he whipped around and ran to my side when I whispered his name.

I asked if Jack could be the one to push the group into the chutes—the more practical work off the farm the better—so that we could check the lambs, one by one, for signs of worms. While Jack held the flock pressed toward the chute's entrance,

Dorothy and I checked the lamb's eyelids for signs of anemia, squeezing white pasty wormer into the mouths of those who looked a little pale.

After we finished, we split out some of the ewes without lambs and went to work our dogs in the big field. Dorothy and her dog, Max, held five sheep for us at one end of the field while Jack and I walked to the other end.

"Yup, you got it, Jack, that's where the sheep are," I said after I smooched him to me so that we could get at least two hundred yards away from the sheep to practice our outruns. Glory hallelujah, damn if Jack didn't stop at the top and do a perfect lift. Twice.

Stopping on a good note, I had Jack drive the sheep down the field for another set of handlers and then turned to go back to the truck. The breeze had shifted; it was stronger now, coming from the north, ruffling the tops of the trees in the woods behind the barn. As we walked, Jack kept turning his head back toward the barn, where Cesar, a 140-pound Anatolian livestock guarding dog, was dozing in the shed. Cesar was used to visiting Border collies coming to work the sheep; they had probably come six days a week when George was alive. After a few perfunctory woofs to remind us he was on duty, he settled down in the shade and pretended we weren't there, a few flies buzzing around his head.

Jack kept looking back toward the barn, its back edge hard up against the woods. I thought he just didn't want to quit working, and said, wearily, "All done, Jack, we gotta go." I repeated, "All done," which Jack learned long ago meant the work was over. Usually, he'd trot somewhere close and lift his leg. But this time Jack planted his feet and began barking toward Cesar, for no reason that I could see. Good grief. I was tired now and just wanted to go home.

"Jack, here!" I said my all-purpose "recall" signal in a low, authoritative voice. Jack turned his head toward me to acknowledge my existence, but then blew me off and kept barking at Cesar. These are the times when I would like to remind him that people pay me to help them train their dogs. Or that I should've taken Jess in the first place, as George had suggested.

"For the love of God, Jack," I said under my breath, and snapped his leash onto his collar. I didn't have it in me to do anything but manage the issue at the moment; the emotions of the memorial had worn me out. Jack grudgingly followed me to the truck and popped into his crate. As I drove away, Jack now whining obnoxiously in the back, I could feel George beside me in the passenger seat, laughing his ass off, always amused when Jack made me feel like an idiot. "That's their job, Maddie, to keep us humble!"

I got home midafternoon, the sun still blazing in a hot-blue sky. I didn't hear a sound as I drove down the driveway; the wildlife being smarter than humans, napping in the shade to avoid the heat. I was tired. Dispirited. The high from being with George's friends was long gone. I went upstairs and lay down with Jack for a nap. Scenes from my time with George played repeatedly in my mind. The time he said "hot damn" when I fixed the starter on his four-wheeler. The time he punched a three-hundred-pound charging ram in the nose and stopped him cold. He was my dad and my uncle and my brother and the only guy I had needed in my life. George used to tease me by saying, "Yeah, I'm just another one of Maddie's old men."

But he wasn't another one. He'd been the only one.

CHAPTER 18

I woke to the sound of a car coming up the driveway. Chris! Damn! I'd forgotten he'd said he'd drop off the collar after I was back from the memorial party.

The house was a mess, and I was little better. My hair, I saw in the mirror as I ran past, had gone feral. I flew down the stairs, almost tripping on the last steps while I struggled to pull a T-shirt over my head. Jack ran by me on the stairs, his barks high-pitched and panicky, unsettled by my mad dash to the door. There was no time to clean anything up—I could see Chris getting out of his car, a dusty black Kia that looked sad and tired.

"Hey! Hi, you found it." I rallied, still trying to straighten my shirt as I opened the screen door.

"No trouble at all." Chris stood beside his car, the sun glinting off his straw-blond hair. He turned his head to take in the view.

"Wow, this is beautiful," he said. He was right. The buildings are run down, but the woods and fields painted a pallet of greens, set off by a cerulean sky. The sheep were cozied up under the lone oak at the edge of the west pasture, as peaceful as a siesta on a hot summer day. The lambs lay against their mothers, ears droopy. We stood in silence, looking at the view, a breeze tickling our faces.

Chris said, "Here's the collar. Sorry it took so long."

I rolled the collar around in my hands. It was thick and wide, made of stitched leather, with a buckle rather than a quick release snap. There were holes where it looked like a brass nameplate had been attached. It was an old collar; the stitching was coming apart at the end, the leather darkened with use.

"If only it could talk," I said quietly.

"No word then about Cisco?" Chris asked.

I shook my head. I stood still too long, looking down at the collar. Chris walked forward and raised his hand as if to touch me on my shoulder, then pulled it back and scratched his head.

"I'm so sorry, Dr. McG. Don't give up, you'll find him." I looked up to answer, but his face stopped me from saying anything. His eyes looked haunted and he had dark circles under them. Too much studying? Feeling shy about being here, even after our trip to Milwaukee?

Jack saved the day by sniffing Chris's pants as if he had a roast turkey in his pocket, making those quiet whiffle noises dogs make when they are serious about investigating a scent. I called him away just before he could make it to Chris's crotch and jam his nose into it. Not the best look for a behaviorist's dog, but one of Jack's favorite ways to introduce himself.

I was about to say thanks and walk back into the house, but Chris had driven all this way . . .

not inviting him in seemed rude.

"Uh, you wanna come in for a minute? The house is a mess but I could make you some coffee." Chris looked away, toward the lone oak at the edge of the pasture. A wolf tree they call it, much older than the scrubby buckthorns growing around it. It had wire grown into its trunk from a fence line given up decades ago.

"Sure, just for a minute."

We went inside, and I bustled in the kitchen, pretending there were no dirty dishes in the sink, left there for more days than I'm willing to admit. I put fresh water and grounds into Dorothy's expresso machine, half expecting it to rise like a small spaceship and pour the coffee into our mugs itself after it was brewed.

"Sugar? Sorry, I don't have any milk."

"That's okay, black is fine."

We took our mugs and settled on the narrow porch, which pitched forward a few degrees to keep water draining away from the house. You always felt like you were about to fall forward if you didn't pay attention. Not very relaxing, but then, old-time farmers in the Midwest didn't seem to favor relaxing much.

Bo Peep kept barking at Chris from the other side of the fence; I let her in, so that she could greet him and let us talk without all the noise. Bonus: I thought it might relax Chris. He squatted down before she got to him and greeted her exactly how I'd taught all the volunteers, letting her come to him without looming toward her. When she sidled up to Chris, all loose-bodied and damn near flirty, he began slow scratches on the underside of her cheeks. I could see her eyes begin to glaze as she leaned into him. She sighed, and licked his face, slowly wagging her tail from her shoulders back. He crooned back to her, "You are the most beautiful dog in the entire world!" Bo Peep moaned a little and rubbed her face against his like a cat.

"Gosh, should I get you two a room?" I joked.

Chris laughed and his face took on some color. As I had hoped, being beside a dog relaxed him. He started telling me about Czar, a Great Pyrenees he'd worked with who was abandoned by a reclusive sheep rancher because he barked away coyotes but loved every human who came on the property.

I countered with an Anatolian guard dog, whose owner told me she began chasing lambs instead of guarding them. He called me the morning he found her with bloody lips and a dead lamb at her feet. It ended well—I found clear evidence that a coyote had killed the lamb, and that the dog had been licking its wounds. Callie, she was called, eventually matured into an invaluable guard dog—I have her picture up in my office with a thank you note from the rancher.

Chris loved the story, added one about a retriever surrendered to the shelter because it wouldn't pick up a ball. A wood thrush began singing in the woods behind the house, its flute-like notes softening the air around us. I couldn't stop myself from asking if he'd thought about what we talked about in the car. "Maybe getting into dog training or professional shelter work?"

He surprised me by turning to look directly at my face. He looked back down at his hands and said, "I have. A lot." I managed to wait out the subsequent silence. "I just don't know how I could do it. I get so nervous around people I don't know well."

I answered: "I know social anxiety can be crippling to some people. You know we both see versions of what looks like it in shy dogs, right? I've seen you turn dogs around at the shelter who were terrified of strangers when they came in." He nodded.

"So, who is helping *you*?" I asked, keeping my voice quiet and low. He shook his head back and forth, as if to say "no one." The thrush sang out plaintively, the trill at the end of its song sounded louder, harsher.

"My dad and stepmom kicked me out a long time ago; they don't even know where I am now. And don't care. I don't have health insurance, and I don't have any money to go see anyone. I'm better off just sticking to coding and working at home, away from people I don't know."

He might as well have waved a piece of chicken in front of a Labrador. I'd spent years working with dogs who were afraid of strangers, and the principles of behavioral change are similar across all species. Fear is fear, whether you are a dog or a person or a penguin. I made myself stop and take a breath when the thrush sang again. I am not an idiot. I knew full well that jumping in to help Chris was not particularly wise. And that not being able to "fix" George's death, nor find Cisco, was pushing me to do something, anything, to feel I could make a difference.

"Well," I said, as if joking, "we'll just have to figure out what your primary reinforcer is and countercondition you to strangers!" He didn't know I was serious, which was my hope. "Hey, you're here with me right now, right? What's the best reinforcement? Chocolate? A beer?"

He laughed, said he should go.

"Well, thanks for coming out," I said, smart enough at least not to push anything at the moment. "I have to get started on the chores anyway. Thanks again for coming all the way out here. I can't imagine that this"—I held up the collar I had been twirling in my hand—"will help me find Cisco. But at least it's something." I stood up, my legs stiff from sitting for so long. Jack leapt off the porch and ran halfway to the barn. *Sheep? Time to work sheep!* I walked off the porch and toward the barn, assuming Chris would follow and go to his car. He stood still.

"Uh, Dr. Mc . . ."

I interrupted. "Maddie, please!"

"Sorry." He grinned a little, his eyes the slightest bit brighter. Although I knew he was in his early thirties, at that moment he looked fifteen. Or forty-five. I couldn't decide which. Either way, in that moment, he looked more relaxed. Kinda cute. A very big golden retriever came to mind.

"Maddie, I've never seen sheepdogs work, and, uh, since I'm out here. . . ." He smiled the biggest smile I'd yet seen on him and said, "That's my reinforcement!"

Chris watched while Jack rounded up the flock, taking my "look back" cue to bring in a straggling ewe who was hiding in the buckthorns. Jack pushed the flock into the sorting chute, and Chris helped me fill the feeder pans full of corn, oats, and protein pellets for the lambs.

"Wow. That was amazing," Chris said as he stroked the side of Jack's head.

"Yeah, working sheepdogs is addicting!" I answered. "But, sorry, I've got to feed the rest of the crew now," I said, assuming Chris would take the hint and go.

Chris stood in place, still petting Jack.

"Honestly, I'm sick to death of studying. Could I stay and help you do the chores?" This time Chris turned and looked straight down at my face. His eyes were as green as mint.

I was going to say no. It had been good to have a distraction, but the truth was that I wanted the farm back to myself. The day had already been full of talking with people at the memorial. I was ready for a quiet night with the dogs, frozen pizza, and bad TV. I started to say no. I say "no" to social invitations at the drop of a hat, especially from men. People learn; I don't get many invitations anymore. Besides, it was time for a break for both of us. While thinking exactly that, I nodded my head: *yes*.

Chris stayed, and helped me feed the dogs, the cats, and Old Horse. Uncle Bert the Stud Duck, rude as usual to all strangers, went after Chris, wings slicing through the air like sabers. I had to use Jack to hold him off Chris, which was difficult, because Chris and I were laughing so hard I couldn't get clear signals out of my mouth. At one point Jack turned his head and side-eyed me with a voiceless canine curse.

After the chores were done and the light got soft and the only bird singing was a robin, Bo Peep came up again to say hello. As we petted her together, I realized how badly she needed grooming. Great Pyrs have coats like polar bears and can get tangled mats of fur that are uncomfortable and cause skin problems.

"Wanna help with one more thing? Give her treats while I groom her out? Then I promise, I'll throw you out of here."

"Sure." Chris sat down with Bo Peep in the front yard while I got the grooming tools and some food. I sat down beside him and we began working on Bo Peep, he giving her treats to keep her still while I cut out the mats starting to form on her belly.

As we worked, Chris began telling stories about crazy things potential adopters had said when looking at available dogs. Like "Could I take her out to potty just once a day? I'm very busy," and "Does this dog come in another color?" I laughed so hard at that one I let my body slump down into Chris's shoulder. He smelled like a meadow.

We kept it up for thirty minutes, taking longer than necessary because we kept cracking each other up. Bo Peep didn't care as long as the treats kept coming, Jack lay a few feet away, drooling. I tossed him a treat every once in a while to keep him from interfering. Finally, Bo Peep looking like a show dog, I stood up and rubbed my back. Chris reached out to rub it for me, and pulled his arm back as if it had been burned.

I watched his back as he turned to go to his car, surprised that I didn't want him to go. He was exactly the type you'd think I'd avoid—your classic American manly-man. Then I realized that Chris's build was the antithesis of my ex-husband's. Tyler was as lean as a whippet, not very tall, but astoundingly strong. But he still exuded testosterone, the kind of guy I grew up with—aggressive, domineering, controlling. And here was Chris, built like a Green Bay Packer, but as vulnerable as a lamb.

I blurted out: "Wanna stay for a drink?" Chris turned back toward me, the light too dim for me to read his face. "I've got a bottle of Johnnie Walker Black in the cupboard," I said. "It's been there forever, but I am pretty sure that alcohol doesn't go bad."

A voice inside my brain asked WHAT THE HELL *are you doing?*

Don't know, don't care, another voice answered. Maybe I

just wanted a life, a life where you can let down your guard and just enjoy yourself. I needed more of it.

Apparently, that wasn't all I needed.

I woke up the next morning at dark-thirty, to the warbling of the house wren, who was nesting, damn her, in a hole right beside my bedroom window. The first thing I saw was Jack's face staring at me from the edge of the bed. Jack always sleeps with me; why was he on the floor? That's when I realized Jack was not in the bed. Someone else was. Chris was quietly snoring beside me, sprawled half in and half out of the covers. I could see an awful lot of skin covering a broad chest between two huge shoulders, the face of a tattooed dog smiling at me from his right arm. The sun highlighted the reddish blond fuzz below his belly button. I stared at him in horror. Holy shit, what had I done?

It is possible I actually asked Jack that very question. If I did, he wasn't answering. I lay motionless in bed, whispering to Jack to go lie down. I lay as still as I could, staring at the ceiling, not ready to face a semi-stranger, literally twice my size, taking up most of the bed. I tried to remember what had happened last night, starting with more shots of Johnnie Walker on the porch. Lots more. I remembered laughing so hard at one point that I began hiccupping, which made us laugh even harder. I remembered putting the cats out because they wouldn't leave us alone. I remembered, when he first leaned toward me, his lips an inch from my ear when he whispered, "I am going to kiss you now unless you tell me not to."

I didn't have to remember the effect that had on me, because it started happening again. Wow, I thought. Your body actually does get hot.

It had been twelve years. I think I actually moaned when I thought about the moment, the night before, when Chris slid my pants down and hovered over me. Maybe that's why Chris woke up.

He opened his eyes, looking bleary and tired. Too much JWB. But then he turned toward me, smiled, and ran his finger down my cheek, tracing patterns between my freckles. So quietly I barely heard him, he said: "You are so beautiful. You have the most perfect skin of any woman I've ever known."

What? Me, the one with all the foolish freckles? The one whose aunt said all the McGowan woman had skin like boiled cod? I'd never felt pretty. Even Tyler, who'd chosen me out of a bevy of beauties, asked me daily when I was going to lose a little weight. Chris's comments were like water in a desert.

I put my hands on either side of his face and kissed him. He threw back the covers, and rolled over on top of me, kissing me back, his lips staying with mine. He moved his hand down my belly and I moaned again.

And then Jack came over to the bed and began to growl. We began to laugh, and Bo Peep began to bark because the LP delivery truck had arrived, and I had to go down to let the guy through the gate to get to the tank, throwing clothes on, yet again, as I ran down the stairs.

CHAPTER 19

The fuel delivered and Bo Peep settled, I began making coffee, the reality of what I'd done kicking in. What the hell was I thinking, sleeping with this young guy I hardly knew? After so many years of pushing men away? But I couldn't deny that, in spite of all the booze the night before, I felt a little frisky, like a young mare let out to pasture after a long winter in the barn.

Chris came down the stairs, sneezing. He did not look frisky. He sat down at the table and put his head in his hands.

"I'm so sorry, Maddie," he said, looking down at the blue plastic place mat.

"For what?" I blurted out, my enthusiasm fizzling. Suddenly I felt sick to my stomach. We'd spent the night together, had booze-infused sex, and, in spite of my brain knowing that my behavior was unwise and borderline inappropriate, my body felt exhilarated. His, clearly, did not. I put a cup of coffee down a little too hard in front of him.

"No, no, I'm sorry," Chris said, no stranger to nonverbal cues after years of working with dogs. "Jeez, I'm an idiot. I didn't mean it wasn't good last night. It was." He turned and took my hand. My fingers got lost inside his giant paw. I started to pull away, but he tightened his grip.

"No, I mean it, it was wonderful. Really. You're amazing."

Amazing? Tyler's response after sex, the first and only other man I'd ever slept with besides Chris, was little more than a grunt, a yawn, and a snore. He never said anything after sex; he just rolled off and went to sleep.

I took a breath and felt my shoulders soften. I let my head sink sideways toward my shoulder. Chris said, "But there's something I need to tell you. If I'm not honest now, I'm afraid I'll lose my nerve and once you find out, you'll never forgive me. And I couldn't bear that."

Which was when Bo Peep burst out barking, loud, furious barks that accompanied the sound of an unfamiliar vehicle coming up the driveway.

"Shit. Who the hell is that?" No one was expected, and whoever it was, their timing couldn't have been worse. I walked to the front door and discovered Joe, Clyde, and Marvin getting out of a rusty Chevy Impala.

Joe strode toward me, his smile reaching all the way to his eyes, fringed by his exuberant eyebrows. Clyde stood beside him, while Marvin hovered behind. Marvin shifted his cap. All three of them looked from me to Chris, who had moved to stand behind me in the doorway. Chris and I stood, disheveled and blank faced, staring at them as if posing for a poster labeled "Two People Who Just Slept Together Who Weren't Planning To and Didn't Expect Company."

Joe grinned, and said, "Uh, wrong day? Wasn't it today we were supposed to come out and collect wood for Harpo's fence?"

Good grief. How many things was I going to forget? My life was splitting apart like a broken zipper.

I rallied. "No, no! You're good! Sorry, I got busy and forgot you were coming. My bad."

"Busy is good!" said Joe, smiling a little too broadly. Clyde and Marvin tried, unsuccessfully, to suppress their smirks.

"Just give me a minute to get some quick chores done and

I'll be out to help. Go ahead and check out the wooden posts that are in the barn, they're against the wall on the top left." I turned and widened my eyes at Chris. He flashed a smile and said quietly, "What can I do?"

We practically threw food at the dogs and cats and let the ducks and Old Horse out of the barn. I explained to Chris that the plan had been to load up my truck and drive the wood out to them today.

"I promised I'd help them build a fence to keep their dog from attacking passing dogs. He's a good dog, really, you'd love him, but he's horrible right now to other dogs. I just have to go."

"What if I went with you? I've never built a fence, but I'm strong and I'm willing," Chris said. Strong, yup, definitely strong. I'd gotten to know his chest and shoulders pretty well the night before. I knew I should say no; I was already starting to feel like an idiot about last night, and now there was this THING he needed to talk about. It all began to feel too complicated. I stared out the window.

"Honestly, Maddie, it's Sunday and I'm not working at the shelter today. I'd really like to help." Suddenly he didn't look so strong when he said it; he looked a little lost again. I'm not sure how a guy who is six two can look like a puppy lost in the rain, but he did. I could've said no, but who would leave a puppy out in a storm?

The five of us spent a half hour digging through a pile of fence posts and random pieces of wood and wire that could be cobbled together to make a sturdy fence. We loaded up the truck and the boys took off. I threw a bunch of tools in the back, checked that the security camera was working and my phone charged, and locked up the house. I let Vince know I'd be gone for most of the day and asked if he'd cruise by on his way to the dump.

Chris wasn't hungry, but I was starving, so we stopped at

Mickie D's for a bacon, egg, and cheese biscuit for me, and coffee for us both. We didn't talk much on the drive; I think we were both in shock over what we'd done. But I thought of little else during that hour, not to mention wondering what Chris wanted to talk about. I asked him about it once we were on the highway; he sipped more coffee and asked if we could wait until later to talk. I said sure—what else could I say?—but I couldn't stop thinking about it the entire drive.

Hearing Harpo bark from inside the house was a welcome distraction, as was the physical exertion of digging fence post holes and straining to tighten the wire between them. By mid-afternoon we had constructed a sturdy four-and-a-half-foot fence, Chris and Harpo had fallen in love with each other, and I was exhausted. And hungry. Chris volunteered to run out for food and came back with a bag full of sandwiches, chips, and chocolate chip cookies.

We each found a place to sit in the dark living room and started in. Harpo went from person to person, saliva dripping from his maw, trying to get handouts. Joe asked, the sauce from his meatball sandwich decorating his chin, "So, Chris. How long have you known Maddie? You two a thing?"

I almost choked out the bite of sandwich in my mouth. Chris finished chewing a big bite of his ham sub before answering. I looked at him and grinned, happy the ball hadn't been thrown to me.

"We've known each for a few years. I volunteer at the shelter where Dr. McG, uh, Maddie, advises us on especially difficult cases. She's pretty awesome."

He didn't answer the second question. I bailed us out by making a fuss over Harpo and saying now that the fence was done the boys needed to start training him to come away from it when called. That was going to take some serious work and was far too much to talk about after spending so much energy on the fence. I suggested that we set another time to get together, cautioned them again about leaving Harpo out in the front yard until they'd done more training, and got up to go. I could barely stand up. The last twenty-four hours had done a number on me.

Seems it wasn't just me. Chris rose with difficulty from the low chair and came over beside me. He put his hand on my lower back, a classic guy move that usually sets my teeth on edge. This time his hand felt like it belonged there.

We were more talkative on the ride home, chatting about Harpo and other interesting dogs we'd run into. I even forgot for a while about the THING after we started laughing again about the behavior of some people, surely the most interesting and ridiculous species on earth. Like the client who called the vet because a weird, wet pink thing had come out of her intact male poodle's abdomen when he got excited. Or the guy who thought he had to train his German shepherd using German words because, well, he was a *German* shepherd.

We arrived at the farm in no time at all. Chris jumped in to help with the chores. Jack gave him a side eye when he walked in, but changed his mind when Chris put down his dinner bowl. Thelma tipped her tail as she walked toward him, in the way that cats do when they are happy to see you, as if pointing their tail toward you and saying, *"You! I want to see YOU!"* Chris stroked her head until she rubbed against him so thoroughly that he thanked her for giving him a bath. We finished feeding all the house critters and moved on to outside chores. This time Uncle Bert the Stud Duck decided that discretion was the better part of valor and allowed Chris to fill the feeder pans and refresh the water.

Chris marveled again at Jack's ability to round up the ewes, standing up unblinking to the ones who turned and challenged him. Once Jack had to lunge at Martha, a particularly feisty ewe, to move her. He never threatened to bite her, just never wavered, and finally Martha gave up and trotted her twin lambs toward the barn. Good boy.

After all the barn chores were done, I asked Chris if he wanted to come on the walk that Jack and I took every evening. It seemed like a good time to talk about what Chris needed to tell me.

The cricket chorus was tuning up as we walked toward the creek, the field crickets chirping percussion to the tree cricket's soft trills, while some robins flew noisily overhead to roost for the night. Bo Peep squatted to mark territory every fifty yards, and Jack insisted on covering her scent with his. At one point he lifted his leg so high it looked like he'd fall over. Chris and I both laughed, and then got quiet. I heard the faint call of a barred owl.

"Okay," I said as I stopped walking and turned toward Chis. "What? What do you need to tell me that is so awful?"

Chris exhaled so loudly that Jack turned away from sniffing a piece of grass and stared at Chris's face. I did too. It looked gaunt.

"I'm a recovering coke addict. I haven't used in over a year, but it's something I have to work on every day. I stopped once, but relapsed. I promise that it'll never happen again, but . . ."

I felt my head dip in a barely perceptible nod, and then I looked away.

Holy shit. That was not good. Drug addictions are horrible things. My father and my ex-husband had been alcoholics. I knew the damage that addiction can do. On the addict, and on those around them.

But somehow, I had expected worse, or at least, something different. Like he was on the run from robbing banks and shooting a teller and was living under an alias. Or maybe he ate kittens for dinner. Something truly horrific.

But wait. If Chris was clean, why did Cisco alert to him when he entered the shelter?

I turned back toward Chris so fast, propelled by that old familiar feeling of betrayal, that Jack whirled around as if there was a charging ram right behind us.

"Settle down, Jack," I said. "Chris," I continued, forcing myself to look directly into his eyes. I knew my own were brittle. "Cisco reacted as if you had drugs on you when you walked into the shelter. That's why I thought he was a detection K9 in the first place. Why wouldn't I think you are lying to me?"

"I swear, Maddie, on the life of every dog in every shelter, that I'm not lying. I haven't used in a year. After Cisco alerted on me, I checked my jacket, an old one I rarely use, and found a stash in an inner pocket. I'd totally forgotten about it being there. I threw it away."

I turned away, sat down on the grass, and stroked Jack's head. I couldn't look at Chris.

He sat down beside me. "Maddie, I would never lie to you. I wouldn't blame you if you never wanted to see me again, but I swear"—he picked up my hands and engulfed them in his—"I'm clean, going to rehab, working on my coding classes, staying out of trouble. I am trying so hard to be the man I want to be. You are the best thing that has happened to me for a long time. Please, please, believe me. I'll go now if you want, but please, please, at least, tell me you believe me."

He gently squeezed my hands, still in his, like a hug. He moved his hands to the side of my face, and said, "Maddie."

Just "Maddie," as my name was a prayer. His eyes were just inches from mine. I could not look away.

I know all about the link between facial expressions as indicators of internal emotions. I also know that people always think they know when someone is lying, or telling the truth, when in actuality, they don't. But I have spent years reading the faces of dogs who could bite my face if I misinterpreted their intentions. And here I sat, looking deep into Chris's eyes. They were velvety clear, and his entire being radiated honesty. I wanted to believe him. So I did.

I looked down at the grass and said, "I have my own sort of awful. My ex-husband did some terrible things to me and it messed me up, but I got counseling and worked really hard and had been doing great until . . ."

I stopped talking because the words were running together and I had started shaking. Chris put his arm around my shoulder. I could not stop myself from leaning in closer. "I don't sleep much—last night is the best sleep I've had in weeks. I've had a lot of nightmares lately. Like I used to."

I picked up a dandelion flower, sunshine yellow, and twirled it in my hand. Chris gently took it and brushed it against my cheek.

"Well, we're both a bit of a mess, then, aren't we?" he said, his face soft and open. So, I kissed him, and he kissed me back, and we folded our bodies together and did it right there in the grass, as the sky turned pastel and the crickets crescendoed, and Jack ran back to the house in horror.

CHAPTER 20

We went to bed early, exhausted by digging fence post holes and extracurricular activities. He left Monday morning, both of us needing to get back to real life. Jack and I watched him walk to his car and drive to the road. I stood on the porch staring at the car's tracks in the dirt, long after the scrunch of his tires on the gravel faded away.

The first client's dog looked to be a good distraction. Three bites, two of them serious. An adolescent fifty-pound heeler cross, he made it clear he'd be happy to make it a fourth as he walked into my office, his eyes like stones. His owners, Helen and Nathan, cooed and chirped about him while he stared at me like a hit man looking for an opening. After getting a thorough history—each bite had been about someone trying to get him to do something he didn't want to do—we talked about what they hoped for in a dog. They wanted a docile cuddler who spent evenings in their lap. What they had was a dog bred to take charge of huge animals, often using his teeth, with a personality on the far side of trouble. I had to suppress asking who the hell let *this* couple take *this* dog out of the shelter.

I worked with him, Justin he was called, for a while, but it wasn't easy. He'd be vaguely interested in chicken for a minute, but then get bored. He ignored toys, dared me to touch him, and left me wondering whether I could get a herd of cattle into the office as reinforcement. I sat down and took a breath, hating what I needed to say. I think they already knew that he was the wrong dog for them, but were afraid to face it by themselves. Better to have an expert's opinion.

Giving up a dog is one of the hardest things a dog lover will ever have to do, but sometimes it's the kindest option. No one is betraying a dog if they know that they aren't a good fit for them. Love is simply not always enough. Justin, a serious, no-nonsense working dog, needed a serious, no-nonsense job. I talked about their alternatives, being clear that it was their decision to make, and that I would support them as best I could no matter what they decided.

They left with Helen in tears, Nathan visibly relieved, and Justin giving me one last flint-eyed glance as they walked away.

The day improved. The next two clients had relatively easy issues and workable dogs. After that, I had lots of emails and calls to catch up on. I got home around six, did the chores by reflex, and climbed up the stairs earlier than usual, exhausted by the events of the last few days. It felt strange going to bed by myself that night. Chris's scent was still on the sheets. It took a while to get to sleep, but I finally did around eleven.

I woke up in a sweat, the claustrophobic nightmares back, Jack licking my face and pawing on my chest. I lay in bed thinking about the faceless man in the dream, the one who stood smiling in front of me, but I knew was about to kill me.

It didn't take a therapist to know that the man was Tyler, the handsome rodeo star who had asked me to lunch so many years ago.

I had scrawled my phone number on the receipt when he asked for it, trying to keep my hands from shaking. He had called a few days later.

We went to his favorite bar, where he introduced me to

Johnnie Walker and dancing two-step to Randy Travis. We started going out once a week, twice a week, and then one night he introduced me to his friends—Karl, the rodeo clown, and Mack, another bull rider—as "his girl."

Tyler was handsome and funny, and even my parents, a car salesman father and Realtor mother, liked him. I couldn't believe that Tyler Jones wanted me, instead of all the tall, slender women with cover girl hair and tiny little waists who hovered around him like wasps on soda pop.

He was all over me like honey. Roses. Steakhouse dinners. A gold necklace with an engraved locket. We'd dance three nights a week at bars with sawdust on the floor and country music on the jukebox. He was a great dancer and a great lover. At least I thought he was. I had nothing to compare him to.

He had hated me talking to men other than Karl or Mack; he said it was because he loved me so much. I'd never felt so special.

Jack pulled me out of my reverie by throwing a stuffed rabbit in my face, his eyes bright and cheerful.

"Right you are, Mr. Wonderful. Time to get up."

The days at the farm and the office went by in a haze of summer sun. Chris texted several times a day, I restrained myself to short, simple responses. I couldn't sort out yearning for Chris to come back while being appalled at myself at the same time. He was too young—I had almost fifteen years on him. Even though I wasn't his boss, he volunteered where I worked. He clearly had issues. This was not an ideal candidate for starting to date again. And yet, like sometimes happens at dinner when you sit down without an appetite, just one bite suddenly makes you ravenous. "Ravenous," the perfect word for how I felt. I ached for Chris to be beside me, to smell him, to touch him.

I hadn't told Dorothy what had happened. I knew what she'd say.

Chris called late in the week. "Please can I come over? I can't stop thinking about you." I said yes, like a woman about to eat a half gallon of Mackinac Island Fudge Ice Cream, knowing she'd be sorry later.

Jack and Bo Peep greeted Chris like a long-lost friend. Clementine licked his hand and went back to sleep. We did the chores together, walked Jack as the sun softened behind the trees, and promised each other we'd only have one shot of Johnnie Walker. I kept to it; I wanted all my senses working for what I knew was about to happen. I led Chris up the stairs, my body practically vibrating. We fell into bed, where I discovered, yet again, what I'd been missing all those years.

I woke up with the sun streaming onto my face, nestled in the crook of Chris's arm. He was awake, lying on his back and staring out the window, his arm around my shoulders. I made a little whimper-moan of contentment, but pulled my head back when I saw his face, ashen.

"There's more."

"More what?" I asked, befuddled by sleep and sore muscles. I sat up and repeated myself. "More what?"

"I've been lying here for hours," he said. "Wishing I didn't have to tell you any of this. But I can't live with myself if I don't tell you the rest of it. It's more than I said before." He sat up, swung his legs over the side of the bed, and put his head in his hands. "I don't know if you'll ever forgive me."

I would like to have been a person who, suffused with compassion, said, "No, no, of course I'll forgive you. You can tell me anything." I was not. I was instantly irritated, borderline furious. Every time I thought life could be good again, I got hit with bad news. I was exhausted by drama and frightened of a life that felt caught on a barbwire fence. Mostly, I was angry at myself. I thought I was done with making stupid decisions about men.

"I need coffee before we talk." I got up, avoiding looking at

Chris. I peed and threw on jeans and a T-shirt. It was warm already, the heat creeping in like a stalking cat. I walked downstairs and started brewing coffee. My hands were shaking. Jack came over and leaned against my leg.

"Good grief, Jack, will this ever be over?" I did not need more revelations. I did not need more melodrama. I wanted to call Dorothy; I wanted my house back to myself. The rosy haze of the last week was turning an ugly orange.

Chris came down the stairs and sat at the table, methodically straightening the blue, plastic table mats. When Thelma walked into the kitchen, the sun shining off her tortoiseshell coat, she made that sweet little trill that cats give to their babies. She trotted up to him, her tail tip lasered toward his face. I stayed silent while he rubbed her cheeks; I could hear her purring from across the room. Jack lay down at my feet, eyes on Chris.

I set two mugs down on the table and sat down. A ray of sun slanted across Chris's hair and forehead. The house wren was still singing, her bubbling song sounding more maniacal than musical.

"Okay," I said, my voice softening as I looked at Chris's face. "What?"

Chris took a few breaths, his chest rising and falling as he looked toward the oaks. Finally, he turned to me and said, "I lied to you about Cisco."

"What, WHAT about Cisco? Do you know where he is?" I had stood up and was yelling. Jack got up from lying down by the stove and stood beside me. He might have growled; I'm not sure. Thelma ran out of the room.

"No, I don't!" Chris said, his voice as loud as mine. "Of course I don't. If I did, I'd rescue him in a minute. Let me explain, okay?" I sat down and stroked the side of Jack's head. "It's okay, bud, it's okay."

"I found him in Chicago, not Milwaukee, in the warehouse of my former dealer. When I quit I still owed them money, and at first they had me pick up drugs and run them to Milwaukee to pay it off. I only did it twice, but hated it, told them I'd pay them off in cash instead. I finally got the money together and went down to pay it off. When I was there I found Cisco lying in a corner, partially covered with burlap, half dead and barely breathing. I picked him up, carried him to my car, and brought him to the shelter. My contact was there when I found him; I asked if he knew who he belonged to. He thought the cartel got him to sniff out competitor's drugs, or to see how hard it was to disguise the smell of them, he wasn't sure. But it didn't work out. They didn't seem to care about him, so I drove him to the shelter. I couldn't bear to let just him die like that."

I was about to ask why the hell he drove me all the way out to a warehouse in Milwaukee for no reason whatsoever, when the light dawned. "Oh my God. Is that who broke in and stole Cisco? Your druggie friends?" I started to stand up again, my eyes locked into his, my chest hot and tight. "You told them? They knew Cisco was here because you told them? Are you f . . . ?"

Chris rose up, saying, "No, no, no," and came around to my side of the table. Jack leapt up and lunged toward him. He could've bitten him; dogs are always faster than we are. But he stopped a foot from Chris, looked up straight at his face, and stared at him with flat black eyes. I'd never seen Jack, the dog who had "never met a stranger," look at a person like that. It broke my heart to see his eyes lose their warmth.

"Jack, that'll do. Lie down." I kept my voice as steady as I could and pointed to the floor beside me. We all saw that my hand was shaking. "Lie down, bud." Jack lay down, his eyes boring into Chris's, his mouth closed tight.

Chris sat back down.

"Listen, Maddie. I never, EVER told anyone outside the shelter about Cisco being here. Everyone at the shelter knew you'd taken him here to foster him, but honest to God, I have no idea how anyone from the cartel could have known."

He sunk his head into his hands again before looking back

up at me. There were tears in his eyes. "I am so, so sorry about this mess. You are the best thing that has happened to me in forever and now I've fucked everything up. I know it was wrong, but all I did was lie about where I found Cisco, that's it. I was too ashamed to tell you the truth. I've been looking for him ever since I heard what happened; asking around, checking out all the storage places that I know the cartel uses."

The wren kept up her incessant singing a few feet from the window. I almost screamed at her to shut up.

"Okay, I believe you," I said. I wasn't sure that I did.

"Look." I took a sip of coffee and leaned down to pet Jack. "You need to go now. I need time to think." I stood up and looked Chris in the eye.

He nodded, rose from the table, and picked up his keys and wallet from the coffee table in the living room. He turned to me when he got to the door.

"I would never do anything to hurt you, Maddie. Or Cisco. I've done everything I could to try to find him, but it makes no sense that the cartel would have either known where he was or wanted him back. It sounded like they thought he was a waste of money. There's no reason they'd want him back."

A lamb who'd lost track of his mom bawled over by the creek. A catbird called. A light breeze came through the living room into the kitchen as Chris stood inside the door, his shoulders practically touching the frame.

Jack stood up. Neither of us moved toward Chris. "Okay. Okay. Just go now," I said.

Jack and I sat back down as Chris walked away to his car. When his car disappeared down the driveway I turned and looked at Jack. "Good grief, Jack, what do I do now?" He shook himself as if wet from a bath and trotted to the back door.

I did the chores in a haze, got dressed for the office, brushed my teeth twice as long as usual, and sent a text to Dorothy. "OMG. Need to talk." I didn't wait for an answer.

I had clients about to arrive at the office. I had to get it together. I popped Jack into the truck, took Clementine out for a last pee, and said good-bye to Bo Peep, telling her how much I loved her.

The day went by in a blur. I did a house call with a Jack Russell terrier who wouldn't walk out the door, a golden retriever who bit anyone who tried to take his stuffed toy away, and a bully breed mix who had been attacked at a dog park and was terrified of any dog with white paws.

It was good to be distracted. I was lucky; the dogs could all be helped, and the owners were all willing to try. I set up second appointments with each of them, a house call for the agoraphobic terrier and office visits for the other two. Dorothy had texted back during the day; I quickly let her know that I had clients and could talk later in the afternoon.

Finally, the last client gone and the notes finished, I called Dorothy, hoping she'd be free. She answered on the first ring.

"Well, you got my attention. What's up? You okay?"

"Uh, no. Yes. Okay, no. Holy shit, Dorothy, I can't believe what's happened in the last week." I told her what was going on, including sleeping with Chris.

"So, you're making all this up, right?" Dorothy said after a long pause.

"I wish. I'm scared and furious at myself for being such an idiot. The guy I chose to finally do it with turns my life, already bad enough, into a soap opera?"

"And this from you, a woman who yammers on about dogs needing impulse control." I let that one go.

"Well, at least there are dogs in the plot," she continued. "And I'm not as surprised as you. You—the one who always says she doesn't trust men, but two thirds of her friends are guys? How about you start from the beginning? How did all this start? Did I actually hear you say that you finally, FINALLY had sex with a real live person instead of a vibrator? Am I dreaming?"

I told her the entire saga, from the drunken night with Chris, the day working together at Harpo's, Chris's confessions.

"Fuck a duck," she said. "I'm coming down. Do not say no. I'm coming, period, soon as I can. Just make sure that the coffee will be hot and ready when I get there."

I hung up and went to do the chores. She wouldn't make it until well after eight that night, so I distracted myself by working Jack on some yearlings in the far pasture. He did fine, but I was slow to respond to the sheep, and twice I said "come bye" when I meant "away." I gave it up after letting him do an easy outrun, not willing to endanger whatever trust he had in me as a handler. We walked back to the house, me sweaty and unsettled, Jack panting hard, his tongue curled up at the tip like a spoon.

As the light began to fade, Dorothy blew in with four dogs, a pepperoni pizza, and a long hug. We divided the pizza slices onto my mismatched plates and talked while we ate.

"Okay, we need to talk about what you do next," Dorothy said, her mouth full of cheese and sauce.

"No shit, Sherlock," I said. "What do I do? Do I tell the sheriff about the possible connection between Cisco's kidnapping and Chris and drugs? Of course I should, but wouldn't I be screwing Chris over for no reason? I don't see why it would help me find Cisco—why would the cartel care about a dog that they'd abandoned? And how would they know he was here at the farm?"

I put what was left of my pizza slice down. "Maybe I should just stay quiet about all of it. I should stop seeing Chris—that's a given. But what about Cisco? What if Chris IS the link to Cisco? I mean, who else would want Cisco beside the dealers?" I liked saying "dealers" better than "cartels." It made them sound less scary.

Dorothy chewed on the ridiculously large piece she had put in her mouth. She swallowed a gulp of Coke and said, "What if you talked again to that cop you're working with? The one with the thunder phobic dog? You keep Chris's name out of it, just tell him the chapter titles of what happened and see what would happen to Chris if you ratted him out." I played with my napkin. Thelma batted a dust bunny from under the table.

"I don't know. Ryan seems like a nice guy, but he's a cop. I can't give him this information and expect him to ignore it. Same with the sheriff. If I tell anyone in law enforcement, what are they supposed to do? Pretend I never said anything? Then why bother telling them? I'm not sure I can ask them to investigate without knowing who Chris is or who his contacts are, so I need to figure this out for myself."

"But wouldn't they already know a lot about who's running drugs from Chicago? Why would they need the name of an 'informant'?" She made finger quotes around the last word. "Or, you could drop it, have a memorial service for Cisco, and get on with your life." Dorothy looked me in the eye. "Maddie, you know you'll probably never find him, right? Maybe it's time to grieve and move on?"

"I know it's crazy, but I swear he's alive somewhere. Waiting for me to find him." This said by the woman with a PhD in science. We both sat in silence for a moment, listening to the hum of the refrigerator and the warning trill of a chipmunk.

"Wait! What if I went to the area where Chris actually did find Cisco and looked around. Maybe Cisco is being held there. If the dealers took him, then surely they'd have him somewhere close by."

"Oh sure, Maddie, great. Let's pack up the Glock and your .22 and go creeping around dark places with bad people hiding in them. Sorry, I'm not playing *Law and Order* with you, that's crazy. But, if you have to do something, maybe talking to Ryan or that sheriff? Doing nothing would be better."

Dorothy took both my hands in hers. "Girlfriend, you need to go to sleep. You need good food and rest and a session with a great counselor and to get laid by someone who is not involved with scary people. I'll take Clementine out and close up the house. Go upstairs and go to sleep."

I went upstairs, and finally, after listening to screech owls calling back and forth for what seemed like hours, I went to sleep and dreamt unspeakable things. Jack woke me up by licking my face when I started to whimper, and I lay stroking his belly until the wren began babbling by the window, long before the sun rose over the horizon.

CHAPTER 21

I slogged through the next couple of days, trying to focus on work and the farm and not obsessing about Cisco. Or Chris, who called every day. I didn't call back. I thought constantly about whether to tell anyone besides Dorothy about Chris's confession. I didn't want to hurt him; he was a good guy who made some bad choices. I kept trying to squelch images of his face—God those eyes—and the unfamiliar peace I felt with my head in the crook of his shoulder.

I wasn't convinced that Cisco's kidnapping had nothing to do with drug running. Who else would want him? Who else would dope a guard dog with fentanyl? Figuring out what to do next about Cisco, much less Chris, swirled underneath everything else I did for the next two days.

On Thursday afternoon I had one more client for the day, an apricot-colored poodle mix who stole dirty laundry from the hamper and bit the owners if they tried to take it away. Like a four-year-old who shows you his new toy but won't let you touch it. Her owners booked an appointment after she'd presented soiled underwear to house guests at a dinner party.

Ruby strode into the office like a rock star. She paced around the office while Paul told me how Ruby had bitten both of them and one of their boys. They'd gated off the laundry room, but having three kids under the age of six made it hard to manage. After getting a lot more information about Ruby and hearing how the family would be devastated if they had to rehome her, I set up a demonstration illustrating how they could teach her to happily give up her "treasures" when asked.

First, I tossed a few pieces of cooked chicken onto the floor to make sure Ruby wanted to eat them. She pounced and inhaled them all. I tossed some more to let her know that good things happen here, and then asked Paul to put down the dirty sock I had asked them to bring. Ruby immediately picked it up and stood glaring at all three of us, her body stiff and her eyes cool. Good! We'd set up what happened at home—something you can't always do in my office.

After instructing the owners to stay seated, out of harm's way, I tossed a handful of chicken several feet to my left. If she wanted to eat it, she had to drop the sock. She did exactly that, snarfing up the chicken lustily, but grabbed back the sock as soon as the food was gone. All good. Now I knew that I could distract Ruby from the sock with tasty treats. Eventually, she'd learn to drop her stolen treasures on cue. But for now, I repeated the exercise several times, letting her learn that dropping the sock led to wonderful things. That was enough for one session, so I tossed a bounty of chicken to the other side of the office, and once she'd turned away to get them, extended my hand to pick up the sock.

No one ever says, "I'm being bitten." At least, almost never. Dogs are so fast, and we are so slow, that it's usually over before you realize what happened. All I remember is a sharp pain in my hand along with a photographic image of her as she bit me. Her eyes, a wolflike yellowish brown, held such fury in them that the memory chilled my blood for hours afterward. Their message was clear. DO. NOT. TOUCH. MY. STUFF. EVER.

My hand was throbbing as I assured my clients that I'd be fine. I told them to stay seated while I went to rinse out the wound. The dog had sunk her canines into the flesh of my hand beside the thumb. Two punctures, deep ones. Shit. Just what I needed. I flushed out the wounds, treated them with antibiotic cream, took some ibuprofen, and came back into the office. Ruby had lain down and was focused on ripping the sock into pieces. Paul and Margo were sitting, white-faced, in their chairs.

I assured them again that I was fine. It was true. I've always had a lot of pain tolerance, and living on a farm full of buried barbed wire, machines in bad moods, and large animals in worse ones, means you get hurt often enough. No big deal.

What wasn't fine was my inability to predict Ruby's behavior. This had never happened to me after working hundreds of cases like this. What dog would leave a pile of chicken for an old sock? I hadn't even touched it, I just reached partway toward it, a good six feet away. In addition, I'd seen a lot of cold eyes in aggressive dogs before, but I'd never seen eyes that contained so much fury. If I didn't know better, I'd say hatred.

I thought of those eyes, and the burning rage that they conveyed, and wondered how Ruby could ever be trusted around the joyful chaos of three young boys. I would never say that Ruby couldn't be trained and conditioned to be trustable, but in this context the risk to the boys couldn't be ignored.

But for now, we had to do something about a dog in warrior mode when she had a sock in her mouth. Easy enough to handle. I tossed another handful of chicken outside the office door leading into the hallway and shut the door once she was outside the room. The sock was put away, I let Ruby back in, and we talked for a long time about their options, and how to keep everyone safe until they decided what to do. I explained that I felt her kids were at risk of a serious injury, and that, in some states, behaviorists would be compelled to report the bite and the danger to the kids. When it was clear that Ruby's owners understood the urgency of this situation, I said goodbye with a heavy heart.

After they left I blew out a lung's worth of air and sat staring at my hand. It was swelling up, so I went to the fridge and put a bag of frozen peas on it. The bag had been there for years, for use in this very instance. I'd never used it since I bought it. Who knows what the peas would've tasted like.

I started to pack up to go home, and found my mind switching back to Chris and Cisco. I decided to talk to Deputy Wallenberg before I went home, hoping that he could describe what would happen if I relayed the information Chris had given me, without me having to give up his name.

Ryan called before I clicked on Wallenberg's number. There'd been a brief thunderstorm in Milwaukee, and Ranger hadn't seemed concerned. As a matter of fact, he played with his toys throughout the entire thing.

"It's working!" I could see Ryan smiling at the other end of the line. "I can hardly believe it—honestly, I was never really sure that it would work. But he didn't look all that worried and was happy to keep playing fetch with his favorite rope toy. Granted, the thunder wasn't very loud, and it didn't last more than ten minutes, but still."

I was truly happy for him; he clearly loved his dog and was determined to keep him on the force. His exuberance was catching, and after talking a bit more about Ranger, I suddenly found myself blurting out a question about Cisco and drug running. It came out of my mouth as if of its own volition. Even as I said it, I wondered if it might lead to getting Chris in trouble, but worry and stress do a number on impulse control, not my strength on a good day.

"Ryan, do you have a minute for me to ask about Cisco?"

"Sure, a few minutes anyway. What's up?"

"Um, so, what if I learned that Cisco had actually been used by a drug cartel to, I don't know, sniff out competitors' drugs, or make sure no one was smuggling out product in their clothes?"

I expected Ryan to laugh, or snort, or to verbally pat me on the head. But he said nothing for a long time. I pulled my hand down from my head; I'd twisted my hair so tightly it was beginning to hurt.

"I've never heard of that happening . . . but that doesn't mean it never could. But guys who pack drugs in cartels are infused with the smell of drugs anyway, so that wouldn't be a reason." He paused. I could feel him starting to think about the implications of my question.

"Where would you get that idea, Dr. McGowan, I mean Maddie? You need to tell me where you heard that, and you *especially* need to not mess with any drug dealers."

"I can't tell you, Ryan. It was from an informant who needs to remain anonymous." I felt very streetwise using the word "informant." "What if the person I talked to was involved, against their will, in trafficking drugs because they owed money to the cartel? Even though they are clean now? What would happen to h . . . this person, if they talked to the police?"

"I couldn't say, it would depend on so many things. It's common for dealers to rope addicts and ex-addicts into doing work for them, but the courts aren't very lenient on people who get caught up. Kevin would know more. I'll ask him and see what he says. I would worry more about what the dealers would do to this person though; that might not go so well."

Oh. Yeah. Them. All I had been worried about was Chris getting busted by the police; I don't know why I hadn't thought about the drug dealers. It occurred to me that sleep deprivation was affecting my brain. Maybe I should just drop it. Maybe I should never have brought it up in the first place.

But I couldn't drop it. Cisco was alive, damn it, waiting for me to find him. "I'll be careful, Ryan, I promise. But would you talk to Kevin? Maybe he has an idea of where to go from here."

"Okay," Ryan said, drawing out the word. "But I won't pretend I'm not worried about you messing around in this. As a police officer I need to tell you to stand down, and as a . . ." Ryan paused here, struggling to find a way to describe our relationship. He started up again. "As a friend, if it's okay that I call you that, you need to drop this and let the police take over. Whatever you do, stay away from that 'informant.' I'll talk to Kevin, see if he has any ideas about what nearby gangs might be involved. Be careful Maddie, this is serious stuff. I know you love Cisco, I get it. I'd do anything for Ranger. Still, this could be dangerous stuff—look what's happened already."

I held onto the phone for the longest time, as I stared out the window toward the parking lot. Two house sparrows scratched in the gravel. I thought for a moment that was I going to throw up. I was scared. Really, really scared, but gradually anger began to replace fear. Anger and fear don't live all that far apart in your brain, and one can switch to the other as quickly as a light switch can be turned off and on.

Someone killed one of the best friends I'd ever had. Someone broke into my home and kidnapped my dog. Someone almost killed Bo Peep. And now, one of the best things that has happened to me in over a decade turned into yet another shit show. Chris, of the haunted emerald eyes, had become yet one more crisis to deal with.

I threw the stapler across the room. It dug a hole in the wall and bounced onto the floor, the staples flying out onto the rug. Words were said. Loudly. I grabbed the next thing I could find, an ancient Rolodex I bought at Goodwill for $1.19, and threw it even harder.

Finally, after slamming some files onto the floor, I sat shaking and holding my head. Breathe. Feel the air come through your nostrils. Feel it leave your body as you exhale. Describe five things you can see: My laptop. The holes in the wall I'd just created. The papers remaining on my desk. A basket brimming with dog toys in the corner. My phone.

Tom. I should call Tom. He'd said he'd ask around and call me if he heard anything, and it had been almost two weeks since we talked at the memorial service. I might as well try again, just in case. And I had to do something. Anything. I sent Tom a text, but also called to leave a message on his landline.

Joan answered the phone, saying, "Oh hi, Maddie. How are you doing?"

"Not great. I'm going crazy about finding this dog that was stolen. Is Tom around?"

"No, sorry, he's in Georgia at a seminar. Anything I can do?"

"Sorry to bother you, but I really need to talk to Tom. The dog that was stolen might have been taken by drug dealers and this guy who found him said . . ." I got a hold of myself, took a breath.

"I just have to find him, Joan. I'm sure he's alive and I don't know where else to turn besides Tom."

"Tom's been so busy lately, Maddie, but I'll talk to him tonight and remind him that you are still looking for this dog." She added, while I twirled my hair, "I'm sorry to say it, but you know that dog's probably long gone by now."

"No, I don't think he is. I have this feeling that he's alive, and I'm not going to stop looking." I blew out a huge breath. "I couldn't save George, Joan, but maybe I can save Cisco."

"Well," she said. "I'll remind Tom to ask around again. Good luck, Maddie." As she hung up, I walked into the next room to let Jack out of his crate. As soon as I put the phone down it rang again.

It was Chris. This time I picked up.

"Maddie," he said quietly. Then nothing. I said nothing back.

"I can't stop thinking about you. I can't study, can't sleep, can't focus in classes. The only thing I can manage to do is my volunteer shift at the shelter." I stayed silent.

"You'd love the little spaniel who just came in. She's a skeleton with two huge eyes and a pink tongue who can't stop licking my face. Hoarding case. She'll find a home in a day once she's released from medical."

I was holding the phone with my left hand. It was shaking. I switched the phone to speaker and put it down on the desk.

"Maddie, say something, please. I am so, so sorry."

"I know you are Chris," I finally managed. "I know. And I don't know what to do. I just want to find Cisco."

I didn't mention that I'd just talked to a police officer.

"Come over, Maddie. We can talk more about Cisco, maybe I can give you some more details that you can tell the cops without my name coming into it. I don't know what else might help, but I'm willing to try."

"I don't know," I sighed. "I don't think so." Ryan's words about staying away from "the informant" rang in my ear.

"Maddie, please? Listen, just come over tomorrow night after work and we can sort out everything we know. I can tell you every detail that I can think of so that you can tell the cops. I'll even fess up and talk to them myself if it would help find Cisco for you."

He paused. "I would do anything for you. Anything."

Jack came over and lay his head on my leg. I stroked his silken head and said nothing.

"Maddie?" Chris finally said after almost a minute of silence.

"Okay, I'll come over," I said. "But just to talk about Cisco." We agreed on eight o'clock the next night, after his classes were over. Jack and I went home, where I tried to get lost in lambs bawling and owls calling and a sunset so colorful it looked like a cartoon.

Chapter 22

I barely slept, but I had gotten used to it. It's amazing how well you can function, at least superficially, on so little sleep. Just two clients that day, a thunder-phobic Chesapeake and a nine-week-old baby Border collie who growled at other dogs. I started the day bleary and distracted, but, as always, the dogs brightened my day. The Chessie wagged from the shoulders back, spreading joy through the room like a sparkler. The puppy squirmed and smiled and learned in ten minutes to look at other dogs on cue for a treat. Soon he was playing with Jack as if they were best friends. He would need lots more work, but it was a great start.

I shook the puppy owner's hand on their way out, wrote up some notes on my laptop, and drove home along country roads decorated with the festive flowers of a Midwest summer.

Bo Peep barked out a welcome from the south pasture as I drove through the dappled shade of the white oaks overhanging the driveway. I took Jack out the back door to relieve himself, walking past Cisco's empty crate. I hadn't moved it since he'd been stolen, even though it was in the way. I had to contort myself to reach the jackets and hats hanging from hooks on the wall behind the crate; but that was far less of a problem than admitting Cisco was gone for good.

Otherwise, all seemed peaceful. Clementine was snoring on the couch and woke up grudgingly when I insisted that she go outside to pee. Bo Peep had settled into the shade of some buckthorn trees, the sheep were sprawled in the grass chewing their cud, and the ducks were sleeping, heads tucked inside their wings. Thelma was curled up beside them. It looked like the farm version of a kindergarten rest period.

I did the evening chores and got ready to go to Chris's. I didn't want to leave, but I wanted to find Cisco more. I grabbed a burrito, chips, and cookies from the fridge, and settled Jack and Clementine in the house. At the last minute I threw Cisco's old collar in the cab with me. I couldn't see how it would help to bring it, but it seemed foolish not to. It was, after all, my only real connection to him. I took off down the driveway, feeling hopeful and pessimistic and nervous and foolish all at the same time. I was especially anxious about leaving the farm, even though I'd been doing it on a daily basis for weeks now and nothing had happened. I called Vince and asked him to check in. He said his son was visiting, but they could stop over in a bit to check on things. I thanked him and tried to focus on driving while I shoved BBQ potato chips into my mouth and washed them down with Diet Coke.

Chris opened the door before I knocked. He stood standing inside the doorway for a moment, silent, looking at me with sad eyes. He might as well have had a sign on his forehead that said "Wanting to hug you but forcing myself not to." I might as well have had one too. But I'd committed myself to keeping things platonic; it was bad enough I was here at all. I had told no one where I was going; I didn't want to hear what they had to say. I did mention it to Jack, secure in the knowledge that he'd be mum on the subject. "They don't talk back" is not on the list about why we love dogs so much, but it should be.

"Okay," I said, still standing in the doorway, "let's sit down and figure out what we know." I strode into the living room and sat on a beige couch on top of a tan rug. Everything in the room was beige, brown, or black, dominated by two computers and three monitors set up on flimsy tables. There were a lot of black cables, snaking all over the floor.

Chris brought me a hot cup of coffee without asking. I took it, grateful for the distraction. I looked toward Chris, trying to avoid his eyes. He sat down beside me and spread out Google Earth printouts of South Chicago, showing exactly where he found Cisco, where he met the supplier, and the location of the two warehouses that sometimes held drugs awaiting distribution.

Chris didn't know much beyond that. He didn't know where Cisco originally had come from. He didn't know who thought it was a good idea to get a K9 to work against law enforcement rather than for them. He'd never heard a word about Cisco before he found him, and his contact had little to say about it afterward. He'd decided not to bring it up after he'd delivered him to the shelter, figuring the less he said the better. After Cisco was kidnapped he did ask, and got a cold stare: "Why the fuck you care about some stupid dog? Maybe you shouldn't be asking so many questions."

"Well, then, doesn't that prove that they do care about Cisco?" I leaned forward, pressing my case. "Why would someone warn you off if they didn't care?"

"I don't know. They don't like me asking questions about anything, ever. That's part of the deal." Chris rubbed his chin and then raked his fingers through his hair. I turned my head away. As hard as I'd tried to focus on what he could tell me about Cisco, it was impossible not to feel his presence beside me. I could smell him, that sweet, earthy scent that had driven me crazy when he was at the farm. It was starting to do that again. I shook my head to get some sense back into it.

I'd been playing with Cisco's collar to keep my hands busy, rolling it around and around between my fingers. I set it down on the coffee table and stood up.

"Can I have those printouts of the warehouses?"

Chris grabbed my hand, hard. "Only for the police, right? You are NOT going there. That would be insane. You are NOT. Promise me."

Of course, he was right. A short, white woman with wild-ass red hair would stand out in a run-down industrial area on the south side of Chicago. But there are hats. And jackets. And the dark. All I'd need to do is go down there in the middle of the night and quietly call Cisco's name. If he was there, I was sure he'd answer me. If he was alive. Which he was.

"I just need them in case I have to talk to the police. I swear I'll keep your name out of it. Surely the police must have an informant or someone on the force who could look around, right?" I knew I was grasping at straws.

"Okay, I have to go." I gathered up the maps and walked purposefully to the door. I turned to look at Chris, standing in the middle of the room, his eyes as soft as rain.

I lost it. I walked to him and buried my head in his chest. His arms wrapped around me and he lifted me up, pressing against me, kissing me. He was warm and strong and radiating so much need that I almost caved. I kissed the cat tattoo on his forearm. But then I pushed him away and said: "I can't. I just can't. It's just too much. Everything feels so fucked up right now I barely know where to turn. But . . ." I struggled to put my angst into words. I finally, weakly, repeated myself. "I'm sorry. It's just too much."

"I'm the one who's sorry." Chris stroked a finger along my cheek. "I get it. I'm just so sorry."

I turned away and left him standing there as I ran away down the stairs, the metal steps clanging. I got into the truck and turned the key, hurrying before I changed my mind. A few miles later I realized I had left Cisco's collar at Chris's.

I kept driving while asking myself why not having it would make any difference. Wanting it was illogical . . . but still. It was the only thing I had left of Cisco besides a wire crate that I swear still smelled like him, even to a pathetically weak human nose. I kept driving a few more minutes, but finally pulled over into a strip mall parking lot. I stopped, texted Chris that I was coming back to get the collar, then turned around and drove back.

As I parked, turning off my headlights, I saw someone trotting down the stairs that led to the upper floor of the apartment complex. A couple came out of an apartment to my right, laughing at something on one of their phones. I trotted up the stairs to discover that Chris's door was cracked open, the lights turned on in the living room.

Cisco's collar was on the table where I'd left it. I picked it up.

"Chris?" I called. Silence. A strange, thick one. I could hear my voice rise in pitch as I called his name again. I walked through the living room into a dark hall. The bathroom door was open. I felt for a light switch and turned it on. Nothing there. I willed myself to keep walking into the bedroom.

Chris lay on his side on the floor by the bed, his knees folded, a bloody mess under his head. I stood still, unable to move. The wall air conditioner kicked on, blasting moldy air into the room. A truck backfired on Harland Road. I heard laughing outside, maybe the same couple I'd seen before.

I ran to Chris, stooping over and turning his head toward mine. His eyes were open and vacant. There was no pulse in his neck.

Hands shaking, I punched 911 into my phone. I spluttered out something with the words "dead" in it, gave out the address, and hung up. I sat in the living room, spinning Cisco's collar in my hands.

I don't remember much after that until I heard the sirens. A cop in full regalia met me outside the apartment and introduced herself—Officer Murphy. She was gentle but professional as she escorted me into the back of her squad car.

There is no comfort in the back of a squad car. It's a tiny space, a black, mobile jail cell, with bars in front of the Plexiglas partition that sections off the back, bars on the side windows. The plastic seat and seat backs were flat and rigid, designed to make cleaning up vomit and blood easy. It felt like sitting inside a small, nasty box. I could feel the gray veil of claustrophobia kicking in, and tried to focus on my breathing.

She asked my name and if I lived here in the apartment. She told me to wait in the car as two other police cars pulled up into the parking lot. Lots of uniforms got out; I barely noticed what kind.

After an endless wait, a woman dressed in tan pants and a burgundy jacket approached the car. Purple tattoos peered out from under her sleeve by her wrist and above the collar of her shirt. She had short, blue-black hair, dark brown eyes, and introduced herself as Detective Garcia. "It would be best to interview you at the station. Would that be all right, if we took you there to talk? We'll get you back here to your car after we're done."

I nodded, numb. She left toward her own squad car, "POLICE" written in blue on three sides. Officer Murphy and I followed behind. In ten minutes we arrived and entered through a door that said EMPLOYEES ONLY. Murphy slid a card across a scanner by the side of the door and escorted me inside, her hand above my left elbow. We walked up two flights of stairs, industrial beige on the walls, and entered a large room surrounded by cubicles on all sides. Each was labeled with name and rank: Det. L. Fahrenbruch, Det. R. Stachel, Det. N. Michelson.

Interview Room 2 was small, and devoid of anything but hard surfaces. Bare walls, painted gray. A table. Four metal chairs. Garcia asked me to sit down and if I wanted water. I said no, then wished I hadn't. A second detective joined Garcia and sat down across from me at the table. They introduced themselves again, Detective Lisa Garcia and Detective Norra Michelson of the Milwaukee Police. I hadn't let go of Cisco's collar the entire time I sat in the squad car.

"I'm sorry to be talking to you under these circumstances," said Garcia. "Any information that you can give us is going to be super helpful. Can you spell your first name for us, please?"

And thus, it began. Question after question after question. Detail after detail. Describe where you parked, draw the apartment complex and parking lot. When did you arrive, when did you leave? Exactly where did you drive, why did you go back? When did you stop to text? Did Chris answer your text? What was your relationship with the deceased? Did you touch the body?

Oh God, the body. All that was left of a big, sweet, messed up man I was an idiot to get involved with. This, after fourteen years of being oh-so careful, staying safe, avoiding men except fatherly types. I had to take some deep breaths to keep from crying. Damn if I was going to cry in front of them.

I told them that I hugged Chris when I left the first time, but I wasn't sure exactly what happened after I called 911, it all seemed blurry now. I said we weren't really dating, but had slept together a few times. It all sounded pathetic. *Dr. McGowan is sleeping around with men she barely knows who are fifteen years younger.*

Gawd. I could feel my face get hot.

We moved on to the people I saw before entering the apartment, starting with the man who came down the stairs. Garcia looked at me intently and asked for a detailed description. It was obvious that he was a prime suspect, unless, of course, they suspected me of making him up and killing Chris myself. I knew I had to be high on their suspect list.

I did my best to describe the guy coming down the stairs. I couldn't say much. He was far away. (How far? they asked.). I had barely paid attention, focused as I was on dashing in to get the collar.

"He seemed pretty tall, over six feet, I think. Dark hair, no glasses, some kind of dark sweatshirt-like thing, no idea what kind of pants he had on. I was pretty far away, still in the truck when I saw him go down the stairs and walk across the parking lot. He seemed to be going toward a truck or SUV parked on the other side of the lot, but I couldn't say what it was beyond being large. I just hadn't paid attention." Now, all I could think about was that I'd gotten Chris killed by the cartel, for asking too many questions about Cisco. My hands started to shake again and my eyes filled with tears.

I took a breath. "I need to explain something to you," I said while Garcia was writing notes. "I wasn't just visiting Chris to chat." Her head came up. The whole miserable story about Cisco and Chris spilled out. Cisco's rescue, the kidnapping at the farm, Chris's former coke addiction, the maps of the warehouses. The entire mess. I realized I was holding the collar up in the air as I talked.

Garcia reached for the collar, saying she needed it as evidence and asked for the maps too. The maps were in the truck. I said I could mail them. Garcia said not to move them, they'd be out to get them. She asked for my keys; I handed them over.

I held on to collar, ignoring Garcia's outstretched hand. I knew it was just a collar, but it was my only link to Cisco, and, irrationally, it felt especially important now. I pulled it back to my chest, and shamelessly begged her to let me keep it. I explained how much I had loved the dog, how much it meant to me to keep the collar. Giving up the collar would be like giving up everything. She shook her head. Sorry. I reached out and gave it away.

I started crying. Everyone and everything was gone. George. Cisco. Chris. Any sense of safety. This was not a pretty cry. I began crying so hard I began gulping for air. I thought I might throw up.

Garcia came over and stood beside me, asking if I would like some water. I took a breath and tried to pull myself together.

"Okay. I'm okay," I said. I wasn't. We took a break, then began again after I'd had some water and tissues and composed myself. Finally, they asked if I minded giving them a DNA sample and fingerprints. I agreed, but asked if I could call someone. "Yes, but make it quick," Garcia said.

I wanted to call Dorothy, but she was hours away. I settled on Vince, feeling like I was the worst neighbor in the world. Surely three in the morning is the last time you should call anyone, much less a neighbor who had already gone over and above helping you.

He answered like anyone would after midnight.

"Maddie, what? Are you okay?" he mumbled. His voice was warm and familiar. I couldn't talk for a moment. I finally blurted out something.

"Stay there," he said. "You are not driving home. My son Liam is here visiting. I can take you home and Liam can drive your truck back." All I could answer was "okay."

They showed up eons later. Vince gathered me up in his arms when I began crying again. I could see his son over his shoulder. He was forty-ish, with vaguely brown hair that curled every which way around his ears. He had big hands like his dad. His arms dangled awkwardly from his body.

"Liam will drive your truck back," he repeated. I nodded numbly. "You come in the car with me," Vince said. "Okay if we leave now?" he said to no one in particular. Garcia nodded, but said I might need to come in for more questioning in a day or two. I said okay, and left with Vince, his arm wrapped around my shoulders.

We got home at daybreak. Jack greeted me hysterically, never having spent a night without me since I got him. He pressed his head against my legs like a burr, following me everywhere. Vince and I did a quick version of the chores. After they were done, I collapsed upstairs on the bed, Jack pressing against me. I thought I'd not be able to sleep, no matter how tired I was, but I fell into unconsciousness as if drugged.

I learned later that Vince had called Dorothy soon as he got home, and that he and Liam had taken turns sitting in the living room until she arrived late that afternoon. I woke up when she arrived and drank the mojito she made me with the mint growing around the root cellar behind the house. Dorothy and I lay on the couch together, watching *House* reruns until I started to doze. She insisted on sleeping beside me in the bed upstairs. Every time the nightmares came, she held me as if I were a child, with Jack on the other side, warm and alive, his heart thumping slow and steady.

Chapter 23

Dorothy stayed all weekend. She made me omelets in the morning and roast chicken at night. We walked the dogs for hours, sitting in the grass when we were tired, watching the barn swallows swoop over the fields, gobbling up insects on the fly. Vince and Liam came over for dinner one night, the first time Vince had ever had a meal at the farm. Dorothy made us roast lamb and asparagus with hollandaise; Liam said it was the best meal he'd ever had and asked her to marry him. We all laughed uproariously.

Dorothy left early Monday morning to care for an injured owl. It was fine. I was overwhelmed with gratitude for her support, but I wanted my house back. House company, no matter how welcome, is tiring.

I had contacted Monday's clients on Saturday, asking to reschedule their appointments because of a "medical emergency." Maybe that was a stretch, but if death isn't a medical emergency, I don't know what is. After Dorothy drove away, I called Jack to come sit on the porch with me. He bounded up the steps, eyes twinkling, and bussed my cheek. His coat gleamed and his huge, bushy tail swayed back and forth. I kissed the crooked white stripe down his face and told him how much I loved him. He sighed, circled, and curled up against me, his ear twitching a fly away.

I sat thinking what a miracle it was that Jack, a predator with a million reasons to run off into the woods, chose to lie beside me. I always feel honored when a dog makes that choice. I began stroking the midline of his head, from the eyebrows back. He sighed again, his head resting on my thigh. When I reached under his head to scratch his neck, my fingers ran into his collar, a blue nylon one with an ID tag affixed to it. Some fur had gotten twisted around the collar, so I unsnapped it to untangle the hairs.

As I did, I thought about Cisco's collar, wishing I still had it. I started rolling Jack's collar around in my hands like I had Cisco's, wondering why the collar had felt so important. It felt more than sentimental, but I couldn't say why. Something had been nagging at me, something subconscious, like underground tree roots talking to each other in voices we can't perceive.

I gave up, put Jack's collar back on, and stood up.

That's when it came to me.

Cisco's ID tag was unique. In one way it was like Jack's—it didn't hang down from a hook like a lot of tags do on house dog collars. The empty holes in the collar made it clear that the ID tag had been a metal plate attached with rivets. Most working dog owners use that kind of ID—no jangling noise to bother the sheep, nothing to get caught on a fence or underbrush. Every ID tag that attaches directly to the collar looks exactly the same: when you take off the metal plate with the ID information on it, you are left with two holes in the collar, one at each end of the plate.

But Cisco's had four, two at each end. I'd never seen that before.

Except, I realized in a woosh, I had. There had been something about the collar on the German shepherd I'd met at Tom's that had gotten my attention. I hadn't known why at the time, but I could see it in my mind now: a thick collar, with four holes for rivets to attach the ID plate, two on each side. Unlike any I'd ever seen—except in Cisco's collar.

My hand actually slapped over my mouth as if in a high school play. Could Cisco have come from Tom's? It made sense. Tom raised detection dogs. He lived and worked only a few hours from Chicago. He had lots of connections in law enforcement with cops who look for illegal drugs. Tom must have, unknowingly, sold Cisco to someone, somewhere, who ended up selling him to the cartel. I called Tom but didn't wait to hear back. I popped Jack in the truck and drove to Tom's.

He looked at me as if I'd lost my mind.

"What the hell, Maddie?" He was laughing as he said that, after I told him about the collars.

"Look, Tom, I know you had nothing to do with it, but somehow one of your dogs got messed up with drug dealers in Chicago. Somebody, maybe some dirty cop somewhere, sold them one of your dogs. Maybe if we went through your sales and tracked down the dogs you've sold, we could get a handle on who ended up with Cisco?"

Tom stared at me. There was a lot of barking in the background.

"Cisco is alive, Tom, I know he is. You must have trained him—"

He cut me off. "Maddie, look." He had stopped laughing. He looked at the gravel between us as if it held the words he was trying to find. "I know you are obsessed with that dog. I get it. And I get how hard George's death has been on you. But Cisco is not George. George is never coming back. Believe me, that's as hard on me as it is on you."

His eyes moistened. His took his hat off and ran his hand back through his hair before he replaced it.

"This dog—I know you think he's alive, but based on what? I'd spend all afternoon looking through my records if it would help, but it's a waste of time. You can't sell a twenty-thousand-dollar dog to law enforcement and then have it disappear off the books. And these collars that you think are so unique? They're not. I order them online; I can show you where I get them. Lots of people use them. Just because you haven't seen them . . ."

"But would it hurt to look? I'd be happy to do it myself."

"And then what, Maddie? I give you the contact numbers for every dog I've sold in the past five years all over the country? You think police departments are going to enjoy having some girl call them to check up on them? This business is tricky enough without you messing up the relationships I've spent years developing. Besides, why me? There must be ten other police dog trainers within a few hundred miles of here."

"Girl." He said girl. I swallowed what I wanted to say while Tom looked toward the kennel of shepherds and Malinois barking behind us. He turned back toward me. "This is crazy, Maddie. You're starting to go off the deep end." Tom put his hand on my shoulder and stared straight into my eyes.

"Are you getting any help? George told me a little about what happened to you years ago. This must be awfully hard on you, living alone like that out in the country."

My stomach turned to stone. I'd told George about my ex-husband in confidence. He swore he'd never tell anyone. I felt like someone had peeled the skin off my body and I was standing outside, in public, raw, bloodred.

"Thanks. I'm fine." The words came out like bullets.

I turned to go back to the truck and drive away, but was pretty sure I shouldn't try to drive right then. I knew what would happen once I started driving. I drive fast enough as it is, but channeling one's fury and pain into a two-ton weapon is never a good idea.

"Okay if I take Jack out of the truck and let him work the sheep a little?" I didn't wait for an answer and walked to the back of the truck to let Jack out of his crate.

As I did, Tom said, "Sure. And, Maddie, I really am sorry. Honestly, those collars are a dime a dozen in the K9 world; it's not going to help you find Cisco. If he's even alive."

I nodded without looking at Tom and spoke to Jack. "Let's go, bud. Let's go work some sheep."

The flock was grazing in a forty-acre field, backlit by the midmorning sun. I could hear a vireo sing in the woods. The sweet smell of new-cut hay drifted in on the breeze.

I had Jack heel beside me as if we were walking to the post at a trial and then sent him "away to me" with a quiet word. Watching his perfect body flow through the grass was better than a therapist. The sheep become aware of his presence one by one, each running toward the center and the protection of the flock. I stopped at the top, and told him to stay while the sheep moved forward. No busting in today, bud. Then I let him bring the sheep to me by himself, without worrying about pace or straight lines, as I would at a trial. It's good for dogs to be able to work on their own, and it's good for us to let go of the reins when we can.

I did a few made up "chores," then called him back. I had planned to work more, but Jack's work was so good I thought it'd be wise to quit while we were ahead. Besides, my stomach had loosened and my heart had quieted, so the important work here—being safe behind the wheel—was done. The wind shifted, bringing the complex scent of the oak-hickory woods behind the barn with it. I said, "That'll do" to Jack, and he came to me, panting hard. He was at my side as we passed through the gate to the pasture, but turned toward the barn as I moved toward the truck.

"Jack, that'll do," I said. Jack stood still.

"Jack, that'll do!" I said more emphatically, patting my leg.

"Maddie!" Tom called as he approached from the house with a catalogue of dog supplies in his hand.

"I just wanted you to see this," he said as he pushed the catalogue toward me. "See? That's where I order the collars and ID tags.... Everybody uses them."

I barely looked at the page. "Okay, Tom, thanks. Sorry." I just wanted to go home.

I called Jack again. He ignored me and began barking, high-pitched with excitement, looking toward the barn. Probably a raccoon, who had been put on earth, according to Jack, to harass and torture him. He cannot, absolutely cannot, keep from obsessing about them. Any scent of one starts him barking, and it took a lot of training to get him to come away from them.

I stopped walking toward the truck. If Jack's behavior was any clue, there was a raccoon in the barn, busy eating away at the grain stored for fattening up the market lambs. As rattled as I was by Tom, and irritated at his condescension, I didn't want one of his dogs to encounter a corn-stuffed raccoon, high on carbs and ready to rumble.

I pulled the leash out of my pocket and snapped it on Jack's collar. He pulled toward the barn, but then veered to the side and lunged his way into a shed beside it, open on one side, more facing the woods than the field behind us. He stopped barking, put his head down, and began sniffing in earnest. The sound of his nose work was amplified by the sides of the shed: *sniff puff sniff puff*. Scent work is hard labor for dogs; Jack looked dead serious as he worked his way around the shed.

I kept a good hold of the leash, not wanting him to surprise a trapped raccoon. He began to concentrate in one corner, turning back toward me and looking in my direction. *It's there! There it is! Can't you smell it?*

Nope, couldn't smell a thing besides the sweet smell of corn and oats mixed with molasses to keep the dust down. I backed Jack up and told him to lie down and stay in the entrance to the shed. He did, his jaw chattering in excitement, as I peered into the corner, looking behind bins of grain, sacks of mineral, and the dusty tools that gather in every shed in every farm in every county.

Nothing. The raccoon probably had scampered out before we got there. I gathered up Jack and walked us back to the truck, while Jack began barking again, still high-pitched and excited, toward the shed.

"I know, bud. Don't worry, I'll tell Tom to put out a live trap."

I sent Tom a text about the raccoon before I drove away, not wanting to talk to him again. As I did, I saw a text from Detective Garcia, who wanted to come out and interview me again.

Would this afternoon be convenient?

OK, I texted back. The day had been crap so far, I might as well keep it consistent. I said I'd be back home by one, giving me time to stop and get lunch at Mickie D's. The salad and roasted chicken from Dorothy were fine, but a girl needs real food in times of trouble.

Chapter 24

Garcia pulled up on schedule at one o'clock. Bo Peep was in the back pasture with the sheep, her low-pitched woo woo woofs bounced off the hills to the east while Garcia got out of her car. I'd put Jack in the crate in the mudroom; the stress and turbulence of the last few months had made him wary of unfamiliar people. It felt almost like another death.

Garcia walked toward the porch with a colleague, a woman in a pants suit with hair in a classic Ricky Martin cut—clipped short on the sides, pouffed up on the top like a pompadour wannabe.

"Ms. McGowan," Garcia said as she shook my hand. "This is Detective Nichols, she's also assigned to this case. Thanks for seeing us today." If I had ten bucks for every time somebody didn't use my correct title, Dr. McGowan, I'd be a millionaire. I ignored it.

Nichols transferred a large bag to her shoulder, so that we could shake hands. I turned and let them into the living room. I picked Clementine up off the couch, and gently put her in one of the dog beds on the floor. She woke up enough to blink a few times and lick my hand, then put her head down and resumed snoring.

"Please," I said, gesturing toward the couch. The two of

them sat down, Garcia unbuttoning her jacket. It occurred to me that no one had ever sat on that couch with a suit jacket on before. I almost laughed, but squelched it by asking if they would like some coffee. Garcia said yes, Nichols no. I brought out a cup for myself, handed Garcia hers, and then sat in the old recliner stuffed into the corner.

"So," Garcia began, "we'd like to go over your relationship with Mr. Norwood and what happened the night he was killed."

Mr. Norwood? Was there another murder I didn't know about? Oh, she meant Chris? I'd heard his last name so rarely it barely registered, but after a pause I got my head together. "What would you like to know?" I sipped my coffee. It was hot and bitter.

"Tell us again about how you met, what you did together, what you know about him."

I went over it all again, but this time in more detail—the shelter, Cisco's kidnapping, our attempts to find him. And, finally, Chris's admission about being a recovering coke addict.

Nichols, who had been quiet up to now, leaned forward and asked if Chris and I had a romantic relationship.

"You mean, did we sleep together?" She nodded. "Yes, three times." Thelma took that moment to stroll into the living room, her tail tip targeting toward me like an arrow. I gave the *churr* sound that momma cats make to call their babies, and she jumped up into my lap. I began scratching her chin; you could have heard her purring from the barn.

"Chris was a good guy," I said. Thelma's purring got even louder. "He just made some bad decisions." I let my own bad decisions speak for themselves.

Garcia asked me again to go over what had happened that night, especially after I left Chris's the first time, where and when exactly I'd turned around to go back. I'd answered all the questions before, but I knew the drill—the cops asking questions over and over to see if there were inconsistencies in your story. Nichols took copious notes as I went through the evening, explaining once again that I only went back because of the collar.

"Can you tell us again about the couple you saw when you went back to the apartment?" I went over it all again.

"And the man you saw coming down the stairs?" Both detectives leaned forward slightly from their positions on the couch. That's when I realized how much dog hair there was on the couch. They both had on dark pants. I got hung up for a moment wondering if I should offer to brush them off.

"Maddie? Can you describe the guy you saw?"

I tried to focus on what I'd seen.

"He was coming down the stairs between the two flights. He was moving fast, not running, but trotting down the stairs. I wasn't very close; maybe seventy-five yards away. I'd just pulled into the parking lot, but he seemed like a big guy. Tall, I think, with a blackish sweatshirt. He had dark hair, pretty short. I can't say anything about his shoes, I didn't notice. But he didn't have a hat on, I'm pretty sure about that."

"Did he have anything in his hands?" Garcia took back the interview.

"No, not that I noticed. But maybe . . . I didn't see anything, but I couldn't swear to it."

"What about the vehicle you mentioned that he walked toward?"

"It wasn't a sedan or a compact car. It looked like some kind of SUV, and dark, I think. It's hard to say, it was across the lot away from the lights. I couldn't tell you a make, just dark, or at least not light colored."

Garcia and Nichols exchanged looks.

"I know," I said, bringing up the elephant in the room.

"That could've been the guy who killed Chris. I'd give anything to tell you more about him, but anything else is just going to be made up and worse than nothing at all."

"We appreciate your trying to stick to the facts as best you can," Garcia said.

She leaned back into the couch. Sipped some coffee. Thelma pushed into my hand for more petting. The clock in the kitchen ticked. I could hear Jack shift around in his crate in the mudroom.

"Here's the thing, Maddie." Garcia leaned forward again, having set her cup down on the scuffed table beside the couch, the tattoos on her right forearm peeking out from underneath her jacket.

"First, your story checks out. Traffic cams show you doing exactly what you said. Given that, the lack of a murder weapon in the apartment, and the timing of neighbors hearing a gunshot, we've eliminated you as a suspect. But Mr. Norwood's murder isn't the only one we're looking into. We still have an unsolved murder from months ago—Mr. George Hughes, a person I believe you also knew well? You knew that George was murdered, right? That it wasn't an accident?" I nodded as my mouth went dry.

"George was killed by a sniper's rifle, not the kind most deer hunters would use. After an extensive search, we found a place in the woods that looked like an area where the shooter cleared out vegetation. We didn't find any bullet casings at first—hoping to match the casing to an individual gun—but the Madison PD came out with a K9 they'd trained to search for casings, and he found it right away. Just one, out of a Winchester long range rifle. It's used by sharpshooters. This was no random accident by a trigger-happy deer hunter. Someone, someone skilled at sharpshooting, targeted and shot him from six hundred yards away. We haven't had any luck finding a suspect though."

Garcia looked at her hands, rubbing them together as she spoke.

"But, now, at least, we have a link between the cases." Garcia stopped moving her hands and looked up me.

"It's you."

I stared back at her. Nichols turned a page over in her notebook. Thelma jumped off my lap and sauntered toward Garcia, who broke the silence by saying, "I'm allergic to cats." I swept Thelma up in my arms just as she was about to pounce on Garcia's lap. I put Thelma out the front door and said, "Sorry. This room is full of dog and cat hair. Do you want to talk outside?"

Garcia didn't answer, and was staring at me so intently that I forgot to breathe for a moment. "You were good friends, REALLY good friends, with both of them."

Everything went still again.

"I don't know what to say," I finally said. I looked over at Nichols, who had stopped writing and was staring at me intensely.

"George was one of my best friends in the world. I still miss him. But he had nothing to do with Chris. Chris was a volunteer at a shelter I consult with, George was a sheepdog trainer and competition coach."

Nichols asked if I had a romantic relationship with George.

"Good grief, no. He was like a father to me."

"It's just that"—Nichols paused—"here you had this super close relationship to these two men, and now they have both been shot." Garcia and Nichols looked at me as if their eyes had the power to make me break down and admit I'd killed them both.

I stared at them for the longest time. Finally, I said: "Look, you don't actually think that I had something to do with their deaths, do you? Do I need a lawyer?"

Garcia answered. "You're not a suspect at this time in either death. We know you didn't shoot Chris, and obviously you couldn't have been the one who shot George."

Then she threw a bomb into my lap. "Have you heard anything from your ex-husband?"

My heart stopped beating. I sat immobile, staring.

Finally, Garcia cocked her head. "Maddie?"

"No, of course not! Why would I?" The wind began to pick up; you could hear it rattling the leaves on the willows by the river. A lamb bleated. "Why would you ask? And how the hell do you know about Tyler?" These last words came out too high. Too fast.

"We know about Tyler Jones because it occurred to us that maybe these two cases are linked, given that you seemed to be such good friends with both of the victims. Given what happened between you and your ex in New Mexico, we have to consider him as a suspect." My mouth was so dry I couldn't have spoken if I wanted to.

She asked, "Is there any chance the guy you saw coming down the stairs was Tyler?"

"No. No. He was too tall. Tyler was, is, five foot eight, this guy looked much taller than that. And bigger, more muscled. Tyler was, is, thin, wiry. Strong as an ox, but wiry."

I blurted out: "Where is he? If you know so much about Tyler, then you should know where he is, right? Doesn't he still have to check in with probation? Where is he now?" I had to stop myself from repeating that question a third time.

"And how do you even know who I am?" I hissed as I leaned forward. "I changed my name years ago."

"We're detectives," Garcia answered quietly. It could've sounded snarky, but it didn't. It sounded almost kind. I stared at her.

"We don't know exactly where Tyler is," Garcia continued.

"He checked in with his parole board in April but missed his last two scheduled meetings. But we're looking for him."

Nichols stood up. "Look, this probably has nothing to do with him. It's most likely that Chris's murder had to do with his involvement with drug dealers. But given what happened in New Mexico, we have to consider Tyler a suspect. Who killed your dog trainer friend remains a mystery, but people have all kinds of complications in their lives that even their best friends don't know about. The two crimes probably had nothing to do with each other. We just have to look at all the possibilities, that's all."

Nichols stood up beside Garcia, whose navy-blue pants were covered in white and gray hair. I thought her eyes were starting to look a little red.

"It would be wise for you to be a little more careful than usual, though. I see you have a security camera, that's good. Maybe have some friends come stay with you for a while, Miss McGowan?"

I rose up off the couch and snapped, "It's Maddie. Or Dr. McGowan. If I can think of anything else to tell you, I'll let you know." I could feel myself starting to shake.

Garcia sneezed. She and Nichols looked at me, looked at each other, and followed me to the door. Each handed me a business card.

"Call us any time you think of anything, Dr. McGowan." This from Garcia. "And it'd be wise to stay in the area. I assume you don't have any plans to travel?"

"Just to some sheepdog trials, all pretty close by."

"Well, good luck then, and be careful for a while. If we hear anything about Tyler or make any progress on the case, we'll let you know. But keep thinking about the man you saw walking down the stairs—he's our best suspect at this point. If there's anything else you can remember about him it'd be helpful. We're looking for CCTV in the area, although there isn't a camera at the entrance to the apartment complex. But maybe something will show up from nearby traffic cams."

Garcia said, "We'll keep in touch." She walked partway out the door, followed by Nichols, but then turned and said, "I'm sorry about your friends." She looked like she meant it. "Take care of yourself."

I gave her a country nod—an almost-imperceptible dip of the chin, no more.

I called Dorothy as soon as they got in the car. She picked up on the first ring.

"Fuck a duck, are you serious?" Dorothy exclaimed. "You? A link between the murders? And now Tyler's in the mix. Oh God, I'm so sorry."

Early on in our friendship, Dorothy and I had traded failed marriage stories—her ex had left her for a woman twenty years younger, basically a teenager. She'd wanted nothing to do with a husband ever since. I was probably the only person on earth who knew she had a friend with benefits, and she was the only one who knew the whole story about Tyler and what had happened in New Mexico. George knew the basics—the abusive ex-husband part—but only Dorothy knew the extent of it. The cops. The press. The court case. Changing my name.

"Do you want me to come down? We could oil your skid steer and the four-wheeler? Keep your mind busy," Dorothy offered.

"No, I'm fine," I said while laughing. We both used farm chores to keep us centered.

"Maddie?" Dorothy drew out the end of my name like you do when you're talking to a dog about to do something wrong.

"No, no, I'm okay, really. It's just all so absurd. Whoever would have thought a few months ago that this would be my life now? It's so insane it's almost funny."

"Okay, but stay in touch. I've got a pissed off baldy to deal with; she got hit by a car and broke a wing. I'm glad she's so rude. It means she should be fine in a few months. You hang in there and call anytime."

I stood in place after we hung up, shaking my head back and forth, just a few millimeters at a time. Was this happening?

Jack woofed, one quiet woof that was easily translated. "Have you forgotten about me?" I went to the mudroom and let him out. It was midafternoon, but I decided to start the evening chores early. No one would mind getting their dinner sooner than usual, and I needed something routine to do. Jack and I gathered the flock, and I fed the lambs, the ducks, Old Horse, and the cats. The dogs could wait for their dinners. But it was not even four o'clock when we were done, so I revved up the skid steer and started cleaning up the chaff in the hay mow. I'd be getting new hay soon, and figured I might as well get things cleaned up before it came. Nothing like having to maneuver in a tight space on a powerful machine to keep your attention off murder. And an ex-husband who had tried to kill you.

I will never forget the first time he hit me. We'd come back from our usual Friday night at the bar, six months or so after the wedding. We'd had BBQ and beer and danced slow to George Strait, Tyler's hand cupping my ass. As soon as we walked into the house he turned and slapped my face, so hard I fell backward and slammed into the wall.

"Don't you EVER do that again," he hissed. I was too stunned to say anything. He reached down and jerked me back up, wrenching my shoulder.

"What? What are you talking about?" I finally found my voice.

"I saw the way you were talking to Karl. Like a slut. I won't have it, not from my wife." He turned and went to bed. I slept on the couch, an ice pack on my cheek.

In the morning I woke to him stroking my hair.

"I'm sorry about last night, honey. Really sorry. I was drunk and I love you so much and it makes me crazy thinking about you with another man. I swear it will never happen again." He kissed me, his lips soft as petals, and went to make us pancakes and bacon. That night he came home with diamond earrings. Little white lights of love. The note inside the box said: "You are the diamond of my life. Please forgive me."

I did.

CHAPTER 25

I went back to the house after I finished up the barn, but couldn't settle down. I turned on the TV, turned it off. Did some dishes. Got out the grooming tools and gave Jack a good brush. Finally, I put everything down and said, "Hey, Jack! Let's go." Walking felt like the only thing that would keep me sane.

We went past the barn; Jack ignoring the ducks searching for grubs. But he sunk his head down in a stalking posture when he saw the sheep in the south pasture.

"That'll do, Jack, just a walk for now."

Jack raised his head and began trotting toward the creek. He lifted his leg on a honeysuckle bush and loped toward an old walnut tree. I listened for birds, but it was late afternoon and they were quiet. The cicadas, on the other hand, were in full voice, buzzing away in the background like a Greek chorus. I walked through a patch of wild catnip, and the minty scent followed me until I got to the creek. It was low, but still flowing. Jack splashed into a quiet pool at the water's edge, scattering water striders right and left. I sat down on the big, flat rock I'd moved to the creek years earlier with the skid steer, creating a place to sit and listen to the water, trying to focus on the present as I'd trained myself. *Every time you think* about Tyler—the set of his jaw when he was angry, the way his eyes went hard before he hit you—gently bring yourself back to your breath. The breeze on your face. The sense of your body supported by the earth.

Jack started barking, excited, high-pitched notes that no meditative state could ignore. Saliva flew out of his mouth as the front of his body leapt up and down, in rhythm with his barks, as if each landing forced a noise out of his chest. For a moment I startled—now what? But Jack was looking straight up into the trunk of a walnut tree.

Raccoon. Had to be. Sure enough, I walked over to see the heads of two baby raccoons peering out from a hole in the tree trunk, about eight feet up. I laughed out loud, at their adorable faces, at Jack's obsession with raccoons, at the relief of having something else to think about.

"I know, bud, raccoons. But you gotta admit, they're pretty cute. That's enough, then. Let's go." I patted my leg and started walking back to the house. Jack ignored me, so I lowered my voice and quietly said, "Jack. Now." He grudgingly turned away and trotted back to me.

My mind was spinning as I walked. George, and who killed him. Cisco, and how I could find him . . . Chris, and if it was my fault he got killed. And now, Tyler. It was all too much.

I nibbled on some cold pepperoni pizza when we got back to the house. I texted Dorothy that I was FINE, and that I'd block her phone number if she asked too often. I went outside with the dogs for their last pee, then sat down on the porch with a shot of Johnnie Walker. Maybe it would help me sleep.

A few nighthawks began swooping high overhead, their nasal *peent peent* calls louder than usual. I could see the white patches at the bend of their wings. I closed my eyes and tried to concentrate on the sounds around me—the calls of the nighthawks, the buzz of field crickets, the muted hoots of a distant great horned owl. I thought I should eat something more, but I wasn't hungry; going upstairs earlier than usual seemed like the best plan. Jack seemed amenable and leapt onto the bed before I took off my jeans. I pulled on my extra-large T-shirt, the one Dorothy gave me that said, "I like birds and maybe three people," and got into bed.

My mind was a circus. George. Chris. Cisco. Drug dealers. Tyler. I tried to channel what George would have said, the man who'd kept me grounded so many times. He told me, once when I was struggling with Jack, "A problem with a dog's behavior is not a bad thing; it's an opportunity."

Okay. I'll go with that. More information—like Tyler being a suspect—is simply an opportunity. It's okay to be afraid, but that doesn't mean you can't use what is bothering you as a road to the solution. What's most important now? I asked myself. I can't bring back George or Chris, and I'm not going to go all Agatha Christie and figure out who killed them. That's the cops' job. But Cisco? I still had a feeling, deep down in my core, that he was alive. And that I couldn't give up until I found him. If I was the link between the murders, then that's information that I could use, whether I was afraid of it or not.

I got out of bed, turned on the light, and got out the journal I kept beside my bed. I started writing, sorting it all out on paper.

First, Tyler. What do I know? He's been out of jail for a while, but we don't know where he is now. He missed his last two check-ins, but that tells us nothing about where he is or what he is doing. Would Tyler find a way to track me down and kill the men I cared about? It seemed unlikely. For one thing, how would he even find me since I changed my name and erased as much of my past as I could?

Sure, the detectives found me, but then, as Garcia said, they are detectives. Besides, Tyler's violence had always been directed toward women—girlfriends or wives, as I learned long after the damage had been done. I'd seen him in an occasional booze-fueled scuffle in a bar, but they were never serious. He never beat another guy into a pulp. And he never tried to kill them.

I finished Tyler's section by writing that it was highly unlikely that he was involved. I couldn't let him distract me from more probable suspects.

I turned to a new page. What did I know about George and Chris that could lead me to Cisco? Could there have been a link between the two of them beyond the obvious? I couldn't imagine how they could have known each other, unless George bought drugs from Chris? That seemed crazy. I spent a lot of time with George and never once did I see any sign he used drugs, or even knew much about them. An occasional shot of whiskey hardly linked him to the underworld of illegal drugs. I rated that as impossible.

Did George somehow get ahold of Cisco and sell him to drug dealers? Equally absurd.

But if I *was* the link between the two, what could it be? I realized, as I heard the faint call of a whip-poor-will in the woods across the road, that it wasn't me that was the link. Or even Cisco.

It was Tom.

Tom trained K9s for law enforcement, and used collars like the one found on Cisco. And he was a business partner with George. He had to be the connection.

But, Tom as the bad guy? Tom, the fun, friendly guy who seemed gutted by George's death? It was impossible to imagine Tom being involved in anything illegal, much less being the guy who killed Chris or George. That seemed absurd. I went back to my first speculation—that Tom had sold someone a dog who turned around and sold it to drug dealers, and they were the ones who killed Chris.

That scenario explained Chris's murder, but not George's. How could George have gotten involved in all of this, whatever *this* was? I wrestled with that for a while, and then wrote: What if Tom wasn't so innocent? What if Tom *was* selling dogs directly to drug dealers, and George found out? Or, what if, God forbid, George was in on it too? Both those ideas seemed crazy, although I admitted to myself that I knew George a lot better than I did Tom.

I turned out the light and lay in bed, wondering how to proceed. Should I go back to confront Tom? Call Garcia? Ask Ryan? I fidgeted in bed for a few hours, and finally began to doze right around the time the dawn chorus of birds started up, the wren in the lead, announcing four-thirty a.m. on the dot.

I said a quiet curse and dragged myself out of bed. I took Clementine and Jack out to pee and made coffee.

I had no idea what to do next.

CHAPTER 26

I drove to the office gritty-eyed and exhausted, but glad I had clients. It would give me something to think about, rather than the spiderweb of worries that gummed up my brain.

First up was Rosie, a Great Dane who came when called to Rick, but not to his wife, Laurie. Rosie, affectionately known as Scooby-Doo, had floppy flews and drooled like a fire hose as she licked my face. Good for the skin. It didn't take long to figure out that Laurie usually called Rosie to come for things she didn't like—baths, going into the house when she wanted to be outside, nail trims. It was an easy fix; we went over how to reinforce Rosie for coming when called with treats, chase games, and play. Rick and Laurie left confident that they could handle the issue; Rosie left with a belly stuffed with liver.

Next, I saw Bangles, a beagle rescued from a research laboratory who was terrified of men. Her owner, Beth, thought she must have been abused by men, but I suggested it was as likely she'd never met any. Dogs who grow up in labs never learn to cope with unfamiliar things, and most animal caretakers in labs are women.

Bangles had begun barking at men from a distance, growling when they got closer, and finally, had nipped a guy when he came to visit. Otherwise, Bangles was your basic sweet, squirmy beagle, and I was confident that Beth could turn this around quickly by teaching Bangles that men, especially those with hats on, meant she was about to get treats. We practiced outside my office, where I asked the guy who runs the bar next door to toss pieces of chicken to Bangles as he approached. By the time we were done, Bangles would've asked for his phone number if she could have.

My next client had left a message to cancel, so I used the time to catch up on other cases. I hadn't heard much from Harpo's owners, so I gave Joe a call to see how things were going.

"Great! Harpo has tried as hard as he can to get over the fence, but he can't come close to getting over it!"

Well, that was something, but letting Harpo launch himself at the fence to get at passing dogs wasn't ideal. I reminded Joe that we needed to teach Harpo to react differently when he saw a dog coming down the sidewalk. Joe agreed we should get together, and we set up a house call for the next week.

"How's that guy of yours doing?" Joe asked as I was about to hang up.

My heart fell.

Silence.

Finally, "I'm afraid he died."

"Died? What the hell?"

"He was killed." I exhaled. "Murdered actually. Look, Joe, I'm sorry, but I'd rather not go into it now. I've got a lot of clients to call, and . . ."

Joe interrupted. "Got it. Jesus, Doc. Sorry."

"See you soon, Joe. Give Mr. Harpo a big, sloppy kiss for me, okay?"

I hung up and looked at the next client on the list, Ryan and his dog Ranger.

I got his voice mail, left a message for him to call back, and proceeded down the list of clients who needed a check-in. By now the evening sun was blazing into the west-side window, so I gathered papers in order to go home and do the chores. My cell phone buzzed as I was walking out the door.

"Maddie. It's Ryan."

"Hi, Ryan. I just called to check in on Ranger. How is it going?"

"Um, okay." Things didn't sound okay. I waited for more.

"Look, as it turns out, I can't really talk right now. There's some stuff going on about that guy you knew who was shot. I've been ordered to stand down for now."

I had been opening the door to the parking area, my big bag over my shoulder, holding the phone in my right hand. I put the bag down and walked back into the office. I sat down at the desk.

"I don't understand. What does any of that have to do with Ranger?"

"Nothing directly. It's just that"—another long pause—"there's a complication, nothing to do with Ranger. I've been told to put working with you on hold until the case is resolved."

"Are you saying I'm a . . . ?"

"No, no," Ryan interrupted before I finished saying "suspect." "I mean, I'm not saying anything, I just can't comment on the case. Or talk right now."

"Okay." I drew out the word longer than necessary. I couldn't help sounding irritated.

"Can you at least tell me that Ranger's okay?"

"He's fine. Sorry, Maddie. I've got to go."

I slammed the door shut as I left the office again, went back remembering I hadn't locked it, and honked aggressively at a squirrel in the road on the way home.

Usually doing the farm chores is like feeding myself; I hold on to the day's rituals like a boat at an anchorage. But this time

I was too distracted to focus. I put Clementine's food into Jack's bowl and had to snatch it away from him before he ate her medicine. I spilled Old Horse's grain onto the barn floor, and groused at Thelma for leaving a rabbit head—*Godfather* style—on the porch.

Chores finally done, Jack and I began our evening walk while the sun sank behind the trees lining the creek. The filtered light softened the ground below it, while a robin sang cheerfully above us.

I looked up and grumbled, "What are you so happy about?"

I called Jack to me and flopped down on my sitting stone once we arrived at the creek.

"I'm sorry, bud. I know I'm a mess."

Jack sat down beside me and leaned against my shoulder. He lay his head on my neck and kissed the bottom of my chin. My eyes filled, and he began to lick the tears from my face.

"Okay, Mr. Wonderful. I gotta get my head together and snap out of this." Jack thumped his tail, turned to pick up his bunny toy, and dropped it in my lap. I knew he probably just wanted me to throw it for him, but I swear it felt like he was trying to cheer me up. I couldn't keep going on like this—not sleeping, drinking more, grumping around. I couldn't bring George back, I couldn't bring Chris back, and I couldn't do anything about Tyler beyond beefing up my security. But I could still do something about Cisco.

I stood up and took a deep breath. "Bud, we need to go back to Tom's; it's that simple." I began walking fast back to the house. Tom had to be the link, he had to be, no matter what he'd said earlier. Jack beat me back to the house, after chasing a squirrel up a tree and then lifting his leg in victory.

Full of resolve, I locked up the house, loaded up Jack, and drove to Tom's. I had called and texted several times, but had to leave messages saying: "I hope you don't mind, but I'm going to drop by tonight...." I figured he didn't answer because he was out doing the chores or had run into town for dinner.

At the last minute I pulled into a Piggly Wiggly market and bought a cake from the bakery. It seemed nicer than just showing up with a lot of questions. I'd gone over and over the questions in my head as I drove—where did he sell most of his dogs, who could I talk to that wouldn't be upset about being questioned . . . ?

The house was dark when I pulled up. Tom's car wasn't in the driveway, and there was no sign of activity around the yard. The dogs in the K9 kennels barked, low and fierce. Jack had begun whining when we turned into the driveway, no doubt anticipating working sheep. I let Jack out of the truck and knocked on the front door. Maybe somebody was home? Maybe watching TV? No answer.

I walked around the side and knocked on the back door. Jack was sniffing around, lifting his leg on anything vertical until I stopped him from peeing on the petunias. No sign of life from inside the house, except the incessant barking of the dogs in the kennels to our right. I realized I heard nothing from the other side of the facility, so I walked toward the barn and the kennels that had held the sheepdogs in for training.

The empty kennels looked forlorn. All the dogs had gone back to their owners or found homes. I was glad they had, but it felt bittersweet at best. The end of an era.

I wondered about the sheep and walked out toward the pastures to see if they were still there. A horizontal line of tiny blue lights was shining just above the ground at the back of the field—the eyes of the flock. It was dark enough now that I could barely see their shapes, black lumps highlighted by their eyes reflecting off one of the yard lights.

Jack had been right beside me, but when I looked down, he was gone. I called him, figuring he had decided to do a bit of independent herding, but then I heard him barking behind me. He was over by the shed—he must have found the raccoon that he'd sniffed out the week before.

"That's enough, Jack," I said.

Jack behaved as if he hadn't heard me. If anything, his barks got faster, louder. This time he wasn't inside the shed, he was beside it, barking into the woods. Perfect raccoon habitat. I walked over, trying to keep it together. I was tired and frustrated, but I didn't want to take it out on Jack. I took a breath and went closer.

"Jack, come on, bud. It's just a raccoon. Let's go." As I walked toward him he turned and ran back to me, his barks high-pitched and frantic. He looked straight into my eyes as he barked. Then he turned back to the woods, raised his head, and howled.

I got goose bumps. But then, howls often do that to me. An owl answered, maybe a great horned.

"What? What is it, Jack?" Jack gave me one last look, his eyes frantic, and dashed straight into the woods, disappearing in seconds into the dark. I could hear him charging through the underbrush, getting farther and farther away.

"SHIT. SHIT, SHIT, SHIT," I yelled." The last thing I wanted to do was follow Jack on some stupid-ass goose chase into the woods after a raccoon. But what if he'd smelled a bobcat? A bear or a cougar was highly unlikely, but not impossible. Any of those could hurt Jack, badly. Maybe kill him. I started to panic. What if I lost Jack, along with everything else?

Hold it together, Maddie. This is no time for a panic attack. I forced myself to breathe slower and deeper, not easy since I was running to the truck to get my flashlight. I shrieked into the night when I couldn't find it, tossing food wrappers and other trash out of the cab onto the gravel. I finally uncovered it lying under some old jackets. I grabbed it, sick with fear, and ran back into the woods where Jack had disappeared.

Running through woods into the narrow light beam of a

flashlight is a surreal experience, like running through a tunnel in a nightmare. What's lighted appears otherworldly; everything else is pitch dark. I couldn't hear Jack at all anymore and had no idea where to run. I stopped and screeched, "JACK! JACK!"

Suddenly, there was Jack, right in front of me. He ran toward me barking, looking straight into my eyes, and then turned and began running back into the woods. "Jack! Wait!" I called. He stopped and looked back at me. He stayed still until I caught halfway up, and then turned and began loping away.

Jack was trying to lead me somewhere; you didn't need a PhD in animal behavior to figure that out. I followed him as best I could, getting swiped in the face by tree branches, slashed by raspberry thorns, burrs sticking to my jacket. I followed him for an hour. Or, maybe it was five minutes that felt like an hour. One or the other. I got a stitch in my side and my lungs were on fire.

And then, suddenly, astoundingly, there was Cisco, licking Jack's face through a thick wire fence, both dancing with joy. Cisco was in a makeshift kennel, set between two huge walnut trees, the ground beneath packed hard by his pacing. Jack was whining short, little sobbing sounds. I was crying before I got to the cage.

"Oh my God, Cisco! Cisco!" I ran to him, gasping, and sat down beside Jack. I tried to pet him, touch him, love him, but only the tips of my fingers could reach through the heavy-duty wire mesh.

He licked my fingers. "Cisco, Cisco, oh my God. You ARE alive. I knew it, I knew it. Oh my sweet boy." I turned to Jack. "You found him! You found him!" I covered him with hugs he barely tolerated, trying as he was to dig under the fencing that enclosed Cisco.

Was that why Jack was barking toward the guard dog and

the corner of the shed when we'd been here earlier? Perhaps he caught a whiff, just a vague sense of Cisco's scent? The wind must have shifted to bring Cisco's scent blindingly obvious to Jack this time.

But what was Cisco doing here? In Tom's backyard? Behind the place where Tom trains K9s like Cisco. What the hell?

While my mind swirled, I got up to open the gate to let Cisco out. It had a padlock on it. I walked around the cage, maybe five by five feet. It had six-foot posts sunk into the ground, super strong fencing on the sides and over the top. Someone had dug the fencing partway into the ground; you could see where Cisco had tried to dig his way out but ran into wire and gave up. Some of the wires on the side of the cage were bent; it looked like he'd tried to climb out after digging but failed. There was a plastic igloo-like doghouse in one corner, every edge ragged from chewing. There was an automatic water bottle attached to one side, the kind that a dog can lick and get water from. It was half full.

I turned my attention to Cisco, who was now sitting attentively, his eyes never leaving my face. He looked to be in pretty good shape—dirty, but seemingly well fed—with one heartbreaking exception. Cisco had on an electric collar, the kind that shocks a dog when he barks. My flashlight highlighted angry, red lesions under the collar around his neck. No wonder he'd been silent when Jack and I were making so much noise. Lord knows how many times he'd barked for help, and received what must have been brutal shocks for doing so.

"Don't worry, bud. I'll get you out." Cisco lay down, put his head on his paws, and thumped his tail. Jack was digging on the outside of the cage. I started to stop him but figured there was no point.

I walked around the cage again. It looked strong enough to hold a bear. I scrabbled up one side, using the adjacent walnut tree for purchase. Maybe I could get the top off? I tried prying the wires apart, ripping cuts in my fingers in the process. It soon became clear that I couldn't get Cisco out without tools. Every edge of the fencing was secured with strong wire. The padlock on the gate wasn't an option, it was the old-fashioned kind with a dial that required knowing the combination. I'd have to cut through the wire.

Which meant leaving Cisco and searching the barn at H & H, where, it occurred to me in a flash, Tom might now be home. Tom—George's best friend, the guy I had totally trusted? Who had kidnapped Cisco and was basically torturing him in a cage hidden in the woods? Why he would do that was beyond me, but I stopped myself from thinking about it. The hell with everything else; what I had to do now was get Cisco out.

I needed tools. I had to go back to the barn and find a bolt cutter. You can't live in the country without one, so I knew that Tom had to have one somewhere. But what if Tom was home now? What if he came home while I was looking? And going back to the facility meant leaving Cisco, which felt unbearable.

If only I had my phone with me! I could call the cops from here. I could've kicked myself for not having it on me. But my phone was in the truck, and it probably wouldn't have had service in the woods anyway. I shook off thinking about it and steeled myself to walk away from Cisco.

"Hey, bud. We have to go find something to get you out." I said this with tears streaming down my face while I crouched down to Cisco's level. I stretched my fingers through the wire mesh again, and Cisco licked them. Jack began whining.

"I'm coming back. I promise."

Cisco let out a quiet whimper as I turned to go, and instantly his entire body startled, one quick shake that told me his shock collar must have been set on high. He lay down, his eyes liquid misery.

Leaving him was the hardest thing I've ever done. I know what it is like to be trapped and running out of hope. I know what it's like to hear someone walk away.

I began running, finding a lightly-used trail that ran parallel to the way I had run on the way in. I called Jack and told him to "heel up." I chanted, *"Get Cisco out. Get Cisco out,"* as I ran, my lungs burning and my legs tiring. I was no longer scared. Or angry. Somehow those emotions had morphed into a white-hot focus that left no room for anything but determination. Adrenaline is an amazing thing.

Jack and I dashed down the path, scattering birds who had roosted for the night in the small trees around us. They chattered in protest as they flew off their perches, startling me until I realized what they were. *"Get Cisco out. Get Cisco out."* I mouthed each word in time with each step, until we reached the edge of the woods and the back of the shed.

It occurred to me later that the smart thing to do would have been to run to the truck, drive into cell range, and call the police. But *Get Cisco out!* had become a mantra that overwhelmed everything else. I could no more drive away than I could have stopped my own heart from beating.

It was pitch black and silent in the barn, except for my ragged breathing and the scurry of surprised rodents. I told Jack to lie down and stay, and scanned the flashlight around the barn until I found an area full of tools. I saw fence post pounders, hand saws, loppers—surely this would be where the bolt cutters would be? I grabbed a huge wrench, but thought better of it and tossed it to the ground. I passed up the chain saw and some smaller shears—too much or too little. The seconds were turning into minutes, and twice I stopped moving because I heard a noise that could've been Tom's car turning off the highway.

Finally, after what felt like an eternity, I found some bolt cutters hanging under some wire panels on the back side of the barn. I snatched them up, called Jack, and ran back into the woods, my heart thumping, chanting, "Please, please, please..."

We ran back down the path. The bolt cutters felt like they weighed fifty pounds. My focus was wavering, and I became consumed with fear that Cisco would be gone when we got to his cage. I tripped on a tree root and hit the ground hard, my head smacking into a rock. Jack stopped and ran back to me, staring at me as I rose into a sitting position.

"Shit," I said too loudly. Then I got quiet, worried I'd give myself away if there was anyone out there who might try to stop me. Who that would be, or where, I couldn't imagine, but the woods felt dangerous now, like when the music changes in a movie. I could feel something wet on the side of my forehead; my fingers confirmed it was blood. I felt nothing; adrenaline is the body's perfect painkiller. I had dropped the light, but found it easily enough in the brush. I got up and started running again, panting so hard I imagined it could be heard for miles.

Finally, when the stitch in my side felt like a knife, there was Cisco, spinning circles in his cage, while Jack ran up ahead of me and whined at the gate.

The bolt cutters made quick work of the wire mesh, but I had to tell Cisco to stay until the hole was big enough to prevent him from being scratched. As I worked, he lay obediently on the other side, but his jaw chattered with excitement. Finally, I dropped the tool and stretched open the wire as much as I could. I said "Okay," and Cisco crawled through, while Jack danced beside me. Once free, Cisco threw himself at me, knocking me over onto my back, while I laughed and cried and rubbed him all over.

I gave us a minute to celebrate, all three of us keening high-pitched expressions of joy, and then stood up quickly. Time to get out of here.

I said, "Heel up!" to Jack, hoping Cisco would get the message and stay close. It occurred to me that he might run off, but the leashes were in the truck, and we had to make a run for it. We wouldn't have won any awards for precision, but both dogs stayed close enough. As we moved through the beam of light surrounded by pitch black, my heart was beating so hard I could feel it hitting my ribs.

Now the trail felt endless again, and every step was a step that increased the chance that Tom would come home. Tom, who, like Tyler, had seemed like such a nice guy. The kind it never occurred to you not to trust.

Finally, we reached the edge of the woods and could see the shadow of the barn backlit by the barnyard light. I put my hand down, palm backward to tell the dogs to stand still, and checked out the barnyard and house. Nothing. Still quiet.

I began to run to the truck when I heard a car turn off the highway onto the gravel driveway.

"Dogs! Run." It was an idiotic thing to say. Neither dog had any idea what "run" meant. But Cisco and Jack needed no encouragement. They sped up beside me and were halfway to the truck when I saw car lights shining through the trees, about to make the turn into the yard.

"Jack, truck up!" I yelled, as I panted behind him. Jack made it to the truck, Cisco beside him, as the car turned the corner and drove by me into its parking spot. I could see Tom and Joan's faces highlighted by the yard light. They looked stunned.

I reached the truck as Tom leapt out of the car and ran toward me. "Up!" I shouted to the dogs as I opened the door to the cab. Jack leapt in and Cisco followed. I piled in behind them, the dogs squashed on the bench seat, eyes like pancakes. I locked the door on my side, and started the engine. Tom got to the truck and tried to open the door beside me, yelling something I couldn't hear. His face was inches from mine; it was contorted with anger. He ran around the front of the truck to try the door on the passenger side.

I hit the gas and almost ran him over. I might have, if he'd stayed in front of the truck for another half of a second. I wouldn't have cared. But he had sprinted around the side toward the passenger's door, and made the turn just as the truck lunged forward. Gravel flew out from underneath the tires, spraying Tom and slowing him down as he ran toward his car. I turned in a tight circle back toward the highway. The dogs scrambled to keep their balance on the seat beside me. I glanced quickly in both directions, then pulled onto the highway as fast as I could.

I turned on the lights and wondered if Tom was going to chase after me. What would I do if he did? No doubt he could overtake me; his Toyota could outrun my old truck in a minute. I punched down the accelerator and felt the truck surge forward. Sixty-five. Seventy. Seventy-five. The chassis began shaking.

Lights appeared far behind me, but coming up fast. It had to be Tom, in a much faster vehicle than mine. Steering with my left hand, I dug under Cisco's belly for my cell phone with my right. I grabbed it just as Cisco lost his balance when we swerved around a tight curve. The phone was knocked onto the floor. Out of reach.

Shit. As we rounded the curve, I spotted an abandoned supper club on my right; you can find them scattered outside any small town in the Midwest. I swerved off the road under a faded sign that said JERRY'S, driving behind the building where I'd be out of sight from the road. The truck bounced so high through the potholes that Cisco fell off the seat onto the floor and the cake I'd bought tumbled out of its cardboard container onto him.

I stopped, turned off the lights, and reached for the phone, now partly covered in icing. I punched in the security code, and hit 911, terrified there'd be no cell service.

"911. What is your emergency?" I got through! A miracle.

"I'm being chased. I'm on County Road MM, a few miles north of Watertown. He kidnapped my dog and I found him, the dog I mean, and the guy is following me and I'm hiding behind an old supper club called Jerry's." This all came out as if the entire sentence was one word.

"Okay. Are you in danger right now?"

"Yes. I don't know, possibly. Probably. I've pulled off the highway, behind Jerry's old supper club."

I saw lights speed down the highway on the other side of the building. It had to be Tom; this road never had much traffic. I had to find a better place to hide, he'd circle back soon enough when he couldn't find me. I told the dogs to hang on and drove back to the highway, going in the other direction.

"I can hear you moving, where are you now?" the 911 dispatcher asked.

"I've turned out of Jerry's and am now going north on MM. I'll find a place to hide off the road. But please send help. This isn't just about a dog. There was a murder. Two actually, and this might be related. Contact Detective Garcia in Milwaukee, she'll fill you in." I gave her my name and license plate number. She asked me to repeat myself; I was still talking at the speed of light.

"Okay," she said. "I'm contacting the sheriff now. Stay on the line. Can you do that?"

"Yes, but I might lose service, so send someone as soon as you can," I said as I drove, passing the entrance to H & H, slowing down to look for a place to pull off and hide beyond it.

Cisco crawled back up onto the seat as I slowed to find a place to wait for help. Jack stayed on the floor, mouth clenched shut, eyes huge. He had cake and icing smeared all over his face.

"Okay," I said. "I see a driveway on the west side of the road, fire number 37904 on a cedar post. I'm turning in. I'll stay close to the road so I still have service."

I drove in, reversed direction in case I needed to drive away fast, and turned the key. Silence, except for the trill of crickets and the heavy breathing of three agitated mammals. Jack was still huddled on the floor, but Cisco's face was more relaxed. He turned and licked my face. If I didn't know better, I'd say he was grinning. K9s are chosen, after all, for toughness under pressure. If he could've talked, I swear he would have said, "This is fun."

"Okay, Tom Cruise, let's look at you more carefully while we wait."

I set the phone down carefully, on speaker, and turned to take off Cisco's electric anti-bark collar. It was tightly attached and I had to pull it tighter in order to release the buckle. Cisco's eyes widened.

"I'm sorry, bud. Hang in there."

The contact points of the collar, little silver knobs, were buried into the lesions in Cisco's neck. Finally, the collar released and I was able to get it off his neck. He shook his head and licked my face again. I was about to throw it out the window in disgust, but realized it was evidence. I tossed it on the cab's floor, telling the operator what I was doing.

"Oh man," she said. "I love dogs. I have a Labrador named Bernie. Who would do that to a dog?" We talked about her dog for a few minutes—her to keep me on the line, me to keep from going crazy. Finally, I heard the undulating whine of a cop car coming from the north.

"I hear sirens," I told her. "Tell the sheriff I'll turn on my lights now and blink them."

Soon the lights from a cop car blinded all three of us. I started to get out, thought better of it, and rolled down my window as a white-blond, six-foot deputy sheriff, tricked out in all the gear, walked toward us. She rested one hand on a black leather pouch on her belt, came to the window, and said, "What's all this about?"

"How long do you have?" I answered.

CHAPTER 27

I tried to summarize things as quickly as I could: Cisco's story and the two murders; Garcia's suggestion that the deaths might be related.

I added: "I can take you to the cage the dog was in, but I don't think we should go in there without backup. He has a lot of guns, and Tom looked . . ." I wasn't sure how to describe his face when he pounded on my window. Scary seemed lame.

"Possibly violent."

While the deputy and I were talking, Cisco had visibly withdrawn from the face at the window and his ears began to flatten.

"Hey, bud." I put my hand on Cisco's chest and rubbed the soft fur under his neck. I could feel a growl generating in his chest. I rubbed my hand in a slow circle on his silky chest as I explained what had happened.

"Pretty dog," she said after I finished the story. "Thanks for keeping him away from me, though. Got bitten when I was five."

"Oh man, I'm sorry," I said, knowing how traumatic dog bites can be.

"Okay," she said as she turned to go back to her car. "I'm calling in another unit. Stay in your vehicle."

She left, talking into her radio, and then sat in her patrol car. I sat and stroked Cisco. He kept licking my face while I talked to Jack, who was still on the floor.

"Hey, bud. It's okay now." I leaned over to pet Jack where he loved it most, that sweet little channel between a dog's eyes. He closed them and leaned into my hand. I alternated between petting him—his body tense, but starting to loosen up, and Cisco, who was relaxing without an unfamiliar face staring at him through the window.

Fifteen minutes later another patrol car pulled up. Two guys got out and went over to talk to the deputy. The tall one, with a pock-marked face, came over, introduced himself as Sheriff Rasken, and asked for my driver's license.

"Has someone contacted Detective Garcia yet?" I asked, wondering if the sheriff could hear Cisco growling at him. I thought not; I could barely hear it myself. But I could feel the tension in Cisco's body. The growling got louder.

Great. Now I was sandwiched between two frightened, aroused canines and an armed man, all trained to react at the speed of light to a potential threat—whatever it was, instantly and without warning. I blew out a breath and turned my head toward the dogs. As charged up as I was, I needed to defuse the energy radiating out from the dogs.

"Hey, boys. It's okay. We're good," I said. I reached out to pet the dogs, but couldn't get to Jack without scrambling over Cisco.

I pretty much fell in love with the sheriff when he said, looking at Cisco, "Poor guy. He must have been through a lot. I had a shepherd just like him." He paused and looked more carefully at Cisco, who looked back with a tight mouth.

"Are those wounds on his neck from this place here?"

"Yes," I answered. "From an anti-bark collar that was too tight and set on high. The dog probably got wet when it rained and it made things even worse. It's on the floor under the Border collie." He leaned closer to get a look. Cisco growled. I had to intervene or things were going to get ugly. You just never want your dog to bite a cop.

"I'm so sorry, but could you back away from the window just a little bit?" I asked. "This dog has been to hell and back, and I can't really do much but try to protect him right now."

He backed up immediately. I would've married him then and there if he'd asked. The percentage of men who did what I requested around a growling dog was small. "Oh, I'm not afraid," they say, while I suppress the urge to answer, "Yeah, but he is and you're not helping."

I said, "Thanks for backing up. That detective I asked about, Garcia? She's the Milwaukee detective who is working on the murders I told you about. Has she been contacted yet? She told me to get ahold of her if anything happened."

"Yup, I heard she's on her way. Okay, I'm going over to this training camp. Normally I'd ask you to stay here for more questioning, but we need you to take us to where the dog was held. You okay with that?" I nodded yes. I wanted to say no.

He turned away and got into the driver's seat. Both patrol cars pulled onto the highway. I followed them the half mile back to Tom's.

I parked behind them as all three walked to the house and knocked on the door. Tom opened the door, with Joan behind him. I couldn't hear what Tom said, but in spite of looking worried, he looked like the friendly man I had always known. Or thought I had. Everyone disappeared into the house, except the deputy who stood outside the door, glancing in my direction every few minutes. Cisco licked the icing off Jack's face. Ten minutes went by. Then twenty.

Finally, Rasken came over and explained that Tom had told them the dog was his. I was the one who had kidnapped him.

"That's ridiculous." I wanted to scream it, but kept my voice calm and low.

"First," I said, keeping my voice measured, "you saw his neck. That's animal abuse. Second, he was hidden in a cage—padlocked!—in the woods with that shock collar on. If it's his dog, why did he hide him? And why didn't he claim him at the shelter, instead of breaking into my home, almost killing my guard dog with fentanyl, and stealing him? I called him several times to help me figure out where the dog came from and to find his owner. He never once said it was his dog. It's insane that he says Cisco is his." My voice was calm, but my stomach was a soggy ball of paper, tight as a fist.

He turned and looked toward the house and said, "Let me get this straight. The dog was at your house. . . ."

I interrupted, and summarized Cisco's story as quickly as I could.

"Did you file a report when he disappeared?"

Thank heavens I had. "Yes, you can contact Sheriff . . ." I put my hands to my head. Too many sheriffs.

"Wallenberg! Sheriff Wallenberg. Dodd County. Contact him. Garcia knows about it too."

"Okay. Let me take some photos of the dog's neck, and then I'll need to see this cage you're talking about."

Cisco's neck got photographed without too much trouble while he sat in the middle of the bench seat in the cab. Jack had curled up in a ball and was pretending to sleep on the truck's floor. I got out and walked around to the passenger side, opened the door, and sat down beside Jack.

"Hey, bud. It's all good. We're all gonna be fine. I've got your bromance boy back, right?" Jack's mouth relaxed a bit while he thumped his tail.

After I rolled the windows up enough to keep the dogs in—thank heavens it was night and not too hot—I asked the big, blond deputy—she never did say her name—to stand by the truck.

"Don't let anyone near these dogs. Promise me. I swear I'd die if I came back and they were gone." I didn't say that she would too, because I'd kill her with my bare hands if she let anything happen to them.

I took Rasken and a deputy down the trail to the cage. This time we had powerful torches to light the way. I showed them where I'd cut through to get Cisco out, and reflexively started to pick up the bolt cutters that I'd thrown to the ground. They told me to leave them there.

Rasken took photos of it, and the cage, from at least ten different angles.

When we got back, there was another car parked beside mine in the lot. Garcia was standing beside the deputy, peering into my truck.

"Garcia!" I yelled from at least fifty yards away, not wanting her to set Cisco back any worse than he had been already.

She turned and began walking toward me. I never thought I'd be so relieved to see a cop again.

I practically ran toward her. "Dr. McGowan," she said. Her face looked neutral, but there was some look in her eyes that I couldn't read.

"Why did you come here tonight?" she asked. It was an accusation more than a question. I instantly felt guilty.

"Because of what you said! It's not me that's the link between everything that's happened, except that I'm a link to Cisco. Cisco links to Tom, who trains dogs like Cisco. I thought about it all night long and came out to talk to Tom. I thought a dog he sold must have been resold to drug dealers in Chicago. But then Jack ran into the woods and we found Cisco when I went to find him."

I ran my hands through my hair. "I thought Tom was a good guy. I still can't believe that he'd kidnap Cisco." I didn't say anything about Tom's face when he ran to confront me. His eyes were as cold as a dog I met once whose owner said, "He'd kill you if I let him." I believed her. I was glad they were talking to Tom and Joan in the house. I never wanted to see him again.

"Okay. Deputy Waylon will take a full statement from you. Then you can go ahead and take the dog back to your place. I talked to Dodd County and your report about the break-in and burglary has been confirmed. I'll take it from here. But, don't go anywhere, and expect to talk to us again tomorrow."

I turned to the deputy, who was looking down at her phone. We sat in her car as she asked me question after question, many I'd already answered. I stayed as patient as I could until she finally told me I could go home.

Garcia called after me as I walked back to the truck: "Next time, maybe call us first before flying off half-cocked?" For a moment, I thought I saw something like amusement in her eyes. Probably just the yard light.

I saluted like a soldier and got into the truck.

"Okay, boys. We're going home."

I didn't call anyone when I got home. It was too late. I was too tired. After I put some ointment on Cisco's neck, I checked on Bo Peep, let the dogs have a last pee, and settled down in front of the TV.

By three a.m. I'd gone through four episodes of *House* and two shots of Johnnie Walker, with Jack and Cisco sprawled on the rug next to the couch. Clementine snored on the big chair in the corner. I thought about going upstairs and getting into bed, but it seemed like too much work.

I woke up to light streaming through the windows, stiff from sleeping on an old, lumpy couch. Both dogs opened their eyes as soon as I looked at them, but it seemed that they had stayed near the couch the rest of the night.

I took them out, fed the house critters, and treated Cisco's wounded neck. The sores weren't infected, a relief, but I didn't like the way one of them looked—deeper and redder than the others. I'd call the vet clinic when it opened. Then I called Dorothy.

She whooped with joy when I told her that I'd found Cisco. And gasped when I told her where.

"Are you FUCKING KIDDING ME? Tom? I can't believe that. Tom? Why the hell would he have stolen Cisco? This makes NO sense. None." I could hear puppies play fighting in the background while I used one hand to make coffee in my fancy-ass De'Longhi.

"I thought he was a good guy, too," I added. "But apparently, I am incapable of reading people like I read dogs. I don't know who I can trust anymore. Are you going turn on me now?"

"Ha! Fat chance," Dorothy said. "Listen, what matters now is that you've got Cisco back. But still, why would he end up at Tom's? Unless Tom is working with the cartel? What if he sold Cisco to them?"

"Maybe. But why would drug dealers need a sniffer dog?" I asked. "It's not like their drugs are going to get up and disappear in the woods or something. Or try to hide in a warehouse where the people can't find them. I mean, really, can you imagine? 'Uh, boss, it seems I misplaced a ton of cocaine. Sorry. Just can't remember where I put it. Do we have a dog who could find it?'"

We both pondered that for a moment. Jack licked himself while Cisco stared at Thelma. No one can win a staring contest with a cat, and Cisco finally turned his head away and scratched his neck with a back paw. Every dog in the world, even dogs with the gravitas of a German shepherd like Cisco, looks like a goofy cartoon character in this posture. I smiled as Thelma threw up her tail in victory and walked out of the room.

Dorothy said: "What if there was another gang who had some drugs they wanted to steal?" "Maybe," I said, trying to think of all the ways a trained drug dog could help people in the business of selling illegal ones. Then it struck me. "Wait! What if they got a dog to figure out how to fool detection dogs? You know, how you could hide drugs so that a dog couldn't find them?"

"Good luck with that," said Dorothy. We both knew that trained sniffer dogs have noses so good they've found three-thousand-year-old bones buried deep underground.

"But wait, your idea could make sense!" Dorothy said. "They wouldn't necessarily know how good a trained dog's nose is, would they? Most people can't imagine it." I thought of a client who was sure that wrapping a steak in plastic wrap would keep his dog from smelling it on the counter.

Dorothy added: "Is this crazy? Are we even making any sense?"

"Got me. I just wish Chris were here to ask." My throat started to close after saying his name. I physically yearned to have his arms around me. Then I thought of George too, and looked at the photograph of him, me, and Jack on the wall. I wanted to take it down and hold it against my heart.

"Okay, look, Maddie. You've gotta call that detective and tell her what you think. And would you please call Vince, fill him in, and ask him to come over? What if the dealers hear about Cisco and Tom and come after you? They killed Chris for God's sake."

I couldn't answer. Maybe they should just kill me too, if my search for Cisco is what got him killed. Tears started streaming down my face.

"Maddie?" Dorothy said, after the line had gone silent while I tried to breathe.

"Listen, girl," Dorothy continued, "whatever is going on, you having Cisco again puts you back in danger. But, at least this takes Tyler out of the picture, right? All this has to do with drugs and drug dogs. Tyler skipping his probation check-ins is just a coincidence."

I got my breath back and managed, "Uh huh."

Dorothy continued. "Call the detective, and then call Vince right away. Or . . . do you want to bundle up the dogs and come up here for a while?"

I told her I was too tired, said we'd talk again soon.

I rallied and left messages for both detectives, asking them to call me back. I got Vince on the first ring, who said "Hallelujah!" that Cisco was alive and back, and "What the . . . ?!!" about Tom. He asked if he and Liam could come to celebrate." I wanted to say no, I was still gassed from the long night, but didn't want to be rude. I said "sure," but I wouldn't be able to chat for long. After we hung up, I went out to walk the dogs and take care of the barn animals. The guys pulled into the driveway just as I went back inside to clean up a little. I knew Vince wouldn't care if my house was trashed, but I didn't know his son all that well. I put away the bottle of Johnnie Walker, which had been sitting out on the kitchen table, squared my shoulders, and went out to greet them.

CHAPTER 28

Cisco was crated in the mudroom, but Jack greeted Vince as if relieved, sidling up against his legs, looking up and grinning. Liam busied himself saying hello to Clementine, who had woken up enough to limp over and say hello.

After we sat down in the kitchen, I poured them some coffee and apologized for not having anything else to offer them. I joked that I could go out to the truck and scrape up the cake that had flown around the cab the night before. We had a good laugh, and then Vince said, "Okay. Tell us: What happened last night? How did you find Cisco? Is he okay?"

"Mostly, but he's got sores on his neck. I'll have the vet check him out this afternoon, but I think they'll heal soon. But he's had a setback about strangers. It's back to square one teaching him strangers are okay."

Liam said: "Happy to help if you'd like. I'll be here for another week before I have to go back to work." Vince turned his face toward him, his eyebrows raising a fraction of an inch, then quickly looked back at his coffee cup. Something shifted in the air, catching me off guard. It took me a few seconds to answer.

"Thanks. We can set up some conditioning sessions after things settle down."

"Soooo, what the hell happened?" Vince asked. "What did you do to find Cisco?"

"I didn't find him, really. Jack did." I described the events as best I could—going to Tom's, Jack finding Cisco, driving away in a panic.

Vince rubbed his face with his hands. Liam shook his head as if it was all too much to take in. I pulled my hand down from my head; my fingers were getting tangled in the hair I'd been twirling.

We all looked out the window as Uncle Bert the Stud Duck chased Martha across the yard, her wings flapping while she squawked throaty quacks of protest.

"There's something else," I said quietly, picking at an old scratch in the table. "My ex-husband might be a suspect now that he's dodged his probation officer."

Vince's face rose out of his hands as he looked up at me. "Jail? He was in jail?"

I gave a tiny shrug. "Yeah. He was abusive." Vince and Liam both stared at me, their faces frozen. "To me," I added, needlessly.

"Oh hell, Maddie, I didn't know that," Vince said. He reached out his hand and rested it beside mine on the table.

"Yeah, well, I don't talk about it much." Jack had been lying at my feet in a patch of sun; I smooched to get him up so that I could pet him. You could hear the baby wrens cheep as a parent came back to feed them.

"Garcia, the detective, thought he might have something to do with the murders, but the good news is—if any of this could be good news—it looks unlikely they had anything to do with Tyler. It's probably all about Tom and illegal drugs, although I still can't imagine Tom being involved in any of this. Much less murder."

As I spoke, I wondered why, if my ex was out of the picture, I'd brought him up to begin with.

Everything started feeling a little too close.

"So, thanks for coming over!" I said with too much enthusiasm. "I promised Dorothy I'd let you know what is going on. The cops are worried about the drug connection, and told me to be on alert. And then, although it's probably meaningless, there's this thing about Tyler." As I stood up I rubbed my hands together, as if to wipe it all away.

Liam leaned forward and said, "Maddie, maybe one of us should sleep on the porch for a few nights?"

My head withdrew, as if my answer physically pushed me backward. "Oh no, really, no. Thanks, but that's crazy. I've got the dogs, the security camera, a rifle in the cellar, and a Glock in the bedroom."

Vince raised his eyebrows.

"But, if you'd check on Bo Peep and Clementine when I'm at work today, that'd be great. I'm taking the boys with me. I'm not leaving them here." Vince stood up and put his hand on my shoulder and assured me they'd be over often. They said good-bye to the dogs, turned away and walked to the truck. Liam was taller than Vince, thinner, a little lanky. Jack didn't take his eyes off him until he closed the door on the truck, then turned to me and looked straight at me. I had no idea what he was trying to say.

I called the vet clinic and made an appointment for Cisco late that afternoon. I packed up the dogs, drove to my office, and settled them in a back room. I tried to focus on the clients for the day: A Lab cross who wasn't trustworthy around a three-year-old child. A Boston terrier who bit if you tried to trim his nails. A brown mix of a thing who killed a neighbor's cat when it wandered into the yard.

I hope I helped them; I barely remembered what I told them. I wrote the notes up as best I could, then checked my phone for a message from Vince or Garcia. Vince had texted that all was well when he'd driven by. Liam had even camped out on the porch for a few hours and seen nothing suspicious. Nothing yet from Garcia, or anyone else from law enforcement.

I left the office as soon as I could, eager to get Cisco to the vet and back home. I gave Cisco enough treats to feed a pack of wolves at the clinic; he came through with only a stiff body and big eyes when the vet first put her hands by his neck. The vet shaved the worst areas, cleaned them up, gave us antibiotic cream, and instructions to keep the area clean and dry. Cisco went home with a belly full of dried liver. I went home in a truck that smelled like dog farts.

Soon after I got home, Liam drove up and asked again if I wanted someone to stay over with me. I thanked him and declined, again. He seemed like a nice guy, but then, that's what I thought when I met Tyler. And Tom.

What I needed was to curl up with the dogs and forget about the rest of the world for a while. I skipped dinner after the chores and slept on the couch again.

Sometime in the middle of the night, I was yanked from sleep by the sound of Bo Peep's barking. That usually doesn't wake me up. Bo Peep barks off and on at night all the time, that's her job. *Don't you dare, coyotes!* But this was different. Her barks alternated between deep, low-pitched notes and higher, almost desperate ones. Something was happening that was out of the ordinary. I leapt up off the couch as Jack and Cisco joined Bo Peep' chorus, barking at the window so furiously that spittle flew out of their mouths. A car was pulling up toward the house, its lights blinding me temporarily as it turned toward the window. What the hell? I could count on one hand the number of unexpected visitors who have driven the length of my rutted driveway. Usually I greet unexpected visitors with curiosity tinged with suspicion. But at three in the morning, it's all about the latter.

I stood frozen for a moment, and then ran to put the dogs into the mudroom, out of danger.

I'd had enough of my dogs being frightened or abused. For a moment all three of us stared at each other, them in their crates, me in the doorway. Cisco was still barking. Jack was looking at me with worried eyes.

I couldn't decide what to do. Call 911? Get a gun? If a gun, the rifle in the cellar, or the Glock upstairs? Immediate action felt best, and the Glock was easier to reach, so I charged up the stairs, my bare feet thudding on the old, wooden steps.

I loaded it quickly, focusing on my breath. In. Out. In. Out. Anything to keep my hands from shaking. I ran back downstairs, clicked off the safety, and peeked out the window. The car sat idling, lights still on. It looked like the driver was still inside, but it was hard to be sure with the headlights shining directly at me. I put down the gun, grabbed my cell phone, and started to dial 911 as I crouched by the window. But then stopped. What would I say? "Help, there's a car in my driveway?"

I picked the phone back up, called 911, gave my name and address, and said: "I might be in danger, might not. Please alert Sheriff Wallenberg that there's an unfamiliar car idling in my driveway, and ask if he could send a car to check on it. He'll know why." I meant to stay on the line, but a wave of fury overtook me. I was sick of feeling like a victim. I hung up the phone before the dispatcher could answer, picked up the gun, and strode out of the house. I knew it was smarter to wait for help. I didn't care.

The car sat idling, a light-colored sedan of some kind. I walked toward it as if in a TV crime drama, as if I knew what I was doing, gun forward, left hand supporting the right. I moved to the right of the headlights, stopped about fifteen feet away, and yelled, "HEY!"

Nothing. I yelled again and walked forward a few steps.

Someone was sitting in the driver's seat, but they weren't looking in my direction. As I got closer it was clear that they weren't looking at all. They were slumped over the wheel, asleep. Or dead. Holy shit.

They didn't stir until I banged on the window with my left hand, gun ready in the right. Slowly, a thatch of yellow hair morphed into a woman's face, eyes scrunched shut, mouth soft and sloppy.

"Whaaa?" drooled out of her mouth. "Justin? Am I late?"

I'd never seen her before in my life. She was drunk. Or, at least, it sounded like it. Maybe there was some other drug involved, but she clearly wasn't capable of doing any harm. I wondered if she needed medical care. I ran back to the house, grabbed the phone again, and called 911. This time I explained that a seemingly drunk or drugged stranger, clearly incapable of driving away, was parked in my yard. Please send a squad car.

I stood beside the fence to the main pasture, where Bo Peep was still barking, and told her it was okay. "Good girl, good girl," I crooned. "You're a good, good guard dog, you are. Good girl."

I stroked her head until the now familiar sound of a siren pulsated from the highway. The approaching squad car bounced over the potholes in the driveway, the flashing lights going up and down festively, as if at a county fair, then screeched to a dramatic halt beside the stranger's car. Sheriff Wallenberg leapt out, right hand on the gun on his hip.

"Maddie?" he asked while keeping his eyes on the woman in the driver's seat. "What's going on?"

"Hell if I know. I have no idea who she is. She just drove up a bit ago, the dogs went crazy, I called 911, and came out to investigate. She was passed out on the steering wheel, so I figured she must be drunk, and called 911 again with an update."

Suddenly, to my horror, and no doubt Wallenberg's, my

body's adrenalin flushed away, and I began to cry. I squatted down to the ground and sobbed into my hands like a little girl.

I could hear him walk over toward me, saw his boots through my fingers as he stood beside me. He squatted down beside me and put his hand tentatively on my shoulder.

"Do you have a friend you could call, Mz. McGowan? I need to get this woman taken care of, but . . . Is there someone I could call for you?"

"I'm okay." I struggled to get the words out. "I'll be fine, really. And thank you." I looked up at him, his Santa Claus belly hiding his belt buckle, his round face looking at me with concern. I stood up, expelled some breaths, and laughed. "Holy shit, I don't know where that came from!

Sorry to make a scene."

"Seems to me you've had a lot going on lately. I heard about that dog that you got back. Is there any chance this woman has anything to do with that?"

"I can't imagine how. Or why. I think she's just a drunk driver who got lost. Happened to my neighbor last year."

Wallenberg helped me to my feet. He asked if I could go back into the house while he dealt with my surprise visitor. I did, watching him through the window as he leaned into the car, sniffed her breath, and fanned his hand in front of his mouth to let me know she'd been drinking. He half carried her out of the car and put her into his squad. She threw up in his backseat. He turned to me and rolled his eyes, made some calls, and came up to the porch. Jack and Cisco went crazy again. I didn't bother asking them to stop.

Over the barking, Wallenberg said they'd send a tow truck out tomorrow to pick up the car and get it out of my way. He added: "You sure you're okay?" I nodded. "And, maybe, stay in the house until one of us gets out here? Garcia told me about you going off on your own to get that dog out. Maybe take a breath and let us do our job?" He did his best to look stern, but I couldn't miss the hint of softness in his eyes. I stood at the door and watched him drive away.

There was no point in trying to go back to sleep; it was almost four and the wren would be starting her high-pitched chatter soon enough. I took the bullets out of the gun and let the boys out of the mudroom for a chance to sniff around outside. They scent marked around the car, with serious looks on their faces, as if they'd been deputized. I watched them while I told Bo Peep again what a good guard dog she was.

I went back in to hang out in the living room; it seemed that Clementine hadn't woken up at all, in spite of three dogs barking their heads off. I got a little worried, went over to check on her. It took a frighteningly long time for me to wake her up, but finally she blinked and licked my hand. I rubbed her pouchy old belly and kissed her muzzle as she went back to sleep. I settled down on the couch for a moment, the boys snoring on the rug, and ended up going back to sleep. I wish I hadn't.

This time the nightmare included a group of men in strange outfits who stood blocking my way home. I tried desperately to tell them that I just wanted to go home, that I wished them no harm, but I couldn't form words in my throat, and nothing came out but wheezes of air. "Police," they said, in unison. "Go back."

There wasn't a cop like Wallenberg in New Mexico. Not the first time I asked for help, when they arrived after I called 911, my jaw aching, my face bloody, after Tyler roundhoused a fist into my face. Tyler opened the door, thanked them for coming, explained that I had been drinking, got nasty, and that he'd had to struggle to keep me from going after him. "You know how they are, Officers," he said, "when they get like that." They all rolled their eyes in synchrony, and one asked, in a flat voice, if I wanted to press charges. I huddled against the kitchen door, mute. Tyler stroked my cheek after they left, said he was sorry, but did I understand why he'd done it? Would I promise to not make eyes at other guys at the bar again? He just loved me so much. . . .

I woke up with Jack and Cisco staring at me, their eyes huge and worried. My guys. I got up and made some coffee, practicing my breathing while memories of those years in New Mexico seeped in like rising flood waters. Pissed that, after years of sound sleep, the nightmares had come back.

I forced myself to focus on the chores, and took a long walk, glad it was a no-client day. I was throwing a load of muck-covered jeans and sweaty T-shirts in the washer when the phone rang.

"Hello, Dr. McGowan? This is Detective Garcia."

"Hello."

"I thought I should let you know that a Milwaukee Police Department detective, Kevin Thompson, is under arrest and is being held in suspicion of the death of Chris Norwood."

CHAPTER 29

"WHAT?" This felt so out of the blue I hardly knew what to think. Kevin, Ryan's friend, killed Chris? I looked at the phone in my hand, as if it was responsible for what I just heard.

"Why? What? What happened?" I spluttered.

"I can't tell you all the details, but I can say it's linked to that dog you rescued. Thomas Hutch's story broke down during questioning about that shepherd, and he finally admitted that he had sold the dog to a drug cartel in Chicago, with Kevin as the intermediary. There is evidence—again, I can't go into any details—that Thompson was the man you saw leaving Mr. Norwood's apartment that night, and it was he who killed Mr. Norwood."

"Holy shit." I sat down. I never liked Kevin, but I didn't expect this.

"But why would the cartel want a drug dog?" I asked.

"Don't know. Maybe they wanted to use him to find ways to hide the scent of drugs from K9s so that they could move it around the country more easily, maybe they wanted to find a competitor's warehouse. My guess is that they didn't know what they were doing, gave up after a while, and just discarded the dog. That's when your friend Chris found him."

"And Tom?" I asked the next obvious question. "What is happening to him?"

"He's out on bail, a pretty hefty one I might add, because it looks as though it was he who broke into your house and kidnapped the dog. He's been charged with burglary, breaking and entering, and dognapping."

I blurted out, "Dognapping? Seriously?"

"Yeah, it's a thing. He'll probably be charged for drugging your guard dog, too, but I don't know what the charge would be for that. Both investigations are ongoing. There are some things that don't add up from what Tom has told us, but I can't say any more. I've told you too much already. But I thought you'd like to know that your ex-husband probably had nothing to do with all this. Maybe it'll ease your mind a bit."

"It does. Thank you."

"I'd still be cautious until all this sorts out, Dr. McGowan. Okay? There's still the cartel; we don't know how involved they are in this."

"Okay. I will. And . . . thanks."

"Uh, wait, does this mean you have any information about who killed George? Was his death related?"

"I'll keep you posted if I have any information I can share." Garcia hung up.

I sat at the table and stared out the window. There were sunflowers starting to bloom along the driveway, the wild kind that line roadways from July to August in the Midwest. Big yellow flowers and blousy green leaves. A flock of goldfinches flew into the elderberry bushes, their bright yellow feathers the color of the flowers. Gold and green, the colors of Wisconsin in late summer. Go Packers.

I called Dorothy and left a message about Kevin. I checked in with Vince and asked him if he'd keep up the surveillance, even though I thought there was less need, now that Tyler was out of the picture and Kevin had been arrested.

The rest of the day went by in a fog. I worked with a Great Dane/collie cross who was terrified of the mailman. I saw a

King Charles Cavalier who, defying all breed descriptions, went after visitors like a junkyard dog. I checked in with clients, including Harpo's owners, Joe and the boys. We confirmed a date for them to come out next week for some training. We could easily start Harpo's training with my dogs at the farm, and I'd be saved a long drive.

After I got home and did the chores, Dorothy and I had time for a long talk, mostly about Kevin. She said, "Ha! See! You were right that that guy is a jerk. But holy shit, there's jerks and there's jerks. I know a lot of them, but no one who has ever killed anybody."

She paused. "At least, not that I know of." Another pause. "Do you think Kevin could have killed George too? Maybe George found out about what Tom and Kevin were doing?"

I'd been wondering the same thing. It was the only explanation for George's death. Did George get wind of what Tom was doing and call him on it? They were business partners, after all. If Tom was doing something dirty it would involve George if it was discovered. Maybe Tom talked to Kevin and Kevin decided to get rid of George?

"That's the only thing I can think of. Tom couldn't have been directly involved in killing George, as much as I hate what he did to Cisco. That just seems impossible."

We hung up, but I couldn't stop thinking about it. I thought of all the nights at sheepdog trials, after we'd run our dogs and the field was dotted with grazing sheep and we watched the stars come out while we told stories and drank beer and ate pie. Pie that Tom had made, and brought over that afternoon, so that he could enjoy the company of George and the rest of the handlers. There was less of that after Joan came onto the scene, but before she did, Tom and George had been so close that some wondered if they were gay.

George couldn't have cared less about the rumors. He liked to tease Tom and say that if he was gay, he wouldn't pick a guy who was as ugly as Tom. He thought it equally funny when talk started that he and I were having a thing.

"Well, now," he'd say. "At least now they think I have good taste!" He'd wink at me and I'd roll my eyes, take another sip of beer.

I just couldn't imagine Tom killing anyone. Kidnapping a dog was horrific in my mind, but still, it was a far cry from murder. Much more likely to have been Kevin.

Except, the next morning, I turned on the TV for the weather report, and heard this: "We have just received information from the Oconomowoc Police Department that a dog trainer . . ." I ran into the living room to see a reporter standing outside H & H, trying to talk over the cacophony of barking dogs. ". . . Thomas Hutch, the co-owner of a facility that trains police dogs, has been arrested as a suspect in the murder of his business partner, George Hughes." I called Dorothy.

"Fuck. That's crazy," she said. "Tom? Seriously? What next?"

We kept talking, repeating ourselves, that we couldn't believe it was Tom who killed George. Granted, I was furious at Tom for what he did to Cisco, not to mention Bo Peep, but I still couldn't imagine him killing his friend George in cold blood. Tom had seemed gutted by George's death; if he was acting, I'd never trust my ability to read faces again. But then, I thought of the shooting range behind his house, and the sharpshooter trophies on his living room wall. And how many times I'd been wrong about men, and that Tom almost killed Bo Peep, and how he'd stolen Cisco right out of my house and lied to me repeatedly. I got angry all over again just thinking about it.

Dorothy and I finally hung up, having exhausted all the ways we could express our shock and outrage. I sat at the table drinking coffee, petting Jack, then Cisco, depending on who got their head under my hand first. "Baaa baaa" drifted through the window; the sheep reminding me it was time to put them out to pasture. Old Horse nickered in response, while the relentless wren warbled while flitting around the bushes behind the house.

"All right, all right, I'll get going," I said to no one in particular.

I called Garcia, left a message. I did the chores and took the boys on an especially long walk. There was a lot of work to do in the office, but thankfully, no clients. I tried to stay busy all day, cleaning up client records, paying bills, vacuuming the carpet, waiting to hear from Garcia. She didn't call—I knew she must be busy, but I was still disappointed. She'd said she'd keep me posted.

I couldn't get Tom out of my mind. Did he or didn't he? I wanted to hear his voice, listen to him defend himself. I couldn't let it go, so I tried calling his cell. I wasn't surprised when it didn't answer. They must have taken it as evidence. But then I remembered the landline number, and called it before I left the office.

Joan answered. "Hello?"

"Joan, it's Maddie. I heard about Tom this morning. I'm so sorry...." I wasn't so sure that I was, but I wanted to hear something, anything, from Tom. If not Tom, Joan was the next best thing. My words were met with silence.

"What happened? Why did they arrest Tom? Is there anything I can do?" I made myself stop; I was talking too fast again.

"Thank you, Maddie, it's good of you to call," Joan answered, her voice hollow. "I'm just as surprised as you are. He was charged, right in front of me, with killing George. First-degree murder, they say, no bail. I guess they found evidence here in the house—they practically ransacked the place—that ties Tom to George's death. They wouldn't tell me what it was, but they took a lot of his guns and ammunition. Along with his computers, his phone, and all of the paper records related to dog sales. I'm not even sure what to do now. We have two dogs ready to go, who are supposed to be shipped to departments out East, and I don't even know where they are supposed to go or who to contact." Her voice began to rise as she talked; I could feel her upset over the phone.

"Do you have a good attorney?" I asked.

"I think so. Our usual lawyer referred us to someone; he might be talking to Tom right now."

"Good. Honestly, Joan, I find it impossible to believe that Tom could have done this." I trailed off for a moment, and then blurted, "Joan? Did you know about Cisco?"

"No! I didn't have a clue! Apparently, things weren't going as well for us as I thought. Tom had sold Cisco to Chicago for double the usual price—fifty-thousand dollars. He took Cisco back in hopes he could sell him for an equal price to another buyer. When he finally had to fess up, he said he had a buyer interested when you came out and ruined the plan." Her voice lowered. "And then, everything went to hell after you came over."

Oh. Was she blaming me for Tom being arrested? But wait, everything went to hell when Kevin was arrested, right? She couldn't possibly blame me for what happened to Tom.

"I won't pretend I'm not upset about Cisco," I said. "And I'm beyond disappointed that Tom got himself mixed up in such a mess. But kill George? I just don't buy it."

She didn't answer right away. "Well . . . none of this makes sense to me either." After we hung up, I sat at my desk for the longest time. I couldn't accept that Tom could have killed George. But then, I couldn't have imagined that he could have kidnapped Cisco either, and hidden him in the woods while trying to sell him again. Tom loved dogs, and how could a dog lover almost kill Bo Peep?

I drove home and did the chores as quickly as possible. Jack and Cisco paddled in the creek's water as I perched on my sitting rock and focused on what I heard around me. Tree limbs squeaking as they rubbed against each other in the breeze. A catbird calling to my left. Cicadas buzzing like a Greek chorus. Jack left the water and came over to lie down beside me. Cisco followed a few minutes later. We stayed there together for an hour, the light softening into a palette of pastels. Then we walked back to the house in silence, linked by a bond deeper than language.

CHAPTER 30

I had a restless night again, giving up on sleep around three, powering up my laptop and watching a colleague's video on treating canine aggression. Aggression seemed to be the story of my life at the moment. So much easier to deal with in dogs. Something I could do something about.

When the sun's rays painted the room golden, I made some coffee, did the chores, and took Jack and Cisco on an extra-long walk.

We crossed over the creek to Vince's field, the dogs tripling the distance traveled by running right and left after interesting scents. I was tired when we got back, but Jack and Cisco were just getting warmed up. Jack was in the best shape of his life—along with working sheep every day, he and Cisco played chase games until they were tripping on their tongues. Overall, he'd seemed to go back to his usual happy-go-lucky self, a big relief. Cisco too looked great: his neck was healed, he'd gained weight and muscled up. But he still needed work to be more comfortable around strangers, especially men. Once inside, I called Vince and asked if he'd have time to come over this morning to help me with Cisco. I'd have the coffee on; he said he'd bring donuts.

He pulled up at ten o'clock, right on time, getting out of the car at the same time that his son did on the other side. Liam pushed a box toward me, a bright pink one from the high-end bakery in Oconomowoc. He said, "I thought you could use some sugar."

He had on a spotless, blue-gray REI shirt that highlighted his eyes, tan corduroys, and a hundred-watt grin. I had on a T-shirt stained with heaven only knows what, over faded jeans decorated with sheep shit.

I took the box, said thank you, and explained what I needed them to do to help Cisco. I gave them each a handful of dried liver treats, and asked them to walk forward, stopping ten feet away in front of Cisco, toss some treats, and then turn and walk away. They each repeated the exercise five times, Cisco learning that approaching men meant good things were about to happen. His body got looser and his belly got fuller with every repetition. We stopped when they got within five feet without the slightest sign of tension from Cisco, having made a lot of progress in one session. Quit while you're ahead.

I put Cisco away in the mudroom and invited the guys in for coffee and donuts. Jack sat at Vince's feet, waiting to be fed from the table, which I knew full well Vince did when I wasn't around.

"Jack, go lie down." Jack gave me a side eye and collapsed in the corner like a disgruntled teenager. He puffed out a sigh, and we all laughed.

Vince asked if I knew anything more about Tom. I shook my head no and said I wished I did. I made quick work of a raspberry-filled, glazed circle of heaven and wiped the sugar off my lips.

"But I think Joan blames me for all this. She sounded cold when we talked, and she said something about me ruining everything. I guess I can't blame her for wanting someone to blame, but surely it should be Kevin." I stared at the box of donuts, forcing myself to put my hands on my lap, under the table. My right arm rose up as if pulled by a puppeteer's string, so I began twisting the lock of hair just above my ear.

"That's crazy," Liam said, in response to Joan's comments. "What were you supposed to do, ignore Cisco in the cage and just walk away?" He pointed to the box of donuts and said, "Have another. They're better fresh."

He picked up his second, a glazed cruller, and took a huge bite. He smiled at me while he chewed, crinkling his eyes, and nodded toward the box. "I know you want another one!" Busted.

I laughed, broke an apple dumpling in half, and ate it in three bites. I was draining my coffee cup when my phone rang. I let it go to voice mail, but leapt off the chair when I heard Ryan's voice.

"Hello, Dr. McGowan? This is Ryan, with Ranger. Ranger has had a setback, and I have permission to see you as long as we don't discuss anything but him. Do you have any time available soon? I could come out."

I told him not to worry, that setbacks were common and he was doing great. Just keep up with the plan. He persisted.

"I'm working the day shift next Wednesday, but I could come out that evening. I think it would help Ranger a lot to see you. Would seven be too late?"

Usually, it would. I hate seeing clients in the evening. I'm up at five a.m., and by six in the evening my brain feels gummed up and my body slow. You can't be at the top of your game all day long working with aggressive dogs and not pay a price.

But Ranger wasn't aggressive to people, and he had an open, honest face that spoke to my heart. The kicker was the chance that I could get some information out of Ryan about Tom's case.

"Sure, I can make that work. Seven next Wednesday at my office. See you then."

I hung up to find Vince and Liam rinsing their coffee cups

out in the sink. "We'll let you get on with your day, Maddie," Vince said, and came over to give me a hug. He smelled like new-mown hay, and suddenly I thought of George and Chris. I began to tear up and pretended to sneeze.

Vince patted my shoulder, while Liam stood at the door, looking at me with his head cocked, just the tiniest bit. It occurred to me, the thought popping up like bread from a toaster, that he had the same kind of open, honest face that I like to see in a dog.

They left, leaving the box behind. I sat down and made quick work of the other half of the cruller, staring at the door long after they walked away.

Next Wednesday came soon enough. I saw four clients during the day, put off writing up my notes to the next morning, and went home to do the chores before going back to the office to meet Ryan and Ranger.

Ranger entered the office on heel, but glanced at Ryan for permission to come over and greet me. Ryan said okay, and Ranger sidled over and nuzzled my hands. I cooed to him. "You are my best boy! What a good, good dog you are!" He rolled over on his back, tongue lolling, face mushy, while I laughed and rubbed his belly.

Ryan watched all this quietly, his face reserved. I didn't know how much was worry about Ranger's setback, or concern about his friend.

"So, tell me about this setback."

Ryan explained that a recent storm caught him by surprise. He was out of the house when the thunder began, and by the time he got home, Ranger was drooling and pacing in the living room. He refused any treats, but did go into the "safe house" with Ryan and settled down while being petted.

"That's all good," I explained. "Setbacks happen, and you handled it well. You didn't try to force food onto him, and you went into the safe house and helped him feel calm and safe.

You're doing great Ryan, really. It takes time to turn thunder phobia around; it's a pretty primal fear after all. Another behaviorist explained it best at a seminar I attended: Dogs must think *God is growling at them*."

"Okay." Ryan didn't look convinced. "It's just that he'd been doing so well."

"I get it. Once things improve it's hard to see setbacks, because your expectations have changed." I kept rubbing Ranger's belly. His eyes had closed and the tip of his pink tongue was sticking out of his mouth. He looked adorable.

Ryan sat unmoving, looking toward me and Ranger on the rug in front of him, his eyes unfocused. I wasn't sure what else to say. All of this could have been easily handled over the phone.

"Thanks for not asking about Kevin," Ryan finally said.

I paused. How do you answer that? I looked up at him, and saw his face was pinched.

"I'm so sorry, Ryan," I said. "I know he was your friend." I left a million questions unspoken. Why did Kevin sell out? When did it start? What did Ryan know? And the worst, the biggest: How could Kevin kill Chris in cold blood?

My eyes got moist. Again. I missed George and Chris so much it hurt too much to think about them. I got up, and excused myself.

"Sorry, have to go to the restroom. Be right back." I splashed water on my face and took some deep breaths. When I got back, Ryan was standing. So was Ranger.

"Look, I know you were seeing Mr. Norwood."

"Chris. Yes, I was. Your friend killed him." The words flew out of my mouth like birds flushed from a bush.

Ryan sat back down. "We don't know that. I think he was framed. What cop would be stupid enough to leave a murder weapon in his own car? That's where they found the gun that killed Chris. It makes no sense."

It didn't. It occurred to me that Kevin's arrest was to Ryan what Tom's arrest was to me.

"I feel the same way about Tom Hutch. I'll never forgive Tom for kidnapping Cisco and almost killing Bo Peep, never." I took a breath. "But killing George in cold blood? I still can't imagine it."

Ryan nodded. "I knew that Kevin was in trouble. He's in the middle of a divorce and has a daughter with leukemia. Insurance has paid for a lot, but he was super strapped for money. He was drinking a lot and, although we've always been best friends, seemed to fade into himself more and more. Now I know he was spending time working with the Chicago cartel, all to make money to help his kid and pay for child support. He isn't all bad, honest."

Just partly bad. As in, becoming a corrupt cop, helping a business that causes pain and suffering to millions, and sending an innocent dog to probable doom. I reminded myself that just because I never liked the guy didn't mean it wasn't complicated. Or that Ryan's sadness wasn't valid. I thought about Tom, and all the pain and suffering he'd caused. I felt both furious and sorry for him at the same time.

I sat back down and stroked Ranger's head. He licked my hand while I scratched his cheek. "Have you been able to see Kevin?"

"Yeah. It's pretty awful. He's terrified, even though they have him in protective custody. A cop in jail? Not a good thing. He swears he didn't do it, and I believe him. But it looks bad. Really bad. He swears the gun was planted in his car, but the evidence is solid that he was there right after you left. He said when he got there Chris was already dead."

Seriously? Doesn't every guilty person say that? I looked at Ryan in disbelief; he knew exactly what I was thinking.

"I know," he said. "But honest Maddie, I know he's done some bad things, but he'd never kill a man in cold blood. Besides, he's smart. He'd never be stupid enough to leave a murder weapon in his car." Ryan bent his head down and rubbed his hands over his buzz cut, back and forth. We both sat silently, thinking of our friends. Both having done horrible things, but both swearing they were innocent of murder. Finally, Ryan stood up, called Ranger to him, and said, "Well, thanks for the cheerleading for Ranger. I guess I just have to be more patient. It's hard though, because my sergeant is not."

"Let me know if you want anything from me. I can write a report that shows substantial progress. Maybe it would help?"

"Thanks. I'll let you know." Ryan stayed still so long that I was about to say I had to get back to the farm, but finally he turned, said, "Maddie, if you ever . . ." He paused to untangle Ranger's leash, looked back up, and said, "Thanks again," over his shoulder. He clucked to Ranger to follow him out. Ranger took one last look at me as a good-bye. I squinted my eyes like a happy dog, told him to be a good boy, and watched them walk away into the night.

CHAPTER 31

Midwest hot and Alabama humid. The electric whine of cicadas buzzed through the soggy air as I walked Jack behind the line of campers at the Sand Lake Stockdog Trial. We'd already run once that Friday, on a high, hilly course surrounded by sunflowers and scrubby buckthorns. Jack had, to my surprise, done a great outrun and a perfect lift, but he got a tough draw—an old bat of a ewe and two lambs.

Jack used every ounce of his ability to control the ewe. At one point, his tail flew up and his mouth opened as he turned toward her, and I thought we were done. But he closed his mouth, stopped, and faced her, holding his ground. She stared at him for a moment, using her years of experience to read his commitment. After what seemed like an eternity, she turned and trotted back to the lambs. I exhaled, not realizing until then I had been holding my breath.

We didn't get a great score, but I was happy with his outrun and lift, and thrilled with his work on a tough ewe. I gushed to him when he plopped into the water tank to cool off. He beamed.

Later that day, I walked with a bit of confidence onto the course for our second run after Jack's great work earlier in the day. And then, of course, it all went to hell. The pressure from the first run got to Jack, and he went back to his old bad habits, busting in on the lift and creating a mess. I raised my hand to signal defeat to the judge and walked off the course. Discouraged and frustrated, I said my good-byes and loaded up the truck to go home.

I should've stayed. Being around friends and their dogs would have been good for me. But although things at home had settled down by the end of August—the killers arrested, Cisco back, Tyler out of the picture—I still felt jangled, like a sparking battery connection that throws out useless energy in all directions. It had been a hard week before I left for the trial. Too many nights with too little sleep. To many difficult clients. Bo Peep had capped it off right before I left for Sand Lake when I found her lying by the west fence, licking a bloody paw. Where did that come from? All I could guess was that she cut it on a stray piece of metal, the kind that disappear in the earth on farms, coming to life like rusty zombies when the ground heaves them out in winter.

The resident pack of coyotes, who I hadn't heard in months, began yipping as I drove her to the vet on the way to the trial. "Great timing," I grumped out loud. The pack starts hunting here just when the guard dog gets injured.

The injury was worse than I thought. After two layers of stitches, the vet suggested that they keep Bo Peep there a few days to keep it clean and prevent her from licking the wound. I walked away with my heart in my throat, saying "good girl, good girl," over and over as she stared at me with soft, worried eyes.

That scene replayed in my head as I left the trial the next day and headed home, along with an ache of grief that George wasn't there for me to talk to after my disappointing last run. I knew what he'd say: "Don't take one regression too hard, focus on what's right and what there is to learn. One run is just one run." And then he'd put his arms around my shoulders and say, "You got this, girl, and I'm always here if you don't." I wanted to hear it out loud, lean into his bony shoulder, feel the warmth of his love.

I started tearing up and shook my head in disgust as I passed a slow-moving truck on the interstate. "Suck it up, Maddie," I said out loud, as I merged back into my own lane. As I did, I saw a sign for the county road that led to H & H, not all that far out of my way. Without thinking, I turned onto it, drawn as if to water in the desert. But the water was George, or the essence of him.

But, what? I show up and tell Joan I just want to be there to . . . what? That's when I realized there *was* a reason to go, one that could help me and Jack. George always knew what to do when things weren't going well, and he always wrote notes to himself after our sessions. Maybe they are still in the house? Maybe they would help me? I could stop in quickly and see if I could find anything about me and Jack. Even if they didn't help, which they probably wouldn't, I'd at least have another piece of George in my life. Just thinking about it made me feel less alone.

I made a quick call to Joan, who said okay, she was home, and I was welcome to search what was left of George's files. The cops had taken most everything, but there were still some files left in a cabinet in his office that they hadn't taken. She wasn't optimistic that I'd find anything useful, but I was welcome to come by and look.

Joan opened the door before I had a chance to knock. She looked so thin and drawn that I leaned forward to hug her, but she turned abruptly and led me through the living room toward George's study at the back of the house.

"How are you holding up?" I asked as we walked through a dimly-lit hallway back to the study. I couldn't imagine what it would be like to have the man you loved accused of murder, but it had to be a nightmare. "Is there anything I can do?"

She turned and gave me a tentative smile. "No, thank you, though. I wish there was." I wanted to do more, feeling closer to her because of what she'd been through.

"Are you able to talk to Tom?"

"Every once in a while. The lawyer has been here a few times asking questions. I guess Tom thinks he's a good enough attorney, but the evidence doesn't look good." She shook her head quickly, and said, "You know, I trusted him completely." She'd been standing in the hallway, looking toward Tom's sharpshooter trophies on the wall, but now she turned to me and said, her voice quiet and sad, "Fact is, it looks like he did it."

"Oh Joan, I'm so sorry. It's just so hard to believe. But then, if he'd do what he did to Cisco and Bo Peep, I guess I shouldn't be surprised." We both stood in awkward silence for a moment, and then she turned and began walking toward George's study. I stood for a moment and scanned Tom's trophies crammed onto an upper shelf on the wall. Most of the trophies were a foot high or so, usually black and gold with a figure of a shooter on the top.

As I turned and followed Joan into George's study, I said, "I guess I should've figured it was Tom who killed George, given all the sharpshooting trophies he had."

"Yeah, he was one hell of a shot," she said, looking as if she felt ill. *"Was,"* she had said. As if he was dead.

She pointed to some file drawers against the wall and told me to help myself, she'd be in the kitchen. I squatted down on George's ancient blue and pink shag rug—I used to tease him about how old it must have been—and pulled open a cabinet drawer. It was mostly empty, with just a few manila files with receipts for sheep feed and lambing supplies. Nothing for me—the cops had taken all his client files.

I opened every drawer in the room, still finding nothing. I was just about to leave when I saw a box of books on sheepdogs sitting on top of a filing cabinet. All the classics: *One Woman and Her Dog,* by Viv Billingham. *A Way of Life,* by H. Glyn Jones. *Eminent Dogs, Dangerous Men*, by Donald McCaig. I had some of these books, but not all, and when I opened them, I discovered that George had written notes on the margins. "Yes! Too hard, too fast!" he wrote, beside Jones's comment that we must never rush a dog's training.

I sat and paged through book after book, hearing George's voice in the words scrawled on the pages. I felt like I'd found a piece of him that I could take home and keep forever. I saw some other boxes in a closet beside the file cabinets, the door cracked open a few inches.

"Joan?" I called as I walked out of the room, then found her stirring something on the stove. "Would it be okay if I took George's sheepdog books? I'd love to look through them, and I'm guessing that they are just sitting here...." I trailed off, hoping—expecting?—that she'd agree right away.

"Sure. I have no use for them."

"Okay, then. Thanks," I said, and went back to get the books. Before hauling the books I'd collected out to the truck, I open the closet door fully to find a partly-opened box with shepherdess Julie Hill's book, *The Natural Way,* sitting on the top. I hiked the whole box up to my chest, loaded the other books I'd selected on top, and walked into the kitchen.

"Thanks, again," I said as I left with an armful of books, feeling like I should say something else. But what do you say to the wife of the man who betrayed you, your dogs, and your best friend? How could she have not known about any of this?

Maybe she did, but couldn't bring herself to believe it. Just like I spent years thinking of Tyler as a good man who had a drinking problem, who just needed my love and support to fight it. After all, he adored me. He told me every day. He bought me an Arabian mare, Neriffa, for Christmas one year. He bought us a gorgeous house in the foothills outside Albuquerque, sent my parents on vacation to the Caribbean. I loved staying in fancy hotel rooms with lush white towels and room service when we traveled to rodeos.

He cried the mornings after, when my bruises couldn't be missed. "I'm so sorry. I just love you so much and I get crazy when I see you with other men. I'll stop drinking, I promise."

He would, for months at a time, and life would be perfect, until the inevitable happened and he came home, his face rigid and his eyes like coal, and nothing I could say would make it better. But I refused to let it define him. Tyler was a loving husband, who had occasional outbursts that he deeply regretted the next day. He'd say, "That's not me, Maddie. I just don't know where that comes from." People do that. They say "That's not me" when they do something they are ashamed of. But that's not true. It is them. Just a part they don't like.

Same with being an abused wife. That wasn't me. I was in a wonderful marriage with a man who struggled with his temper and occasionally took it out on me. Clearly, some of it was on me. I knew not to make eye contact with other men, and to stay quiet when we were out together, but sometimes I forgot. I stayed home more. I created a massive garden, and rode Neriffa for miles and miles across the hills. I'd run my hands over her silver-gray shoulders and kiss the baby-soft spot between her nostrils. I thought I was happy.

I refused to let the bruises and pain define either one of us. I understand it better now, now that I see clients who rave about how loving their dog is—even though he ripped the lips off the babysitter or put the postal carrier in the hospital. It's seductive to live with an individual who can be loving most of the time. I say to my clients: "It's not what your dog does ninety-eight percent of the time. It's how serious the other two percent is. Does he bark and growl? Okay. Or, did he tear someone's face half off, or almost kill the Yorkie down the street? No matter how hard we work to turn a dog's behavior around, one has to accept that if shit happened once, it can happen again. The question needs to be, how dangerous is the shit?"

If only I'd asked myself the same question.

Chapter 32

It was a relief to get home from the trial with George's books. An indigo bunting hopped along the driveway in front of the truck, his blue feathers flashing as he flew to an oak tree. As I parked, Vince walked out of the barn, holding some wire and a post pounder.

"I thought I'd see if I could fix that fence over by the creek while you were gone." Vince stopped and adjusted his cap. Today was a Packer day. He had a Chicago Bears cap too, just to get a rise out of his friends.

"Back a little early?" Vince asked.

"Just a little tired, glad to be home."

"I'll just go ahead and get in a few new posts since I'm here," Vince said. "The ground's pretty soft right now after the rain. Good time to do it. By the way, I bought some onions and potatoes at the farmer's market yesterday, put them in your root cellar."

"You are crazy kind, Vince, like you don't have your own farm to take care of. But I'm beat, so I'm going to crash. How were things with Cisco?"

"You mean my new best friend? I know your Jack is smart, but I swear Cisco could graduate college. Damn, Maddie, he is one cool dog. I did just put him in his crate and locked the back door, cuz I was planning to run home for a few hours this morning as soon as I finish this."

Happy to hear how things had gone with Cisco, I let Jack out of the truck as Vince went to the barn. Jack promptly lifted his leg on the nearest vertical object, ignored the sheep, and waited for me on the porch to let him in. Guess he felt tired too. Cisco went all Disney movie on me when I let him out, play bowing and swirling around my legs, cry-whining with happiness. I plunked down on the floor and joined both dogs in a moment of bliss.

I woke up Clementine and took her out to pee. She squinted in the sun, squatted, and ambled back into the house as I unloaded the truck. In the living room, Thelma bunted her head against my leg; I reached down to give her a good chin scratch. I stood in the living room for a long minute, staring out the window toward the wolf tree by the creek. Finally, I unloaded the truck, leaving a mess of jackets, boots, and dog supplies on the mudroom floor. I couldn't resist opening up the box of books I'd brought from George's office, and was disappointed to find only a few books on the top; otherwise, it was full of trophies. I sighed and made a mental note to call Joan and see if she wanted them back.

"Hey, Jack, let's go take a nap." I patted my leg and trudged up the stairs with him behind me. I fell into bed, something nagging at me, but I didn't know what. Did I leave something at the trial? I finally let it go and slept like the dead, the sun dappling the covers through the blinds.

It was the coyotes that woke me, the banshee chorus sounding closer than ever. I lay in bed for a moment, waiting to hear Bo Peep counter with her deep-throated threats. Jack never barked at coyotes, apparently understanding it was not in his job description, so I thought nothing of his silence as he lay at the foot of the bed. Then it hit me: Bo Peep was still at the vet clinic, and my lambs were unprotected. Shit. Outside the window I could see that the sun had dipped below the horizon, the light fuzzy and dim. The sheep had moved themselves close to the barn, milling in a tight circle to jockey for the safety of the middle.

I threw on clothes and ran down the stairs to let Cisco out of his crate. I thought he might start barking and get Jack going. Two big dogs barking, even inside the house, might help a little. I thought of running to the basement to get the .22—a few warning shots into the sky ought to do it—but thought I could get away with just a few good yells. If it didn't work I could always go get the gun. I ran out to the porch and yelled, "HEY! HEY!" in my deepest, growliest voice.

The howling continued, and the dogs stayed silent, looking at me as if I was falling down on the job. It occurred to me to imitate Bo Peep, so I followed with my best imitation. "WOOF! WOOF! WOOF!" I yelled, as loud and low-pitched as I could make it. Silence from the coyotes. Ha! I speak guard dog! Impressed with my victory, I turned to go back inside when car lights appeared in the driveway.

A red sedan pulled up and parked behind my truck. Now the dogs began barking behind me at the window, ramping each other up. Cisco was barking furiously, borderline out of control. I wondered if somehow he'd had a setback when Jack and I were gone. He seemed more aroused than he had before when visitors came.

I wasn't up for company, and cursed under my breath at the intrusion.

"Joan!" I said, surprised to see her. "Can I help you with something?" I asked as I walked out the gate to greet her.

I stopped when I saw the Glock, pointed at my chest.

Terror is different than fear; it compares to fear like agony compares to discomfort. The first time I was truly terrified was when I stood up from being punched in the stomach to see Tyler pointing a gun at my head. My insides went liquid, and then he smashed me in the head and everything went black.

But now, I had time. Maybe only a few seconds, but a lot can happen in just one of them. I took a breath. *Think. Breathe. Look at her face, not the gun.*

I rallied enough to stutter something, maybe "What?" or "What's wrong?" As I did, I backed up toward the gate. I needed to get back into the house, to my own gun, to cell service. There was a whooshing noise and a thump. It took me a second to realize she'd shot at the fence post beside me.

"Don't move," she said.

"What the hell, Joan," I said. "What is wrong? Why are you doing this?" But I already had a guess about why she was here.

She stared at me for a moment, walking forward a few steps, the gun pointed at my heart, her eyes flat. The dogs were still barking, Cisco's low, growly notes running a bass line under Jack's higher ones. Their nails scrabbled against the glass.

"Ah, Maddie. If you just hadn't come to the house . . . But no, you had to go looking into the closet and find my trophies."

"I just wanted to borrow George's books," I said, trying to keep my voice steady. "What do I care about any trophies?" Everything fell into place. Tom wasn't the only sharpshooter at H & H.

She shook her head, slowly, back and forth. "I'm not stupid, Maddie. And you're not either."

"Whatever it is, Joan, I'm sure we can work it out."

"Work it out? That's not going to happen. I know how stubborn you are. George described you like a dog with a bone." The light was fading. We stared at each other; the gun was still pointed at me. I didn't know what else to do but stall.

"So," I said. "You killed George."

"He figured out what Tom and I were doing—selling dogs for twice the price, to anyone willing to pay. He threatened to go to the cops."

"What about all the evidence against Tom? You set him up? Your own husband?"

A band around my chest started to tighten. The world started to swirl. I knew, from long experience, that my legs were about to crumple. Forcing myself to take some deep breaths, I looked behind me at Jack and Cisco, still barking hysterically at the window, their eyes reflecting the yard light that had just come on.

Joan moved one step forward, the gun still pointing at my heart.

"Wait. Wait." I held my hand out, as if asking a dog to stay. As if it would make a difference. The snowy tree crickets starting to sing.

"Wow, Joan," I said, trying to keep the tremor out of my voice, desperate to keep a conversation going while my brain came up with a plan. Or for James Bond to run in and save me. "I gotta give you credit for setting Tom up! I can't imagine how you managed it." I tried to put a look of admiration on my face. Just me and Joan, in the sisterhood.

I had to do something, now or never. Running for the truck wouldn't work, I'd have to run past her. The house was out, I'd have to get through the gate, run up the porch, and open the door. I'd be dead before I got there. Still, handguns are famously inaccurate; if she shot me maybe it wouldn't kill me. I eased my right arm behind my back and began trying to open the sticky gate latch without Joan being able to see what I was doing. Ease up the latch, then push the wooden post toward the center with my right elbow. I tried scratching my head with my left hand to distract her from what I was doing with my right.

I had just gotten it open when something slapped me, hard, on the shoulder. I looked down to see a circle of red on the T-shirt over my upper arm. It took a moment to figure out that it was blood, and then the pain hit and my brain screamed *YOU GOT SHOT. RUN!* I slammed the gate shut behind me and ran around the side of the house, bullets pinging into the house. As I ran, I saw Cisco throwing himself against the window.

"No, no, no," I chanted to myself as I got behind the house, terrified Joan would switch from shooting at me to killing the dogs. Once out of Joan's sight, I pulled up for a second, remembering that Vince had locked the back door. I could hear Joan trying to open the gate on the front of the house, rattling it back and forth. I think she screamed "fuck," but it was hard to hear over the dogs.

I had nowhere to hide before Joan got through the gate and around the house. I could run for the bushes to the east, but she'd have plenty of time to shoot me before I got there.

And then I saw the boards over the root cellar, looking like a few pieces of old wood stacked against the house. No one would know what it led to without being told. I ran and pulled on the wood; thank God Vince had opened it up today and loosened the lid. I jerked it up with my left hand and scrambled inside, pulling it back down as fast as I could.

I curled up as tightly as I could, but the wooden lid still rested on my head. My back was pressed into the round globes of potatoes and onions, my feet squished underneath me awkwardly. I had just enough room to move my left hand against my injured right arm to try to slow the bleeding. The blood felt warm and sticky. I tried desperately to quiet my breathing, imagining Joan standing just inches above me, sure she would hear me, open the lid and finish me off.

The dark was overwhelming, stifling. I couldn't move. I was in a tiny, black box, about to die. Again. Like in New Mexico.

* * *

I am told I was trapped in the chest freezer for a day and a half after Tyler beat me to a pulp and threw me in there to die. I knew it was going to be bad the instant he walked in the door the night before. Like that moment when you hit black ice on the highway, and you know there's nothing you can do.

When I came to, I was thirsty, desperately thirsty. The pain undulated in waves, my head throbbing and my ribs burning. I went in and out of consciousness in a timeless haze, but eventually became aware that I was trapped in a small, dark space. There were hard, unyielding walls on all sides.

At first, I was so woozy I felt only vaguely curious about where I was, how I got there, my mind covered in velvety fog. As time went on, my head began to clear, and I realized I was trapped in the equivalent of a coffin.

I tried to push my way out. I could move the cover up a quarter of an inch, but no more. I kept trying to stretch out my legs, as if magically what they were up against would disappear. Not being able to extend them made me feel crazy, almost as bad as being trapped. It was flat black inside, like Tyler's eyes before he shot me. The air was musty, moldy, and felt thick going down into my lungs. I couldn't take much of a breath anyway; my ribs hurt too much to expand.

I screamed. I screamed until my throat was sore, my ribs furious at the exertion. I'd yell and pant in pain, then yell some more. I finally stopped, exhausted, and passed out.

Our neighbor Simon found me. He'd seen Tyler careen away in his truck after hearing him yell at me. He wondered why no one had walked our dog the next morning, or that next evening, as I always did. First he looked all over the house and the garage, using the key we'd given him for when we traveled, then called the cops. They found blood on the kitchen floor and began their own search. I heard them talking, at least, I think I did. It's all so hazy. Not finding anything, they put out an APB for Tyler and his truck. It was assumed that he had driven off with me.

Later, Simon told me that he couldn't sleep that night, something kept nagging at him about the house. He sat up with a start at three in the morning, went into the garage, and smashed the padlock on the freezer lid with a sledge hammer. That's what had woken him up, the padlock. He'd asked to store venison in the freezer one fall, but we explained it wasn't working anymore. It just sat in the garage, waiting for us to cart it away. It never had a lock on it—no kids in the house. But now it did; his unconscious had recorded that and woke him up in the middle of the night. He found me curled up in the bottom of the freezer, barely breathing.

My body recovered in a few months, but it took my brain a lot longer. At one point my therapist said, "Find what makes you feel happy. Ask yourself what makes you feel safe." I began to focus on helping animals, especially ones that had been traumatized. I bought the farm. I got Jack and Bo Peep and Clementine and sheep, and spent my evenings walking in peace and listening to birds.

But now, trapped in the pitch black again in the root cellar, my old friend, terror, was back. I tried to breathe deeply, silently, but began shaking so hard I was afraid I'd cause the cover to move. I had to put my hand over my mouth to keep from shrieking. I could hear the dogs barking, as if underwater, and Joan milling above me.

Desperate, I remembered what I'd learned since New Mexico. Don't run from an emotion, welcome it. Identify it, acknowledge it, give it space.

"Hello, Fear," I said to myself. "Oh sorry, is your name actually Terror? My apologies." The absurdity of this almost made me smile. It's hard to scream when you're smiling, so there was that. At least I wouldn't die in the middle of a panic attack.

The terror subsided, but my arm was throbbing and getting wet from all the blood. I knew I couldn't stay down there for long. And then something above me exploded in a cacophony of breaking glass.

The dogs had gone through the window. Joan would shoot them in a heartbeat.

Chapter 33

I jerked up, using my head as much as my good arm to raise the cover. "No, no!" I screamed, sure that I was about to see Jack and Cisco die in front of my eyes. Joan was to my right, her gun moving toward the dogs, who had just turned the corner and were charging forward. She turned briefly when I emerged like a bloody corpse out of the ground, but then turned back to Cisco, his head down, eyes blazing, running straight at her. She couldn't miss him at this distance.

I lunged toward her, scrambling halfway out of the cellar, and managed to grab her left ankle enough to pull her off balance. It gave us just a second, but that was all Cisco needed. He was on her instantly, knocking her over backward, the gun flying from her hand. She lay on her back, Cisco's paws on her chest as he growled into her face.

She screamed, "Get him off, get him off!"

I was frozen for a moment, trying to settle myself and decide what to do next. Cisco stood still, his eyes on Joan's face. Jack stood beside Cisco, head down, his mouth tight, staring at Joan as if she was a ram about to charge. "Good boys, good boys," I crooned, trying to keep things calm.

"Steady, boys," I said, my voice wavering, as I crawled fully out of the cellar. I kicked the gun further away, picked it up, and pointed it at Joan.

"Don't move or I'll tell him to kill you," I said. As if he would do that. As if I would ask him. "If you don't move, he won't hurt you," I said to Joan. "Just stay still."

"Get him OFF!" she panted.

I stood still, torn about what to do next. I had to call the cops, but I'd have to go into the house to get the phone. I'd either have to leave all three of them alone to do that, or call Cisco off and control Joan with the gun. Cisco side-eyed me with a look that couldn't have been clearer if he'd spoken. "You do your job, I'll do mine. But get to it."

"Stay there, boys, stay there," I finally decided. I wasn't sure if Cisco had a signal to stand down—he was a detection dog, not one trained in protection—but things seemed in control the way they were. "Joan, don't move or it won't go well." I turned and began to run around to the front of the house, but stopped when I heard Cisco's growls escalate and a scream from Joan. Joan had tried to stand up.

"Jesus, Joan, stop moving. I told you. . . ." I began walking backward to the corner of the house, as I repeated, "Hold 'em, Cisco, hold 'em, Jack." As if they knew what that meant. I dashed through the house and into the mudroom, where I could see the three of them out the window.

"I can see you, Joan, don't move," I cautioned. "Good dogs, stay there, good dogs," I repeated, as I grabbed some leashes from hooks on the wall, found the phone, and dialed 911.

"I've been shot, someone tried to kill me. She's still here, send help right now."

I added my address, hung up without waiting for an answer, and opened the back door to find all three motionless. I put the gun down, my hands shaking now, and tied up Joan's ankles with a leash as best I could. My right arm was dripping blood and screaming at me. I stood up with the gun in my left hand and said, "I'll call Cisco off, but if you move, I'll send him back in. Or shoot you, take your pick."

I said, "Leave it!" to Cisco, the cue I use to stop Jack from eating rabbit poop. I hadn't gotten around to teaching it to Cisco yet, but the tone of my voice was clear. He turned his head a half inch and looked into my eyes. *You sure?* I wasn't, but I was afraid he'd get shot by a cop if someone came and saw a dog "attacking" a person. Whatever I said, I needed to say it with authority.

"Cisco, that'll do," I said, using the signal I use as a recall. I kept my voice low, breathed deeply, and repeated it.

Jack came over first, his ears sideways, his eyes pancaked. He'd been taught as a young pup that you never, ever, ever, herd humans. Everything that just happened violated that, and yet, I would've bet the farm that he knew I was in danger and wanted to protect me.

"Cisco, that'll do. Leave it. I got this." My word salad of mostly meaningless cues seemed to have an effect. He turned his head toward me. "That's a good boy, good boy," I crooned, reinforcing the first step of what I wanted. "That'll do, Cisco. It'll be okay."

He backed up, then stood still, a few feet away from Joan, who was glaring at us. I figured that was good enough for the moment. "Good boy, Cisco, good boy."

"Now, Joan, you can sit up, very slowly, but why don't you stay seated on the ground until the cops come?"

"Fuck you, bitch," Joan snarled as she began to rise. Cisco leaned forward. Jack growled.

All three of us stood still, staring at Joan, until enough adrenaline left my body and my arm began to throb in earnest. After much too long, the operatic wail of a squad car stopped some sparrows squabbling in the brush.

"Over here!" I shouted as loud as I could after I heard a car door slam shut on the other side of the house. "Don't hurt the dogs!" I added, terrified that something would go south and Jack or Cisco would get shot.

It was Wallenberg who ran around the corner of the house, after smashing through the gate. Gun drawn, pointed toward Joan's chest, he said, "Maddie, an ambulance is coming. Can you call your dogs off now that I'm here?"

"Will do," I said, pretending confidence. "Okay, boys, that'll do. Let's go." I turned and Jack swirled beside me, like a competition obedience dog showing off his perfect heel. Cisco hesitated. "It's okay, Cisco, the sheriff has got it now. That'll do." I patted my leg and ducked down a bit, to encourage him to come.

Cisco's body relaxed a bit. He walked over to me, turning his head every other step to look at Joan. All three of us went inside the house, where I dissolved onto the couch, saying "thank you thank you thank you," and kissing their foreheads. Cisco started licking the blood on my arm while Jack bathed my face with his tongue. I hated to crate them up, but was worried about what would happen next, so, after thanking them again, I put them away. As soon as they were in, Jack whining heartbreakingly, I called Vince. Liam answered.

"I need help. I'm okay, but Joan came to kill me and I've been shot. The cops are here and I'm worried about the dogs. Can you..."

"Coming. Now."

Good thing, because I was getting woozy.

CHAPTER 34

Liam burst into the house and ran over to me, collapsed on the couch. I was too light-headed to get up; shock was settling in. He sat beside me and gently put his arms around my shoulders, avoiding my bloody arm.

"I've got you, I've got you," he repeated. Bleary as I was, I thought this was a ridiculous thing to say. The dogs had saved my life, Wallenberg was arresting Joan, and an ambulance was on the way. I turned to look at his face, about to say something sarcastic, but the warmth on his face and the fuzz in my brain won out. I lay my head on his chest. He smelled good, woodsy.

I snapped out of it when an ambulance arrived a few minutes later. Two EMTs charged into the house, carrying big, rectangular packs. An older guy—buzz-cut gray hair and an earring in his right ear—sat down beside me and said, "What's going on?" He asked if I had any other injuries beyond my arm, and made me yelp when he pressed a gauze pad onto the wound. I shrieked when he splinted my arm to my body.

"Do you think you can walk out to the ambulance, or do you want us to use the stretcher?" "I'll be okay," I said. He braced me on my left side as I rose to stand, my knees wobbly. A younger woman with electric yellow hair walked next to me on the right, her left arm held out to catch me if I wobbled. Liam followed close behind.

It didn't hit me until we got to the front door: they were taking me away from the dogs. I turned toward them so fast I almost fell over. I took a breath, not wanting the dogs to hear the fear in my voice. "Take care of the dogs, Liam, you and Vince, promise?" He said of course they would, they'd take care of everything. It didn't matter. Being ripped away from them felt almost as bad as being shot, but there was nothing to do but blow out a breath and walk to the ambulance.

They took the bullet out that night; I don't remember much beyond bright lights and someone holding my hand as they wheeled me into an operating room. The bullet had shattered my humerus, but missed the brachial artery. If it hadn't, they told me, I would have bled out in the root cellar.

I woke up with a clunky cast on my right arm, brain fogged and miserable with needles poking into me all over. My arm hurt like a bitch, but I didn't want more pain meds to make me groggier than I already was.

Dorothy, who had driven out in the middle of the night, came to see me the next morning with Vince. They didn't stay long, just long enough to swear to me that the dogs were fine. I believed them, and it made no difference. I wanted to see the dogs as much as I've ever wanted anything. Ever.

Garcia came by that afternoon to get a statement. She pulled a chair over beside the bed and shook her head. "Damn, Maddie, you are something else."

"What? I didn't do anything! I just stopped by Joan's house to pick up some stuff. I did NOT go off half-cocked, and I didn't realize she was the sharpshooter until she drove up last night." I wagged a wobbly finger at her with my good arm. "How come you guys didn't notice her trophies in the closet? You went through the house, right? Twice!"

"Yeah, well, you got me there. Tom told us that the shooting range was for training K9s, so we just assumed they were all his." She grimaced and tilted her head in apology. "I need to take your statement first, but I can fill you in on some things once we're done. Okay, ready to talk?" I nodded and described all that had happened as best I could while she wrote copious notes, even though she'd set up a phone to record what I said.

"Okay," she said finally, after I'd gone over and over everything until I was exhausted. "Here's what I can tell you. Joan admitted to not just killing George, but killing Chris as well. She practically bragged about it. Chris knew too much about the business to not eventually link things back to her, so she went over to kill him. Kevin pulled up into the parking lot as she was leaving the apartment, when Chris was already dead. She saw her chance to pin it on him, so when Kevin was inside, she broke into his car and "hid the gun"—Garcia made finger quotes—after she wiped it. She was literally smiling as she told me all this. I've seen a lot in my time, but that bitch is something else."

"But what about all the evidence against Tom?"

Garcia nodded. "Impressive, right? She told us that after she killed George she wiped the rifle after she used it, got Tom to handle it to get his DNA on it, and hid it in the barn. She actually bitched about the 'damn sniffer dog finding the effing casing' in the woods, also with Tom's DNA on it. After you found Cisco, she put the gun in a more obvious place so we'd find Tom's fingerprints on it." She looked out the window and shook her head.

"That woman is scary as shit."

I lay for a while in silence; I didn't know what to say. Poor Chris. Poor George. And, even, poor Tom. What a nightmare, being set up for murder by the person you thought you could count on the most.

Garcia put her notebook down on her lap and leaned forward. "You okay?" she asked.

"Sure. Thanks," I said.

She raised her eyebrows.

"Well, sort of. You know." We both looked at the view out the window, all blue sky and skinny clouds, when the nurse came in to take my vitals. As she did, Garcia said, "By the way, that's one cool dog you have there." I knew she meant Cisco, but felt like Jack wasn't getting the credit he deserved.

"It was Jack who found Cisco, you know," I said, turning to look right at her. I could hear the defensiveness in my voice as I said it. *Good grief, Maddie, get it together.*

"They're both amazing," I added. "I am the luckiest woman in the world to have them."

"You are indeed, Maddie. Except for, well . . . getting shot."

We both let that sit. I turned my head back to the window and said, "I just want to go home."

"Don't blame you there," she answered as the doctor came in to tell me they wanted to keep me one more night just to be safe. Something about my blood pressure. I snoozed when Garcia left, waking up late afternoon to find Vince and Dorothy sitting at the foot of my bed, staring at me.

"Good grief, you two, don't you have anything else to do?"

"Nope," said Vince, pointing out the flowers they'd brought and a box of chocolates on the bedside table.

Everything was fine, they said. Dorothy had even gone to the vet's and picked up Bo Peep, whose paw was healing well. I laughed when she told me that Bo had barked for at least an hour after she got home. Even Cisco and Jack seemed relieved when she finally shut up. No one had heard or seen a coyote since she'd been back.

Dorothy drove me home late the next morning, and there has never, in the history of the world, been a more emotional greeting between two dogs and one person. When we pulled up, the dogs were in the house and saw or smelled me walking through the gate. I had the presence of mind to ask Dorothy to stay close to my injured arm once I got inside, so that the dogs couldn't hurt me when I sank to the floor. Jack sobbed like a person. Cisco made squeaky noises that could've come from a teacup chihuahua. Even Clementine joined the party. I laughed and cried and did all kinds of things that dogs usually hate, like hugging and kissing them all over everywhere. They didn't care. I looked up and saw tears in Dorothy's eyes, and pulled her down beside us.

Vince and Liam came over every day to help out with chores and "just to visit Cisco." Liam regaled us with "fun at the farm" stories from his childhood, including a county-wide search for their high-producing cow who went on the lam for three days, finally showing up in a suburban garage. Dorothy came down on weekends and entertained us with stories about her rehab patients. She told us that snatching the food away from the red-tailed hawk to get him to eat had worked miracles, and added sweet stories of baby raccoons and a tiny, saw-whet owl who kept falling asleep on her shoulder. We laughed a lot. They plied me with elaborate, healthy meals until I finally begged someone to go get me a Big Mac and fries for lunch, and a frozen pizza for dinner.

I took a month off from work. I didn't have to explain why to my clients; the story was all over the news. As stories go, this was a good one. "Woman, trapped in freezer years ago, almost killed a second time by jealous wife! Saved by dogs!" Inaccurate and sensationalized, but I couldn't blame the press; we humans love drama as much as any other primate. I avoided the news when I could, spent hours walking the dogs and with Old Horse, her velvet nose tickling my cheek after I brushed her out with long, slow strokes. Still, some nights I lay in bed, remembering the feel of Chris's warm chest under my head. Some nights I avoided the empty bed and slept on the couch. I took to kissing George's face every morning in the photo of him, me, and Jack.

I was doing okay. I worked with a meditation teacher, did

eye movement desensitization and reprocessing with a great therapist who called me out on focusing more on healing my dogs than myself. We worked on my guilt about Chris's death, and acknowledging that it wasn't men so much that I mistrusted, it was the decisions I made about them. I went back to the creek, sure now that the "man" I saw was a mirage created by exhaustion and trauma.

In a way, Jack and Cisco struggled more than I did. As horrible as the attack by Joan had been for me, it almost felt like some kind of release. I'd gone back to my worst nightmare, and come through stronger and semi-sane. I had access to therapists specializing in trauma recovery. But you can't do talk or EMDR therapy on dogs, and both had been restless, nervy, sleeping for short periods and waking up with a start. For a while, both barked hysterically, pupils huge, when someone drove up. Jack began having what looked like nightmares, his legs jerking in REM sleep while he emitted yips and growls. Cisco got clingy, didn't want to leave my side. He began licking his paws when I got ready to leave the house.

They were improving, though, both physically and emotionally. They played together hard twice a day, sometimes playing tug, sometimes racing. Their play growls alarmed the sheep, who lined up to watch them in a phalanx, keeping an eye on the predators. I taught Cisco to "take a bow," a posture only a relaxed dog would naturally take, and asked both dogs to do it when mildly stressed. Jack, who had known it early on, began bowing himself as a way to self-soothe. I knew Cisco wouldn't be far behind. We walked over the fields every day for hours, turning our mouths purple with late season raspberries growing along the creek, watching the flocks of starlings starting to gather.

People came by to help countercondition them to cars pulling into the driveway and unfamiliar people walking toward me and the house. Joe, Clyde, and Marvin came by and threw pieces of chicken to the dogs as they approached until Jack and Cisco treated them like family. Even Garcia and her partner, Joyce, came by, tossing treats and eventually rolling on the ground with the dogs, giving them belly rubs on the threadbare rug in the living room. After a few months Jack was back to acting like his old self, and I guessed that Cisco wasn't far behind. But I knew from my years of work with trauma that those memories would never be erased, that I'd always need to keep working with them, watching for triggers that could set them back.

Tom, out on bail for burglary and canine kidnapping after Joan's confession, had called me repeatedly for a few days after I came back from the hospital. He said it had all been Joan's idea, that she had the idea of selling dogs on the black market, and she was the one who kidnapped Cisco and drugged Bo Peep. But he was a part of it; it wasn't like Joan held him at gunpoint. If not for the two of them, George and Chris wouldn't be dead, Cisco wouldn't have suffered so much—twice, and Bo Peep wouldn't have almost died. I know how important forgiveness can be, especially to the person who provides it. Maybe someday I could be that person, but not now. Maybe not ever.

Liam had flown back to Wichita after I'd been home a week, but came back a few weeks later, the same weekend Dorothy came down again to help out. "The guy may be a sweetheart, Maddie, but there's just so much help a person needs," she said after raising her coffee cup in a toast as he drove away after the second visit. When I accused her of being jealous, she rolled her eyes and got up to clean out the barn.

"I'm going with you," I told her as she started out the door. "Don't try to stop me. It's long past time that I started getting back to normal."

The grass was dewy as we walked to the barn, the paws of Jack, Cisco, and Dorothy's dogs sopping wet by the time we went twenty feet. The starlings were beginning to gather on the electric lines, as they did every fall, their raucous chattering a brash addition to the soundscape. Old Horse ambled over and pressed her head against my chest. We breathed in time together. In, out. In, out. I kissed her forehead and looked up to follow my friends, two-legged and four, backlit by the morning sun, before they got too far away.

EPILOGUE

Early October, sandhill cranes flying overhead, their dinosaurian voices breaking through the crisp air as I arrived at the Minnetonka Sheepdog Trial. A bevy of pink and orange maple leaves surrounded the field, fluttering in the breeze like Easter ribbons. The course was massive—five hundred yards long, with an undulating landscape that hid the sheep and your dog from view for an endless twenty seconds. Some of the sport's greats—dog and human both—were there to dazzle us with their skill. Jack and I had our work cut out for us.

A lot of friends would be there watching. I'd said yes when Vince asked if he could come out to the trial and watch me and Jack run. He told me he'd always wanted to go to a trial and watch us work, but didn't want to make it hard for me to find another farm sitter. I'd had no idea he was interested. I said of course he should come, and found another neighbor who could help out.

I brought Cisco along too, unwilling to leave his care to anyone but Vince. He'd been doing well with visitors at the farm, and I knew the trial, where people don't allow their dogs to run up to others, would be a good next step. Vince volunteered to help take care of him when I was busy with Jack—he and Cisco had a hell of a bromance going on. I loved seeing them hang out together, sort of father and son-like, if the dad smelled like weed and the son had a tail that could sweep coffee cups off a table. Vince said he hadn't realized how much he'd missed his old dog, Sadie, and was grateful to spend time with such a smart, beautiful dog.

He arrived at the trial early that morning with Liam at his side. I was surprised to see him; Vince hadn't mentioned he was coming to visit. "Couldn't let Dad come alone! I'm afraid he'll catch the bug and buy a flock of sheep before I can stop him." Vince's smile in response didn't reach his eyes. Something was going on between them, but we all pretended, following the rules of "Midwest Nice," that it wasn't. Besides, what family doesn't have issues? Not my business.

Liam and I had talked a few times in the last month, he calling just to check up on me and chat. He talked about his work as a landscape architect in Wichita, I whined about keeping farm machinery working. We laughed about eccentric clients we had had. He asked often about the dogs.

We watched some early runs with Dorothy, who had high hopes for her young dog, Butch, running in the Open class for the first time. While the guys marveled at the beauty and skill of our competitors' dogs, she and I talked strategy about our runs, sitting in our high-end camping chairs. Dorothy pulled out a thermos of coffee and homemade coffee cake from a tote bag; we spent a few relaxing hours watching and chatting.

It was Jack's turn late in the morning. After one last nervous pee in the porta potty, I gathered him up and opened the gate to the field. A red-tailed hawk swirled circles in the sky as we walked to the post, my stomach tight. It was the longest outrun we'd ever done, and I was worried he'd never find the sheep. Plenty of dogs that day had run in desperate circles trying to find them, their handlers whistling and calling, trying to redirect them to the right spot. Many had failed. "Just find the sheep, Jack, don't worry about anything else."

Jack scanned the field. It didn't look like he'd located the sheep, who were barely visible at the far end. "Look," I said, his cue to find the tiny white dots who looked a million miles away. His head kept scanning left and right, as if he had no idea where they were. I began to feel panicked about what to do. Send him? Or keep trying to help him find them? My heart started its all-too-common racing, while my brain began yelling *WHAT TO DO? WHAT TO DO?*

Out of nowhere, I remembered George's voice, like a whisper: "Trust your dog." He'd said it repeatedly—to me, to other handlers at his training clinics. "Do the work you need to do in training, but open your heart and trust them at a trial."

I let out one long, slow breath and whispered, "Away to me!"

Jack burst away from my side, his beautiful black and white body flowing like water over the emerald-green field. He ran, bless him, a perfectly gorgeous outrun, circling far behind the sheep and lifting them carefully but with commitment.

He'd been perfect so far, but it didn't matter. The lead ewe, through no fault of Jack's, took off toward the rest area behind me at a run, chin raised in defiance, the ovine equivalent of "make my day." Jack's only chance was to power around in a semicircle to stop her, which he barely managed to do halfway down the field. That allowed the back two, as slow moving as hay bales, to put their heads down and graze obliviously, ignoring everything else. The fourth ewe disappeared in the swale. Jack pushed the runner back toward the laggers, but had to circle around to the back of them to move them forward. As he did, the sprinter, eyes gleaming with victory, ran past me and leapt over the fence like a gazelle into the rest area. Impressive.

I turned to look at the judge, who smiled a rueful smile, shook her head in sympathy, and said, "Thank you," trial-speak for "you've been disqualified." Jack, refusing to give up, found the one hidden in the swale, joined her up with the others, and brought them down the field to me.

All I could do was laugh. Jack had done nothing wrong.

Sheepdog trialing is like gambling at a casino, and sometimes the house wins, if the "house" is a group of sheep who have rejected the concept of flocking.

Jack cooled off in the water tank, his head up, mouth open, looking as proud of himself as I'd ever seen him. Dorothy came over with Vince and Liam, shook her head, smiled, and said, "What are you gonna do?!"

I didn't care about the score, or lack of it. I felt happy, joyous even. Jack had found the sheep and done a great outrun and lift on a tough course. I had kept my wits about me and focused on my dog and the sheep, rather than drowning in anxiety. My friends Vince and Dorothy were there, Liam was looking, well, sort of interesting, and Jack had been wonderful, in spite of our score.

I turned away to call Jack out of the water tank and cool his muscles down with a walk, telling the others to go grab some lunch. Liam said he wasn't hungry and asked if I needed any help. Dorothy said, "Oh for fuck's sake, just go walk with her if you want to; she doesn't need help walking her dog around a field." Liam looked at me and raised his eyebrows.

"Sure," I said, and we walked side by side, Liam on my right, Jack on my left, toward an open area where I could cool him out.

"Um," Liam said, running his hands through his hair, "I'll be going back to Dad's for a few days after this. Any chance I could take you out to dinner?"

"No" rose up in my throat reflexively. I opened my mouth

to say it, but then stopped myself. I looked up at his face, his hazel eyes full of questions I wasn't ready to answer.

"Could I take a rain check? I don't think I trust myself to make good decisions right now." I didn't say "about men," but, of course, that's what I meant. Trusting your dog is one thing. Trusting yourself is another.

"But," I added, "thanks for asking."

"No worries." He smiled. "I can wait."

I nodded and kept walking. Jack lifted his leg on the closest bush.

Dorothy ran that afternoon, putting down a glorious run with Shae that earned her a third and an automatic slot in the Nationals later that year. We all celebrated that night at a BBQ joint, and got sauced on margaritas. Vince got sentimental about his dairy cows. Dorothy stopped the restaurant's conversational buzz when she said, "Fuck yes!" to the server who had asked about another drink. Liam started doing dog breed imitations and had us clutching our sides.

Jack and I ran again early the next morning. We didn't place, but we got through the course credibly enough. Although Jack and I lost points here and there for zigzag lines and missing a gate panel, I was thrilled. Doing "well enough" on a tough course was a victory at our stage of the game. Jack seemed to know it too; he left the course and threw his tail up toward a sweet little bitch standing by the gate. You could practically hear a red sports car gunning its engine outside the bar.

As I turned to call him away, I saw a man standing about fifty yards away, looking straight at me. About five feet eight. Western shirt. He had on a white cowboy hat, not something you see often at a sheepdog trial in the Midwest. He tipped his hat, as if to say hello. I startled, like a horse frightened by a snake in the grass. Startle responses rarely go away once you have PTSD, but they get easier to manage. As he turned away, I shook my head as if bothered by flies, took a few breaths, and laughed. The ghost of Tyler wasn't going to haunt me now; I was done with that. The guy was too heavy, walked with a limp. I called Jack and walked past my friends, who were congratulating us on a good run.

Vince and Liam left after our run, while I stayed around to watch Dorothy's second run with Shae. They got a lousy draw, handled the sheep brilliantly, but they weren't able to do better than twelfth. Still, they got lots of compliments on Shae's skill and heart, and I knew Dorothy was happy. She nodded when I said I'd be leaving right away, having packed everything up before her run.

"I'd be nice to get home before dark," I said. She said she was packing up too, happy to get home in plenty of time to do chores and relax a bit.

The drive home was uneventful and lovely, the highways a tunnel through the orange and reds of fall. Yellow poplar leaves drifted down like confetti, swirling over the highway when they got caught up in the slipstream of traffic. I got home midafternoon, happy to be back with plenty of time to unpack, do the chores, and relax. Bo Peep *wurred* in happiness when I got out of the truck, then spent several minutes sniffing over Jack and Cisco. Assuaged all was well, she lay down in the shade of an ash tree and resumed her nap.

She woke up when a car pulled into the driveway, barking her excited "announcement" bark to the heavens. Jack and Cisco were out in the yard with me; I called them to me, saying, "Oh good! Visitors!" the phrase I'd been pairing with tasty treats to make them more comfortable when cars pulled up.

"Ryan?" I said, as he got out of his car. Possibly the last person I expected to see. "Is Ranger okay?" *Now what?* I thought.

"No, no, everything is fine! I was just driving by on my way to visit a friend in Madison and realized I was going right by your farm." He turned and looked back toward his car, took a step toward it. "I'm sorry, I should've called," he said, in response to my stunned face.

"Oh good," I said nonsensically. "I mean, oh good, nothing's wrong. It's fine." Meaning it was okay that he just showed up unannounced. *Good grief, get it together, Maddie.*

Jack and Cisco stood beside me, trying to read the room. *Is she okay? Who is he?* Concern about them got my head together before my social skills kicked in.

"Wanna say hi to the dogs?" I asked.

"Oh, of course!" Ryan answered. I said "okay" and the dogs ran to Ryan. Jack's tail wagged from the shoulders back as he swirled around Ryan's leg. Cisco was a bit less relaxed, but by then I was comfortable letting him greet unfamiliar people on his own. Cisco sniffed Ryan's pants as if on a job. Jack twirled around a couple of times, then lay down for a belly rub.

"Well, um, wanna tour of the farm?" It seemed like the thing to say.

"I'd love it, if you have the time," Ryan answered, getting up from crouching down beside Jack.

An hour later Ryan walked back to his car, saying he shouldn't have stayed so long. But, after introducing him to Bo Peep—he said he felt like he'd met celebrities after greeting the dogs—it was me who asked if he'd like to see Jack work.

"Man, that was something," he said, after watching Jack work. "I can see how it's addicting. I love watching dogs being dogs, doing something they are better at than us.

"Speaking of working dogs," he added. "You'll never guess what I found out. Remember when I asked you why Ranger gave me such ambivalent signals in that warehouse, the one that supposedly was full of coke? Well, it HAD been. There were drugs there the day before, but Kevin had warned them about a raid, so they moved it. So, Ranger was right! He was alerting to residual odors but couldn't find a source. He was trying to tell me, in the only way that he knew how, that there were drugs there once, but not anymore. I wonder if Cisco had been there the day before too. Maybe that's why Ranger lifted his leg, trying to tell me that another K9 had been there?"

I wouldn't put it past him, given the intelligence of dogs like Ranger. Of course, maybe not, but the fact that he did it while staring straight into Ryan's eyes makes you wonder. Ryan laughed when I presented an alternative explanation: Ranger was going to overmark another dog's scent come hell or high water, and stared straight at Ryan to dare him to stop him.

We'd run out of things to say. Ryan was petting Jack with one hand, holding his car keys in the other. He gave Jack a last scratch and turned to open the door.

"Um. Maddie . . ." He stood still, looking at his hands fiddling with the keys. He looked up, and his eyes locked on mine.

Oh. I couldn't believe it hadn't occurred to me until now. Why he kept calling about Ranger. Why he wanted an in-person appointment instead of a phone call. I knew what he was going to say before he said it.

"Um. Could I come back over sometime again? I'd love to see Jack work again. Maybe give Ranger some time to be off leash in the country?"

"Um, well, sure, maybe. Sometime." I might as well have scuffed my feet and said "garsh." We stared at each other for a moment, transfixed by my ambivalent word salad.

"Okay then, see you later," he said as he got into his car.

I waved good-bye, called the dogs, and walked back to the porch. I sat there, Jack and Cisco lying beside me, for the longest time, as the light dimmed and the air softened.

* * *

"Every house needs someone to watch the swallows," the poet Wendy Barker wrote. Someone to sit and just be, with no agenda except to let their eyes follow the birds as they curve effortlessly through the air. There must have been twenty-five of them; the last babies had fledged a few weeks ago, their nests littering the barn's rafters. "Muscle up, kids," I said. They had a long flight to South America for the winter, and they were late. Some of them wouldn't make it back.

But they trusted themselves to try, and maybe, just maybe, that's enough.

Gratitude

My husband and best friend, Jim Billings, is the person most responsible for this book being written and published. I could never, ever—never ever ever—have done it without his love and support. If I thanked him every day for the rest of our lives, it would not be enough. But I will watch soccer on TV with him, as if I cared deeply about it, from here to eternity.

Maddie McGowan and I would like my literary agent and cherished friend, Jennifer Gates of Aevitas Creative, to know how grateful we are for her unwavering support of my first venture into fiction. Without her wisdom, literary chops, and encouragement, this novel wouldn't never happened, or been so awful that we all, especially me, would pretend we had nothing to do with it. Thanks also to all at Aevitas Creative Management for their unwavering support; I am so lucky to have you in my corner.

What would I have done without my friend, colleague, writing companion, and cheerleader, Cat Warren? Cat and I spoke every month for years as a first-time-fiction writing group of two: reading and critiquing each other's drafts, thinking through plot twists, refining word choices, and supporting each other through the miasma of creating good fiction. Keep your eyes out for her first foray into fiction in the years to come.

Lucky, lucky me—out of the deluge of manuscripts that overwhelm the desks of every publisher, Editorial Director Wendy McCurdy of Kensington Books took a chance on a first-time fiction writer and has been behind *Away to Me* from the word go. I am grateful and forever indebted to Wendy for her excellent editorial suggestions, and the support and guidance of many at Kensington, including always helpful Editorial Assistant Sarah Selim, the eagle eye of copy editor Ellen Winkler, Madeleine Brown in the publicity department and the entire marketing department, especially Kristin McLaughlin and Kait Johnson. This novel is all the better for their wisdom and commitment.

Susanna Daniels of the Madison Writer's Studio also played a vital, and deeply appreciated, role in the novel, especially in its early stages. Writing fiction was a mystery unto itself when I first started. I've written many a non-fiction book, but was clueless to the riddle of crafting an actual mystery. I can't imagine how I could have started without her coaching and support.

Thanks too to the Driftless Mystery Writer's Advisory Group, also known as some good friends of mine who are smart, literate lovers of mysteries, and whose thoughtful feedback of earlier drafts helped me untangle plot lines and character development issues. Scones forever, to Judy Borree, Eleanor Flinn, Donna Huntington, Sylvia Peterson, and Anne Topham.

I am a lucky person indeed to have had so many great readers throughout the process of creating this book. I thank Jim Billings, Meg Boscov, Nicholas Butler, Randy Brown, Maggie Ginsberg, and Melissa McCue-McGrath, all of whom have improved my endless drafts substantially.

I am also indebted to the many experts who provided essential information (and lots of patience), including Karen London, a colleague and kick-ass animal behaviorist; Cat Warren, Mike Baker, and Melissa McCue-McGrath about scent detection K9s; Detective and Crime Scene Analyst Colleen Michelson; forensic psychiatrist Dr. Rebecca Barkhorn; Shannon Barry, Executive Director of Domestic Abuse Intervention Services; Terry Barton and colleagues of Dane County District One EMS; and fire arm expert Logan Deaton at Wilderness Fish & Game, (thank you for the introduction, Peter Eisch!). Thank you to the town of Clear Creek, Wisconsin, whose name I borrowed—because it is just too perfect—and whose location I moved to fit in with the rest of the novel. I promise to come visit soon. I thank Steve Dahlgren of Dog Grin Photography for taking a photo of me that actually looks a lot like me. On a good day.

Thanks too go to the many brilliant animal behaviorists and trainers who have taught me so much, and continue to inspire me, including Suzanne and Dan Estep, Karen London, Melissa McCue-McGrath, Pam Reid, Zazie Todd, John Wright, Nancy Williams, and a host of others who have moved mountains through their advocacy of compassionate and science-based training. A tip of the hat and a play bow of gratitude goes to all of my Certified Applied Animal Behavior colleagues, and organizations like the Association of Professional Dog Trainers, and the International Association of Animal Behavior Consultants.

I am a much better writer than I am a sheepdog trial competitor, but for the skills I have, and for years of insights, companionship, and a mutual love of working dogs, I thank my sheepdog friends and mentors, including Rose Anderson, Scott and Jenny Glen, Adrian Espinoza and Diane Davis, Julie Fitzpatrick, Janet and Paul Henning, Donna Huntington, Tresa Laferty, Vicki Peterson, Lori Perry, Dan Reuter, and Roxanne Tapaninen. Special thanks go out to Scott Glen, Adrian Espinoza, and Diane Davis for coaching me on Maddie's challenges with Jack

I would also like to thank the handlers and trial hosts who

do a great job taking care of their sheep—good shepherding should always be the core of what sheepdogs and sheepdog handlers do.

I have so many friends and family members who have supported me through the highs and lows of life that a full listing would take up several pages. Know that your love and kindness buoys me up every day. I hope you will forgive me for not listing all of your names. I cannot neglect to mention my beloved, deceased sister Wendy Barker, a brilliant poet and creative writing teacher, who continues to inspire me with her bravery, honesty, and sense of humor. And, where would I be without my other amazing sister and nieces—Liza, Wendy, Annie, and Emily, along with BFFs Cat, Julie, Meg, and Melissa? You are like water and oxygen to me: Essential, and appreciated every moment of every day.

To Skip, aka Skipperdeedodah, and to Maggie, aka Princess Margaret: no one deserves dogs as funny, smart, loving, and talented as you. And beautiful. Yes, Skip, you are the Ryan Reynolds of dogdom. So noted. (We'll talk about eating bird seed and rolling in sheep shit at another time.) I love you, not to the moon and back, but to another galaxy

I am sure I have forgotten several people who deserve to be thanked. I promise I'll remember the day after the book has gone to press.

I will end, full circle, where I began. To Jim Billings: My partner. My friend. My lover. My travel companion. My farmer, mechanic, builder, and problem-solver. My Wordle master. The love of my life.